Published by Griffyn Ink

www.griffynink.com

For ordering information or special discounts for bulk purchases, please contact Griffyn Ink at Mail@GriffynInk.com.

SoulFire

SAVANNAH KADE

CHAPTER 1

R ae was standing in a long line at the lingerie store when she felt it again. That feeling of a finger sliding up the back of her brain. The universe telling her "pay attention."

She didn't ignore that. So she looked around the store, but saw nothing else. For a moment, she panicked. Was it a bad feeling? Was something about to go wrong?

Fifteen years ago, she'd been a kid in a clothing store with her family. She and her older sister Sloan had been sent to the back aisle to pick something out for the weekend. Rae had been looking at a red top with white stripes when she felt it. That slide up the back of her senses that always put her on alert. Only that time it felt bad. *Bad.*

"Sloan!" she'd whispered it harshly, terrified even though she didn't know what of.

"Rae?" Sloan's voice had been at a normal volume, just confused.

All Rae had wanted was for her sister to be quiet and for her parents to be in the same aisle. Her eyes must have told the whole story, because Sloan's whole expression went round when she looked at her little sister. They had to go find their parents, even though Rae still didn't know *why* she felt this way. She only knew that she did. And that she was never wrong.

Dropping the shirt she'd been admiring, she reached out and met Sloan's hand where it was on the way to grabbing hers. When they touched, they connected. Rae felt things, but Sloan saw them. She only saw snippets and pieces, but it was sometimes enough.

As their hands joined, Rae heard Sloan gasp. She felt the churning in Rae's stomach, the gut clenching dread that something was wrong. Rae saw the pieces that Sloan saw. Gunfire. Bodies. A square, armored truck.

Holding hands, they ran toward the back of the store. The two girls spotted their parents and made eye contact as the sounds started. The handful of store employees on duty abandoned their stations and began running toward the rear doors, holding them open for patrons to escape. There had been gunfire at the front of the store.

They'd learned later that two, armed men came in and gunned down the guards from the armored truck. They'd come to collect the deposit money at the bank next door. Despite being in full Kevlar, the two guards had been killed instantly. The robbers had made off with the entire set of four bags of money. They'd never been caught. And Rae had never forgotten it.

She still had some mild PTSD when she saw an armored car. To this day, she'd never felt anything that strong again. But now, standing in a checkout line at the back of the lingerie store, her first thought was, "Is it bad?"

She stopped, almost ducked, but managed to stay upright and attempted to look normal. She didn't want to have a panic in the checkout lane. But a few slow breaths later, she realized the feeling wasn't bad. Not at all. That was just her memory being worried.

Someone was in the store. Someone she knew? Rae couldn't quite tell.

After a moment's debate, she turned around and acted like she'd forgotten something. Despite having all her things neatly folded and ready, she headed toward the middle of the store. There was someone the universe needed her to see, and Rae didn't ignore the universe.

She heard them before she saw them, though the voices didn't trigger any memories, just the feeling.

Luke and Yasmin.

The couple that got married at the B-n-B last year. That feeling she got demanded that she stopped dead still in the lobby of the beautiful old house. Then she'd seen the pictures, of Luke and Yasmin, from infanthood all the way to their wedding day. The photos of Luke looked like they could be pictures of her grandfather. And here the two were again.

Rae stopped, stunned. She hadn't been able to find them, and she had looked. She'd even used her boss's database, but with no last name, and no knowledge of even what state they were from, "Luke and Yasmin" wasn't enough to get her anywhere. Now here they were.

She followed them around a corner debating what to do. Was he the cousin they'd lost track of? She didn't know. She didn't even know if maybe Yasmin was the one that triggered the feeling. All Rae knew was that she felt it.

Still, here they were. In the lingerie store. That put really high odds on them living somewhere near here. It could be they were visiting and had lost all their luggage or something, but to Rae it looked as though they were shopping like locals.

She was trying to figure out what to say, how to introduce herself when she didn't even know what she was to them—if anything—when they turned another corner. Rae followed subtly, not wanting to spook them. She didn't think she was scary, but stalking people was not kosher.

She almost had a plan by the time she turned the corner. But in the end it didn't matter. They had disappeared.

CHAPTER 2

R ae Woodward's jaw hung open, and she couldn't seem to get it to close. Tears were welling up in her eyes and her boss was looking at her in that way that men did when females were crying for no apparent reason. That look that was partway between *what can I do to help?* and *what the hell did I do now?*

Rae understood his concern. She was acting out of character —Rae Woodward was stoic, normally. And to top it off, her anger, irritation, and general shock were greater than that of the average person. Any Joe walking down the street could easily take the comfort of a friend saying, "You couldn't have known." But Rae could have. And should have.

What she shouldn't have done was walk in here today. She shouldn't have sat down and showed her boss the photos and asked for the next assignment. She should have said to herself, *My life is going great. My rent is paid, my boyfriend is wonderful, and my friends are always there for me. What's a little extra money?*

But she didn't do that, did she? Clearly not, because she was sitting here with Lincoln handing her a tissue that she absolutely did not want even though she needed it. She was hurt, she was angry, and maybe worst of all, she felt stupid.

Had Lincoln known what she was going to see? He had seemed a little distracted when she held the generic thumb drive and the eight-by-ten glossies she'd printed out in the front office. The usual hallmarks of a completed job, they'd slid nicely across the scarred desk and given her a feeling of satisfaction. It hadn't lasted much past the moment when he traded her pictures for the business-sized check. Lincoln had some odd preferences; he believed in digital cameras and paper currency. Now the check was getting worried between her fingers and she wasn't even looking at it. She had asked him the same thing she always asked. "What do you think?"

"I think you caught him cheating on his wife." Lincoln usually gave her the commentary he knew she was looking for, but not today. This time, he'd just thumbed through to the next photo and the next, studying each as he went.

Rae wished he had really looked. The composition on the top photo was gratifying. The close up of the tall man kissing the willowy blonde was a study in the play of light on the planes of two faces. Passion perfectly captured. It would make the viewer cry.

Rae sighed. Unfortunately, it *would* make the viewer cry—because the viewer would be the kissing man's wife. The wife, however, was clearly a brunette, and shorter than the woman being kissed in the photo. Rae, too, had almost cried as that particular shot had popped up on her screen at home. She wished she'd taken it with good old fashioned film. She would have loved to watch it bloom in the bath of developer the way she had as a kid.

But no matter how beautiful or well-framed this photo was, it would never be used in a gallery or sold to an admirer. It would likely be seen exactly once, by a woman whose heart it would break, then it would be locked away in Lincoln's files, never to be looked at again. Except maybe at the divorce proceedings.

Sometimes Rae felt like she showed her naked soul in her art photographs. But this was just as excruciating. To know that she had captured *the perfect moment*. And to know that it would be forever hidden. She blamed the husband. He should have been kissing his own wife and not someone else's. Then again, if he'd been kissing his own wife, she wouldn't have been there. Suspicion was Lincoln's bread and butter, and therefore hers, too. She needed to sell some real work. This P.I. stuff was going to kill her.

Just as Lincoln pushed the file into a tray on the corner of his desk to await his next meeting with the client, Rae had leaned forward and made the fated bad move: "Do you have another assignment for me?" She knew that getting a gallery opening was something that wasn't going to happen to her very soon. Lincoln at least admired how she framed her pieces. And mostly it paid the bills.

"Actually, I do." He pushed his swivel chair back toward the rickety file cabinet behind him, and rolled open a drawer, peeling the top folder from the stack within. The man liked his paper. Less hackable, he said. So far, nothing had tipped her off that this folder would be far worse than opening an anthrax envelope.

Nothing had tipped her off. That's what burned. She got that feeling. Almost like someone was tapping her, in her brain, to get her attention. She hid it, because people didn't like that, but that's how it worked. She'd known when Sloan broke her arm in seventh grade. She'd known when Bobby Brannan dumped her in the ninth grade, though there was argument that anyone could have seen that coming from a mile away. And she'd known when her mother died in a car accident five years earlier. So how had she not seen this coming?

"Annette Lipscomb. Came in two days ago. Will be back next Thursday." Lincoln thumbed through the papers that Annette had filled out by hand, then pushed the file across the desk as though it were just paper.

Rae glanced over the neat script that stated the reason for hiring Lincoln Cardman P.I. Still nothing about the assignment tipped her off that it was out of place.

I suspect my husband is having an affair.

Well, these days it seemed they all did. She flipped through a short list of reasons that Annette thought Roger might be seeing another woman. Then Ray began studying the longer list of preliminary paperwork that Lincoln already had in order. The credit card reports and other pages would help her know where to start. Maybe tell her what time of day to tail the guy. Where he had frequent haunts.

According to his credit card statements, he liked Le Bistro. Rae smiled. Le Bistro was one of her personal favorites. She could have the tuna steak sandwich while she worked.

Potential Cheating Husband Roger apparently also had an apartment elsewhere in town. On March Street even. Rae knew right where that was. He had also purchased a piece of jewelry recently: a ring, according to the receipt. Not that Annette had gotten any jewelry lately.

Rae had seen enough. Roger was clearly a right asshole. He didn't sound like a "potential" anything; he seemed to be the real deal. So it felt good to take the assignment; she and Lincoln would nail the guy to the wall. He'd get what he deserved and she'd get enough to pay the rent and take off a few weeks to do her own work. Cheating Roger would pay for her next round of camera equipment.

Still, she should have said *no*. She should have been listening to the universe, but she wasn't. Because when she turned the page her jaw opened to its current state and words became impossible to form. She felt her stomach knot, unknot and knot again. Cheating Roger was *Roger Barett?*

The photo of him was clear as day.

Lincoln just kept looking at her. His head tilted a little to the side. He had been married a long time and he knew when to wait a woman out. He also knew when he didn't want to be involved. Clearly, he had decided that this was one of those times.

Rae's jaw worked up and down, more like a fish than anything, and finally she croaked out a noise. "Lincoln?" Her voice sounded shaky even to her own ears. "Who is this?"

"Huh?" He finally focused on her face, coming out of the trance he had entered while waiting for her to make sense. "That's the husband. Different last name."

She took a deep breath in, mentally recited a spell for strength, and started to feel better. Then she had to talk. "Well, I can tell you for certain he's cheating on his wife."

Lincoln's teeth pulled back. It wasn't really a smile, of course. He was too confused to truly smile at her, but he was trying. Sort of. "Of course, he is. He'll be covering that DVD player my kid wants for Christmas."

"No." Rae tried to sit up straight. It didn't seem to be working. Despite casting a quick spell on herself for steel in her spine, she was wilting like spaghetti. "I *know* he's cheating on his wife. I just can't get the pictures."

A frown marred the man's thick brows. She had never refused a case before. "You know the girlfriend or something?"

She nodded.

"Me."

It was barely a squeak. She shook her head and twisted the ring that had adorned her right hand for the last month. She'd thought the ring was sweet, the three sapphires beautiful, the sentiment genuine. After a moment, Rae realized what she was doing and yanked the thing off, tossing it on top of the file. "That's the ring in the accounts. That's what he bought. It lines up with the date."

Lincoln picked it up and looked it over, turning it this way and that. The motion mimicked the rolling of her stomach as she thought about those Le Bistro salads and the creme brulee they had shared. He was the one who'd introduced her to that place. *That bastard!*

"Are you sure this Roger is your Roger?" Lincoln held it back out to her. "Because this ain't the ring."

"What?" Confused now, she didn't take it back.

"You're sure you've been seeing *this* guy?" Lincoln's lips were pressed together and his large finger landed square on Roger's face in the school-sized photo. If only actually squashing him were so easy. After she nodded, he looked her in the eye and solemnly asked another question. "Are you in love with him?"

How could she be in love with someone who currently inspired a feeling close to vomiting? She shook her head this time. She wasn't in love with him. But he had seemed to really be falling for her. And he was the first man she had truly liked out of the last fifteen or so she had dated. Go figure. The only one that hadn't seemed to be a jerk turns out to be the biggest ass of all of them.

"Rachel, let's just both stay calm." Lincoln used her given name, warning her that she wasn't going to like this. He still held the ring between his fingers. "I've been in this business a long time. And I have to say that this is a first for me."

She nodded. What else could she do?

"Honey, I hate to break it to you, but you aren't the only one he's cheating with."

"*What?*" She practically barked it out as her brain absorbed the ramifications of Lincoln's words. *There was* another *other* *woman?*

"This ring isn't the ring from the receipt." He held it up. "I know my cheating husbands, which means I know jewelry. . . . And I hate to be the bearer of bad news, but *this* ring didn't cost *that* much."

So Mr. 'I'm falling so hard for you' was falling harder for someone else? Not only was there another other woman, but he liked her *better*?

Rae couldn't believe it. She couldn't speak. She was going to get disowned from her extended family for such a major misstep. Even her friends would think she was a fool. Sloan would still love her, she thought. At least she could count on her sister. Then the implications hit her and her jaw unhinged again. She croaked maybe, but she didn't make any real words.

"Do you still think you could tail him? There might be some real satisfaction in doing it."

Her cold confusion heated to rage. "Oh, yes, I will." Cheating Roger was going to pay. And pay. She'd never had a job that was personal before. "I'll start tailing him tomorrow."

"Wait 'til Monday, honey." Lincoln pushed the file across the table at her. "Give yourself a little time to simmer down. This still needs to be a professional job."

Though she nodded in response, basically agreeing to wait, Rae didn't want to simmer down. She wanted to march right over to Roger's real house, the one where he kept the kids he had blatantly denied having, and tell Mrs. Annette Lipscomb a thing or two about her husband.

But Rae had always known Lincoln to be right about these things. And if Lincoln said 'wait', she should wait, no matter how good a baseball bat would feel sliding along her palms right about now. Common sense told her that fantasy was the exact reason Lincoln wanted her to wait.

She knew if she were ever on the other side—if she was ever a wife who found out that her husband was sleeping with another woman—she would want Lincoln on the case. He had the touch. And he'd never cheat on his wife. As he said, you'll always get caught . . . . eventually. And then you'll pay.

Rae pocketed the now rumpled check she'd wadded and flattened while not paying attention. Then she managed a nod before letting herself out the door, her copy of the Annette Lipscomb file firmly in her grasp. At least it was Friday and there would be plenty of designated drivers on hand tonight. They'd all be willing to give her a ride home after she told them about her day. Hell, they'd each buy her a round. They were good friends.

CHAPTER 3

S am felt the hit but didn't flinch as Sheree punched his bicep. Her words were a harder smack than her fist, though. "Lighten up, Sam. You just need to get laid."

He mustered up a half-assed smile but was sure it came out looking more like a grimace, and he tried to hide it behind the beer bottle he was drinking from. If only she hadn't hit the nail on the head. And also managed to miss by a mile at the same time. He had tried *just* getting laid, and that hadn't worked out so well.

The fistful of times he'd given it a real shot had been lackluster at best and emotionally painful at worst. He'd felt like a complete asshat when one woman had fled his apartment crying. Never mind that it was after a round of orgasmic sex. It had still left him dissatisfied and she'd picked up on that. She began with petulance and worked her way into full sobs, saying things like *you seemed different* and *what do you mean you want to be alone?*

Another woman had played the cold-hearted card to him, pointing to his clothes on the floor with one graceful hand while using the other to light her post-sex cigarette. That one started to say something about needing her space, but Sam had been out the door before she finished. Two others had wound up having awkward goodbyes in the middle of the night and he'd never spoken to either of them again. He deleted the first woman's number and had never even gotten the second. That just said it all, didn't it? It was the end of his forays into 'just getting laid' he decided.

Now, his eyes scanned the bar, settling on the door, and willing it to open.

Eventually, it did.

"Lisa!" God, Sheree had a loud voice. It sliced clean through the noise at the crowded bar on a Friday evening. His friend somehow managed to be high decibel and dulcet at the same time. He loved it. Lisa turned their way, recognizing the sound, and waved at them, then tugged Jack along behind her. Jack was becoming a permanent fixture in their little circle. Which was interesting, because in the two years that he had been doing this Friday-night-thing Lisa had never brought a guy. Not until Jack. And Lisa was a notorious serial dater.

The couple reached the table after pushing their way through the crowded bar, turning heads as they went. Sam could understand. Lisa was beautiful and men wanted her. Enough to ignore the young stud on her arm. Jack looked like a typical bad boy. And the women swooned. Not just because of Jack's looks or his grin, but because of the way he and Lisa turned toward each other. Always aware and in tune with the other. Everyone around them wanted that. It seemed Sheree was included in that group. But she was happy for her friend and so she waved and smiled and Sam saw her envy pass in the slightest waver before it got folded into a genuine smile.

Lisa beamed as she came close, Jack's hand still tucked firmly in hers. Jack used his spare hand to clap Sam on the back. "So what has our favorite super-lawyer been up to this week?"

Sam tipped his beer at Jack as the couple slid into the vinyl booth across from him and Sheree, and smiled. "Right now, I'm saving the world from patent infringement."

"Patent infringement?" Jack ordered a beer for him and a different one for Lisa, then turned back to Sam.

"Yeah, I'm working for a foreign guy who designed an easily movable ski rack. It goes on the back of the car instead of the top for easier access. One of the big companies ripped off his design. And we can prove it."

"You on barter with him?"

Sam nodded. "Part of it, yeah." 'Barter' wasn't the right word, but Jack always used it. Then again, getting paid later and only contingently wasn't even as solid as knowing he was getting an actual thing. He sighed. His clients often gave him something of what they were working on, so maybe Jack had used the right word. Sam smiled imagining that one day he would wind up with a flock of chickens in trade for legal work. "He gave me three of the ski racks."

"Can you get me one of those? I'll buy it off you."

"Sure." Sam made a mental note to get one of the spares out of his garage Tuesday night. He really should consider a storefront and a resale license given the amount of stuff he passed on to his friends from his clients. He was wondering if he should pay taxes on it, but just then his breath hitched. He knew she was there the briefest moment before he felt her brush against his elbow. He didn't even have to look. But he did.

Rae looked tired. No, more than that, maybe even upset. Her auburn ponytail was rapidly falling apart, a handful of wisps had broken free around her face. Her hair was fighting the straightening she'd put it through earlier, and winning. Waves and curls formed at the tips where her fingers had undoubtedly played havoc in their standard nervous fidgeting.

His mouth didn't work.

But Sheree's did. She leaned out from the back of the booth

and started the inevitable conversation. "Rae, honey, what's wrong?"

"Oh, you won't believe the day I've had!" Rae braced her hands on the table in front of her, leveraging herself down into the chair pulled up at the end to accommodate all six of them, as though even just sitting down was more than she could handle. She opened her round mouth, the bottom lip looking a little bruised from its forays between her teeth, and she started to talk, "I—"

Just then the waitress showed up again, her bare curvy midriff even with their eye level. This time Sam didn't look; he just watched in awe as Rae ordered two Top Shelf margaritas with a shot of Patron Orange on the side. She was a tiny thing, and he wondered where she would put it all. He also began to wonder about her sanity. Rae wasn't a heavy drinker in the worst of times from what he'd seen.

"Rae!" It was Sheree's voice, but everyone's sentiment. All eyes at the table were on the weary redhead. Anyone whose attention she hadn't gotten with the bad-day comment, she got with the margarita order.

Rae shook her head as though shaking out a bad thought, then looked back out into the crowded bar impatiently, as though the waitress couldn't get back fast enough. Finally, she turned back to Sheree, "I'll tell you everything if you'll drive me home."

Sam found his voice at last, the sound turning Rae's head so she locked eyes with him. "*I'll* drive you home, just tell." He hoped that bastard boyfriend of hers was finally getting hung out to dry. He was just so *wrong* for her.

Rae nodded at him. "You're on!"

Her grin, the first one of the evening and not quite full enough to reach her eyes, still made his heart kick. But he didn't get to moon over her long. Which was good, he didn't need anyone catching onto the things he thought.

"So? Spill!" Lisa had leaned almost all the way across the table, her long, super-blonde hair nearly hanging in the salsa. Not that she noticed. Even Jack waited impatiently.

"Spill what?" Alex slid in across from them, casually bumping Lisa and Jack down a bit, not that they noticed, before he signaled the waitress for his beer.

"Rae's bad day. Now Shhhh." Sheree again turned intently to her roommate.

Sam watched as Rae spent almost a full minute licking her lips, carefully folding the edge of a beverage napkin and gathering her thoughts before starting the tale. "So, I finished that last case. I caught the guy openly kissing his girlfriend in front of the hotel. All very sleazy, you know. And I asked for another job." She paused and waited while the waitress lined up the two drinks and a shot in front of her. Then she continued, her fingers moving to the shot glass that she swirled and coddled as though subtly casting some kind of spell.

"So, stupid me went and asked for it! Sure enough, another wife suspects her husband of cheating. No surprise there. I look through the wife's suspicions list, and the credit card statements. The guy likes Le Bistro—"

"Oh, I love their Salad Nicoise!" Lisa put in, "Ow!" She turned to Jack who was removing his elbow from her side. That was another first for Lisa. Normally she didn't put up with *anything*, deserved or not. But when Jack called her on her shit, she listened.

Rae went on. "Cheating Husband Guy also has these mysterious jewelry purchases, his wife hasn't gotten any new jewelry and it's been about a month or two since the purchase. So she's pretty suspicious." So far, this all seemed pretty normal to Sam.

He couldn't help listening when Rae talked and he knew about how she wanted to get out of this job, but how it paid the bills. He knew she was trying hard not to lose faith in marriage and relationships, but sometimes what she saw pulled her down. He was waiting for why today was so bad, though. He didn't have to wait long.

"He just seems like your average cheating bastard. Then . . ." Rae paused, seeming to think for a moment. Instead, her small, perfectly manicured fingers quickly wrapped around the shot glass and she tossed it back.

"Whooooo." Her breath rushed out of her as the light blush climbed her cheeks, and she went into a small tequila shudder, and a raspy "Oh, that's good." Before any of them even realized what she was going to do. After a deep breath she spoke again. "I turn the page and who is staring back at me from the family photo but . . . *Roger!*"

"No."

"Roger?"

"That bastard!" Sam was surprised to recognize that it was his own mouth moving for that one.

Alex had managed to keep his own voice out of the chorus until then. But he added in an even better observation. "*Family photo?*"

Rae nodded and gulped at her margarita. "Two kids, a boy and a girl, ten and seven." She swallowed half of one of the 'ritas on the spot, then licked away the salt that had clung to her lips.

Sam almost shuddered. She was going to be the death of him and as far as he could tell, she had no clue. Then he heard his own voice again. He was grateful he could form coherent words, even as he felt the soft rub of her sweater against his arm. Her jeans clad knee was drawn up under her, and her chair was scrunched close enough to his that her leg brushed his jeans. Surely she wasn't aware of any of it. "I'm so sorry, Rae."

He reached out to hold her hand, or touch her in some gesture of comfort. But she was reaching for the stem of her margarita glass, her eyes focused on her next dose of liquor.

"Don't be." She didn't look up, just licked the salt from the edge of the wide glass and drained it. She held the empty glass up to him finally making the eye contact he craved. "In a few minutes I won't even remember his name."

Another murmur of pity rolled across the table and she started on her second drink before her head popped back up. The grin she was wearing was a little too true, and was certainly incongruous with the story she was telling. But he didn't get to ask her about it. She gushed, "And Monday morning I have to start tailing the guy."

Sheree leaned across him again. "What? To catch him with *you*!?"

"Nope. His *other* girlfriend."

CHAPTER 4

S am lifted Rae's limp body out of the passenger seat of Sheree's car and carried her through the lobby to the elevator.

Rae gave a little sigh and curled into him. "I love you, Sam. You are so good to me."

He would have thought it sweet if he hadn't been able to smell the tequila coming off her in waves. As it was, she was simply drunk. And she was drunk because she'd been in love with her boyfriend and he'd turned out to be the lowest of pond scum.

Sam couldn't decide if he was happy about things or sad. On the upside, Roger was officially gone and he wasn't coming back. Sam had disliked Roger from the first moment he'd met him. Of course, he would have disliked any man that Rae introduced as her 'boyfriend,' especially when he was kicking himself seven ways to Sunday for not stepping up a little sooner. He should have at least *tried*. But he'd not gotten his shit together enough to ask her out and she went off with Cheating Husband Roger.

On the downside, Rae was clearly smashed, both

emotionally and alcoholically. On the upside, she was single. Although, on another downside, not really and she probably wouldn't really be "single" for a while. Another downside: he might have to watch while she made her way through a rebound guy or two and he didn't know if he could handle that. On the upside, at least she was in his arms now.

Sheree opened the door to the apartment the two women shared. "Thank you so much, Sam. I never could have carried her."

That was true. After she'd snuggled against him, she'd gone completely limp again in his arms. He didn't think Sheree would have been able to lift her in the first place, but now she was just dead weight. "She'd have spent the night in the car, huh?"

Sheree smiled sweetly. "Nope. I wouldn't leave her in the car. I would have drug her in." She held Rae's bedroom door open for him, revealing mussed bedcovers and a dresser with a large mirror. Several perfumes and a couple of hairbrushes were scattered across the top.

Sam set her down across the covers, her limp form melting against her incredibly soft sheets she must have spent a chunk of change on. They were nicer than anything else in the room.

"Sam?" Her voice sounded as limp as her body, but Rae surprised him by smiling up at him and grabbing his neck. "Thank you."

Then she surprised him even further by pulling him down to her and planting a sweet kiss against his cheek.

He was grateful the lights were off or Sheree might have seen his face. Rae certainly could, but he could have started singing showtunes or playing the drums in her room, and she still wouldn't remember a scrap of it in the morning. As much as he wanted to climb in beside her, it wasn't the direction he wanted to go. He'd never taken advantage of a drunk woman before, and he wasn't about to start now. So he pulled off her shoes and tucked the covers around her. "'Night, little drunk Rae."

Sheree laughed.

Sheree walked with him back to the door, and he took the elevator back down and out the front of the apartment complex. He climbed back into his coupe waiting for him at the curb.

All in all, it had been a very interesting evening.

CHAPTER 5

R ae felt her heart harden a little with each photo she snapped. It was her third day on the job, and she'd finally managed to go the whole day without her jaw unhinging and swinging open like she was trying to catch flies.

Right now she was watching Roger dip his tongue into this woman's throat with enough motion for a solid tonsil inspection. Nope, the jaw unhinging had definitely passed. Rae had worked her way up to a good case of the willies. How had she ever kissed this man? And she was thanking every god in the heavens that she hadn't slept with him. He'd been just a little too pushy on that front. If he'd backed off, he probably would have had her. She was grateful now that he hadn't. She was still beating herself up for missing the signals, too. How had she not felt what scum he was.

Unless he somehow didn't actually think he was doing anything wrong? Maybe she'd had no signal because he didn't give one. That thought was almost scarier than the idea that she'd missed it.

Sighing into the empty car she was doing her stakeout from, she reconsidered. Most jobs didn't make her this pessimistic.

Sure the thoughts always crept in. Did every man cheat on his wife? Were there any good ones left? What was the point in trying for a monogamous relationship, let alone a marriage, when so many failed so disastrously? Was betrayal the norm?

But she had answers to all of those questions. No, not all men cheated. Case in point: Lincoln. He was a rock for his family, and his eyes still sparkled when he talked about his wife of almost twenty years. Of course, if anything ever happened to them, Rae was certain her whole world would fall apart.

She always reminded herself as well of the cases she'd had where the husband hadn't been cheating. One man had been raising champion cocker spaniels on the side, because his wife was allergic. One wife had just been shifty, Rae had been *certain* she was cheating, but they had never been able to prove anything. Of course, there was a high percentage—of men *and* women—who were sneaking off for trysts with same sex lovers. But about one in ten of her assignments actually *wasn't* committing adultery. Still, nine in ten were.

It was enough to make anyone give up on true love.

But Roger Barrett was about as low as it got.

So far, she'd only seen him with women, but at this point there was little she could find out about the man that would surprise her. His apartment seemed to have a steady flow of women in and out. Some with very little passing time. How did he not get caught?

Then she smiled a fiendish little grin. Oh yeah, he *was* caught.

He'd called her last week and she'd done what Lincoln coached her to do. She hadn't tipped him off, just said her grandmother had died and she would be out of town for a few days. Lincoln was a little too good with the lie. He'd thought the whole thing up. The dying Grandma gave her an excuse not to see him before she left, and to sound upset, or at least not like herself on the phone. All without letting Roger in on it.

Rae wasn't a good liar, but it disturbed her how easily this one rolled off her tongue. She found it was easier to lie to a liar. She canceled their plans for Monday night quickly and cleanly and at the time he let her.

Now it appeared she'd been replaced by a blonde-haired, blue-eyed paralegal just as quick as you please. Rae figured all this would make her cry or make her heart break. But it didn't. Instead, she just got angrier and angrier, which just went to show how much she had loved Roger. Probably not much at all. Maybe she'd just liked the idea of Roger.

And Roger had been a great idea. Good looking, charming, falling in love with her. But all that was a shame, because the real Roger wasn't good enough to lick the bottom of her shoes after a walk across a farm. The real Roger was giving one more quick peck on the mouth to the woman at her front door.

Again, she thanked the gods that she hadn't slept with him. His pushiness in that category had been a clue. And there had been little rubs along the way, things that made her think she should be attracted to him, but she wasn't. It had been so nice to have a boyfriend, though. So nice to get flowers and be taken out on lush dates. Still, she'd missed the spark and fire that she thought she should have felt.

Rae was tired. She had enough dirt on this man to open her own mud bath. With a sigh she sat back and felt her shoulders slump while she watched him get in his car. He was picking up his cell phone even as he drove away, probably calling another of his little doxies on the way off. She was still watching him even though she was done taking pictures. Roger on the phone didn't incriminate him. Unless...

Rae jerked to attention when her cell phone rang. Wouldn't you know it, she'd been right. He was calling *her*. Shaking her head, and unsure why she was she was even doing it, she punched the button and connected the call. "Hello?"

"Hey, Baby. I'm glad I got you." He sounded like an oil slick now, and Rae wondered why she'd never heard it before.

"Yeah, I'm here." She let her voice drag out and it wasn't hard to play the part.

"How are things at your Grandmother's?" That was one of the things that made him so good at cheating. He remembered all the details.

But Rae knew the game now and she laid it on thick. "I miss my grandma and all, but I think I'm all cried out. So, I'm just hanging out and watching a show."

He laughed a little. "Anything good?"

"Just one of your typical revenge plots. It's really good, I'll tell you about it when I get back. I have to go." She couldn't stifle the little grin as she watched his car hang a left at the light in front of her. He didn't see her or recognize her car.

"All right. I miss you, Baby."

"I've missed you, too." *But now my aim is better.*

She hung up just as a mini-van pulled into the spot that Roger had vacated. A father and three sweet small kids climbed out one by one. They ran screaming for the front door of the house. It swung open as they got there, and Roger's girlfriend greeted all four of them with hugs and kisses.

Rae's stomach turned and she reminded herself that neither of these people was her client. But she felt so bad for the father. Her chest was full of lead weight as she cranked the engine and turned the wheel. The woman looked up at her with a frown on her face as she closed the door behind her family. Rae just hoped the wife was nervous enough to quit what she was doing.

But then again, if there was one thing that she had learned from this job, it was that you never knew what was going on behind closed doors.

CHAPTER 6

"I'm not leaving." Sam crossed his arms, looking like a black and white photograph of himself where he stood bathed in the red light of the darkroom.

"I need to be alone." Rae sighed, thinking it was better that way. Alone with the developing photos of Roger. She'd used film. Good old fashioned film. Though Lincoln preferred digital, there was a case for film. The courts ruled in favor of film if there was a question of altering the photos. Film meant the lawyer wouldn't even have to call in an expert. Roger's attorney could suggest that they'd been manipulated, but Annette's lawyer would only have to button his jacket and smile and say, "it's film." Rae was handing it to them. She had a soft spot for Annette Lipscomb now.

So she stood in her small room that she sometimes converted to a darkroom. Roger hung from every clip along the drying lines and stared out from every plastic tray of solution. Roger full of smiles and passion. Roger at Le Bistro. Roger at the park with his children. Roger and the blonde. Roger and the brunette. Roger and his kids' pediatrician, of all people.

He was going to fry.

As soon as she handed these photos over to Lincoln.

"You shouldn't be alone like this." Sam hadn't moved.

"And why is that?" Rae turned, gesturing with the tongs, "Don't go thinking I'm going to drown myself in the vat of developer."

A rough breath made its way past Sam's lips, and his blue eyes flared. Rae watched as the muscles in his arms clenched a bit. His brown hair was the perfect warm shade of chocolate, but it topped an angry expression. "If I leave you alone, you'll just cry."

"So?" She turned back to the tray where another page of photo paper had gone from blank to incriminating in thirty seconds.

"So, he doesn't even deserve that much attention from you."

Pushing down her frustration, Rae reminded herself that Sam simply had her best interests at heart. Her voice was barely a whisper. "What if *I* deserve it?"

She hadn't realized that she was shaking until she felt him remove the tongs from her fingers and set them on the countertop before turning her and putting his arms around her. The cotton of his T-shirt was soft over his wide chest. Probably the remnants of his college football days...the shirt and the chest.

"Don't beat yourself up over him. You don't deserve that."

"No." She flattened her hands against him and pushed back to look up at his face. "I mean, what if I deserve the opportunity to cry about it? So *I* can get on with things."

He nodded, and she waited for him to leave but he didn't even make a move to go. He just pulled her against him again, saying, "Then cry."

Already the tears were making marks down her face against her will. She had planned to do this by herself, rant and rave, taunt Roger's photos with the demise she knew was coming, maybe even start a small bonfire and burn something. Sam would never understand a good ex-boyfriend ritual. But he wasn't letting her go. Her voice was tinny and hollow. "He had me so fooled. He said he was falling in love with me."

"I know." Sam leaned back against the counter, pulling her with him, his legs and arms bracketing her on either side. "And of course you believed him."

"It just didn't even occur to me that he would lie like that."

She had believed she would *feel* it. She'd counted on being warned by her own intuition if something bad was coming. It didn't just happen with events, it happened with people, too. She'd avoided some people over the years simply because of that feeling, even though she'd not gotten confirmation that was the right move. She'd simply never had anything that proved her instincts wrong. She hadn't felt anything about Roger. Now she felt Sam's fingers in her hair, stroking it, soothing and calming. "Eventually, you'll get over him."

Rae snorted, she hadn't meant to, but it was too late to take back her very un-lady-like response. "Get over him?!" She looked up into Sam's startled face again. "I am over him. I was never really in love with him in the first place. I just . . ." She shrugged a little. "If not Roger, then who? I liked him better than any of the other guys I've dated in the past year and a half. And, of course, it turns out he's *married!*" Her tears started coming again, making small wet dots on the front of Sam's shirt. But he seemed not to mind. "Why couldn't he have just been *gay?*" she snuffled.

Wisely, Sam didn't grace that with an answer.

She got angrier as she talked. "I asked him if he'd been married. He said 'no'. But I think that I asked if he'd been married *before*. It never occurred to me to ask him if he was married *now*."

"Rae, he lied. That's all there is to it."

She heaved a big sigh. "And I'm the fool because I believed him." Stepping back out of his embrace, she waved an arm around the room, "Look at all of them! *Us*, I mean 'us' because I am one of those women. How did he even have the time? How can he hold a job with all the women he's seeing and how did I not see it?"

She felt his hand against the back of her head again. "Because we all see what we want to see, and you're a trusting person who believed a man who seemed sincere. It was a mistake, but don't let him make you cynical, okay Rae?"

She wasn't sure how long she stood there, plastered to Sam's chest, sniffling and crying. She couldn't very well tell him the truth. Tell him about the instincts her parents had taught her about. Her mother hadn't wanted to talk about it, but Rae had inherited it. Sloan had, too, despite the fact that she had a different father. Sam knew that Sloan and she were half sisters, but he had no idea about the rest. So she sank into his arms and held her tongue.

Her frustration had passed by the time she felt his arms uncurl from around her so he could push her back from him, checking her face for signs of sincerity, for just a moment. "Feeling better yet?"

She nodded, and turned back to the photo still soaking in the stop solution. It didn't make her stomach turn anymore. Maybe Sam had been right: she shouldn't have cried alone. She clipped the paper to one of the lines strung across the back wall. The room was peppered with black and white evidence of her error.

His voice was soft in the red haze, "I'm sorry but I need to get going. You can come with me if you want."

His question hung in the air behind her, but she was involved in the photograph and replied only with, "Hmm?"

"I have to get home. I babysit my sister's twins every other Wednesday." He was backing toward the door, but knew enough not to open it without her permission.

"No, that's okay. You go." She covered her exposed photo

paper in preparation for the light he would let in. "I should finish up here, so I can hand these off to Lincoln tomorrow."

He nodded. "Ready?"

She knew he was asking about more than just letting in the light. So she added a smile to her answer. "Yeah."

Rae glanced around the room one last time in search of anything that would suffer from exposure, but she didn't see anything. She felt better, a little bit of weight removed, as Sam backed out the door. "Lock the front door behind you please."

CHAPTER 7

Rae stood in her kitchen chopping vegetables in preparation for her usual Tuesday night. Lisa was beside her, doing her own prep on Rae's limited counter space, and chatting about something Rae wasn't paying enough attention to.

Instead, she was focused on the stiff paper of the formal note in her back pocket. It matched the woman, she thought. The four-by-six card with her full name printed across the top in script. It looked like it had come from a woman who wore pearls and cooked for PTA potlucks. It had a certain Southern feel that was out of place in Los Angeles, but not bad. Rae was certain that the words on it had not been the intended use when the note cards had been ordered.

It was a thank you note and it had come in the mail yesterday, although Rae hadn't found the guts to open it until today. The small neat script filled the front of the card. And Annette Lipscomb's signature flowed across the bottom corner. At least the woman wasn't angry. She was glad that Rae had come forward. Not only with the photos, but with her own story.

Lincoln had set up an interview with Mrs. Lipscomb's attorney and Rae had given her statement. She told the whole thing. How she and Roger had met. How he had lied point blank about not having kids. How she had been to his apartment. Lincoln used that information to get his hands on the lease and turn that over to Annette's lawyers as well.

Rae had even been invited to the mediation. Annette had requested it personally. Rae had never been to a divorce mediation meeting. It was a preliminary hearing of both sides, so she wouldn't be involved in the whole thing. But while it was awful to tell what she'd done, it felt really good to see that her statements had been damning. She also handed the ring over to Annette to be sold, and the money put into the kids' college funds. Not that it would net much money, because Roger was a cheap bastard, but she hoped that ten years in a fund might turn it into something.

Annette had hardly looked at her that day. She had been in tears. Her expression contradicting her statements that she was glad it was all getting resolved so quickly. Her lawyer had been sympathetic, putting an understanding arm around her in a woman-to-woman hug. While they commiserated, Rae had been left to walk out of the meeting room and into the front office where Sam was waiting, reading a magazine.

He had again ingratiated himself. Not letting her drive. Trying to convince her that she didn't have to go through with it. Then he argued that it was going to be more difficult than she thought. He was a lawyer, she thought he must know what he was talking about. But she hadn't listened.

Rae had railed. *I'm prepared* and *trust me, no one wants to make him pay like I do.* But Sam had insisted that he had the afternoon off and that he drive. And then he further said that he would wait in the lobby.

Now she was glad he had. She'd never been so happy to see

him. Walking up and sinking into the soft leather beside him, she sat for a few moments reveling that it was all over.

Sam spoke when her eyes finally slid closed. "Did you feel more than you thought you would?"

Her mouth had twisted up into a parody of a smile. "Only for the wife, and then for those kids. I was glad I could help, but it was grueling." Air filled her lungs involuntarily, and with it came the leather and paper scent of the large, lush office. "Can we get out of here?"

He stood and offered his hand like a true gentleman. Luckily Rae didn't wave him away before realizing that she was drained and allowing him to help pull her to her feet.

They said nothing else all the way home, except to order at the drive-thru window where he had known instinctively she would want to go. That night, Rae slept like a baby for the first time in a long time.

She'd continued to sleep well, until last night when the unopened note had stared at her from her nightstand. It mocked her for having no idea why Annette Lipscomb had written to her. Rae had helped when requested. She'd even showed up to the deposition and confessed to every sin. So what else could Annette say?

She had read it an hour ago, knowing that if it was bad tonight's party would take her mind off it.

But it hadn't been bad. Mrs. Lipscomb was as formal as her pearls and stationery. Rae found it to be the epitome of class, writing a thank-you note to the girl who had dated her husband. Annette was even gracious about Rae's help with the divorce. And lastly, letting her know that no blame was directed her way from either herself or her children.

Rae sighed and went back to chopping veggies, still barely participating in the conversation with Lisa. She only hoped that one day she was together enough to reach out to someone else even when her whole world was shattering. She was trying to turn her thoughts away from the note still burning a hole in her pocket and back toward getting in gear for the party when she heard Sam's voice from the entryway.

"I have corn chips and salsa, and potato chips and onion dip." The front door clicked as he sauntered through with grocery bags tucked in both arms.

Sheree eased one out of his grip and headed over to lay the snacks out on the second-hand dining room table. "You are such a guy." But she went back to arranging things on the already heavy-laden table. Stepping back she surveyed her work, and must have declared it acceptable. Next, she got to the usual job of pulling the mismatched chairs out from the table and dragging them into the living room. Sam was perfectly capable of opening the chips and setting them out, and Sheree just sort of waved him at his new job.

His smile was a little unnerving to Rae, even though she only saw half of it from her vantage point in the kitchen. Not the smile itself, but maybe it was just that he had seen her crying over Roger. She wasn't ashamed of her tears, but she wasn't by any means proud of the fact that she'd been caught dating a married man.

Sam's response to Sheree carried in to where Rae was prepping more food with Lisa. "Hey, I make a mean potato chip, and you wouldn't believe the effort it takes to seal my onion dip in those little pull-tab cans."

Lisa's voice hissed at her eardrums. "Rachel Woodward, you haven't been listening to me!"

"Sure I have." She hadn't, and she blushed terribly when she lied. All her friends knew it.

A few decibels lower, Lisa started again, "I think Jack is going to ask me to marry him."

The knife clattered to the cutting board before Rae could stop it. But she didn't watch the knife fall, instead her gaze was squarely on Lisa's face, "Why do you think that?"

Eyes narrowed, Lisa tilted her head a bit as she stopped mixing. "Do you think I'm wrong?"

Rae shook her head, "No, . . . I don't know. I'm just really curious what made you think that."

"Well," She went back to calmly stirring a little more dill into yet another batch of dip. "He wants me to meet him in Vegas after we each spend Christmas with our families."

Rae felt her eyebrows raise. She had so little control over her expressions.

Lisa's happiness bloomed as she clapped and jumped little hops in a small circle. "See, you don't think I'm off my rocker." She took a few breaths and forced herself to calm down, but just a touch. "I knew everyone else would warn me about getting my hopes up." She held a palm up to Rae as she started to speak. "Do not, I am already warned."

"No, it was the 'getting my hopes up' part that had me shocked." She tried to keep her voice low, really she did. "What happened to love'm-and-leave'm-Lisa?"

CHAPTER 8

Lisa shrugged in response to her question. "I think that maybe that was the Lisa that loved-and-got-left talking."

Just then, Sam walked through the old, swinging, saloon style door that almost separated her kitchen from the dining room. "What is this, ladies?"

Rae, unable to answer him honestly, leaned further over her green peppers. She let Lisa continue on as though the weather had been their original topic. "I just don't know if the whole usual crowd is going to show up. It's supposed to *snow* tonight. And you know what everyone's saying. . . . that the sky has been saving up. . . . We should get the usual L.A. downpour of rain, but with the temperature, it could turn to snow. Which would be insane!" When Lisa stopped being amazed, she got practical. "You do have a lot of spare blankets around here, right Rae?"

"Yeah." She nodded and looked up. At least Lisa was smart enough to give her a question she could answer without a lie behind it.

"Anything I can help with?" Sam asked as he glanced around the mess of a kitchen.

Lisa waved the dip covered spoon his way, "I think you've done enough, chip-boy."

"Actually," Rae reached across the counter, glad for a topic that didn't involve Lisa and her suspected marriage proposal. Sam would have an opinion about that. She handed him a jar with the notecard she had written on, and motioned with a piece of greenery. "You can hang this somewhere—in a door arch or something. But near a surface where you can put the jar and sign out right under it."

He turned the twig around, looking it over. "What is this?"

"Mistletoe." Rae went back to chopping but didn't fail to notice his frown. "It's real mistletoe. Not that plastic stuff."

He grinned at her. "All right Martha Stewart: explain the jar." He motioned to the little sign that Sheree had plastered to the front. *Abused Children's Fund.*

Rae glared. They all knew that she hated Martha Stewart. Didn't anyone realize that the domestic goddess was *divorced*? She'd been in *jail* for Pete's sakes. The whole Snoop Dogg friendship was cool, but in general, the "it's so easy" was a big crock of crap with glitter on it. Who had time to make marzipan vegetables for a peter rabbit cake? It was not "a piece of cake"; the stupid thing had taken three hours.

Rae shoved down her distaste, not wanting to let him bait her. "A kissing fee. You kiss, you contribute. If you don't want to kiss someone, contributions accepted anyway. It's for a worthy cause."

He nodded. "Good idea. Are these the people who helped with that kid in Sheree's class last year?"

"Of course." She gathered the veggie wedges and scooped them onto the platter next to the bowl of yet another kind of dip. At least she'd made this one herself. Lisa sailed from the room as the doorbell sounded and Rae heard her friend greeting the first of the guests.

Sam pulled her attention back as he often did. "All right then, where do I find string?"

"Not string, ribbon. You can choose from the handful that are on the desk in my room." Sauntering into the blue-bulb lit dining area she called back to him over her shoulder. "No more Martha cracks either!"

She sighed. She did have three really nice ribbons laying out on the desk. At least her old college roomie Zoe had appreciated her cool, budget décor.

Rae made a few more trips back and forth through the out of date swinging doors. By the time she had the table set, Sheree was in the middle of the living room and it was thick with people. Jack still hadn't arrived, but that hadn't seemed to slow Lisa down. It also seemed the dire predictions of snow wouldn't hold true. Or at least they hadn't stopped anyone yet.

Rae tried to shove her thoughts away. There were days that she felt all powerful. That her very thoughts that something was going well would make it go bad. The last thing they needed now was snow in Los Angeles. People here weren't really prepared for the cold, let alone snow. The front door was already letting in a cold blast with each new guest. But the way everyone was packing in the small apartment was getting almost too warm. The gust of cold was becoming more and more welcome.

She was standing by the door when the buzzer rang again just as there was a knock at the door. Rae hit the button and pulled the knob simultaneously. "Jack!"

"Hey Rae." He gave her a quick peck on the cheek. "Is my girl here?"

She pointed. "Over by the CD player. Near the Mistletoe."

He smiled and stalked off, peeling his scarf as he went. He was clearly nuts about Lisa, not even stopping to set his coat down. Rae couldn't not watch as he grabbed his girlfriend and kissed her. It was sweet and soft and made Rae bubble with jealousy while at the same time she chided herself for looking. But apparently she wasn't the only one.

"Hey!" Sheree called over the music. "That's a dollar for charity!"

"A buck, huh?" Jack got everyone's attention, as he laid Lisa back over his arm and proceeded with a kiss hot enough to have some of the guests fanning themselves, and Rae thought that maybe Lisa had been right. After a moment, they came up for air to shouts of "That was worth more than a buck!" and "At least five!"

Jack made a big show of opening his wallet and putting the five in the jar, before everyone found their way back to what they were doing before the spectacle.

Just after that, her old roommate Zoe showed up. "Rae!" She threw her arms around her friend and Rae hugged her back. It had been a while. Zoe was in grad school in chemical engineering. So while they'd both graduated two springs ago, Zoe was still a student. Rae was just a private investigator's assistant.

"I brought my friend Jessica," Zoe announced and introduced her friend to Rae before getting sucked into the crowd. Though few of the people were left over from school, Zoe did know a few and it was a party. If you couldn't meet new people at a party in Los Angeles, what could you do?

Rae talked to people as they came in. Introduced herself to the ones she didn't already know and munched a few of the carrots and green peppers she'd cut up. Eventually, the knocks slowed down and she wound up mingling her way through her own party, talking to one friend after another. All the while the apartment was filling with more and more of her and Sheree's friends. She also was seeing a handful of people they didn't know. But they were all bringing food and drinks and everyone was having a good time. Even opening the balcony doors and going out to smoke or just to escape the crush of bodies that had started moving to the music.

Eventually Rae had eaten enough munchies to call it dinner. And soon found herself in the middle of the red lights Sheree had added, dancing with Liam, another P.I. from Lincoln's office. She'd had a crush on him about a year back, but he had been dating someone else. And by the time he had broken things off with the girlfriend she was neck deep with Roger. Sighing, she pushed the thoughts away and glanced over Liam's shoulder to the wall clock in the still brightly lit kitchen. 12:10.

Rae bumped into the crowd and turned to find Wendy, another teacher at Sheree's school. She introduced Liam and stepped away as he began flirting shamelessly. Rae stopped and did a gut-check. Nope, not even a little twinge at the thought of Liam dating the teacher. She guessed the crush hadn't been as big or important as she'd thought at the time. Just a place holder, probably.

Watching him take an obvious interest in the woman made her think about her own love-life or lack thereof. The problem was, while she was well and good over Roger, she hadn't even given a thought who to turn her attentions to. Which was probably a good thing given how far astray she had managed to get last time. Singlehood would be good for her. Real singlehood, the kind without someone to chase.

"You look like you're holding up alright."

Rae spun around abruptly at the sound of Sam's voice, and he trailed her to the speaker set-up where she'd plugged in her iPad. She smiled at him as she tapped her way through the lists and swapped out one that had already played through. "Actually I am. There's just a lingering feeling of stupidity. But no love lost."

"Can you look me in the eyes and say that?"

"Of course." Rae propped her hands on her hips and stared him down, repeating herself word for word. "There's a lingering feeling of stupidity but no love lost." Sam laughed at her, but she continued. "I'm not hung up on Roger." She shrugged as though it didn't mean anything, but it felt good to say and mean it. No one else even asked, they just neatly skirted around the issue.

"Well, that's good to hear." He took a sip of his beer, then glanced over her head. "Uh oh, Rachel."

Her breath caught. No one ever called her Rachel.

But it didn't seem any big deal to him, so she followed his gaze up.

Caught under the mistletoe with Sam. She laughed a little to quell the bubble inside her. There were worse fates.

CHAPTER 9

"All right." Sam looked up at the mistletoe again, then set down the beer and rubbed his hands together, while Rae wondered what the hell he was doing. "I'd better do this right."

Feeling her eyebrows start to raise was all she got to do. His hands were warm and unexpected on her cheeks and she stood paralyzed. He tipped her face up to his just as his lips brushed hers. Her breath sucked in at the sudden jolt she felt.

Sam? Oh Lord, Sam.

But he didn't give her time to think it over. He barely made it an inch away before pulling her back and kissing her again. This time he leaned into it. His mouth melding to hers, so that when his lips parted, hers naturally followed. She inhaled his breath and her legs were folded softly under her with the wave, leaving her washed up against him, upright only because he held her there. Her breathing had entirely stopped, her eyelids dropping closed. And she let whatever was controlling her push her mouth against his for more.

It had started at her lips, but instantly spread everywhere.

The heat that had swept through her made her fingers clutch at the front of his shirt. His hands slipped away from her face, leaving her sad, until they slid down to her back and pulled her closer. She sighed into him, not meaning to. Not meaning *not* to. It just happened and she was rolling with it.

Suddenly, without warning, he let her go. The cold of the air gusting through the balcony doors snapped her back to a red reality where all the pulsing was from the people dancing around her and not from anywhere inside her.

Her calves were taut where she had been straining up on her toes, and a quick scan of the room showed that no one had been paying any attention. Rae plastered on a weak smile and pointed at the jar. "Charity."

Charity? What? That's all she could say? The guy had robbed her of her ability to form sentences?

But it was just Sam, she reminded herself as she gathered the courage to look up at him. When she managed to force herself to look she saw he was digging intently in his wallet. He caught her gaze as he held up the bill. A *twenty*. Casually shoving it down in the jar, he gathered his beer before calmly turning and walking away.

Rae turned herself back to the music lists, grateful for something to focus on. For the fact that no one was paying any attention to her. The red lights would mask the telltale flush she could feel on her face and under her skin, but her rapid breathing would have given the whole thing away.

A twenty!? Was he just being generous to the abused kids, or was he making a statement about that kiss? God, she wasn't going to be able sleep tonight. She had a second thought that she was glad Sloan hadn't made it. Her sister would not have missed that show.

"Hey Rae!" It took a moment to recognize it was her own name and she turned to find the source of the voice, while at the same time trying desperately to take stock of the situation and discover if anyone had seen anything. Sam had disappeared into the crowd, and the voice came again before she located Wendy, the teacher from Sheree's school.

She danced up with a half empty beer in one hand and Liam in tow in the other. "Can you play something that's a little slower? But maybe with a good heavy beat?" Her head tilted prettily and Rae started listing a few titles for her, before realizing that it just wasn't going to happen with all the conversation and dancing and music that was already swirling around them. So she pointed to the iPad and hit a few buttons to bring up the list and had Wendy pick out a few on her own.

While the girl was bent over the rack of neatly stacked cases, Rae glanced up at Liam, who simply shrugged in return. *That little player!* The thought was through her head before she could do a thing about it. *He's planning on getting laid tonight!* While she desperately wanted to be offended, Wendy didn't seem like the type to think much more of it than that herself. So Rae mouthed the words *Good luck* across to Liam and walked off wondering what she would think if she knew her kid's second grade teacher was picking up strange men at parties.

In a few minutes, she made her way to the front door where she found Sheree already saying good-bye to people. Then she looked at the clock and saw it was approaching three a.m. When had it gotten so late? And even standing at the door she was still warm. From the alcohol? Or that kiss?

Unable to answer any of that, she joined in with hugs and "Merry Christmas" and "Happy Holidays" to the people leaving. Lisa and Jack exited a little while later with mischievous looks on their faces. Zoe and her friend Jessica left together, and Zoe promised they'd get together soon and catch up. Alex left with a woman Rae had never met before tonight and one by one the guests headed out the door, until Sheree was shoving Sam out, insisting that they weren't going to clean anything up tonight anyway.

Rae looked up and tried to keep her expression neutral. They said a casual *good night,* all while she was wondering if there was any visible place on a person to detect a pulse rate. But Sam left with the same smile he'd been wearing when he showed up and it all seemed pretty normal on the surface.

Suddenly, lethargy closed over her. It was so late. Her shoulders felt the weight of it all within that span of a few moments as they began shutting off lights and picking up the beer bottles left in precarious spots and the cups still half full of who-knew-what. Then she was turning off the music.

Sheree leaned her weight against the balcony door as though it were made of thick lead instead of standard issue sliding glass. She forced the lock into place with a grunt then spied her charity jar on the bookshelf as she turned back to the dining room. "I'm exhausted, but I desperately want to count this before bed."

Rae followed her to the table with slow shuffling steps and plopped down into a chair after dragging it up. They pushed away chip bags that turned out to be empty anyway, and stacked a few paper plates to make room. Then Sheree turned the jar over, unconcerned with the few rolling coins and such. A good handful of bills mounded up and tumbled out in a small radius. Sheree held up a few fives then exclaimed, "A twenty!" She turned it over. "I wonder if somebody actually donated that or if they took change back."

Stacking the bills by denomination, Sheree found she had almost two hundred dollars for the cause. Not all of their friends were like them. Rae was making ends meet, but without a lot extra. Sheree was an elementary school teacher, hence the reason she had an adult job and a roommate. Zoe was still racking up student loans. But some were rolling in the black. That was good. There were solid donations for a good cause.

Rae didn't mention that she knew where the twenty came from. Her tongue wouldn't work.

Instead, she grunted and got up to walk down the hall to her room, suddenly wide awake and grateful that Sheree didn't seem to be any the wiser. She had been exhausted just moments before, but now she knew she would never get to sleep.

CHAPTER 10

Rae sat across a concrete picnic table from Sloan as they watched the dogs run around the two acre park. Some of the owners threw balls for the dogs. One even had a stick that grabbed the ball on the end then lobbed it far into the distance.

"I want a bag of chips," Rae lamented, hungry.

"You can't eat here." Sloan waved her hand around to the dogs rushing by. There was a section fenced off for smaller dogs, but maybe thirty to forty medium to large to very large dogs played in the open section of the park. "You'll become bait."

Sloan was sitting her boss's dog again and Rae had to wonder what was going on. Was her sister getting abused as an underling? Was she also picking up his dry-cleaning or worse? Or was she maybe having an affair with the boss?

"Ew." Sloan made a face and said the word almost into the air. But Rae knew, Sloan had heard her. They were remarkably connected for half sisters. Though, in their hearts, the "half" was a mere technicality. It only meant they had different last names.

Sloan's father had died when she was very young. Her mother had re-married to Rae's father. But he was their father.

He'd adopted Sloan before she was two, and her older sister didn't remember anything of her birth father. Supposedly, he'd been a great man and she carried his name as a keepsake. But that was all she had of him. Apparently, she had a full connection to Rae, and the sisters sometimes heard each other's thoughts.

"I would never. Ew."

Rae grinned, wondering whether she should have held that thought back until later.

Sloan smiled at someone in the distance and tipped her head. Then she turned back to Rae. "If you want the truth, he got stuck without his dog sitter one day and I volunteered just to be nice. Just so my boss would *owe* me."

"But you're still doing it?"

"Well, now he owes me a lot. And . . ." She looked around. "Have you seen the men?"

"Oh my God. Sloan Ellis! You are picking up men at the dog park?" Rae tried not to bust out with indignation, but she was having a hard time keeping it in. Sloan was much more proper than she was herself. Her sister would never sit in a car and take pictures of married people cheating on each other. Sloan wouldn't pick up a camera and pursue an artistic career by the skin of her teeth, either. But here she was, scoping guys at the dog park.

Sloan shrugged. "Do you have any idea how hard it is to meet a real man in Los Angeles?"

"You mean like a lumberjack? Or a cowboy?" Rae teased.

"No, like someone who is really who they say. Someone who isn't just collecting phone numbers to see how many he can get. Or isn't on a dating app and judging everything about you." She looked around the park again. "Gruber and I are getting to be recognized."

Rae looked around, spotting Gruber, the little flat faced bulldog playing with a pit mix and a dane. Then she looked back at her sister, who looked a little melancholy for a sunny day at the park. Everyone was out, the place growing more and more crowded as the day got warmer. It was the first decently warm day after that cold snap with the threat of snow. So everyone was doing what they were doing—getting the dog out and enjoying the air.

Sloan continued, "I mean, this just feels more organic."

At that moment, a guy came over and sat down on the other end of the bench, on Sloan's side. He smiled at them, then immediately looked down at something that had pinged on his phone.

Oh well, Rae thought. She was looking away, checking out the men now and wondering if Sloan had the right idea. While many were factually attractive to her, she found she wasn't actually *attracted* to any of them. She wanted to ask why, but somewhere down in her, she understood what it was. None of them were Sam.

Shit. She couldn't do that. Could she? Had that kiss meant anything? And how could she spend another minute asking that same question when she already knew damn well she had no answers for it.

"What are you thinking?" Sloan asked her with those narrowed, big-sister eyes that seemed to see too much.

But just as Rae looked back at her, trying to think of what and how much to say, Sloan jumped up. "Oh, Gruber! No!"

She was at the other end of the bench grabbing at Gruber's collar as he jumped his squatty little legs up onto the man on the other end of the bench. He'd even dropped a ball into the man's lap.

Sloan was hauling the short but strong dog back and apologizing as she did. Rae hopped up to help but then found she wasn't needed. The man didn't seem to care.

"It's the dog park. I didn't wear anything that isn't washable." There was a smile in his voice. Which was good. The second thing she'd noticed was that Gruber and the other dog had found a mud puddle. She was glad her sister had driven.

There was a hose at the park so they could wash the dog off, but Gruber was going back in that car either muddy or wet, and Rae was glad it wasn't her car. She wondered if Sloan would tell her boss just how much he owed her.

Listening in with half an ear, Rae heard the two talking. The other dog was his, and everyone needed to get hosed off. They were walking over to the drinking area and wash platform as Rae sat back against the table looking around.

She was thinking once again about how the men here stacked up to Sam—and that they really didn't—when she felt it. She almost popped up to look around. It wasn't as strong as usual. If there was a usual.

She'd first seen that Luke guy at the B-n-B, apparently at his own wedding weekend. But it was the same feeling she'd felt around Los Angeles before, several times, though she hadn't been able to pin it to anyone. Then it had happened at the lingerie store when she'd seen him again.

Maybe it was Yasmin who was triggering the feeling.

Rae scanned the park for either of the two, hoping to sort out this mess and maybe even say hello and start to figure out what it was. But she didn't see Luke or Yasmin, last name unknown.

Instead, her gaze landed on a couple that was walking by in conversation. Their dog was a bit of a misfit but he clearly was in love with his people. They called him "Redford" which almost made Rae laugh. And they called each other Tristan and Megan.

She didn't know what it was. She just kept getting this sensation. It had been several years and she was anxious to figure it out. Then she'd seen Luke and he'd looked so much like their mom. Like her grandfather. He wasn't here now. She looked again as Sloan came back to the table.

"Let's go. Gruber is clean and he won't stay that way if I let him off leash again."

Rae stood up noticing the smudges of mud and wet patches on the side of Sloan's jeans. "So how's the other guy doing?"

Her sister smiled. "Pretty good. He has my number now." Her eyebrows quirked right as Rae's stomach growled. "Come on. We'll drop Gruber at home and pick something up to eat at my place."

Sloan had a decent patio with actual furniture. And a better job. Perks of being the big sister. She'd buy the lunches. Rae smiled. Free, good food. Perks of being the little sister.

But as they walked out, she looked over her shoulder at the lovely but enigmatic Megan. The woman had dark, tightly spiraled curls and a skin tone that defied description. Her eyes almost slanted, but none of that was what got Rae. It was that "Megan" was looking right back at her.

CHAPTER 11

G od, he hadn't slept in three days.

Sam ran his fingers through his hair and stared into the mirror over his sink. His image looked haggard and lovelorn, and it was a little too accurate of a reflection, he thought. He had actually spent time considering that the color of his shirt might bring out the blue in his eyes.

He was a sick, sick man.

Tonight would be the first time he had seen Rachel since that kiss. Well, since he had left that night. The rest of the night had gone on as if nothing had happened. Three days he had wondered if she understood what he meant by putting that twenty in Sheree's kiss-and-donate jar. If he was a lucky man, then he would find out tonight. And he would find out that she *did* understand. If he was very lucky, she would feel the same.

Deciding that it was time to give up and hit the road, Sam pulled on his heavy jacket and was brutally warm for a moment as he jogged down the steps. But when he opened the front door, the cold sucked the wind out of him and set his thinking on a clearer track. Nothing to do but wait and see.

He climbed into his low black coupe, and pulled the long door closed behind him as he revved the engine. The car was one of the few remnants of his fast-track-to-partner days. Sitting for a minute while his thoughts gathered, he played with the radio stations and the navigation system. But his thoughts didn't sway to where they were going and whether he knew the way. They turned to Rae, like they always did lately.

Somehow he'd managed to hold her at bay up until recently. She had always hovered at the edge of his interest, from the moment Sheree had brought along her new roommate and introduced Rae around the group a year and a half ago. He hadn't wanted to get involved with a friend from his circle, fearing it would screw up the dynamic. At the time, he had just weaseled his own way out of his old life. He wasn't stable. Wasn't sure he'd be able to pay his rent every month. And when it came to Rae, he knew he wasn't ready at the time for what he knew he was headed for. There had still been too much of his own mess to work out.

But a year and half had changed the mess. It had sorted nicely. He left his big firm and his break-neck speed job. He hired a paralegal/office worker of his own. He rented his own space and not in the posh area of town. Still, it was Los Angeles, rent was never cheap. This time, he was trying to take cases he believed in, not just the ones the partnership thought it could make money off. He'd worked to do pro-bono work still.

Instead, it had taken six months of taking every reasonable case that walked through the door and two that weren't. He'd dug into what little savings were left after down payments on the rent on his smaller condo and the office just to pay his assistant. The young man hadn't seemed to catch on that his check wasn't always covered by billing. But then it happened. Sam was stable enough to turn down a crap case he didn't want and didn't think had merit. Then it happened again. He'd started to get a reputation for integrity, and his old firm even started referring some cases they didn't want his way. They weren't cash cow cases, but that had been the point of leaving.

Sam finally breathed easier. He saw that he could still pay his bills and as the year wore on—in spite of concerns about paying the rent—he found that he was actually happy again.

Until Roger came and pushed him over a ledge he hadn't known he was standing on. Rae had dated around so at first Sam hadn't thought anything of it. He hadn't been worried about losing her. But then, she just kept seeing Roger, and odd little comments she made about him convinced Sam that the guy wasn't right for her. It hadn't convinced her, though.

And until two months ago Sam hadn't been sure that all his negativity toward Roger wasn't just that he wanted Rae to himself. He still honestly wasn't sure about that one. But he had been right about Roger.

The man made him seethe, but luckily Roger was now gone for good, so Sam threw some of his energy into slicking the car into reverse and heading out for the usual Friday night. This week Lisa got to choose and she'd voted for dim sum. The car clock glowed unearthly green, 5:57. He'd be a little late. Too much time spent pondering his shirt color.

He had to admit he'd lost it. The scary part was that so far he didn't mind so much. Samuel Levi Brock was living the definition of pussywhipped. With one major exception, he wasn't getting any. *Any.* All he had really accomplished was an open door and a sharp eye out for possibilities.

He cursed under his breath as he passed the exit for *Sumthing Good.* He'd have to double back. He'd had a lot of practice with that over the last three days. Rae had thrown him for a loop with that kiss. Though he'd known it would be hot, and he'd known he'd wanted it for a while, his knees had almost buckled.

As he finally locked his car and headed inside where it was

warm, he wondered if she'd be able to do it to him again. His lips curled up lazily at the thought.

"Well, you're in a good mood." Jack reached out and caught his coat as he went by.

"Oh." He turned and found them all tucked around a table hidden just behind the entrance. "I would have totally missed you."

Lisa tilted her pretty blonde head. "Nah, we saw you coming." She and Jack each shuffled over a space, leaving him the empty seat at the end, and further from Rachel than he wanted to be. It was probably a good thing. He wouldn't want to seem too eager, right?

He peeled off his coat and slung it over the back of the chair, before picking up the local amber lager that his friends had waiting for him. And that, he thought, was exactly why he had chosen this life.

He'd never had time for his friends when he'd been at the other job. He'd made plans, sure, but he'd always been late. Finishing up this deposition for the next day or that filing for the judge that evening. If he'd made it at all. In fact, it had been missed plans that had snapped him. Everyone sent him a picture of them out without him and put it up on social media and he'd realized they hadn't even missed him. They'd gotten so used to him not making it to things—just like he had—that no one even noticed he wasn't there. Now he was.

He stuffed his face while the conversation rotated around food, then turned to Sheree's class. "So then Jacob looks up at me and says 'Miss Lester, you should take a Viagra if you don't feel good.' Well, I didn't know what to say to that, so I just stayed quiet. Then this little angel of a boy just smiles at me and goes on, 'My daddy takes them whenever he feels achy and the next day he's better!'"

Sam laughed until Rachel brought up her job. "Lincoln gave me a huge bonus for nailing my ex-boyfriend's ass to a tree."

There was a slight pause in the conversation so she continued. "Sooo, I have decided to spend it on myself."

"New lenses?" Lisa asked. "Filters?"

"Nope." Rae shook her head and her dark red curls, loose tonight, bounced happily. "That's all business related to me. This is just for fun, and because I was never brave enough before."

"Do tell."

They all glanced at Sheree, who seemed to already have the inside scoop but wasn't talking.

"I've decided to take swing classes. They have this club where they have lessons in the back room, and then afterward you can go out and join in on the dance floor."

"Sounds like fun." Jack rubbed his shoulder against Lisa's, ignoring the fact that she seemed almost stunned that he would say such a thing.

Rae sighed wistfully. "Yeah, the only problem is that I'm still not quite brave enough to do it now."

Alex laughed. "Come on Rae. I've seen you. You aren't hopelessly uncoordinated."

She shot him a dirty look. "Gosh, thanks." Then she sighed again. "It's just that more women than men always show up, and I want to have a partner, so I'm hoping one of you guys," she eyed Sam and Alex pointedly, "or better yet, both of you, will go with me. My treat."

Alex and Sam looked at each other. And Sam did his level best to feign indifference at being handed such a perfect opportunity.

Sheree looked around the table. "I keep telling her that men will ask her to dance, but she doesn't believe me."

Rae shook her head. "You haven't been there. There are *always* more girls than guys."

"I've been out with you." Sheree rolled her eyes. "Honey, it doesn't matter how many other women are around. Someone will ask you to dance."

Sam stayed quiet, grateful that the words had come from Sheree's mouth and not his own.

Rae turned back to the guys, the pleading in her voice hard to turn down. Not that he could have anyway. "You can even pick up whoever you want. There will be a lot of extra single girls around. But you have to dance with me some, too. Okay?"

Alex shrugged, so Sam followed suit. "When?"

"Thursdays at seven-thirty."

"That takes me out of the running most weeks." Alex leaned back in his chair, and took another swallow of his beer, while Sam silently thanked providence. "I have that business class."

Rae nodded, and her brown eyes turned to him. There was no heady glow of lust, but they were in a public place. *A man could hope, right?* At least she was asking him along. "All right. But I'll warn you. I can already swing."

"What?" She laughed, her wide smile catching in his throat. "You got your groove thang, white boy?"

"Ha ha. What I mean is that I can actually swing dance. East coast, west coast, and a little lindy hop."

He was leaning toward Rae, but was put back in his place by Alex and Jack, who were now hooting hysterically and making motions of bowing at his feet. Jack could barely contain himself. "Pray tell, why do you know how to *Lindy Hop?*"

"Why else? I was trying to impress a girl."

This time it was Alex. "What? Leading USC to victory three years in a row wasn't enough?"

He started to answer but Rae's voice broke in. "USC? University of Southern California?"

"Yeah." Lisa looked like Rae had gone insane and she spoke a bit slowly. "You know, . . . football. Guys in those tight pants and shoulder pads, patting each others butts?"

Sam laughed, that would be what Lisa got from the game. But it was Rae's face he was watching, everyone was.

"You played for *U.S.C.*? You were a quarterback right?" Lisa asked him while Rae still stared at him like he'd suddenly grown a second head.

He barely finished his nod wondering where this was going, and clearly he wasn't alone.

Rae's stunned voice broke his shock with a squeak. "You're *Samuel Levi* Brock?"

"Yes." It was a slow answer. Had she really not known? All this time. He nodded, and put the pieces in order for her. "Samuel Brock, Sam. You've always known I was Sam Brock."

Clearly, she was just making the connection. "You were all over TV as the what? . . . spokeslawyer in that code copyright case that wound up in the supreme court."

He nodded again. She really hadn't known. A few swear words flitted through his mind. It might change everything.

She was putting the pieces together. He could see it on her face. He could also see she was still confused. "I thought he was blond."

He nodded. "I was." It was a sore point with him. Before she could ask he volunteered. "I've tried to stay out of the sun for a while. I got recognized too much." The whole table was watching him and he didn't like it. It was a big part of the reason he had left it all behind. As he watched, she buried her face in her hands shaking her head.

His heart sank a little at the prospect that Rae would see him differently now. Whatever it was, she wasn't happy that her friend was ex-star-quarterback in the NCAA. OR that he'd gotten his face all over TV going directly from college football into a high profile legal internship. *Shit.* Clearly, the way she was upset, things would be different. She'd demand to know what kind of fool he was giving that all up. A lot of people hadn't understood. Most people hadn't.

Her voice carried through her splayed fingers. "You all knew didn't you?" She glanced around at the others who were shaking their heads. How had she *not* known? With a sigh of disgust, she continued, "I can't believe this. My friends and I used to watch those games when we were in high school, and we talked about your ass!! This is so embarrassing."

He laughed. Maybe there was hope.

CHAPTER 12

Rae sighed, watching as the two swing dance teachers stood together in perfect form. Their arms managed to stay stiff without looking robotic, each finger, each muscle in exactly the right position to demonstrate how a man should hold his partner and how she should hold herself. Add to that Meredith and Ken were decked head to toe in fabulous swing outfits, including obviously expensive dance shoes. The outfit showed off not only perfect physiques but also perfect style.

Rae's own jeans and slightly heeled loafers just didn't seem as cool as they had when she'd chosen them earlier tonight. She'd liked her own outfit, right up until she'd entered the front door.

"Come on." Sam's voice pulled her back to reality. Which, to be honest, wasn't much better than the slow downward spiral of jealousy and self-doubt she'd been riding all evening. "You need to stop slumping."

Excellent. She was slumping in front of a guy who had kissed her senseless. She didn't think poor posture had ever made anyone's top ten ways to catch a man list. "Hmmm." It was all she could think to say without incriminating herself.

His hands left her, vacating their positions at the small of her back and holding her other hand out. The raised hand felt odd, hanging out in space.

He's given up on me already. The thought flitted through her mind, but dissolved when both his hands appeared at her waist, just resting on her hips. His voice was low, and difficult to pay attention to, as his hands were running up her back, slowly but surely causing the intake of breath that was straightening her spine. Maybe slumping was underrated. Maybe she should do it more if it earned her this.

His words were not seductive. Crap. "We're not going to look like them right away, that takes years of training."

"And a great wardrobe." She murmured back, noting the brief warm smile her comment generated.

Teacher Ken's voice cut through her thoughts, "We'll be learning two moves tonight. A more basic move . . ." He didn't finish the sentence, just started dancing with no perceptible motion to Meredith. They moved in perfect time to nonexistent music, after a moment of simple steps he spun her out slowly, then wound her back in close and dipped her. "And a more difficult move."

Their feet never stopped, and he and Meredith realigned, but only for a heartbeat. Then he spun her fast enough to show off the perfect flare of her skirt and the ruffled matching panties she wore underneath. He continued to speak while moving his feet and still leading Meredith through a series of three turns in different directions and a variety of holds.

They finished side by side with Meredith not looking the slightest bit winded or dizzy, although Rae had experienced both sensations just watching them.

"All right," This time it was Meredith's dulcet tones that rang out over the crowd. "Let's take the beginners on the entry-side of the room with me, and the more experienced dancers on the window side with Ken."

Rae let go of the near-death grip she had on Sam and went back into her slump. Sam belonged on the advanced side of the room. She did not. "I guess I'll see you later, then."

But he grabbed her hand and pulled her back to the appropriate position, facing him with about two feet in between. "You paid my way in, I'm going to earn my keep."

"Oooh," she smiled, "I got me a man-ho for the evening."

"No."

Just that one word and she knew she'd been put back in her place. She should not have said that. It was offensive. She was opening her mouth to offer a truly sincere apology, but she was honestly afraid that opening her mouth would let her put her foot right back in it.

Her fear only lasted a moment until Sam eased her concerns. "I don't man-ho for this cheap, and my man-ho moves are certainly far too good to use in public."

Her fear and tension dissipating, Rae laughed and almost missed that Meredith had asked them to line up all facing the same way and she was showing the basic footwork and they should all practice by copying her.

There were a few people who instantaneously began doing the proper moves, Sam among them. But within a few minutes, Rae could keep up with the music and didn't embarrass herself. There were a couple people who obviously had zero sense of rhythm, and Rae tried not to look at them, afraid they would throw her off beat. At the same time, she was fascinated with how a person couldn't feel the thrum of the music.

A short while later, Ken left the advanced group doing a few minutes of practice, while he joined Meredith to show the proper hold again and add in the footwork.

Rae watched for a few measures, finding Ken to be an amazing dancer with moments of blinding fabulousness. As she watched, she sent up a quick prayer that she could follow along.

Then another that dancing with Sam would undo whatever spell that Christmas kiss had visited upon her.

Even as she was having that thought, Sam took her hand in his, tugging her close. First, he used his free hand to position her fingers in the proper hold over his own, then he ran his fingertips down her arm creating the proper dance space and calling to mind wicked images of *Dirty Dancing*.

She fought to hide the shiver that shimmied up her body at his touch.

Competing sensations warred in her brain. Sam's hand, creating a warm pressure on her lower back, or her own palm collecting heat from his well-muscled shoulder, through soft cotton. Her legs, almost locked from her inability to think about anything else.

Oh yeah, and she was supposed to be paying attention to her feet? That was not going to happen.

After a few minutes Rae gave up wishing that something here would snap her out of it. Sam didn't have a femme side. He wasn't rude or pushy about her lack of ability. He didn't even seem to mind being stuck on the beginner side of the room. She wasn't getting over that kiss. If anything was happening, the *opposite* problem was occurring. She was getting more tangled up in it all. Even though she really had no idea what *it* was. But broad muscles, soft T-shirts, and a ready laugh weren't helping her let go of her growing fantasy.

Then Ken suggested they each pair up with a more experienced partner. And Sam was suddenly gone. Off to find a more experienced partner than himself. Rae stood alone, looking around the class, knowing she needed to find her own partner. Just as she'd told Sam she would do.

Instantly there was a broad palm, with a light dusting of hair on the forearm, and a voice, "Hi, I'm Oscar." And she looked up and smiled into a handsome set of brown eyes and shook his hand, even as she felt the bucket of ice water douse her. Oscar was hot, friendly, and even sweet.

Still, he was no Sam.

Rae tried not to watch Sam performing the same set-up on a thin, dark-haired beauty who beamed at him with a smile that reached to her eyes and beyond. Sam smiled back at the woman, as casually as he had with her. And why shouldn't he? He was used to this. It was just her. Just that stupid Christmas kiss that pulled the rug out from under her. She fought to find her own voice and her own decency for the nice man who'd rescued her from being left over.

"Hi Oscar, I'm Rae, short for Rachel." And with that she put her arms and her mind into Oscar's capable hands.

CHAPTER 13

R ae thumbed through the jumble of mail she pulled from the vertical mailbox in the lobby. It had practically fallen out in her hands, there was so much of it. She stood in the lobby, tucking business size envelopes under her chin as she chucked pieces of junk mail into the overflowing lobby trash. When she looked at the bin she could practically reconstruct the tree that had been killed to offer everyone in the building that low, low interest rate credit card. Knowing her friend didn't want a new credit card or plastic surgery either, she threw away some of Sheree's mail, too.

With letters laced between her fingers in three categories—Sheree, Rae, both—Rae climbed the steps. There was an elevator, but it wasn't fast by any stretch. And there was no better way to a great ass than climbing actual stairs. She wound up through the stairwell that the manager clearly didn't expect anyone to use. It was neglected and dingy compared to the rest of the building, which as a whole was pretty nice for the mid-level rent.

She wanted to thumb through the catalogues that had arrived, but they stayed tucked in her left hand, as she didn't have a fully free hand to open the heavy fire door from the staircase and she didn't have enough fingers to operate the key to the apartment door. Setting all the mail and her camera cases at her feet in the hallway, Rae searched her purse for her keys before remembering she'd shoved them in her pocket.

Pushing the door open, she spilled into the unit, smiling at the bright colors she and Sheree had painted the walls last summer when work had been slow for both of them. Bit by bit, she hauled all her things inside, cameras, mail, catalogues.

Managing to get Sheree's mail into the inbox she'd set on the entry table, Rae held onto her own. Then she sorted her own bills into the other box and started shredding through her own mail while sitting at the dining room table. The chair was hard and the mail wasn't all that fun. She had a bill for her student loans. Which she could cover, but she'd forgotten about it, and there went those leather boots she wanted. She frowned when she saw the return address on a plain white envelope. *The Webber Gallery*. The Webber was a local place for fine and semi-fine art. Rae had a piece there on commission and another in the back room, that she hoped they'd get out and dust off soon. Neither had sold, and it had been a while.

With a deep breath she steeled herself to open the letter, just praying it didn't say they hadn't been able to sell either piece and could she please come reclaim them?

But the letter didn't say that at all.

In fact, she wasn't certain what the letter said at all, because a beautiful baby-blue business check was clipped to the front. For a good handful of hundreds of dollars.

Holy shit.

She had to shake her head to clear it. Wondering if it had all been a mistake, she gingerly lifted the edge of the check and began reading the attached letter. Her mouth formed a round 'o'. She had sold *The Towers*. At full asking price. And she'd been pretty certain it had been the one they'd initially put in the back. Maybe they had rotated it out front instead of *Butterfly*.

"Hey! I'm home!" Sheree's voice came from just beyond the wall.

Rae assaulted her with a huge hug.

CHAPTER 14

Sloan took her out to celebrate. Rae thought it was only appropriate that she buy the dinner with her fat check, but Sloan wouldn't hear of it.

"Fat checks are awesome, but they can go through your hands like water," Sloan had told her over shrimp scampi. "Put as much of it into savings as you can. But you can get one pair of boots."

Rae grinned. She had the best big sister.

Sloan went on. "When I first got this job, the pay was definitely higher than I'd gotten before. And the first three months, I did nothing of value with it. I could not tell you where that extra money went."

Rae nodded. Big sister wisdom to the rescue. "At least yours was steady."

Sloan nodded. "But I'm doing the nine-to-five thing. It's not for you." However, she smiled and raised her glass of wine. "Here's to your first big sale, and may there be many more!"

Rae could drink to that. By the time she left, Sloan had piled all the to go boxes into Rae's hands and told her to take them for herself.

"I can feed myself!" she protested.

"I know. I do. But I also know how it feels to be concerned about money."

Yes, Rae thought, there was a rough two months after she graduated when she was just starting out with her first company. Then Sloan had stepped in. But that's what you got when you had a math degree that she got in three years, followed immediately by an MBA. So she took the food. She was the creative one.

She leaned back against the headrest in Sloan's nice sedan and moaned. "I think dinner gave me the body shape of that cannelloni."

Sloane laughed at her. "Stuffed to the gills? Me too. But it was so good. It was worth it."

"I won't be able to climb up the stairs," Rae moaned.

"Shall we go walk along Hollywood Boulevard?"

"Oooh. Yes." Though she drove it often, it had been a while since she'd gone crawling in the various shops. A lot of them turned over rapidly, so there was plenty to explore. She directed Sloan to a side street near Zoe's apartment, and they climbed out. Rae felt it as she unfolded. She almost moaned again. She'd definitely over-eaten and walking would do her some good.

They crossed to the south side of the street and ducked into a shop full of kinky shoes first. Next, they passed a jewelry store, then a t-shirt shop that would spray paint anything onto a shirt for them. They graciously refused. They made it all the way down past Vine, before turning around to head back.

As they crossed at the light, Rae grabbed Sloan's hand and tugged her diagonal across the road. "Look, we have to go in there."

"Blessed Be?" Sloan was running, though it wasn't that easy in her heels. "What is it?"

Rae had better vision. "It's a magic shop."

"What? I don't need magic tricks." Sloan was on the corner

of the sidewalk now, having made it across, but no longer following Rae. The shop was less than half a block down.

"No. It's for real magic. Like witchcraft and stuff!" Rae was still moving forward. She wanted to see what was in that shop.

"Witchcraft. That's not safe." But her sister had caught up and was now reading the gold lettering on the sign.

Rae turned and frowned. "What do you mean?"

"That stuff's dangerous. You shouldn't play with it if you don't understand it." Her expression was deadly serious. Moreso than Rae would have expected.

She stopped on the street and looked at her sister with a serious expression. "Have *you* played with it, Sloan?"

"When I was in eighth grade, one of my friends got out a Ouija board. It was not okay."

"Wow, you never told me."

"We didn't tell anyone." Then Sloan's eyes darted away before her next confession. "My friends said they used it all the time and it only went nuts when I was there. Even if I was just in the room. But by themselves? It didn't do anything." Sloan met her eyes then. "It scared the crap out of me, Rae."

"I didn't know." She paused, standing there on the corner of Hollywood and Vine. "I still think we should go in."

"Why?"

"Because I do."

"Is it one of your feelings?"

Sloan would trust her if she said yes, but Rae wouldn't lie to her sister. "Not quite. But think about those feelings that I get. I know we can't always prove that I'm right, but nothing has ever proved me wrong."

Sloan nodded solemnly.

"And you see things. You know it. You've told me. It's probably why the Ouija board went wonky around you." Rae crossed her arms, not comfortable venturing into this territory for the first time with her sister. "Mom always knew where we were and when we weren't okay. And remember that time Dad canceled our trip? And that plane went down! Both our parents had it, too. That's why we never really thought it was so odd. But I think we need to go into that store and learn more."

"Why more? Isn't it enough to be the weird kid? To learn not to tell people what I see, even when it would help them? Because it doesn't help them. They get so caught up in how I got the information that they won't *use it!*" Sloan's voice pitched, and Rae realized they never really talked about it. It was an open secret in the family.

The day she'd called her sister and said, "Something happened to Mom, and it's bad," Sloan had only replied, "I know."

Still, Rae's curiosity had gotten the best of her and she'd done some digging. "Sloan, Mom was an Alberti and her mother was born a Tavani."

"What about it?"

"Nonna was like us, too," Rae pushed. "And the Tavanis and Albertis are some of the biggest known families in witchcraft in the old country."

"What?"

Had Sloan never looked this up? "Were you never curious?" Her sister shook her head, but Rae couldn't stop now. "You're an Ellis and I'm a Woodward."

"Is that supposed to mean something?" Sloan was in full avoidance mode now, her blond hair looking perfect around a face that looked wary, scared, and almost angry at her little sister for bringing it up.

"Yes, they're families known to be associated with American and English wicca."

"You can't be serious."

But she was, and Rae was reaching out to take her sister's hand. "Mom is gone, Dad is gone, your birth father is gone. It's just us now. Maybe we should find out where we come from. And maybe they can help us find our lost cousin."

Sloan had looked at her weird. Though she'd never agreed, she eventually let Rae pull her along. A bell jingled as they opened the door and Rae looked up but couldn't see it. Cool trick. Something about the little shop made her feel immediately at home.

CHAPTER 15

"All right." Rae sighed and gave up. Sam had been pushing her to try out her new swing dancing skills on the main floor for three lessons now. Always before she hadn't felt up to joining the other dancers who were showing off their moves. They were good. Some were pros, just keeping up their skills or enjoying the sheer fun of it.

Alex hadn't shown up once, as he was just too busy with his grad school classes, but that was understandable. Sam, on the other hand, had come every time. He always danced with several of the other girls and had become quite a favorite. Though she and Sam usually stayed after classes and watched the other dancers on the floor, she'd never worked up the courage to get out and try it. So mostly they sat at the bar, enjoying some drinks and the show.

Until last week. One brave girl had come up to them while they were talking. She had danced with Sam in class a few times, and last week asked politely if she wasn't interrupting anything. Then Rae had had to watch while the skinny blonde had hauled Sam out onto the floor and let him swing her around and over and under.

Rae had been brutal to the ice in her drink. Sam hadn't made a move on her since the party. Her goal had been to learn to dance, and she wanted to get out and try some of her new moves, but the blond had beat her to it. To top it off, Rae had spent her swing dance lessons alternately trying to learn the moves and quash her fascination with Sam. Oh, and trying not to watch him dance with other women. Two out of three of those things had not been part of her goal. She'd just been stuck mooning over Sam and trying not to show it.

It wasn't like he had asked her if she was available. Clearly, the Christmas kiss—as she had come to refer to it—was just a kiss for charity. So now, she sighed, knowing that it was time for her to try out her skills on the floor. It was either that or watch Sam dance with the stick. And while she felt she had made admirable progress in denying whatever she had felt for him, she wasn't up to watching the blonde drape herself all over him while they danced in some perfect rhythm Rae had yet to achieve.

She finished the tail end of her drink and was startled when he tucked her hand in his and led her through the throngs of people that covered the floor. Rae had always enjoyed that first moment when he would take her hand in his and then place the other at her waist. But that was all she had ever gotten to enjoy of it, because then she had to concentrate on what the teachers were saying and where her feet were supposed to be going.

The band was taking a quick water break as Sam rattled off a few moves to her. She nodded. He had picked fairly easy ones. Not letting go of her hand, he pulled it up into the proper position and let the other slide around to just beside the small of her back. Then, suddenly the band members were all back, and with a quick word from the leader, the horns started up and they were off.

Her toes kept getting in the way. Rae would make it through the first few moves, but then lose a step and wind up going the wrong way. It seemed, just when she would get it together a little, she would start enjoying the pressure of his hands touching her and her feet would drop steps again.

Mercifully, the music ended, and she slouched, defeated, off the floor. Only to have her arm yanked back, her hand still caught in Sam's and apparently he wasn't going anywhere. His voice said so. "Come back."

"Oh please, that was so horrible." She tried to extract her fingers, at least she told herself that she did. "Dance with someone who can dance as well as you can."

He tugged at her fingers again. "Come back."

"Your feet will be black and blue." But she obeyed and returned to standing in front of him, hand still firmly tucked into his. Though she enjoyed that feeling immensely, the rest of it felt like crap. She was failing miserably and she'd so wanted to be good at this. She also had wanted to impress Sam and that ship had sailed. Full of dancers doing perfect steps and not stepping on each other's feet.

He smiled. "It's time for the lecture."

"Lecture?" Her eyebrows rose as he nodded. "This is my dance space—" she pointed to in front of her, then him, "—this is yours?"

"No. Listen: It's dance, not a democracy. I lead, and you follow."

"I'm trying."

He nodded. "Yes, but you're doing it wrong."

"Clearly." The droll word fell out of her mouth before she could stop it.

"You can't and shouldn't anticipate me. This psychic method you're using is poor, at best."

"But then how do I know where to go?" She was whining, frustrated. This wasn't the Rae that she had wanted Sam to see. She had hoped to wow him with her natural ability. But that dream had gone out the window and led up to him lecturing her. Ugh.

"I'm going to push and pull you where I want you to go. You just worry about hitting the steps, the rest of you will go where I tell it." He moved her hand back and forth in front of her, controlling her shoulders. Just like in class. But in class they had been doing specific moves and not just whatever the man felt like.

She gave up. "I've been trying."

"I know." He placed her hand on his shoulder and found her waist, setting the little butterflies in her stomach free again. "But this time, you're going to close your eyes."

"If I can't do it with my eyes open, then how am I—"

"Close them."

She did.

"One, two, ready."

Rae just paid attention to her feet. Just like he had told her. Shockingly, it was *much* easier. She simply paid better attention to where his hands pushed and pulled her. She could tell even in class, from the few other guys that she had danced with, that he wasn't what the teachers called a 'mushy' lead. But now he actually had her going where she was supposed to. Suddenly, she made only a few minor errors, and the ones she made were somehow easier to correct with her eyes closed.

She made it to the end of the piece finally. "Oh, my God."

But the music started up again and so did Sam. She was moving before his voice found her over the wail of the horns. "If you feel like you're up to it, try opening your eyes."

She kept them closed again at first, but then peeked a little. Every time she did, her feet wound up tangled in each other again. She finished the song with her eyes squeezed shut in an attempt to prevent any more errors.

"Okay, it's getting weird with yours eyes closed."

"But I mess up when they're open."

Sam laughed. "So, find something to look at." She opened her eyes, as the singer announced that this would be the last piece. She found that the collar of his shirt was a steady unchanging point while she was facing him.

Just above her view she saw his head shake. "That's just as bad as having them shut. Look here." He pointed at his own eyes.

Her breath hitched as she was caught in his gaze, and her chest filled with some odd warmth, but there wasn't any time to think about it. The music had started up again. Sam's steady stare penetrated her soul and kept her from thinking too much about her feet. What she did think was that she was falling, into some wide-open space, some place where she and Sam were far more to each other than they were in the real world. Some place where the butterflies inside her meant something. But the poor man was just trying to help her learn to dance.

Still, Rae was excited. She was dancing, which was great. That alone felt like a kid getting a good grade or shooting that first basket. But underneath were the gushy feelings for Sam. The ones she was finally admitting weren't just a silly crush. The kind she'd never had for Roger. Roger had been stable and steadfast and full of shit. Sam was her friend. Part of her inner circle and if she went there . . . well, it could easily mess everything up.

Her feet stumbled as she wondered if Sam could read the passage of thoughts across her face. But his arms looped around her and his hands applied gentle pressure, and for the briefest moments she wanted to believe it meant something more. But he righted her, and set her feet back into rhythm, and Rae realized that she was reading way too much into it and so she forced her thoughts back to her feet.

She made it through the whole song with only a few missteps. And it really was fun, just like she'd hoped it would be.

Although after all the spins he put her through at the end, she felt utterly drunk.

"I did it!" Gleefully she hopped a few times, only to have Sam pick her up and spin her around. She didn't even get to think before his lips closed over hers and melted her like butter. It was a good thing he was holding her up or he would have had to mop her off the floor.

Then he set her down and the band was thanking everyone and saying goodnight. She turned away from Sam so they could join everybody in the applause. It was as good an excuse as any to get her breathing back under control. Before she could take stock of the situation they were washed along with the crowd, getting their coats and her purse and heading out the door.

"Where are you parked?" His voice was as casual as it could be. Apparently, the kiss hadn't affected him at all. Which was a crying shame because she couldn't think straight.

"Huh? . . . Oh! I'm just down the street. The lot was full." Rae shrugged and turned to head down the steps from the lot.

"I'll drive you." Sam tried to steer her over to his coupe.

"I'll be fine, Sam, really. I'm a big girl." She stuffed her hands in her pockets and tried to convince herself of that. She also told herself it didn't mean anything to her that the kiss didn't mean anything to him.

"And I'm from Georgia. Southern gentlemen don't let women walk down alleys by themselves."

She nodded and reluctantly climbed into the passenger seat. Silently, they followed the slow moving stream of cars heading out of the lot. Nothing was said until he pulled up beside her little red terror of an old coupe and leaned over as she hopped out. "Next week?"

Rae nodded. "Sure, if you're up for it."

With a final nod from Sam, she closed the door and turned the key in her own car door, before sinking into the seat and putting on a good show of getting the car started and driving off. She didn't want him to see how much he kept rattling her.

By the time she pulled into a spot at her building, Rae thought she had herself pretty much together. At least outwardly.

CHAPTER 16

"Look!"

Mrs. Brock led her only son through the kitchen and into her sitting room. She beamed and pointed at the huge framed, black-and-white photograph that she had just acquired. As usual the whole room had been rearranged to accommodate her new piece, and Sam was afraid eventually there wouldn't be any visible drywall left, just a series of art photos. The question was, would there be so many holes that the room would collapse? Luckily his parents would never sell this house; they loved it here. But he was not looking forward to the day when they would have to hide the millions of punctures his mother had put in the wall over the years.

To her credit, his mother had a great eye and managed to acquire some amazing pieces. All black and white. Some by unknown artists who remained unknown, but the vast majority were original prints by artists before their time. She had some Ansel Adams pieces that the man had actually printed himself. And an Annie Liebowitz piece from when everyone was saying 'Annie who?' Now, her latest treasure was this odd shot of New York City by some new unknown.

It was of people walking down a busy street, with the World Trade Centers in geometric form in the back. A man and a woman stood facing each other in the foreground, perfectly aligned to the buildings. Throngs of people crowded the street, but they didn't look quite right. He had to admit, for a simple shot it kept you staring.

"See?" He felt the smile in his mother's words. "Do you want a Coke?"

"Sure." Coming from Georgia, he'd grown up with Cokes. He'd often wondered if Georgian women put Coca Cola in the babies' bottles rather than milk.

"You just keep looking, it gets more interesting," She called out from the kitchen over the hiss of a glass bottle being opened. He swore that she would be offering him Coke until he was seventy. He could remember her pouring whiskey for his father when his dad was still younger than he was now. He shook off the thought to keep assessing the photo before him. Something wasn't right about it, but he couldn't figure what.

A bottle with a striped paper straw appeared at his left shoulder, and his mother's voice started again. "Do you see it?"

"It's not right. But . . ."

"Look at the trade centers." Her finger pointed. "They aren't there. You can see the clouds through them." He blinked and suddenly it was obvious. She kept talking. "And look, this side reflects Chicago, not New York. This side L.A. The other building reflects Miami and D.C. And none of the people are going toward the towers on the street. Normally traffic would go both ways, but they're all coming at you. And look at the water. The towers are missing in the city's reflection." She finally took a breath. "I haven't figured anything else out yet. So, if you spot something new, let me know."

He shook his head. What had seemed to be just an old photo of New York clearly was anything but, and he tilted his head this way and that, trying to catch other hidden things in it.

His mother laughed. "I've been doing that, too. . . . It's a local artist, you know."

He could take Rae to the gallery show. The thought was instantly there in his mind. But wasn't it always? What excuse could he dream up to go out with her? The touch of her lips could be conjured in his senses in a heartbeat. But he couldn't be entirely convinced that the feelings were mutual. Sometimes it did seem like it couldn't be anything else, and sometimes it seemed as if she'd never notice him that way.

Luckily his mother didn't notice that his brain had gone missing from the earth momentarily. "He doesn't even have a gallery show yet."

How did she do that?

"So are you going to hop on your bandwagon and get him one?" Some days it seemed that his mother just enjoyed exercising her connections. He'd always pondered the idea that she should create an artist just to see if she could literally sell anything. Maybe pass off her own photos as belonging to some young hotshot she had conjured. Maybe turn a five-year-old into the next big thing.

"I haven't met him yet. The gallery owner had another piece out front, which honesty was just as stunning. He had this one in the back room. You know I always ask what he's got in the back. Sometimes that's the best stuff. Apparently, he doesn't think this artist has enough work to carry a full show yet. I think I'd like to meet him, though."

Sam laughed as he polished off the soda. His mother had simply been biding her time, waiting for another crusade. The last photographer she backed had moved to New York eight months ago, hitting the big time and leaving her without a pet project.

"Good luck, Mom."

"Mr. Woodward will get his own show soon. He's so

talented. I can feel it." She nodded to herself, and Sam didn't doubt her.

Then he stopped dead. "Woodward?"

"Mmm Hmm." She turned off toward the kitchen, hollering for his sister and father to come to dinner. "Ray Woodward."

He almost choked. "Ray Woodward?"

CHAPTER 17

R ae froze. "Your family? For dinner?" Meeting Sam's family? Had she missed a step somewhere? Didn't only girlfriends go to meet the parents? Was she his girlfriend and she somehow didn't know it?

"Yeah. You can meet my mom and dad, and you already know Christy." He seemed to shuffle from foot to foot. If he was nervous about her answer or maybe just worried that everyone beyond the kitchen would hear, she couldn't tell.

"All right." She wasn't sure why she said it, but it was already out there. Why was she invited to dinner at his parents' house? She turned back to the living room with the bowl of popcorn he had caught her with, and suddenly everyone cheered. For a brief moment she was unsure why they were celebrating. Then she realized that something had happened on TV. The TV cops had solved the crime or nabbed a bad guy or something. It had nothing to do with her.

Alex, Lisa, Jack, and Sheree all sat in various places on and in front of the sofa. All oblivious to the fact that Sam had just cornered her in the kitchen and asked her to meet his family.

Crime Night just kept going on around her. The weekly Tuesday evening get-together didn't hold her attention anymore. She found she was glad that she and Sheree were hosting this week. Rae didn't think she'd be very safe behind a wheel if she'd had to drive home tonight. Not the way her brain was wandering around untethered. If only the clues in real life were as straightforward as they were on TV. There was always a telltale toenail, or a bit of blood. Sam was nowhere near as easy to read.

She just settled into her spot to stare at the tube like everyone else. Hoping that they wouldn't notice that she wasn't paying any attention at all.

Sam didn't kiss her in the kitchen. And why would he? She was just making ideas up. Maybe because she wanted to. Then again, maybe he wanted to, too, and everyone else had been swarming the place like they usually were, getting in the way. But he did wear a kind of a funny smile for the rest of the evening.

For two whole days, she thought it through. She tailed the next cheating husband Lincoln had assigned her. And she was glad to know that this one left her without the residual anger. Or that feeling of vomiting. It just made her a little sad, like usual, to see another marriage fall apart so badly. Why didn't people just get divorced? Not that that was great, but it sure beat cheating.

Sam wasn't the cheating kind. She could feel her lips curl up a hint at that thought. Hell, he was hardly the dating kind. One or two, here or there. At least that was what she knew of his history. But he had always been honest and straightforward as long as she had known him.

So, what was with the asking her to his parents' place for dinner? His mother was cooking, for God's sakes. That indicated a certain level of . . . a certain level of . . . what? Commitment? They had hardly kissed!

Mind you, those kisses had turned her insides to jelly. And made her happy that whole business with that smarmy Roger was over and done with.

Rae snapped a few photos of the husband as he entered a motel room with a woman who was not his wife. You would think they would be smart enough to get a room with inside entry so that it would be harder to prove they were getting a room together. But hey, their stupidity paid her bills.

She checked her watch and at five called the other P.I. she was sharing shifts with and told him where to trade out with her. In half an hour, she was racing home to change and overanalyze the whole situation all over again.

As she was getting dressed she had decided that he *must* be interested in her. It was the only explanation for dinner with his family, right?

Okay, *getting dressed* was the wrong term for what she was doing. Throwing her clothes around the room while she tried on outfit after outfit was more like it. She was more mimicking a tornado than an adult woman.

Then Rae finally realized that what she wanted to accomplish with her clothing was actually a completely impossible task. There was no outfit to catch Sam's eye that wouldn't also clearly not be a good meet-the-parents outfit. Jeans and a tight tee were far too casual. The low cut dress? Far too sexy. Pants and a sweater were far too frumpy. In the end, she was caught in a meet-the-parents type outfit that she only hoped wouldn't turn him off, when the front door buzzed. So she guessed this was what she was wearing.

"Accckk." Her hair! She bolted to the front door and pushed the talk button, maybe it was the Avon lady, right? "Hello." She could always hope.

"Hey, it's Sam. Buzz me up."

She didn't know any Avon ladies.

Oh well, at least she would have a few minutes while he came up the stairs.

Managing to run a brush through her hair, she stuck a few tiny, cute clips in just for show. Why had she agreed to this?? She touched up her makeup from that morning. It would have to do. She racked her memory for a magazine article about a stakeout-to-steak-with-the-parents transformation. Day-to-night, sure. But none of it had ever really applied to her. This wasn't the typical office-to-dinner-with-champagne date.

He knocked at her apartment unit, but she carefully finished applying her lipstick first. He would live.

Rae forced herself to be calm on the way to her front door and then began to wonder if he would kiss her. Calm fled out the window. *Oh god.* How would she handle that? How *should* she handle that? Throwing the door open before she could get too worked up, she tossed him a casual smile as she grabbed her jacket and purse. "Let's go."

Even the air hummed between them as he leaned in. "You look great tonight."

"What? These nice, pressed pants? I just grabbed them out of the back of the closet." She shrugged as though she didn't wear ripped jeans and sneakers most days.

He chuckled but didn't say anything else as they made their way down the back steps to where his coupe waited by the curb. Ever the southern gentleman, Sam opened the door for her and then headed around to the driver's side.

Somehow, they didn't say a single word to each other until he pulled up at a quaint house painted a bright, clean white with blue trim. It could have been the Cleaver's house from Leave It To Beaver. And it was the perfect place for a blond-haired, blue-eyed quarterback to have grown up, even if he'd actually grown up in Georgia.

He announced, "We're here," as though it wasn't fully obvious.

She just eyed the house, unable to make a move to get out, and he seemed to psychically gather her thoughts. "Yeah. They've only been here ten years, but it looks like every other house I grew up in. All-American."

"Like you." God help her, but she didn't know where that came from.

He just grinned and threw open the front door ushering her in as though it were the most natural thing in the world. The butterflies in her stomach began a mass migration.

"Sammy!" Christy threw her arms around him then roughed his hair, before being a perfect lady to Rae. "It's good to see you again. You look great." And so on.

Rae's jacket was taken and hung up and she felt like she had wandered into a perfect TV show. It was so different from the jumble that she had grown up in. If she hadn't experienced it occasionally at friend's houses when she was younger, she would have sworn that the TV show she had entered was actually the Twilight Zone.

"Oh hello. You must be Rachel. Sam has told us all about you."

"Mom." He sounded kind of embarrassed. But Rae smiled, maybe she would get lucky and get kissed again. Even as she shook hands around and uttered niceties her stomach did little flip-flops.

"Come on." He grabbed her hand and tugged her through the house to the sitting room. There was a little swirl of satisfaction in the pit of her stomach at having him take her hand like this. She hardly noticed the photographs on the wall in the room. She would ask his parents about it later. But Rae filed it under 'small talk' and looked up at Sam, waiting.

He'd tugged her along until they were alone in the back of the house. Maybe he would say or do something now. She took shallow breaths as she looked at him and waited.

He raised his eyebrows at her, sending her into even more

flutters. But his mother walked in behind him before he could even speak. Rae took a solid step away so Mrs. Brock wouldn't think their guest had been trying to seduce her son in the back room. Like she actually had been doing. She tried to gather some coherent thoughts and decided to start with the small talk. She waved her hand around at the walls.

"Are you a collector—" She didn't finish.

The piece on the wall drew her in. Huge, black and white, with all those familiar faces. It made her heart sink.

"Oh yes, I just love finding new artists."

Rae cocked her head, barely registering Mrs. Brock speaking, or that Sam wore a huge grin. Her Trade Center piece stared down at her. Sam had bought it for his mother? She hadn't *really* sold it then. He must have thought he was doing something nice, some sort of favor, but she'd believed she had an actual patron. Now she would have to return the nice fat check to him. She couldn't keep that kind of money from Sam. Not now that she knew.

This sucked monkey balls. One second she'd thought she was becoming a real artist and that Samuel Levi Brock was interested in her. The next she realized it was all a lie.

"What's wrong?" His voice was soft and low in her ear. But before she could answer his mother spoke again.

She didn't listen, even though it was rude. She couldn't muster up the manners she'd been taught. In a rough whisper, she tried not to give herself away, but she could hear the hurt in her own voice. "Why did you buy this? Why didn't you tell me?"

But his mother, gazing at the wall and unaware of their exchange, piped up before he could answer. "I just acquired this piece a little over a week ago. Sam tells me that he knows the artist, Mr. Woodward. Do you know him, too?"

Now Rae was utterly confused. Turning to Mrs. Brock, she placed a hand flat to her chest like an old woman and said the only thing she could think of. "What?"

But Mrs. Brock continued to smile. "He promised to introduce me."

"Rachel—" Sam started, but this time she turned to him, still without a clue.

"What?"

He grinned and it began to sink in. She wasn't his girlfriend, there was never any intention of introducing her to his parents. Well, not that way. The butterflies all came to an eerie standstill. Her voice was low and mean. "You didn't buy this?"

Even as she heard the sound from her mouth, she wished desperately that she could take it back. Open mouth, insert foot. *Shit.* Her anger was all from her disappointment that he didn't bring her here as his girlfriend.

She wouldn't have guessed it, but finding out that his mother was the one who bought the Trade Center piece didn't begin to make up for not being asked to meet his parents for the traditional reasons. Apparently, she'd really wanted to be his girlfriend. Even though the sale of her art was at least partially legit, she was hurt. And in her hurt, she sounded mean.

He didn't deserve that. Honest, up-front Sam hadn't led her on in any way. She had concocted that story all by herself.

He even smiled in response. "No. *She* did."

"But you told her to."

"No." Sam shook his head. No guile. "My Mom collects art. She found the artist herself." Then he grabbed Rae by her shoulders and turned her to face his mother.

At least as the older woman spoke again, Rae found a smile. *A real buyer.*

"I paid quite a few hundred for it. Good money. But I tell you I stole it. It was worth more."

"Oh, my god." She heard it before her brain acknowledged the words.

"Mom." Sam's hands steadied her, soft and firm on her

shoulders, even as he moved around behind her. "This is Rachel Woodward."

"Oh. Are you related to—"

He cut his mother off. "*Rachel*, Mom. This *is* Rae Woodward."

CHAPTER 18

"Jeremy." Sam fought to keep the exasperation from his voice, but it was a losing battle. "I *know* that your mother set this up for you. But I'm not defending your mother. She didn't commit a crime. You did. I'm defending *you*. And *you* can pay me or go to juvie. I'm not going to work for a client who doesn't want to be defended."

The boy stuck out his lower lip. He was all of fifteen and would have looked almost a man if not for the utterly childish expression on his face. Sam had the strong desire to help the kid back onto . . . the right track? Hell, any track would do. But at what cost?

His mother lived in the same townhouses he did, two units over, and she didn't have much time after working too many double shifts. Jeremy here had clearly fallen through the cracks a while ago. His little brother would follow soon if something wasn't done.

But Jeremy didn't see it that way and he just shrugged his shoulders indifferently. "Why don't I just pay your fee?"

Sam bit his tongue. It was all he could do not to blurt out that he didn't take drug money or stolen money or any of the kinds of money Jeremy was likely to offer. "My fee is in labor." With great force of will, he managed to not grind his teeth. He also managed to stop his brain from thinking up chores for the boy. When clearly that would be a waste of time, as Jeremy would rather go to juvenile hall than do actual work for anything.

After a long pause, Jeremy nodded. "Fine, you get me off and I'll pay you."

"No. You need to pay your lawyer a retainer."

"What the f—"

"No swearing." Yeah, like he had never uttered a swear word. Well, he sure hadn't done it in front of an adult when he was fifteen years old. He'd have had his backside tanned.

Jeremy sneered. "What the frickin' hey is a retainer?"

"It's the fee you pay your lawyer to take your case. So that I won't just drop you like a hot rock if a better job comes along." Sam purposefully leaned against the doorway into the hall. He wanted to exude calm. He wanted to. Surely, he could fool one surly teenager.

Again, Jeremy shrugged. His leather jacket a little too big and bunching at the shoulders with the movement. "I don't know."

Sam was about to motion him out the door when he spoke again. "You're cheap. I should just go pay a better lawyer."

A better laywer? What? One who argued before the supreme court *before* the age of twenty? Who would charge Jeremy here *less* than labor from a kid? But Jeremy and his mom didn't know the whole story, and wasn't that what Sam had wanted? Wasn't that very anonymity the reason he'd quit his old job and moved here? So, he just sighed. "Fine."

Again, the overly casual shrug. "I'll think about it."

Just then the doorbell rang. And thank God. Sam needed a break. He brushed past the kid to open the door without looking. He was hosting the Tuesday night get-together this week. It had to be one of his friends. He needed it. He needed this meeting to be over. He'd done all he could to help. Crime Night would be a very welcome reprieve from the ill-mannered attitude of Jeremy. If only he hadn't agreed to the boy's mother's pleas.

"Hi!" Rae held up a twelve pack of soda and a bag of unpopped popcorn as she made her way to the kitchen.

Jeremy's eyes followed Rae's ass, then his whole body followed her through the doors. He actually licked his lips. "Hey, hot stuff. You look positively ripe for the—"

He didn't finish the sentence.

As Rae whirled to confront the voice that had trailed her, Sam grabbed that sturdy leather jacket and used it to shove Jeremy against the wall. He pushed his face within inches of Jeremy's. "You will *not* speak to her like that."

"Dude!"

"You will not speak to *anyone* like that in my home." After a moment, Sam let the kid's feet slide down to the ground. "Apologize."

Jeremy held his hands up. "I didn't know she was yours."

Sam chose to ignore that statement. How could he respond anyway? And wouldn't Jeremy just dance knowing that he had that kind of dirt on his neighbor-slash-lawyer. "Don't you *ever* speak to *any* of my friends that way."

"Okaaaay." Then the kid turned to Rae. "Sorry, babe."

Clenching his fists to keep from popping the kid, Sam watched as Rae nearly managed to keep her jaw from dropping open. Clearly the best course of action was to see Jeremy out the door as fast as possible. Then Sam came back in to where she stood with one jeans clad hip against the counter and a very questioning look on her face.

"I'm sorry. I'm defending him. . . maybe."

"Defending him?" She frowned but then rifled through his pots for something to pop the corn in. "Do you have vegetable oil?"

"Of course I do. You left it here last time."

She smiled, "Good for me. . . what did the kid do?"

"Stole a car."

"I thought you were an intellectual properties lawyer." She poured the oil in a layer on the bottom of the pan, then dropped in a handful of kernels. No microwave corn for her. Something about the workers getting yellow-lung from all the butter flavor powder. That and her innate Martha tendencies. Which she always vehemently denied.

"I am an IP lawyer. But his mother begged me, and they really need the help, and there's nothing that says I can't take the case. Besides it's small."

"Small? I thought you went away for a while for grand theft auto." She shook the kernels into the pan, but to him it was a brief glimpse to the future, when she would cook him dinner, when they were an old married couple. He could hope, right?

"Let's just call it petty theft auto."

She turned to face him, her brown eyes wide. *"Petty theft auto?"*

He nodded. "The blue book value on the car was only eight hundred."

She threw her head back and laughed. Just then the doorbell rang again. Sam left her there with the kernels popping in the pan, giggling to herself. He heard her coughing as he opened the door to face Sheree and Alex who had come up the stairs together. Sheree sauntered past him with a bag of veggie chips in hand. "What is she cackling about?"

Rae stopped coughing long enough to call out from the kitchen, "Sam's client got arrested for . . . for . . . Petty Theft Auto!"

Sam shrugged as Sheree looked him up and down like he should be locked up. He explained again. "The blue book value was less than eight hundred."

But Sheree didn't laugh. Her tight curls just bobbed their

disappointment. "And what kind of idiot steals an eight-hundred-dollar car? And how is this idiot going to pay for your services?"

Sam agreed with her. "Not with cash. I'd put my whole bank account on the money being stolen. Or possibly drug money." He shoved his hands down in his pockets and followed his way back into the kitchen, where he could watch Rae. "He'll have to work it off."

Sheree raised an eyebrow again. If she did that often enough they'd get stuck. "Work!? Doing what? Stealing cars?"

"Nope. If he actually does the work, he'll be cleaning mine. Taking out my trash, scrubbing my floors."

Rae toed the old linoleum, "They need it."

He winced. He'd have to scrub them himself before the next time she came, if Jeremy didn't do it. He was rescued by the doorbell again. Lisa and Jack showed up, hand in hand, just before eight o'clock.

He heard the soft sounds of popcorn falling into a large bowl, but the image it conjured wasn't of popcorn, but of Rae, comfortably cooking. And for that brief moment he could imagine his home place plastered in her artwork. Filled with the smells of the Italian food she loved to make. Recipes she always said were embedded in her genes. And he decided in that moment that that was the way things were meant to be. He just had to figure out how to make it so.

Standing there, staring into space, he'd missed his friends rearranging his furniture and turning the TV on without him.

"It's on!" Jack hollered even before he set the remote down. Crime night had begun. And it was February. That meant sweeps. His crowd was all huddled on and in front of his couch, passing the chips and popcorn, opening beer and soda.

This was exactly why he'd strayed from the path to partner. The fast track left little room for friends. Well, friends that you didn't want anything from, who didn't want anything from you except your company. On that path, his Tuesday nights were spent around a table watching his co-workers pretend to drink foreign beers they probably didn't even like. He'd never know them well enough to find out the truth. He'd spend his other evenings alone, or eating cold take-out during an impromptu meeting to plan the next case or talking mergers as though they were the important things in life.

Mergers were not the important things.

This was what it was about. This condo was older and cheaper than what he'd had before. Less chrome, less granite, less money. More love. More free time. The carpet wasn't perfectly clean. And his linoleum had stains, but that was because he had friends over to spill stuff on it. Friends, food, and TV.

Even better, Rae was on the floor with her back to the base of the couch, and Sheree had softly slid over to make a space for him, right behind Rae. If he didn't know better, he would have suspected his friends were onto him. He hopped over the arm of the couch and settled his legs one on each side of her, as she settled back against his shins and passed the popcorn up his way.

He no sooner had grabbed a handful when she sneezed. He felt her chest contract against his legs.

"You okay?" It wasn't his voice. His mouth was stuffed with popcorn.

She nodded, but held up a hand as she sneezed again, then went into a coughing fit. It was all he could do to keep from whacking her on the back, but after a moment she turned around to look at him. Her eyes were red, but she managed to speak. "Thanks for not whacking me on the back. I'm fine. It's just a little cold."

Sheree waited until the commercial, before speaking. "I told her to take something but she won't."

"I hate cold medicine. It says it tastes like cherry, but it tastes like lies." Sam laughed even though she'd said the sentiment to the room in general. Then the show started up again, and they all got still. Except Rae who coughed or sneezed every few minutes.

At nine they changed the channel, but Rae kept sneezing. Then she coughed over a line that explained exactly how the evidence showed who the killer was, and it was all Sam could do to keep the others from massacring her.

"Hey, go back, listen again."

They did, and she managed to sneeze this time.

"Dammit, Rae!" Jack and Lisa offered it up in perfect sync as Jack hit the jump back button yet again.

Sam fended them off by promising to put cold medicine in her, and dragged her to the hall bathroom before any damage could be inflicted.

CHAPTER 19

R ae whined at him, looking pitiful and slightly sick. "I don't want cold medicine."

Sam had her elbow in his hand. "If you don't take some you're going to get drummed out, and I can fight one or two of them—I'd do it for you—" He mockingly put a solemn hand to his heart, even though he really would have done it. "—but I can't take on all four of them."

She almost pouted. Even with her nose red, that lip looked inviting, but he held himself back. It was not the right time. It was never the right time.

"Have you ever taken that stuff?" She eyed the bottle of thick red syrup that he pulled from the cabinet. "It tastes like nasty candy and a hospital had a baby."

"Wow, that's a serious indictment." He put the bottle in her hand. "Stay." And went out to the kitchen for a cup of ice water, then returned to find her in exactly the same position he had left her in. He held the cup out to her. "You can wash it down."

She nodded and sighed, clearly resigned to the horrible tasting liquid. Rae watched warily while he poured her a shot in the plastic medicine cup. He could almost hear her counting as she eyed the cup for a few seconds before tossing it back, then she made the foulest face he had ever seen while gesturing wildly for him to hand her the water. She guzzled the whole thing before slamming the empty cup bar-style onto the counter.

"There. I hope everybody's happy." She stalked out of the bathroom, making little disgusted shivers as though she could still taste the cough syrup. It was all he could do to stifle a laugh. She was adorable.

Everyone in the living room turned to him. "Did she really take it?"

"You're not covering for her are you?"

He swore that she had, in fact, swallowed the syrup, but no, he had not checked to be sure she wasn't faking it. Rae offered for anyone to smell her breath. No one took her up on it, and Sam settled back into his spot on the couch with Rae tucked right in front of him on the floor.

Eventually she melted back onto his legs, leaning her head on his knee. He figured that the medicine had worked, as she hadn't so much as sputtered in the last twenty minutes. A little while later they all realized that it had worked too well.

"What happened?" Her head popped up from where it had been 'resting' on his leg.

Sheree explained to her how the bad guy had done himself in. But Rae just pouted as Sheree shook her head. "You aren't going to be able to drive yourself home, are you?"

"What? No. I'll be fine." Rae lowered first her arms, then her head onto his lap completely negating her statement.

Well, Sam thought, at least he was content with her there. But his mouth opened before he could stop it. "Do you want to go sleep it off on my bed?" *Where had that come from?*

"Bed?" Her eyelids fluttered.

"Come on." He half lifted her and guided her toward the back room. "Sheree can drive you home when we're done." She mumbled something about 'bed' again, then half-tumbled/half-crawled along his sheets, before tucking her arms and legs around his pillows. Sam sighed to himself. Of course, she was voluntarily in his bed, but it was because she was medicated and *tired*, of all things. Hell, she was stoned. He reminded himself to word his wishes a little more carefully in the future.

An hour later, when everyone was packing up, Sheree wandered out of his room. "She told me to 'go-way'. She's out cold, and I can't lift her."

"I can carry her down to your car." Sam volunteered. He didn't think he could stand to have her sleeping here. It would be better if she were a real guest.

Sheree shook her head. "Sure, but that's not enough. Unless you ride home with me, how will I get her out, and up to the second floor?"

Jack just grinned, a wicked male grin. "Sam, just climb in with her. You finally got a woman in your bed again!"

"That's gross, Jack." He made a fist at his friend. "She's drugged." Luckily, Lisa punched him in the arm so Sam didn't have to. But he did think he'd have to leave Rae there. "I'll send her home in the morning when she's slept it off."

When Jack raised his eyebrows again, Sam glared. "I'll sleep on the couch."

"Thanks." Sheree hugged him and headed out the door. "Tell her I tried to wake her up but she wouldn't listen to me."

He nodded and found himself alone a moment later with Rae curled up on his bed, the light glaring over her head. Standing in the doorway, he tried hard not to stare, afraid that she would wake up and catch him. He had already admitted to himself that he had it bad. He was in way over his head. But there she was. Auburn hair floating around her face on the pillow. Looking even more red against the black of his sheets. Her hands curled around his pillow, long artists' fingers pale against the dark fabric.

Sam shook his head to break the stare, before making his way into the room and pulling his shirt over his head. There was a blanket in the hall closet. He kept it for friends who wanted to crash on the couch. He figured no one would be able to fault him if he slept in a tee shirt and sweats, so he went to grab them quietly, but the closet door creaked awfully as he tried to open it.

He'd never noticed that before. But then again, when had he ever tried to be quiet? There was no one to not wake until now. He'd oil it in the morning. Admittedly in hopes that he'd be in a similar situation soon. Minus the cough syrup, of course. He left the closet door where it was—barely open at all—and decided that sleeping in his jeans would have to do.

"Is it time to go home?"

Her voice startled him and he jumped around to face her. Rae was propped up on her elbows, her hair wild around her face, her eyes half closed against the bright light. "No, go back to sleep. You can drive home in the morning."

She half started to push herself upright. "I should go now."

She mumbled the words unconvincingly. She clearly wasn't safe to operate heavy machinery. Or maybe even a toaster.

"You're not in any shape to drive, baby. Go back to sleep."

"Okay." She fell back against the pillow, instantly even more deeply asleep than when he had come in, it seemed.

Sam walked as softly as he could across the room then reached up and flicked out the light.

"Where are you going?" Clearly, she hadn't been anywhere near as deep asleep as she looked. But she still sounded very groggy.

"I'm going to go sleep on the couch."

She was slurring her words, but he still understood her. "You're too big for the couch."

Got that right. But he didn't say it.

"You should stay here. The bed's plenty big."

Sam froze, his back to her, on his way out into the hall. She hadn't just asked him to climb in with her, had she?

When he turned, she was passed out again. Unsure if he was relieved or disappointed, he turned again toward the living room. He didn't make it more than three steps before her voice caught up with him. "You're too big. You can't sleep on the couch."

"I'll be fine." His voice protested.

"No. Stay. I dond wanna kick you outta your own bed."

His mind told him he shouldn't. He told himself to firmly say he would be fine sleeping on the couch, but the words wouldn't come out of his mouth. His feet turned and started walking back to the bed. She *was* curled up to one side of the mattress. Although, if he could stay off her side, he didn't know. Lifting the covers, Sam slid in, the king size bed plenty big enough for the both of them. As long as he stayed on his half.

It turned out he *could* stay on his side. It was Rae who scooted across and tucked herself into him, her head on his shoulder. She sighed as she placed her hand on his chest. Sam felt her body go entirely limp again. He, on the other hand, was wound tight as a spring.

CHAPTER 20

R ae rolled over, not wanting the haze of sleep to retreat. But against her will the world around her pushed into her senses and formed itself. The bed was magnetic and the warm smell and heat beckoned her back into the soft folds of her subconscious. She snuggled down under the covers, a small thought trying to take hold in her brain. She rolled over into the luscious heat and rolled smack into a wall of muscle.

She blinked. Twice.

And froze.

Sam.

The heat was his. The deep smell that she hadn't been able to put her finger on, it was man. And not just any man, either. Sam. And not just any Sam, shirtless Sam. Oh, Lord.

After a moment, realizing that he was still asleep, she tried to think through how she had gotten here. Vague memories of crawling into his bed pushed to the surface. Along with hazy feelings that the black satin pillow was her new best friend. Rae could only find a few clear thoughts from the night before, and one of them was Sam saying he would sleep on the couch. But he wasn't on the couch now.

He shifted in his sleep, causing her breath to suck in, just a little, even though she didn't move. *Couldn't* move. The arm that had been loosely draped around her waist now burned a slow journey along the side of her hip. The heat rattled loose a memory of lying in this bed on her back, her arms out at her sides, and asking him to stay. No, make that *arguing* that he should stay. And then a fuzzier memory of curling up into him.

Well, at least it appeared he had no complaints.

Rae stayed stock still, whether it was from fear of being found out, or fear that he would stop the rich torment, she wasn't sure. Her slow breathing stilled as his hand stopped midway down her thigh then began to slide back up, over her hip, up her side, fingers feeling each rib. Her eyes and mouth widened as it approached her breast.

Suddenly she was jolted to action and, without input from her mind, Rae tucked and rolled away, as though it was a sniper after her and not Sam. The breathing she had so carefully controlled just moments ago set up a rapid intake and she perched on the side of the bed, legs dangling, chest heaving. She already knew that she wanted Sam that way, so why had she ducked and run?

Because she wouldn't be able to stand it if she found out he had been dreaming about someone else.

"Rae?" Her name was soft and long on his lips, his voice still slurred with sleep. "Morning." He slowly pushed himself up on his elbows where he lay.

Without even turning her head she answered him. "Morning, Sam." And wondered if her voice sounded half as good to his ears as his did to hers. Somehow, she conjured the nerve to turn and take a look at him. But there was something magnetic about the man on the bed behind her, and the glance turned into a thorough perusal. The sheets didn't cover him, his jeans peeked out from satin edge, the only thing telling her eyes he wasn't completely naked. Rae didn't dare move as he rolled himself to a sitting position, his thigh brushing hers. Her train of thought derailed as her eyes swept the rumpled man beside her.

He stretched his neck, arms resting on his knees, still waking up, wearing only his jeans. His bare chest moved with each breath, and she forced her eyes up to his hair, seriously suffering from morning head. She watched as her hand reached up to touch it and tried to cover the unauthorized action with words. "You're getting blond streaks again."

He moved as though to duck away.

But she grabbed his arm. "You look great either way."

Sam's eyes opened all the way, finally. But they were burning holes in her. Rae sat dumbfounded as he reached up to her cheek and pulled her to him. His fingers curled into her mussed hair, and she began to think that she must look a fright. But the thought disappeared as his lips closed over hers.

His skin beckoned her hands, her fingers tracing their way up the back of his arms, finally resting on his shoulders. She leaned into him hard. Sank into the kiss. Into his hold. But in a moment, it was over. And Sam looked like he didn't know what to do. She probably did too.

Willing her mouth to say, "kiss me again," Rae only managed to stare at him. She couldn't force the words to come.

It was Sam who broke the contact as he stood and walked to the closet before turning back. "I didn't get a chance to tell you last night, but my mother wants to know if you can meet this coming Friday evening. She thought the two of you might go to the Webber Gallery and see about getting your own show."

Rae blinked again, her brain desperately searching for the missing link in their conversation. But it was nowhere to be found. Perhaps she had simply dreamed that kiss. Maybe she still had a narcotic level of cough syrup in her blood and she was hallucinating. So she focused on the topic in reach. "She can just do that?"

He nodded and grabbed a shirt from the neatly folded piles inside. He spoke again while she was still befuddled by the fact that someone could just walk into the Webber and demand a show for an unknown artist.

"Rae, I'm really sorry about last night."

"What?" Her confusion ballooned, taking her down new paths, and odd thoughts raced through her head. Had she slept with him? She didn't remember! She glanced down quickly to see that she was still fully clothed.

"You asked me to stay in here with you, and I just didn't want to sleep on the couch." He shrugged his way into the t-shirt while he spoke. "I don't even know if you're dating anyone who might get mad."

She smiled in automatic response to the relief that coursed through her system. "No, I'm not dating anyone who might get mad."

"Good." He turned away from the closet and came back to the edge of the bed. She hadn't been able to move, while he'd wandered the room restlessly.

But now he was back, cupping her face in his hands again. Then his face was close to hers, his breathing coming in shallow sighs. She could hear her own breath escaping her. Then he closed the distance and he was kissing her until she was butter. Butter desperately trying to melt into him. Onto the floor. Anywhere.

His mouth sought hers and she leaned into the sensation, the soft touch of his lips working some kind of magic on her. It held her in place and at the same time made her bend and move toward him. His lips opened over hers, moving restlessly, his tongue chasing the sensations. His hands held her in place as though she might actually want to move away. *Never.* Rae kissed him back, forgoing all rational thought.

Her fingers crept up the front of his chest, now covered with the soft cotton of a shirt washed too many times. The heat and the hardness of him were evident behind the thin layer and she let her hands wander.

His breath sucked in, moving his chest beneath her touch and she felt her fingers clench at him of their own accord. Her hands slid up to his neck, pulling him closer as though she might devour him. And she wanted to. She'd waited for this. Known it would be so good. But she hadn't anticipated it would be this good.

Sam caught her lower lip in his teeth and softly made his way to the side of her mouth. Her head tipped slightly, following his lead in a way she'd never been able to on the dance floor. Right now, in this moment, she had nothing more to care about, no right steps to hit, no one watching, only the desire to not stop, to move wherever he led.

Then, when she led, he followed. Her hands had slipped, open-palmed down the front of his chest until she hit the bottom edge. The frayed cotton moved like sand through her fingers and she scooped it into her grip and tugged upward.

Sam's mouth was on the side of her neck, his lips and tongue tracing erotic zones she didn't know she had. Then he was gone. Blue eyes caught hers, fire making them burn, one last moment before he raised his hands and let her tug the shirt off him. For a moment, she stilled at the sight of him. He'd been bare to her just minutes ago, lying next to her in bed, she'd even had her hand on his chest. But it was different now with permission to touch him, to feel, to explore.

With her right hand, she kept pulling upward on the shirt, but her left reached down to trace lines on his skin. Her mouth followed, sucking and tasting, licking at the little hollow at the base of his neck. He moved then, his arms pinwheeling to get out of the shirt and at last tossing it to the side without even a glance to see where it landed.

His hands stroked her hair, small sounds coming from his chest as she nipped at him. Then, with a gentle tug on her hair, he silently implored her to look up at him. No sooner than she'd made eye contact with him, his mouth was on hers again. Where before he'd been hungry, now he was ravenous.

Her whole body tipped back, all thought centered on his mouth on hers, his tongue begging her to open her own mouth and meet him halfway in this quest. Her fingers clutched the hot, bare skin at his waist and she held on for dear life until his own hands made contact with the skin along her ribs.

He'd pulled up her own shirt, and she rolled her shoulders, turned her head and lamented the loss of his mouth on hers as it was her turn to tug off her own clothes. He played her own game back at her, his mouth closing along her neck as one hand came up and cupped her breast.

Her breath gasped in, raising her chest into his touch, a motion he took advantage of. She was twisted, sitting sideways on the edge of the bed, she'd gotten as close to him as she could, but it wasn't working. In her heady state, it felt only natural to climb across him and straddle him. Then she was on him, her head thrown back in wanton release as his thumb stroked the peak of her breast through the lace of her bra.

Score one for good underwear. Her panties weren't the same color, but they were the same style and she thought about them as she moved her hips closer. That thought fled as she felt him, hard and ready through his own jeans and hers. His hands clutched and they were airborne for a second before she felt the mattress at her back, the weight of him pressing into her. His thumb still stroked her and she sunk her fingers into his hair as his mouth moved from her neck downward.

She sucked in a breath as he nipped at the top of her breast, then again as he got closer. Then, as his mouth closed over her nipple, she let out an audible gasp and arched her back. Her body had taken over, she didn't think about it, just moved against him, into him, trying to get closer.

His hand slid behind her back, lifting her, and it took a

moment of confusion to understand that he was going for the clasp on her bra. *Oh, dear God*, please, she almost said it out loud as she raised up onto her elbows to help him out. As she did, she caught sight of the alarm clock on the bedside table. 8:07.

"Oh God!" Rae jolted under him, causing Sam to back up suddenly. Despite the completely confused look on his face, she scrambled for her things. "Liam is going to be so mad at me."

"Liam?" Sam jerked all the way back, completely out of her reach now. An instantaneous cool caution replaced the hot blaze he had been just a moment before.

"Yes, he's going to kill me!" She didn't know what was going on with Sam. And she didn't have time to stop and try to find her center and listen for him. Instead, she was scrambling to find her shoes. She began a mental list of what it would take to get out the door in twenty seconds or less.

"You could have just said so."

Rae's flurry of energy froze at the reserve in his voice.

Oh, God, it had all come out wrong. She had to make him see, and she had to get out the door an hour ago. "Where's my purse?"

He stalked down the stairs and to the front door with Rae hot on his trail, jumping into her shoes and buttoning her top button as she went. He held both her purse and her jacket out to her, his mouth a firm line. Rae double checked. Everything else she needed she was either wearing or could claim later. She grabbed for the door knob but then reconsidered her tenuous position. She was already dead in the water with Liam, and she *had* to straighten things out here. She couldn't leave Sam with that look on his face. She couldn't ruin this before it got started. And she wasn't going to leave him for the whole day thinking she'd lied and was dating someone else.

"Listen, Liam isn't going to be mad about . . . anything that happens between us. He'll be mad because we're on twelves, and I'm su—"

"Twelves?" He still looked disbelieving.

Rae nodded. "Continuous twelve-hour shifts, round the clock surveillance. I was supposed to relieve him at *seven*." She sucked in a breath hoping Sam would understand. "He's been in a car for over thirteen hours now!"

"Oh." A little of the ice in his features began to melt. But not enough, not all the way. Not back to the Sam who had kissed her to oblivion about one minute ago. Rae couldn't stand to leave it like this, it wouldn't be enough. So she grabbed for his shirt, but only got bare chest. For the briefest of moments, she looked for something to hold on to before settling on a belt loop. She pulled him toward her even as his head bent down for a quick solid kiss. For a split second their eyes held, and she saw that things would be okay.

Then she bolted out the door, digging for her cell phone. "Liam! Where are you? I am soooo sorry. . . . yes, you're right. I *am* late. Yes, you win, I owe you the five. . . . I'll be there in twenty." She snapped the phone closed and threw a brief look over her shoulder.

Sam was standing, propped in the doorway, exactly as she had left him. Except the expression on his face had changed. "You pay him?"

She yelled back over her shoulder, "Running bet!" Then she turned and waved, before diving for her car.

CHAPTER 21

R ae sighed to herself. She wished that she could have found time for some sleep, but this guy that she and Liam were tailing apparently had caught on that he was being watched. Finally, this afternoon she managed to get the drop on him.

She had to actually stop tailing him for a while. Instead of following him, she tried to get ahead. She went straight to a motel that had shown up on credit card receipts and waited for him there. Sure enough, she caught him with another woman. A hooker nonetheless.

And that was a last straw for her. She had to take some time off from cheating husbands to do her own work. Especially now that there might be a gallery show.

Rae tamped that thought down. She was very lucky to have had that one piece sitting out in the back office. It would be overly hopeful to think that she might get a show.

She had at least managed to shower and change before heading out the door to meet Sam and Mrs. Brock. She was thankful for the opportunity. And she was thankful for the chance to shower first.

Her energy level picked up steam as she drove out to meet them. Her large portfolio was stuffed into the passenger seat beside her. It was plum leather with stickers like a suitcase, from every city she had photographed in. It wasn't the typical black, but it wasn't bizarre. It didn't scream *free-spirited artist*. It suited her.

And Sam would be there tonight. She had hardly spoken to him since she had fled from his room two mornings ago. Just enough to set up this meeting with his mother. Maybe tonight they could work something out. Maybe she would find the guts to ask him if he wanted anything other than a few casual kisses here and there. Mind you, casual kisses that reduced her to smoldering ashes.

She cranked the little red terror to a stop in front of the Webber Gallery and did a quick scan for Sam's car, but didn't see it anywhere. Maybe he was late, or maybe he had ridden in with his mother. Maybe with a few deep breaths she could calm herself and find something other than this lovesick floozy to fill her head before gathering her portfolio and climbing out. Rae put on airs of respectability and belonging as she pushed through the front doors and into the gallery proper. She felt like a huge fraud, but as long as she managed to keep that to herself, she might just come out ahead.

Mrs. Brock was in the back room talking to Martin Webber when Rae entered. A quick glance around the room revealed the absence of Sam, but just as quickly she shoved the worry aside and braved ahead. "Hello."

Mr. Webber held his hand out, and started right in. "Linda was telling me about a piece of yours that she snagged from me a while back, and was curious why you didn't have a show yet."

Nodding, Rae decided to do nothing else, as she wasn't sure if it was a question or not.

Mrs. Brock started in on the man, transforming from the

mild-tempered housewife that Rae had seen the week before into a fierce businesswoman.

In short order, she laid out organized plans and generous pay scales. Rae didn't speak at all. And why should she? Mrs. Brock was clearly in charge here. Rae had never seen Webber appear to play any part other than the snobby gallery owner.

At Mrs. Brock's command, Rae quickly and quietly unzipped her portfolio and showed off the pieces they had chosen the evening before over tea. Ceding complete control of the room seemed to be in her best interests, and Rae found she hardly opened her mouth. Just nodded and smiled more like a display model than a photographer.

Twenty minutes later when they left, it had been decided that Rae would be part of a now five artist show that would open in exactly seven weeks. The show had previously held only four artists, but Mrs. Brock had conceded to the multi artist show when Martin Webber said that getting Rae her own showing would have to wait until he had an open slot, which would be at least five months away. Secretly, Rae was glad she wasn't the only artist in the show. It lifted a little of the now enormous pressure she felt. And the other artists would bring in patrons when she wasn't sure she could fill the gallery. She could hardly breathe.

Linda Brock, however, was all wicked smiles. "I knew you deserved a show."

Rae laughed nervously. "I think he has faith in you, if not me." Her stomach turned. But she reminded herself that this was what she wanted. What she had prayed and worked for. And now she had to deliver. Now she had to sell pieces. The fear came tumbling out. "What if they don't sell?"

Mrs. Brock beamed at her, looking for all the world like Sam's soothing mother again. "They will, sweetheart."

In that instant her thoughts snapped back to Sam, and she asked where he was.

"He's actually at home. I was so in the thick of it with Webber that I forgot to tell you. He's sick." They were already at Rae's car, "I was going to offer to take you out to dinner, but I thought you might be more interested in checking in on my son."

Rae suppressed a smile. Barely. She had learned some time ago that she wasn't nearly as slick as she liked to think she was. It appeared that Mrs. Brock had read the situation as clearly as if it had been in print. "Maybe Sam and I can take you out later. So I can thank you for all this." On impulse she threw her arms around the woman. "This is my dream."

Linda hugged her back, but shooed away the compliment. "It would have happened for you sooner or later, I'm so happy to help make it happen sooner. I'm just glad I get to claim credit for *discovering* you." Then she broke the hug, "Now do me a favor and go check in on my son. Tell him I sent you if you wish."

Rae grinned. Yup, not nearly as slick as she thought she was. "Thank you." She climbed into her old red economy car and started it, the air in the vents hadn't even cooled, the meeting had been that short. Within a few minutes, she was standing huddled on Sam's doorstep waiting for him to answer the bell.

But he didn't answer.

Rae didn't like the feeling at the back of her brain, so she pushed the button again. She looked into the windows, and tried the knob, knowing he was sick. She was ready to go around back, but that would require going through his fence. Instead, she hit the doorbell again. She'd heard it, it would alert him if he was home, but probably wasn't strong enough to wake him if he was asleep. She told herself to give it three tries. If he didn't answer by then, she'd have to come back the next morning.

Ring two didn't bring any luck, but the third one did. Just as she was about to turn around, the door slowly opened and he blinked at her a few times. His hair was mussed and he was bundled in sweats. "Don't come near me." He held his large hand palm out to ward her away. "How did it go?"

"Your mom got me a spot in the next show."

He grinned, even though he still looked a little pained. "That's great, I'm sorry I missed it."

Looking past him into the living room, Rae spotted a large powder blue blanket in a wad on the couch, and an open bag of chips on the coffee table. "What's your temperature?"

"Hot." He saw where she was looking and tried again to send her away.

"And you're eating chips?"

"I'll be fine. Now leave before you get sick, too."

But she couldn't overcome the urge to take care of him. And when he coughed a few times she knew she couldn't just go. She shoved past him and grabbed the spare key he kept on the hook just inside the door. "I'll be back in a little bit."

She bolted down the steps, not looking back to see how Sam felt about that. A few seconds later, the little red terror chugged to life again, the engine warm in the cooling night air. Rae wound her way to the nearest food store. Forty minutes later, she was back. Using the key, she let herself in. Then she spread her groceries out on the table. Sam was out cold on the couch, which was a good thing, or he might have been yelling at her for stealing his key.

CHAPTER 22

His head pounded, and he fought a groan as he rolled over. Grabbing his temples, and squeezing his eyes, Sam racked his tired brain, but couldn't remember being this sick since he was a kid. He ached. And when he opened his mouth just to breathe, he started coughing. Which didn't help matters at all.

He huddled on the couch, pulling the blanket tighter against the cold, and coughed his way through the whole set of commercials that were blaring from whatever channel he'd left the TV turned to. His throat was raw when he finally stopped.

Taking a deep breath and being grateful to not start coughing again, he paused. He smelled something. Not that he would be able to recognize citrus from burning rubber with his head in this state. But something definitely smelled. He sat up, and regretted it instantly. "Ehh." He put his hand to his head as if he thought he might actually be able to physically quiet the pounding by touch alone.

"You're awake."

It was Rae's voice. He could recognize it because it was still reverberating in his head. "Wh—"

The word didn't even get out. She appeared in front of him with a tray that held a bowl of steaming soup. That was what had smelled good.

Sam tried to open his eyes all the way, and then remembered what he had told her earlier. It hurt, but he got it out. "Why didn't you go home?"

Her face showed that she had been expecting that, and she looked him right in his eyes. "You're sick. And you aren't taking very good care of yourself. I'm staying."

"Then you'll be sick." He didn't want her to argue. He wanted her to leave. And then he would eat the soup. He could imagine the proper smell now, and in his mind it was heavenly.

Rae didn't argue. She just crossed her arms and went to the kitchen. "I'm not going anywhere." She returned with a glass of something bright red. He eyed it for a minute before she spoke again. "It's Gatorade. When was the last time you had a Tylenol?"

He sank back into the wicked couch. "I'll call my mom. Please, go."

"Your mom sent me. Add to that, I'm quite certain this is *my* cold you have, so I *can't* get sick from you."

He was going to kill his mother. Sweet little Linda Brock with her knowing little smile. Except that she hadn't counted on the fact that the last person he wanted to see now was Rae. He blinked a few times slowly before admitting that that wasn't the case. He was wonderfully glad to see Rae, he just didn't want Rae to see him. And it looked like she was setting up house. God forbid.

She asked again. "When was the last time you took anything?"

"A while ago."

"An hour? Two hours?"

"Maybe an hour." He wanted to shrug, but it hurt. And he

could feel himself getting crankier with every question she asked. Why didn't she just leave like . . . ?

Like a what? he had to ask himself. Honestly, a good friend would stay and take care of him. But he didn't want to her to be his friend. A good girlfriend would stay, too. Only she wasn't his girlfriend yet. And this sure as hell wasn't the way to get her there. He wanted to groan in frustration, but didn't want to suffer the consequences of groaning. His head was pounding enough already.

She held up the tray that he finally realized she must have brought with her. He sure didn't own one. Then she set out the drink and soup bowl and a piece of bread.

"You cut off the crust?" *Oh, dear God.*

Rae tilted her head. "I don't like French bread crust when I'm sick. But the bread is great."

"What's in the soup?" It looked homemade. He desperately wanted to hug her, and he also desperately wanted her to disappear. She could come back when he was healthy.

"I made it. Chicken broth, actual chicken, spinach and rice."

"Thank you." He might not want her here, and he might be mad that she wouldn't listen to him and leave, but he wasn't an ass.

She wouldn't leave until he ate, that much was clear. So he carefully picked up the spoon, even though it hurt every joint, and he took a sip. It tasted even better than in his imagination, if seasoned a little by his fear. He ate the entire bowl and the bread without a single sideways glance at the chips. He thanked her again. He tried to send her home again. Then he decided that if she was staying a shower was definitely in the works. Not that he felt like standing. Not that he wouldn't have been asleep in front of the game shows half an hour ago if left to his own devices.

Sam announced his intentions and Rae went ahead of him to get the water going and set out towels for him. He was glad that his coughing fit was drowned out by the sound of the water, but it felt like his grandma was there. He walked as carefully as possible down the hallway, trailing his hand on the wall to stay upright. When he at last made it into the bathroom, he found it empty. Peeling his clothing carefully and slowly, he climbed under the spray.

He was thankful for the small favor that she hadn't insisted on sitting in the bathroom and keeping watch. He was thankful again that she wasn't watching when he went to shut off the water. The old fashioned knobs offered more resistance than usual, and he felt positively arthritic. Every move hurt.

But he wrapped himself in the fluffy towel that he realized wasn't his either, and headed into the bedroom. She rushed in as he approached the bed. "Here." She held out a dose of the same red awful cough syrup that had knocked her out earlier in the week. He had blessed the cough syrup then, now he cursed it.

"I heard you coughing in there. Just take this." She held out the tiny cup and he decided not to argue with her. That hadn't gotten him anything but a sore throat and the growing conviction that all his plans for them were going to hell in a well-tended handbasket.

"I'm going to bed." Maybe she would leave him alone if he was asleep in his own room. He hunched his shoulders in to ward off the chill, even though he had dried himself completely. He spotted a fresh pair of boxers laid out on the bed, and managed to be both thankful and angry at the same time. It all flew from his mind with the brush of her fingertips down his bare arm. Good to know *that* was intact.

"Oh, you're cold." She pointed to the boxers. "I'll turn around."

And she did, all tense and toe-tapping until he said she could turn back. Rae barely looked at him as she pulled back the covers to reveal a wadded blanket in the bed. She grabbed it, "Climb in."

He sighed, but did as she had ordered. The fight was gone. And the bed was warm to the touch as he slid in. Rae smiled as she pulled warm covers over him. Her hair was loose around her shoulders and her smile was everything that was slipping away. "I put the electric blanket in to warm it up for you." She proceeded to unfold the ugly mustard colored thing and lay it over the covers. "Sleep."

It didn't take five seconds.

CHAPTER 23

"Sam." Rae shook him gently, the small plastic medicine cup in her hand brimming with cough syrup. He was coughing even in his sleep.

He didn't rouse.

She tried again, but his breathing simply kept coming in long uneven rasps. She climbed onto the bed beside him, but didn't touch him. Resting against the headboard, she wrapped her knees in her arms, then rocked slowly, hoping the motion would wake him. She also hoped it would soothe her. She didn't know what to do.

Sheree had dropped off another bottle of cough syrup yesterday, since he had polished off the first one. It had been three days, and she had put as much soup and fruit and juice into him as he would eat. Luckily, Sam had slept most of the time. He'd managed to get to the living room and watch some TV. But that was yesterday. After the first twelve hours he'd even stopped fighting her and trying to get her to leave. She was glad now she hadn't left.

Reaching out, Rae nudged him again. His sleeping bulk felt like dead weight, almost unmovable. Again he didn't respond. If his breathing hadn't been so loud she would have leaned down over his face to check that he was still doing it. As it was, he positively rattled with every breath, and that couldn't be good.

Lisa had called yesterday, wondering if she could help. But there wasn't really anything to do. Unless Sam didn't wake up. Rae shuddered at the thought, sending the small movements through the bed.

Though she hadn't been able to stop and listen for the feeling in the back of her brain, it had come anyway. Something was wrong. It had been a little wrong when she'd showed up a few days ago. Now it was bordering on very wrong. But she didn't know what she was supposed to do.

She'd called Sloan. While she wanted to tell her sister about the gallery opening, instead she'd asked for any secrets for treating fevers or coughs. Sloan had only begged off saying she was no nurse and had no idea what to do. She'd volunteered to do internet Reconn, but Rae thanked her and called Sheree. Sheree worked with kids, she had to know what to do, right?

"Honey, if their foreheads feel hot, I send them to the office. That's all I can do. I don't know. Do you want me to call my mother? She's a nurse."

Rae had said not yet. But she was getting ready to pull that trigger now. Then she heard Sam for the first time in hours.

"Hmmmm?" His voice sounded far away, and probably he had been. But her rising panic quelled for the moment. Now all she had to do was get him awake and lucid.

"Sam?"

"What?"

God, he sounded bad. Finally, his eyes fluttered open and he looked at her. If she hadn't known how sick he was she would have believed that they were full of defeat. She held out the small measuring cup to him. "It's time for another dose."

"No." He tried to sit up. Groaned. Then tried again, finally succeeding in propping himself against the pillows. "I just keep getting worse."

She nodded. "But your fever's so high." It was like sitting next to a space heater, yet he stayed huddled under about five blankets.

"There's got to be another way. This isn't working."

Setting the red syrup on the side table, Rae nodded. "A cool bath helps sometimes."

He just shook his head. She understood; it was a technique used on fussy babies, not grown men.

So, she uttered the one word that struck terror into her own heart. "Hospital."

He shook his head again. "No doctors."

But she felt that streak of something . . . anger? . . . fear? . . surge up again even as that feeling of touch in the back of her brain swiped down. Wrong. Very wrong. "You need to see a doctor. Sam this isn't going to clear up on its own."

"Sure it will." He didn't move from where he huddled against the headboard.

"Then take the bath. Get your fever down and I won't take you."

"No."

"*Sam.*"

"Fine." It was just one word, but it held a world of sentiment as he ground it out between angry teeth.

Rae nodded, relieved to see that he could still muster up anger, and went to start the bath. The water surged into the tub and she wondered if it would work. She was afraid that they'd be spending the evening in the ER, but at least if they did she'd have a better idea what she was up against. And professional help.

Tepid. That was what she was going for and she wound up with a bath that she herself never would have climbed into before she called him into the bathroom.

He didn't come.

"*Sam?*" She stared to panic again, then told herself the water was still running and maybe he hadn't heard.

But he had. His voice was faint. "Coming."

But he didn't come.

Brows knit together, Rae stood and rounded the corner into the room. Sam stood, barely. Leaning on his dresser, he was clearly considering steps out into the wide expanse of the room, but he hadn't yet made them.

"Sam?"

He was gruff, angry. "My head hurts. Been sleeping too damn much."

She came up to assist him but was stopped short by the look in his eyes. He was so mad. She saw it now. He really hadn't wanted her here. But at this point she was beginning to worry about whether he'd make it. That feeling slid down the back of her brain again and she tried to push the fear aside. Instead, she used it fuel her own anger. "You need to go to the hospital!"

"No."

"Sam!"

"I agreed to take your stupid bath. I am not going to the hospital." He shoved past her, and for a brief moment she was happy that he had found enough strength to stand, no matter how he found it. Then he wavered.

Rae rushed to grab him around the waist and steady him. She managed it—barely. He tried to shove her away, but she held on and won.

That was when she got really scared. She could feel his muscles beneath her arms, but he couldn't seem to gather the strength to push her aside. She knew Sam. He couldn't fight *her* off?

She led him into the bathroom where he sat down gingerly on the edge of the tub. She desperately wanted to take him to the hospital. She wanted to call his mother. Anything not to be responsible for him. Anything for help. She completely avoided thinking about what might have happened if she hadn't stayed. She wanted to drag him out of there, and down to the car, or call 9-1-1. But clearly, he was upset enough. So she kept her voice soft and calm, maybe too calm. "Can you get undressed?"

"I'll be fine."

She nodded and headed for the door. She didn't believe him. "I'll come check on you."

"No, you won't."

"Sam, I have to."

"Rae . . ." He hadn't said her name since she had arrived three days ago. And now it gave her the chills. He hated her. It was clearly a warning, but she wasn't leaving. "Sam, you didn't wake up in there. I can't just leave you—"

"What?"

"I tried to wake you up and you wouldn't." She left it at that. "I'll come in to check on you. Here," She held out a towel, "just take it into the water with you." Turning, she pulled the door almost shut behind her and ducked around the corner before all her strength failed her.

She felt the wall solid behind her back and slowly slid down it. By the time she reached the floor, tears were pouring out of her eyes. Sam hated her. But more importantly he was sick. Very sick. Sam the quarterback, with probably four percent body fat, could barely stand.

She shuddered and bit her tongue to keep the noises from her crying from carrying into the bathroom. Rae barely made out the sound of him sliding into the tub. What if he died?

Why hadn't she had the guts to tell him how she felt?

Curled in a ball, huddled on the floor just outside his bathroom she shook for a full minute. Sam was lost to her. It was in the way he said her name. When he looked at her, he was so angry. So she tucked that away somewhere safe to cry over it later, and made the decision to take him to the hospital when he got out.

The feeling at the back of her brain was getting worse. She had to save him, even if he hated her for it. Sam was in danger. She *knew* it. And she'd never been wrong.

CHAPTER 24

Mrs. Brock rounded the corner with her husband in tow. The instant she saw them, Rae snapped awake and jolted out of the hard hospital chair. She clutched at her purse as she almost knocked it off her lap in the process of jumping up. Unable to find words, she pointed to the door just behind her that led to the room where Sam was sleeping, fully expecting the couple to brush past her and go in.

But Linda Brock did no such thing. She didn't stop, but in one fluid motion, approached and drew Rae into a tight hug. "Oh, thank you so much for taking care of him. I never thought it would be this serious." She pulled back and looked Rae straight in the eyes, then hugged her again, tighter.

If it had been her own father, Rae would have expected him to hang back, maybe look a little out of sorts at being in the hospital. But Mr. Brock was anxiously waiting his turn to hug the girl his own son hated with all his heart. His embrace included a few soft claps on the back and a "we can never thank you enough for this."

Then they took a few deep breaths before opening the door. They looked out of place in the hospital hallway. Rae was in maybe too comfortable clothing—yoga pants and a sweater. But the Brocks were too far the other way. They must have been out when she called. Mr. Brock's pants still held the crease and Linda had every hair in place. She ran her hand through it without messing it up in the slightest before turning the knob and entering.

Rae could hear their muffled sounds of the family talking, although she couldn't make out Sam's voice. His must have been the gaps in the conversation, his voice not loud enough to carry around the corner. Or maybe it just sounded so much like his father's. She sighed wishing she could hear better. At least the horrible feeling that Sam was in danger was gone now. That was the only upside to this. Still, she wished she could hear the conversation. Know what Sam was saying.

Not that it mattered. She was sitting in the hallway because he had ordered her out of the room. Out of the hospital in fact. But she had stayed until his parents showed up. Just in case.

Since they had, Rae knew she should pick herself up and go home, but she just didn't have the strength. This was it. Sam was entirely in someone else's care now. She could feel the tension seeping out of her, her energy draining into a puddle there in the hallway. If the hospital chair hadn't been flat-out uncomfortable, she could have just curled up and gone to sleep right here.

But as it was, she craved her own bed. She desperately wanted to get away from Sam. Away from that look in his eyes. Away from the smell of the hospital and the bustle of the nursing staff, always walking by, but always with a purpose somewhere beyond her, going back and forth in their bright scrubs.

She could feel it coming, the tears pressing at the back of her eyes. They had been there for a while, waiting for the chance to shed. But now they were so close and she had to blink to hold them back. It was so much harder now that she didn't have to be strong. Now that she wasn't the one in charge. Rae had tried to help Sam down the stairs and into the car, but he was too heavy for her to support him. She'd been petrified they'd stumble and fall down the long staircase. She hadn't even been able to get him out of his room.

That had all happened *after* the argument about him going to the hospital in the first place. The rough part had been that Sam hadn't really argued. Mostly he just quietly said "no." Rae had sat on the edge of the bed and gotten in his face. She threw every argument in the book at him. Made him agree that he was sick. That he hadn't eaten in over a day. That if anyone he cared about had done this he'd take them to the hospital.

He'd finally—*finally!*—relented. And they made it about three feet from the bed before they both gave up and turned around. When she had him back under the covers, shivering and sweating from the exhaustion, and her guilt had ratcheted up another ten degrees, she picked up the bedside phone.

But the Brocks hadn't answered. Neither had his sister, Christy. If he was this mad at her, she had no idea how Sam would react if she called Alex and Jack. So she had told Sam to go back to sleep, and had calmly walked downstairs to the kitchen. She put a few things away, washed the two cups in the sink, and called 9-1-1.

When the ambulance arrived, she was in her coat, with her purse slung over her shoulder and a bag of the medicines she'd been pumping into Sam for the past few days waiting by the door.

She could tell he was shocked to see the paramedics, but not as shocked as she was by their actions. While he was still in bed, two of them converged on him and took his vital signs. They ran an IV into him within that first minute. But the scariest moment was when they placed an oxygen mask over his mouth and refused to say anything other than he was stable.

Sam hadn't wanted her in the ER room with him. So she had

read the entire newspaper, headlines through to the obituaries. Next she followed him up here to the inpatient ward where they admitted him. That had scared her as much as anything. Finally, one sweet nurse in pink scrubs had come out holding a clipboard and asked if she was Rae. When she'd nodded 'yes,' the nurse had said "Of course you are. He said 'gorgeous redhead'." Which had instantly endeared her. "He wanted you to know that it's pneumonia."

Even the memory both scared and relieved her. It was dangerous, but she knew what pneumonia was and that it was survivable.

"Rae?"

She startled. She recognized the voice, but hadn't realized that she had nearly fallen asleep. Mr. Brock shook her shoulder. "Let me give you a ride home?"

CHAPTER 25

"Hey, it's good to see you back!" Jack clapped him on the shoulder, although Sam could tell it lacked its usual vigor.

He worked hard to smile at everyone as he came in, then looked around Jack's apartment, surveying the changes Lisa had made to the place since Jack had asked her to move in on their New Year's trip. At least that's how he wanted it to look.

Like he was taking in the whole room. Not like he was trying to place Rae and see where she was sitting, and what look she had on her face. She was emerging from the kitchen, a bowl of fresh popcorn hugged to her chest. Sam did his best to drag out the process of hanging up his coat, but she still hadn't sat down, so he turned to go into the kitchen for a drink.

Her voice floated to him from behind his back. "It's good to see you again."

"Thanks." He didn't turn, disappointed that she had singled him out, when he was working so hard to be invisible to her.

"You look great."

He didn't really acknowledge it, just grunted a little. He had already thanked her repeatedly for saving his life. The ER doctors had told them it was a bad case of pneumonia. One of the worst they'd seen and that he could have died if Rae hadn't brought him in. He'd been held prisoner in the hospital for five days, with his mother and Christy taking shifts. It was just another good reason to hate hospitals. That and the damn gowns. He was finally back up to speed for all his day-to-day activities, but even a game of touch football was still out of reach. Thank God the weather hadn't pumped back up to its usual L.A. sunniness this year so no one would really expect much of him.

With a soda in hand, he went back into the living room, not even caring that he had missed the first ten minutes of crime night. He had been purposefully late so that he could position himself away from Rae. Sam chose the opposite end of the sofa and sank in, the little bubbles in the soda of more interest now than his favorite TV show. But it was Rae that he couldn't ignore.

Like a prism in the light, every move she made caught his attention. He could even hear the soft, rhythmic crunching as she ate popcorn. The way she kept brushing her ponytail back over her shoulder and it kept sliding back forward anyway. Her facial expressions, from giggles to her friends to a gasp at an explosion on the screen. Even a cringe here and there.

Each move was a reminder of what had slipped through his fingers. But then again, he could be dead, right? He had tried time and again to count his blessings but he kept coming up short. The reason he had left his old life behind was for a real chance at family and friends—the kind he had grown up with—and ultimately a family of his own. Rae was the first woman he had really imagined in that role. Not that she had expressed one iota of interest in it. Not that it mattered a bit now, because at this point all his hopes for him and Rae were gone.

Alex's voice finally cut through the wall of his thoughts.

Probably because the question was aimed at Rae. "How goes the getting ready for the show?"

"Oh!" She lit up. "I'm putting together a series I always wanted to do. Sheree and Lisa are going to be in it. And Sam's Mom and sister, too."

"Huh?" He heard the sound come out of his mouth before he thought it. A grunted monosyllable was not what he wished he had said.

But she turned her smile at him and brushed her ponytail back over her shoulder again. "Well, you'll see. When I saw them I realized that they would add an extra dimension to the series. And they agreed to be in it. So . . ." She shrugged. "That's all I'm telling you." The smile lingered at him a moment before she turned away and began a conversation with Sheree. Then they were both absorbed back into the second show.

He tipped back his soda again, only to get nothing. So he crushed it in his fist like he always did. A force of habit, backed by a little lingering anger. At least no one made any comments about him being strong enough to do that again. Then he got up and wandered out to the kitchen for another drink.

Three sodas later, the shows were over and he couldn't recall the plot of any of them. But he could tell you exactly how many times Rae had played with her ponytail and how many times she had smiled at him. And he could tell that he was in a deep hole with only a shovel.

And there was only one thing you could do with a shovel. So he could keep digging or he could put the shovel down.

Instead of doing anything about his problem, he got up and followed his friends like sheep as they headed out for the night. He was at the door just behind Alex when the fingers brushed his arm. He knew it was her. No one else shot sparks through him with just the touch of her skin. Her voice lilted up to him. "How are you feeling?"

It wasn't what he had wanted to hear, and he forced the answer out through his teeth. "Fine."

Then again, what had he expected? Her arms around him and her breathy voice coming from open lips? *Sam, I love you, take me to bed!??* Yeah, right. Apparently not in this lifetime.

She turned away at his gruff tone and slipped out the door and down the stairs to Sheree's car.

Sam watched as her auburn ponytail bounced and blocked his view of her face. Rae didn't turn around once. He followed her down the stairs, disappointed in the evening, and only after he was halfway down did he remember to turn around and say something to Jack and Lisa. "See you guys Friday."

Rae stood behind a table at the back of the room. Though Sloan stood next to her, she still felt little zings of nerves. The class was offered every Monday evening, and luckily the fact that she'd missed the last two hadn't caused any harm. She'd been too busy with Sam the first week, then too exhausted the second, to make it here. She'd intended to come, really she had.

Rae had even told Sloan to go without her and scope the place out. Sloan had refused.

"This is *your* thing. You wanted to come. I'm not going to a witchcraft class without you."

"Maybe you'll meet a nice guy!" Rae had offered up. Sloan had been single a little too long.

"Oh, yeah," her older sister had scoffed. "A wizard or a warlock is such my style."

"Do they even call them that? Aren't they all just 'witches'?" That had begun a serious debate on semantics of male witches. Not that they had solved anything. But Sloan had not come without her.

So tonight was the first time they'd come. Beginner class.

The sign on the door said tonight's lesson was simple scrying spells. When pressed, Rae had told Sloan that she hoped to learn a little. Though she'd missed the "Parking Karma" class last week about small practical spells, this was one she'd looked forward to. So, though she was still depressed over Sam completely ignoring her, she wished she would get something useful out of this class.

"What do you need to scry?" Sloan had asked while they looked for a spot. All the good ones were taken, probably because everyone else had made it to "Parking Karma" last week.

Rae had confessed. "If we can scry, then we can find this Luke guy."

Finally, pulling into a spot, Sloan had turned and looked at Rae with an unexpected seriousness. "You're putting a lot of pressure on this class."

"No, I—"

"Yeah you are. I think you need to remember that our ten dollars is buying us entertainment. Like a movie. Like when you go to the place where you paint your own picture while you drink. Just like that, we're just pretending. And it's entirely possible that these people are too."

"They aren't!" Rae had protested. "Remember when we came in. They were helpful, and they really seemed to know what they were talking about."

"Please, Rae. They're preying on your hope!" Sloan cut the engine but didn't get out. Only later had Rae realized her sister didn't want to be overheard by any would-be witches or even shop owners. "They sold you a product. You bought that little herb thing for the kitchen to clear your apartment of bad energy. You gave them money. And they sold us both this class. They're good salespeople. They told you what you wanted to hear." Sloan shook her head. "You know, it's worse. They didn't just sell you a product. They sold you hope."

"You're right. Hope is terrible. I shouldn't have it. We should drop it." Rae had gotten out of the car. It was all she could do not to slam the door. "Let's stop looking for Aunt Emilia's baby. Everyone else is gone, but, hey, let's stop looking for Mom's niece or nephew. She wanted us to find them, but let's give up on it."

Sloan shook her head over the top of the car, angry that Rae had blown things out of proportion. But her sister didn't give her enough credit. She was an adult now, too. Sure, Sloan had gotten there first. She got to every milestone first—it was just part of being the big sister. But sometimes it seemed she still saw Rae as a ten-year-old who couldn't sort her wishes from reality.

"I'm *hopeful*." She countered. "I'm not sold. I'm not dead-set. I have no idea if this will work or not. I'm not going to hand them my life-savings!" She was grateful when Sloan didn't clap back with a comment about how much that wasn't worth. It was hard to prove adulthood when she was still living hand-to-mouth and trying to "make it big" as an artist. "I just wanted to come tonight and see what it was all about. It's ten bucks. Don't stay if you don't want to."

That was when Sloan relented. "I want to stay. You just sounded like you wanted to put all your eggs in this basket."

Rae almost blew up again. She was not stable. She was angry that Sam was angry at her. She was brokenhearted that he'd kissed her like he had and then dropped her like a hot rock for doing what any friend would do. She was mad that her life was such a roller-coaster. In a matter of months, she'd discovered she was an adulteress, fallen hard for the first man in a long time, thought she'd actually gotten him only to have it ripped away, gotten her first gallery show, which was a ton of pressure, and was working with the mother of said angry man. Easy peasy. Right? She might barf from all the twists and turns.

Sloan had touched her back gently, as though sensing the

cloud Rae was living in. "Let's go in. Let's waste our ten bucks and learn about scrying. Who knows, maybe they'll have a crystal ball that we can see our cousin in."

So they'd come in, written their names and emails on the sign in list. Rae wasn't certain that Sloan hadn't written a fake email, but they'd been brought into this back classroom and given a choice of seats. Rae had picked one of two back tables. Each table had two seats, so she and Sloan were a unit.

She looked around the room at the other beginning witches. Most looked a lot more comfortable here than she and her sister did. They had likely been coming more often and gotten to know each other. Rae desperately wanted to meet some of them, ask about the class. She was curious how many of them would tell her about the healing power of crystals or that essential oils could cure cancer.

She'd expected the room to be full of earth mothers and stoned millennials. Instead, she saw high end jeans, low end sneakers, button down shirts and t-shirts with band names like the Foo Fighters and even Journey. Still, Rae wanted to meet people by having them come up to her. She wasn't one to introduce herself around an unknown room.

Just then, the low conversation in the room slid to near zero, and the teacher walked in.

"Hello beginners! I'm Delilah." The petite blond woman commanded the room. "I'm filling in for Allison tonight." She looked around the room, her gaze landing easily on Sloan and Rae. It was as though she knew they were the newbies, even though she was clearly a last minute sub. Delilah continued. "My last name is Goodman and my parents started this shop before they passed away. My family still runs it. My brother and I are eighth generation practicing Wiccans. I'll be happy to answer any questions after class. First, if we could do a real quick round of introductions."

They went around the room, Delilah keeping the pace up, a

natural teacher. Again, Rae was shocked no one was named Moonbeam or Alder. Everyone seemed normal. Some were in for mercenary reasons—they wanted promotions, money, to get a house in a rough market. Others were more casual and came because it was fun. By the time they got to the back row, Rae was relatively at ease. "I'm Rae and this is my sister Sloan." She knew Sloan did not like speaking in public, not off the cuff. "We saw the shop a few weeks ago while we were wandering Hollywood Boulevard."

She laughed as she realized how that sounded. "As far as scrying goes, it would be good to learn because we are looking for a lost family member."

CHAPTER 26

Rae shuffled the tripod over a few inches trying to center it behind the two-way mirror. She had been thinking about how to best capture this without using actresses, and it hit her one day when she was reading while Sam was sick. Something about watching witnesses in the interrogation room when they were alone and they thought no one could see them. Or maybe they knew and just forgot.

She had sketched this idea out on the notepad beside Sam's phone and stuffed it into her purse. With a few modifications from the original concept, it stood before her now. At its heart it was just a dressing table with a two-way mirror and her camera behind it.

Sheree was puttering around on the other side. God bless her, she seemed to think that she was getting the good end of the deal. Rae had bought her best friend off for the chance to be in the show as a model. She at least felt good about the fact that Sheree had known from moment one that it wasn't meant to be an attractive picture.

"Okay, Rae." Sheree spread her makeup out on the small white counter they'd set up together. "What do I do?"

Rae grinned, it had begun. She'd had the idea for this portrait series a long time ago, but she hadn't had the time or money to pull it off. That was the problem with a lot of art. It cost a lot of money to get to some of it, and there was no guarantee of return. She was giddy that she was finally producing this one, though.

"You sit down and put on your makeup and forget that I'm here." Sheree did as she was instructed and, in a few minutes, Rae had snapped off hundreds of photos. It wound up taking Sheree fifteen minutes to go through her makeup routine.

Lisa buzzed up from the front door to the building halfway through Sheree's photo shoot, but Rae didn't move from behind her camera. Mrs. Brock answered the door for her, letting Rae keep focused on Sheree doing what she would naturally do in front of the mirror in the morning. Lisa slid past Rae in the limited space behind the two-way mirror and went into the bathroom to scrub her face clean as instructed, then waited. Rae barely noticed the movement behind her. She adjusted a light once, but that was it.

It had been difficult setting up the shot so that she had light —which naturally came in through the wide sliding door. But also so that she didn't capture the trees of the park and the starting-to-rust rails of her balcony. Facing the other way, she got more light directly to the subjects, but had her old, old saloon style kitchen doors in the background. In the end, it had taken rigging and professional batting blankets to obscure the background of her apartment.

Then it was Lisa's turn. "I'm only the second one?"

"Well, you and Sheree are the two people easiest to get back for re-shoots if I need to fix anything. Since that's most likely with the first people, yes, you're only second. And thank you in advance." She motioned Lisa to the seat and hid herself behind the mirror.

Lisa peeked around the side. "I just put my makeup on?

That's all?"

"Yes." Rae managed to hide the fact that Sheree had just about cracked her up with the faces she had made, contorting this way and that. Rae knew she would never put her own makeup on the same way again. No wonder it was an unwritten law that you didn't let a man watch you put on your makeup unless you were never, ever, ever going to date him.

The day sank by with more and more of her friends, and then her friend's friends, showing up. It was good steady work and it looked like she would manage to get all the subjects photographed today. Which was good, because she really didn't want to tear-down and set-up again. That would most likely ruin the continuity. And there was no way she could leave that scrim up for several days. This was killing the apartment and Sheree was a prisoner in her own home while Rae used it as studio space.

Then the knock at the door made her head pop up. It was six in the evening and she hadn't thought about him all day. But that knock.

Mrs. Brock opened the door and Rae could hear the smile in the woman's voice. "Sam."

It *was* him. And she had recognized his *knock*? She was in way too deep. Forcing herself back to the task at hand, she hurried to catch a shot that she almost missed.

She kept her eyes glued to the small screen on her camera. She had the system set up to give her a digital view, but capture the picture on high speed film. Though she could look at her set up and act as though she was engrossed in the math of it or the art of the shot, it proved harder to keep her focus on the images that filtered to her through the two-way mirror and her lens. She tried, but her mind strained for the conversation between Sam and his mother.

"You're not finished? I'll just come back later."

"No, just wait."

"Mom." There was a lilt to his voice. A *don't-ask-me-to-do-that* tone, that made Rae's heart sink a little lower in her chest. He didn't want to be around her. That much had been clear for a while. He was that upset about her taking care of him while he was sick.

At least he was alive. Now she pushed down anger. She'd felt that feeling she got. He'd been in actual danger. The doctors said he could have died if he hadn't come in when he did. And he hadn't gone in, he'd been carted in because she forced it on him. Fine. She told herself she would make the same decision again. And she would. Then she told herself she didn't care, which was a bald-faced lie.

Rae squeezed off a few more shots while Jennifer, one of the teachers at Sheree's school, put the finishing touches on her face. She didn't want to make Sam suffer. If he was that uncomfortable around her, she would let him go.

She motioned to Mrs. Brock. "You can go next, you've been here all day. Then Christy. You'll be quick, but Christy will need to do all her makeup before her pictures because she's the final shot. The one with all her makeup on. Have you washed your face?"

Mrs. Brock went off to the bathroom, and Rae felt Sam behind her shifting from one foot to the other while he waited.

Jennifer sat straight up, her face completely painted to what was supposed to be her "normal" and she smiled at the mirror, just as Rae instructed. As soon as that shot was done, she hopped up and started gathering her things. Christy took over her mother's job of thanking everybody and handing out cards that had been printed with the Gallery information as well as the date and time of the show. Rae had to admire Mrs. Brock. The woman was an unstoppable force.

Rae had wanted subjects for the shoot. Mrs. Brock was the one who pointed out that they would want to see themselves in the finished product. They would come to the opening. They would likely bring dates. And a packed gallery sold art. Then she'd showed up with printed, business-sized cards and handed them out. Rae admitted it was far easier than handing them out herself.

A half hour later, Rae finished with Christy and sent the Brock family on their way. Sam hadn't said one word to her in the entire time he had waited. Although she had heard him talking easily with Sheree, about cars, work, Jeremy of the petty theft auto case, and all sorts of things. But the girl he had kissed senseless, the one whose shirt he'd plucked off as he bent her over his bed, didn't even rate a "hello."

She had a hard time focusing for the rest of the evening.

Relief and disappointment flooded him when Sheree answered the door. Sam knew he should just let it go, but he couldn't.

"Are you here to see Rae?"

"No. Why would I be?" Okay, so he wanted to see Rae. But he had made up an excuse to see Sheree instead. Mentally, Sam kicked himself for thinking he was getting any of that by any of his friends.

Sheree wandered into the kitchen passing the dining room table where she was working on grading the papers she had spread everywhere. "What can I get for you?"

"Advice." He glanced around, not seeing Rae at all. He hated how his heart sunk at the loss of something he'd never really had. Just a few stolen moments, and now . . . nothing. "I just needed some help. Someone to tell me how to deal with this kid Jeremy."

"The kid who stole that car?" Sheree pulled a pale ale out of the fridge for him. He smiled, at least he still had his friends. And Rae was still his friend. If he could ever just think of her that way.

"Yeah. You're the only one I know who works with kids. I thought you might have some ideas." *And I thought Rae might be around,* but he didn't put voice to that thought.

"I'll do what I can. But my kids are in fourth grade. There's a big difference between nine years old and sixteen." She tilted her head. "Then again, maybe there isn't."

They made themselves comfortable on the couch while she explained about Sam needing to stand firm to his principles and decisions. "You should just call it like you see it. You can read the situation. You're the one who knows what to do here, so just tell him what to do. Don't ask. Don't say you don't know. I mean, you'd get upset if you called your doctor and he said 'Yeah, well, I just can't make heads or tales of this test result. What do you think?'"

Sam laughed. Thank God he'd been paying attention.

Sheree smiled. "You have to be in charge and stand firm, even if it means you kick him out and cut him off. He'll respect it."

Nodding, Sam finished off the beer. "It sucks for his mom, though. I'd love to help her out."

"Sure, but you can't put a criminal back on the streets just because his mom is a good person. You have to do what you can live with," Sheree pointed out.

That felt good to hear. He'd been leaning that way, but honestly, he'd felt awful about it. But if Deana couldn't control Jeremy, then why should he have to make up for it if the kid really didn't care if he went to prison? He felt a little of the weight on him lift. "You're right."

"Of course, I am." Sheree let out a wide grin. Maybe she liked her own humor. "Will you answer a question for me?" Maybe she had something up her sleeve.

"You need legal advice?"

"No." She glanced quickly down the hall, almost like she

didn't want him to catch the move. He felt his brows pull together, then she whispered. "Rae's in the darkroom."

"Oh." So, she had been here the whole time. His senses hummed now, and he tried to tamp them down. It wasn't like it would get him anywhere.

"Soooo," Sheree drew out the word as she tucked her legs up to get comfortable. "What's going on with you and Rae?"

"What?" He practically jumped back. It wasn't what he'd expected her to say.

"Come on. Something was up."

Sam shook his head since he couldn't think of anything to say. He wasn't so slick. Sam knew now that he was, in fact, transparent. But he gave lying his best shot anyway. "Nothing's up."

"Really? You two looked a little on the cozy side to me there for a while."

He shook his head again, not expecting her to believe him. But he did it anyway. Oh yeah, he was a fool. Seven kinds.

"Hmmmm. Honestly, we all went to check on you when you were sick, just to be sure you really were sick. The way you and Rae had been, we all sort of figured you two were just disappearing for a bit."

If only. He had to bite his tongue to keep that one in.

He shrugged and offered the only honest answer that didn't spill his feelings like marbles across the table. "Sorry, no such luck."

He considered asking her what Rae thought, but that would be just as bad as spewing his hurt all over. He stayed quiet as she chewed her lip, thinking. So Sam decided it was time to go. Clearly, he couldn't stay here and have Sheree pecking apart his carefully constructed shell.

Hugging her goodnight, he left, wondering what they had all seen between him and Rae. Then forcing himself to face facts. Whatever they had seen sure didn't matter now.

CHAPTER 27

Rae stood in the dark room. The tongs in her hand held a black and white photo dripping from the stopbath. Her eyes didn't see the red all around her, didn't see much of anything. They had glazed over while her body had strained piano-wire-tight to hear every last piece of conversation between Sam and Sheree. She had forced herself to continue the rote movements of developing pictures. As though acting like she didn't care would make her really feel that way.

And, of course, the only thing that she could remember now was Sam's last sentence. "No such luck." It had just been a kiss. A make-out session. A spur of the moment shot of heat. Whatever it had been, it was gone as soon as she was. Or else it had died with his illness. It wasn't enough for him to acknowledge it had even existed.

Through sheer force of will, she focused again on the picture in front of her. The darkroom was illuminated by its standard, non-damaging, red bulb, but her eyes had adjusted and she saw the shades of the photo as clearly as anyone in a natural light would. She could easily read the bright hues captured in the still gray planes. In her own eyes, it was one of those perfect photos.

Where the paper she held now was exactly as she had expected it to be when she had snapped the shot. And she hoped that other people would see it that way, too.

Looking up at the photos hanging around the converted closet, she tensed and focused her eyes again at the handsome blue-eyed man laughing beside his car. She liked that she could see Sam's generosity and humor in the photo. And she hoped that other people would see him as she did. She would have to get his permission to hang the photo in the show. She would have to have a real conversation with him.

She wondered again at the quality of that photo. She most likely wasn't capable of sound decisions, because clearly she was blind. Maybe it was perfect simply because it was Sam. She would have taken it out of the show, except that she was certain she had liked that particular image even before she had thought of Sam in those terms. Or maybe just before she had *realized* that she thought of him in those terms. But that was of no concern now. She had heard plain as day through the door, that he hadn't ever thought that there was anything between them. That Christmas kiss under the mistletoe must have been as much a fairy tale as it sounded.

This time, Rae met Sloan at Blessed Be. They were over a block down the street, on opposite sides of Vine. Rae at least got a spot on the same side of the street as the store and she headed to the corner to wait while Sloan caught the light.

She stood there, waiting with her hands stuffed into the pockets of her lightweight hoodie. Looking around at the people on the street, she tried to not get asked how much she cost. It was one of those LA things, to get mistaken for a hooker, just for being on the street.

The weather had turned for the better, making her happy

with the sunshine again. It was what she'd signed up for when she'd picked this place for school. Her bragging had even gotten Sloan to choose a job offer here in the city. She'd had two excellent prospects, but her sister was here—her only family left —and Rae had bragged about the weather and the beaches. Anything to get her sister with her.

She'd thought she might leave after graduating, go somewhere with a bigger art scene. But that would have been New York or Chicago. It would have been away from Sloan and all her friends. No, this was the place for her, watching her sister debate whether she should jaywalk, and eventually settling on just jumping the light a little.

Rae grinned at her. "We really should not have missed the *Parking Karma* class. Everyone is out-performing us."

Sloan shook her head. "You're the reason we missed it. You and that hunk of man you have a massive crush on."

"I told you, that's way over and done with." Turning away, Rae started up the gentle slope of Vine Street. "So over."

"Uh-huh, so over that you have to repeat it. A lot."

"Yes. If I keep telling myself, maybe it will sink in. Nothing I can do about it anyway." She shrugged, but Sloan put an arm around her shoulders.

"I'm sorry. I know you really liked this one." She sighed the way only a big sister can, irritated at the world just for Rae. "After the craptacular mess that was Roger, I'd really thought this one was better. Men. If only you could poke a stick in them to see if they were done."

Rae grinned. "You actually can, but if you find a good one, it's too bad, because you'll be in jail for assault."

Sloan nodded. "Men."

They got to the door of the shop and Rae had actually managed to turn her thoughts to last week's class in scrying. This week was about protecting your home. Rae didn't really need or believe in that too much, but she wanted to become a regular. Everything helped. Scrying hadn't really told her much except that she was right. The only problem was that she didn't know if the scrying itself was right. As Delilah had explained, it took practice to get good at it. Rae had practiced all week. She had plenty of spare time, not having a boyfriend and all. But it kept telling her that the man she'd seen twice now was, in fact, her cousin and that he lived in L.A.

It all sounded like wishful thinking to her.

Until she entered the shop and stopped dead.

Sloan ran into her back, not knowing what was going on, and it occurred to Rae for the first time that Sloan had never seen these people in the flesh. Only phone snapshots of pictures of this Luke guy. But there behind the desk stood Yasmin.

Someone else came up behind them at the door and Sloan jostled Rae, pointing out they were being rude. Rae walked forward, unable to look away from the woman behind the desk. She remembered the loose curls, dark hair with shots of blond that were likely an afterthought. At the time, Yasmin had been all smiles, getting married the next day at the beach. Now, she was staring at Rae, ignoring Sloan and about everyone else at the store.

"Welcome to Blessed Be." She tilted her head as though listening for something. "Do I know you?"

"Oh no," Sloan said from over Rae's shoulder. She was grabbing Rae to steer her, not understanding what was going on. "We were in the beginners' class last week. For scrying."

Another shove to get Rae moving, but she shrugged her sister's hands off. And stepped forward as Yasmin's expression got more wary. "Maybe you do recognize me. This is going to sound weird . . ."

Of course, when she started like that, it sounded more than weird, it sounded creepy. She sighed. Yasmin didn't help. Didn't offer a flip "oh, it's a wiccan store, we get 'weird' all the time!" Nope, she just looked at Rae and her eyes narrowed a bit.

Hoping for the best since this might be her one shot, Rae launched in.

"My college roommate and I were at a little B-n-B up the coast for spring break two years ago. We stumbled upon your wedding. The wine was great, thank you." She grinned and tried to put the situation at ease. It almost worked.

Yasmin nodded at her, but Rae jumped in and continued.

"Your husband, Luke . . . um, he looks like my mother. Like my grandfather." Shit. She was totally blowing this. Could she just say she had a *feeling*? She wasn't psychic or anything. She'd never called it that. Her mother hadn't, though it had always been treated as legitimate and never brushed off when Rae got a *feeling* or if Sloan *saw* anything.

Yasmin's eyes narrowed.

Rae tried again. "My mother's sister had a baby that she gave away. He would be about thirty-five now. Or she, we don't know." She hated confessing that part. The baby had been born in Italy, on another continent. Getting the birth information from a sealed adoption had been next to impossible. They weren't even close relatives, cousins didn't have much sway with the system. *Shit.* "But the baby was born in Italy, then my aunt died. We've been looking . . ."

Other people in the store were starting to gather around. The man she'd seen at the dog park—*Tristan!*—came out from the back. He put a hand on the counter next to Yasmin's almost like a signal. He looked at Rae but spoke to Yasmin. "Is everything okay out here?"

"So far." Yasmin didn't look at him either. Her brows furrowed.

For a moment Rae thought she might have said something that triggered the woman. Sloan was now watching in rapt attention. She jumped in to back up her little sister. "Look, we just want to meet this person. To find them and let them know they have a family."

Rae didn't add that everyone in their family seemed to have some odd little *gift*. She hadn't really thought anything of it, until her mother pointed out how both girls had learned early not to speak of it outside the family. That people thought they were weird even when they were giving useful or even vital information. Then her mother had told her that Emilia had been the strongest in her family. What *gift* might her child have gotten? Rae didn't know.

Yasmin was speaking up. "My husband has a family."

Her heart sank and Rae nodded in accepted defeat. "I'm sorry. If he's not adopted, then it's not him."

She'd felt *that feeling* when Yasmin and Luke were together, and she hadn't known which of them it was. Trying to be subtle, she stilled and listened to the feeling in the back of her brain. Was Yasmin frowning because it was her own story? Had they simply found someone who happened to look like their family, but Yasmin was the one they were related to?

Rae didn't feel anything. Was that because she was stressed? She surely was, she could feel the nerves thrumming as she stood in the middle of the shop surrounded by strangers listening in. She wanted to simultaneously charge forward to make her case and sink through the floor to disappear forever. Or did she feel nothing because it was never about Yasmin? Was it always Luke? God, he looked so much like her grandfather.

Yasmin was still staring at them oddly. "Give me your number. I'll give it to my husband. He can reach out to you if he wants."

Nodding rapidly like an idiot, Rae stepped forward and took the notepad Yasmin was pushing across the desk at her. She plucked one of the pens from the holder by the register and started to put her info down as Yasmin turned back to her non-stalker-like customers.

"Let me put my info, too." Sloan pushed up next to Rae. Though Rae started writing her sister's address and number,

Sloan shook her head and snatched the pen away. Rae blinked. Sloan wasn't one for acting odd. She didn't catch on until her sister ripped the top sheet away and waited for Yasmin to finish talking with someone.

"Here's both our information." Sloan sounded sweet and kind. Rae wondered. "Thank you so much for helping us out." She held out her hand to shake a thank you, and Rae got it. She watched the subtle shift in Sloan's body as the two women made skin contact. Then they split and Yasmin took the paper, admonishing them to get to class before they were late. She promised to give it to her husband.

In class, they had just a moment before Allison, the usual teacher started speaking.

Sloan leaned in first as she peeled her jacket. She whispered, "Do you think she suspected anything?"

"Honestly? Yes. She looked like maybe she read you, too." But it was too late to change that. "So what did you see?"

"A big Italian family with a bunch of people around a full table. Most of them dark Italians, some Americans. Yasmin and that Luke guy in the pictures there. I can't be sure, but if that's his family, he's definitely adopted."

CHAPTER 28

R ae climbed the steps to Jack's place again. It was Lisa's turn to host, but they were at Jacks. They hadn't yet decided how the whole hosting go-round was going to change after the two of them had moved in together. Would they meet every third time here? Rae didn't know. Teetering in her hands was the platter of seven layer dip. She prayed that Sheree would arrive right behind her with the chips and graciously open the door. But when she looked back over her shoulder all Rae saw was the street.

Maneuvering her elbow around, she aimed it for the doorbell, then almost smashed the dip in her face in sheer surprise as the door opened, with Sam filling the space and almost stepping on her.

"Rae!"

Breathing quickly, she re-balanced her precious dip. "Yes?" Where had that cold tone come from in her voice?

"I didn't see you—" The sentence ended as though he didn't know what to say. Like an apology or an offer of help was too much to have hanging between them. "I— I was just on my way out to my car."

Sam held the door wide for her, pressing himself back out of her way, as though a mere touch from her would be more than he could bear. She noticed through the haze of irritation as she slid by that he wasn't wearing a jacket.

Why should she notice that kind of thing? She shouldn't. She'd heard him the other day, perfectly clear. She didn't look back as he closed the door behind her, and she made her way in to set the dip down. She was done being responsible for it. Rae loved to make it, and loved to eat it, but carrying that dip was a lesson in nerves.

As usual when Lisa hosted, the place was set up for a party. A real party. None of Rae's popcorn was even to be found. Biscuits and honey and jellies were arranged around the table. There were small strawberry shortcakes. Cream cheese and feta stuffed bell pepper slices and of course a big block of cheese set out with a cheese knife and crackers. *And this crowd thought to accuse* me *of being a Martha Stewart?* Maybe it was because they all knew that Lisa was a black belt, and no one really wanted to tangle with her.

A snap of warm air buffeted her from behind, and she turned to see who was coming in the door. She had her answer by the sound of the voices even before she saw them. Sam and Sheree were chatting up a storm about whether or not Jeremy could be trusted to wash Sam's car.

Rae stole the corn chips from Sheree's hands and pulled the bag open. It wasn't fair that Sheree got to have easy conversation with the man that she wanted. And he wasn't really speaking to her. Why? Because he was mad that she made him homemade soup, and put a warm blanket in his bed when he was sick. Okay, more likely he was angry that she made him take that stupid cool bath that didn't work, and that she had stayed and watched over him when he told her to leave. Sure, he was furious. But if she hadn't done all that, he'd be dead.

Ungrateful ass.

She picked up the biggest chip she saw and found a perverse satisfaction in marring the perfect surface of the seven layer dip. Then she did it again.

"It's on!" Lisa plopped onto the overstuffed couch with such force that it nearly bounced her back up. She pointed the remote and cranked up the volume to catch the 'scenes from last week.'

It was just as well. Rae would have been forty pounds heavier by the end of the night if she had continued to take out her anger on the dip. She grabbed one of the small strawberry shortcakes anyway and headed to the couch. Tucking herself into the crook of the other arm, she looked up as Alex burst through the door. "Did I miss anything?"

"Not yet! Shhhh." Lisa pointed the remote again and scooted over a little to make room for Jack between them.

Sam waited until just about everyone else was seated then cleared himself a spot on the floor in front of Sheree's spot in the armchair. He was about as far away as he could possibly be. If that was a good indication of how angry he was, well then, she didn't stand a snowball's chance in hell.

Well, she hadn't ever stood a chance. The problem was she kept checking back in as though that would change. It wouldn't. She was angry at herself for hoping.

The strawberry shortcake was going to pay for her sin, too. Had she been alone, Rae would have apologized to the little cake first. Instead she just began lifting the strawberry slices from the top and eating them one by one. If it could be called eating. She bit in with fervor, chewed it to a pulp and went back for the next one. Halfway through the top shortcake round Jack's voice cut through a commercial. "Rae? What are you doing to that cake?"

"Eating it!" She wished she hadn't sounded so irate. She'd like to blame that on Sam, too.

"You do know where the forks are?"

Five pairs of eyes were turned to her, as she sat with another slick strawberry between her fingers. "I like it better this way."

Jack shook his head. "It just seems silly that Lisa went to all this work to stack those little things." When Jack hosted crime night there were Doritos and beer. Rae had to make her own popcorn those nights.

"Hey!" Lisa smacked him on the arm with an irritated grin. "I did go to a lot of work to make them, and Rae is clearly enjoying it. There's no fork law in this house, and you should be the first to admit that."

Rae beamed at Lisa. "Thank you."

Right then Alex's voice cut in, "Besides, I'm enjoying watching her eat it that way."

Her fingers stopped just at the moment the strawberry hit her lips. Her eyes widened. It hadn't occurred to her that there was anything involved here other than a shortcake and a vengeful tongue. She hadn't meant to be giving any male persons any ideas.

Her gaze flew instantly to Sam, but he was watching the commercials, not her mouth. Rae resigned her lips to their lonely existence, and went back to polishing off the cake. If Sam wasn't watching, then it could only be about the taste.

A few commercials later, Lisa asked whose turn it was to pick Friday night.

"Mine." Sam finally pried his eyes away from the television and turned to Lisa, making solid eye contact. It seemed he would talk to anyone but her.

"So what's your pick?"

"Bowling."

"Hmm!" Lisa perked up. "We haven't done that in a while."

"That's why I thought of it."

"So," Lisa looked back and forth between Rae and Sheree, "Should I make nail appointments for all of us for Saturday morning?"

Rae smiled. That would be good. It would take her mind off how grumpy Sam would most likely have been to her the night before. "Count me in."

"Me three." Sheree managed to squeeze in before the show came back on and the two cops were back to running down the street after the perp.

Rae took the next commercial break to get up and get more food. She wasn't that hungry, but it always tasted so good when it was Lisa's night and it gave her something to do with her hands beside fidget like a nervous twit. Sam was up and on his way to the table when she stood. But the second she approached him he waved her by and turned to go down the hall toward the bathroom.

Her breath sucked in and she fought for control of her jaw which was desperately trying to open to a great cave. He had been headed to the dining room. He couldn't even stand to be at the same table with her? That ass!

She almost chased him down the hallway just to yell at him, but decided that it was all better unsaid. Clearly, she didn't want anyone else involved in this little fantasy world she had constructed where she believed she'd stood a chance with champion quarterback and hot shot lawyer Samuel Levi Brock. Weaseling in when he was sick was probably just too much for him, from a girl he'd made the mistake of kissing senseless. A girl who would read that kiss as something that it definitely wasn't. She'd taken it as better than it actually was. Certainly as more than he meant it to be.

She told herself it was all for the best, finding this out now. He was such a jerk that she couldn't possibly have any feelings for him. She decided that she'd made a terrible mistake. She repeated this to herself like a mantra and told her heart to pay close attention. She attacked the stuffed peppers.

~

"For God's sakes!"

Sam stood in the open doorway of his garage looking out over the wet driveway where Jeremy held the formerly fluffy towel he had just blackened to pitch. It was one of the nice ones Rae had left him. Sam sighed. At least the boy was actually doing a good job of getting the car cleaned.

"What?" Jeremy managed to make a shrug look righteously angry.

"It wasn't your fault." Sam sighed again and sucked it up. He *had* told Jeremy to use the white towel. He had just meant from the *other* bathroom. Where the old, good-for-nothing-but-car-washing, already grubby white towels were. "I like the glow. How much longer?"

The little coupe would shine like oil. So that Sam could drive it out tonight to not pick up his hot girlfriend that he didn't have. He would go out bowling and watch Rae not speak to him.

Another shrug from Jeremy and the boy and his beat-up leather jacket turned back to the car. He didn't acknowledge Sam now in any way other than voice. "Twenty minutes."

"What? Oh." That showed where his mind was these days. The same place it always was. In the gutter. With Rae.

At least before when it had been in the gutter, Sam had believed he actually had a chance of getting in the gutter with her. He trudged back inside. Jeremy was seeming to be more trustworthy this week. But Sam left the blinds open anyway. This was a kid who had stolen an eight-hundred-dollar car. Who knew what he'd do with a nice black coupe in front of him?

Pulling a blue short-sleeve shirt out of his closet, Sam held it up in front of the mirror. It brought out the blue in his eyes. Which only made him disgusted with himself. Why should he wear anything to make her notice him? Clearly, there was no point. He shoved the shirt back at the closet as though it were all the shirt's fault that his love life had gone south. South Pole south. Grabbing a green shirt, he pulled it on instead. He didn't know whose eyes that matched and therefore declared it okay.

Rae had come in here and seen him at his worst and ordered him around like a child. He was still in knots over that. The twist that happened in his gut every time he thought about it couldn't be ignored. The anger seethed just below the surface. More than anger, he was just upset, gnawed at by the feeling that he had lost something valuable that he couldn't replace.

The expanse of the black comforter called to him. It was neat, spread out smooth, and entirely un-rumpled. She had sat there beside him with her arms curled around her knees and waited for him to wake up. It was hardly the image he had conjured for how he wanted the two of them in his bed together. His ideas involved a lot less clothing and a decided lack of thermometers and mothering. More like the morning they'd woken up together. But that had been fleeting. Had she run because it hit her what they were doing? Or had it really been about the clock? He'd never know now.

He tried watching TV for the remaining few minutes, flipping through all the channels at least three times before Jeremy announced he was finished with the car and could he go home?

Locking up and sending Jeremy on his way, Sam headed out to go bowling. Why hadn't he suggested a movie? Then he wouldn't have to watch her. He knew she would wiggle her butt and he wouldn't be able to avoid looking. Neither would anyone else, for that matter. She was a terrible bowler but tried to steer the ball through some kind of wiggle-witchcraft. All it did was distract everyone from her awful score. He should concentrate on bowling. He could take his anger out on a thirteen-pound ball. That was enough weight to work out some nerves, right?

The drive over was lost to him. For all he knew he had been abducted by aliens and deposited in front of the fun center. All he could think of was the hour he'd spent at her apartment last week. He'd watched her work, all focus and talent. She was amazing, pure drive. She hadn't even noticed him at all. It was just Rae and her camera looking through her two-way mirror and capturing human faces. He already knew how talented she was. How she could hold her camera up and snap a shot and get better pictures than he could when he lined up his shot carefully. She always seemed to know where the light was and what it was worth to her picture. She said she just "saw" it. To make things worse, his mother couldn't stop talking about the show and what an amazing artist Rae was. There were already two new pieces that Rae had given her hanging in the house.

He couldn't escape her. Some image of her always came forth. At his mother's. In his condo. He could see her in the kitchen making him soup, or hear her come down the hall to check on him. She even haunted him away from his own home. Like in the car, when he remembered driving her away from dance lessons. Even without something specific, she haunted him in his mind.

She hadn't asked him to attend swing dancing class with her again. Sam didn't even know if she was still going, or if that big black-haired guy had finally asked her to dance now that Sam was no longer there to make rude faces over her shoulder.

The red and neon of the bowling alley sign was suddenly overhead, and he cut a sharp right at the last moment into the tiny lot. He was the first one here, as he should be. It was his night and he had to get the lane and wait.

A parking spot opened up before him, which was a good thing. In this state of mind, he might have driven in circles for a while. The last of the Santa Ana winds blew warm air at him as he hurried inside, but he was grateful. It brought him back around to the earthly plane. To what was going on here, and not in the world of his imagination. Which had grown very rich of late.

Inside, he looked around and grounded himself with the

sounds of smashing pins and the low rumble of the ball return. The round man behind the counter handed him shoes and directed him to one of only two vacant lanes.

Taking up otherwise empty time, he staked out the wood surface, and ordered a few beers and chips, then entered a team name into the computer. Next, he went around to find a ball. He chose his own easily. The heaviest thing he could find. It would give him the best aggression workout. Then he set about gathering balls for the rest of the crew. No one was serious enough to have their own.

Jack and Alex? Having no clue what they used, he got an assortment of about four heavier balls and lined them up in the return loop. Sheree and Lisa were as much a mystery, and he grabbed a few of the lighter, girlier colored ones.

But Rae . . . they had all come here about four months ago. And he even remembered that she had a "lucky" ball. An eight-pound black and pink swirled thing that said "Sweetie" on it. Someone must have left it behind, she'd mused. Rae and "Sweetie" had gone on to her best score, crappy though it still was. She had reluctantly set the ball back in the corner when they had all left.

Sure enough, he spotted Sweetie in the middle rack behind a family and went to retrieve the stupid thing. How could he pass it up?

As he headed back, he spotted Jack, Lisa, and Alex at the chairs drinking the beer that had arrived without him. Feeling like a complete idiot, he grabbed another random ball off the shelf, and carried it with his fingers laced in the holes. He couldn't even get his fingers into the ones the girls used. But he couldn't very well show up with Rae's prize piece and look like he knew it, could he?

"Hey!" Yeah, sure, that sounded casual. How about a nice *"Where's Rae? Do I stand any sort of chance with her? Never mind. I know I don't."* Softly he set the two balls into the ball return loop and picked up his beer. Soon they would start playing, maybe then his mind would work. *Yeah, Right.*

His head turned even before he consciously recognized her laughter. He wanted to whack himself over the head with the beer bottle. Because that was clearly what it would take to get him to see things clearly.

But he did see things clearly. Clearly his own way. Whatever Sheree was wearing he couldn't have said, but Rae was in her soft blue gingham shirt. Her hair in a ponytail, bouncing as she walked. With her white slim pants and socks she could have stepped right out of the fifties. He forced himself to turn away, and began inputting their names into the computer.

He wouldn't put hers first.

When he looked up, the girls all had their shoes on and everyone was ready, and he had put Rae's turn right before his.

CHAPTER 29

"No! Left, Sweetie, left!" Rae leaned in hopes of conveying her message to the bowling ball. They had done so much better last time. Well, there would be a second game. Sweetie guttered and Rae frowned. "You're up." She grumped to Sam.

At least in his black mood he didn't seem to notice that she was just as foul.

As she swung back, her ponytail curled around the side of her face and receded. Revealing Sam's tight, sculpted butt in a great pair of jeans. Rae watched as he focused down the lane and threw the ball hard enough to smash pins.

"Strike!" It was Jack, Alex, and Lisa all together. Rae didn't get in on the cheering in time. She hadn't watched the ball make its path down the lane. She'd been watching Sam's backside. It was far more interesting. She clapped in what she hoped was a show of good nature before finding a chair and nudging Lisa up for her turn.

After three more rounds, Rae was ready to give up. Grabbing her wallet, she headed up to the concessions counter for a beer. Drinking more could only improve her game. She had hit fifteen pins total in six tries. It was a better average if she didn't count the three gutter balls. At least no one so far had made comments about getting the kiddie bumpers out for her. Sam, of course, had stood up and made short work of her disaster by throwing his own ball so hard that she thought the pins would burst.

But instead they had flown out to the sides like spinning blades and mowed down everything in their paths, including all the other pins. That strike gave him a total of three, plus two spares and a split that had left him cursing. Lisa pointed out that maybe he shouldn't have chosen bowling if he couldn't have fun. He had grumbled that he was having plenty of fun, and they had all left it at that.

Rae took the beer from the concessions guy, thinking again that showing her ID was a waste. It was clear to both of them she'd passed twenty-one a while ago. By the time she got back to the lane she was surprised to discover a third of her beer was already gone. She drank while everyone else proceeded to get up and roll the ball and hit pins.

If only she could hit pins. Ah well. When it was her turn again, Rae tucked her fingers into the pink and black swirled ball and hefted it in her hands before starting down the aisle. She did three steps, swung her arm back then forward and let the ball fly. Sweetie, of course, spun leftward and guttered. For some unknown reason Rae decided to give actual bowling just one more try. This was how you were supposed to do it, though it clearly wasn't working for her. If she didn't score something worthwhile with this roll, she was going to revert to granny method and set the ball down and shove it. She did her three steps again and let the ball fly. This time, it stayed in the lane.

"Go Sweetie!" She yelled as the ball swirled its way down the course slowly but surely. Finally headed in the right direction, it looked as though it might not get there with enough force to actually knock over pins. But it did. Seven in all. A cheer went up behind her. An even bigger cheer than for Sam's strikes. Seven pins.

As she whirled with her fists up in the air, she spotted her friend. "Liam!"

Rae ran several lanes over where he and a few people she didn't know were getting set up and she jumped into his arms. She hadn't seen him since they had worked those rotating twelve hour shifts just before Sam had gotten sick.

"Rae!" He swung her around and finally set her down facing him.

"What have you been doing? I haven't—"

His voice was low, but he was clearly cutting her off. "What's with the tall, brown-haired guy?"

"Huh?" Rae swung around and saw that he meant Sam. The word choice was never how she would have described him. "Oh, Sam. It's nothing."

Liam grinned that cockeyed charming smile of his. "Believe me, it's not nothing."

"Oh, believe *me*. It is."

He laughed at her, clearly not agreeing. "You still got the five?" He was asking about the five-dollar bill they constantly tried to win off each other and that she had won back from him recently.

It was her turn to giggle. "In my purse."

"I'll get it back."

"How?"

"Okay." He tried to look like they were in casual conversation, but his voice was more conspiratorial. "You just go along with me, and I'll prove to you that it's not nothing."

Sam? Not nothing? Well, sure, it wasn't actually *nothing* but Rae already knew what it was. "He's mad at me."

"No, it's not that."

Her brows pulled together. "Really?"

He nodded. "Watch and learn." Without warning, Liam

swept her into his arms again. This time, kissing her full on the mouth and spinning them around a few times. Gently setting her back on her feet, he dipped her low and made the kiss look like a lot more than it was. When he let her up, she was still clinging to him, and he faced them so his back was to her friends and his chest blocking her view of their faces. "Now, look over my shoulder."

Rae did as she was told. Sam's fists were jammed in his pockets, and his head was turned away. His jaw was clenched. It didn't prove anything other than that he was mad. And she was just about to say so when Liam spoke again.

"What are all your other friends doing?"

This time, she looked at the rest of them. They were all jumping, shouting and cheering her on. She told Liam.

"Exactly. All your friends think it's great sport, except one who's mad. Why would he be mad that you're kissing someone else?" He held his hand out for the five. "I can kiss you again, he'll only get more upset."

Rae blinked a few times. The entire makeup of her universe shifted just a little, and things were clearer. *Better.* Sam wasn't just avoiding her, he was mad. Which meant he felt *something.* She felt the smile as it grew across her face, but then she blinked and crashed back to reality. Her memories cleared that fantasy up real fast. "He's mad because I took care of him when he was sick. He didn't want me to."

Liam threw back his head and laughed. Maybe guffawed was more like it. "What? Did you make him soup and take his temperature?"

Rae felt belittled, although she wasn't sure why. "Yes." She slouched just a little.

"You should owe me ten for that. Or twenty." He could barely control his laughter. She would have paid it, if it would help her figure all this out. Liam went on for free. "Rae, you played nurse to a guy who wants you? You are so naive."

"*What?*"

Just then his girlfriend—Rae couldn't tell—came up behind him and gave Rae the once over. Even as she sidled up to him as though to claim him, Liam kept laughing. "Lucy! Tell Rae that she can't take care of a man who's interested in her when he's sick."

Lucy started to say just that, but Rae stopped her. "Why? He was really sick." It was all she could do to keep from being loud enough to sound like they were having the conversation over the PA system. She didn't want to blare that he'd had pneumonia and might have died if she hadn't taken care of him. So she simply shut her mouth and waited.

It was Lucy who answered her. "Men want to be seen as big and strong, and if you nursed him, you destroyed that." Then Lucy looked her up and down again, though her expression showed she reached a less negative conclusion this time. "And clearly you want him, too, or you wouldn't still be here having this conversation."

Dear God! Had her ribcage become transparent and everyone could just read her heart like that? She would have been upset, if they hadn't been making sense. This time she didn't have a good argument against their conclusions, and that made her happy.

"Wait right here." She turned, feeling her ponytail bounce behind her in her new happiness, and went back to fish the well-handled five-dollar bill out of the back pocket of her billfold.

Sam's jaw stayed clenched while he spoke. "It's your turn."

"I'll be just a moment." Wow, he really was angry.

She handed Liam the five and hopped back to bowl her two throws. Only, she couldn't. Sam stood sentry in front of Sweetie, a disbelieving look plastered across his features, arms crossed over that oh-so-nice chest. "You *paid* him for that?"

"No, I—" She looked at him, *really* looked at him. Suddenly he made sense. "I owed him the money."

Weaseling her way around Sam, she managed to get to Sweetie. Rae guttered both balls but this time she didn't care.

"Honey!" Sheree hollered out over the whir of the machine picking up and dusting under every pin. "We should get Liam here to kiss you every round. You're in a much better mood."

How could she not laugh at that? She could see it made Sam even more upset, which in turn made her happier. By the time she looked up, Liam and Lucy were deep into a game. She hadn't even seen them get started. She'd been so focused on her own interactions.

While Sam bowled, Liam called out to her. "Are you going to do anything about it?"

A quick glance at Sam assured her that he was paying every ounce of attention to the lane. "Yes. Thank you."

That garnered a few questioning looks from Lisa and Sheree, who had overheard the last exchange. Rae paid their expressions no attention, she just watched as Liam and Lucy smiled and draped their arms around each other as another guy that Rae didn't know came up and joined them. She turned, nearly colliding with an appalled Lisa. "Well, you can bet I wouldn't be that free with my boyfriend."

Rae glanced to Jack for the briefest of moments. "I'm sure that you'll never have to be."

Sam guttered the ball and swore violently.

Maybe he hadn't been paying as close attention as she'd thought.

Twenty minutes and a lot of confidence later, Rae got her opportunity.

Sam had just turned from smashing another set of pins, still miraculously not having actually splintered any of them. "Hey, my sister wanted to know if I could babysit her twins this weekend over Saturday night."

Lisa and Sheree were looking at him like he was nuts. So what, right? But Rae guessed what was coming.

"I'd rather not do it alone—" He probably wanted advice, or the name of a sitter to help him be a sitter. She didn't let him finish.

"I'll help." She heard her own voice in her ears, sounding all sweet and innocent. Like she wanted to help out a friend, no ulterior motive necessary. Not like she had been a lion in waiting, ready to pounce.

A Saturday overnight. She'd be able to say something then, she just had to screw up the courage to do it. And she had to, she couldn't let a golden opportunity like this pass. Rae just wished she'd have another witchcraft class before this weekend, but it wasn't to happen. The next one was called "The *Big Wish*." She could use a little of that. Only, she'd have to dig it out of herself.

She would just hold tight to what Liam told her and pray that he was right about Sam.

CHAPTER 30

Running her fingers through her hair, Rae tried to make it look like it was just naturally gorgeous. Not like she'd spent an hour fixing it for tonight. Sadly, she already had a lie in place. If anyone asked she'd just say that she had worn her hair up all day and had just taken it down. It wasn't really a lie. She had worn her hair up all day. And that did make it curl, just not quite like this.

She touched up her lipstick hoping she'd finally get a chance to put the "long wearing" claim to the test. Maybe she should have used her *"Big Wish"* spell on that. She hadn't, though.

First off, the magicks store made them sign a paper that they wouldn't use a *Big Wish* spell on people. Ever. That was some pretty serious stuff. She thought about letting Sam look over what was essentially a contract, but she wasn't ready to confess what she was doing. Secondly, she'd used her *Big Wish* on the gallery show. It was getting closer every day, and she needed people in the event on opening night. She needed buyers. So the Sam thing would have to untangle without spellwork. She was left with the regular methods. So she'd done her hair, told herself she was going to say something, and pray she got an opportunity.

A girl could hope, right?

Sliding her arms into her gray, hooded sweatshirt, she looked it over. It looked casual enough and yet still clung enough. God help her. She had to quit this. She needed to leave her apartment right this minute and stop obsessing. What she needed to do was figure out how she was going to have this conversation with Sam with everyone there. She wasn't going to declare her love/lust in front of everyone. Sighing, she realized that all she could really do was be ready for an opportunity.

None had come over the weekend. The twins had been too much of a handful. The few times they slept, she and Sam had smiled briefly at each other before passing out. Trying to hit on him while babysitting crawling infants had not been her brightest idea.

Zipping the jacket, Rae locked the door behind her and headed down to the garage. It seemed her car knew the way to Sam's by heart. In a few thoughts, she was standing on his doorstep, even though she didn't remember the drive or getting out of the car. But she could remember each photo she had thought through on the way over. Each way she had imagined to get to talk to Sam alone tonight. Each line she had rehearsed.

She knocked lightly, then turned the knob, letting herself in at the same time hearing his voice call out, "Come in!"

The living room and dining area were empty, and she turned to hang up her coat, and set her purse by the door.

"In here!" She loved the sound of his voice coming from the kitchen. That alone could send a small warm fuzzy sensation through her. He still didn't know it was her. But she could imagine that it would continue to be just them. That he *did* know it was her, because who else would it be?

"Hi, Rae."

She paused. He hadn't even turned around. And the words

tumbled out of her mouth before she could stop them. "How did you know it was me?"

He shrugged. "Your walk, and now I can smell your perfume."

"I'm not wearing perfume." She frowned.

"Shampoo, then?" He still hadn't looked directly at her.

The world slowed on its axis for a moment. He knew her walk? Chalk up another vote for Liam. She had to find a way to get Sam to talk to her.

It was all she could do to watch the way he moved as he reached up and pulled a glass from the cabinet. He poured a pale orange liquid into the tumbler and turned to press it into her hand. There was a soft smile that encompassed his whole face, and again she felt like she had the morning she had woken up in his arms. Cared for. Warm. Maybe . . . *Hot*.

She took the glass from him, unaware that she was standing there giving him the worst googly-eyed look until he spoke. "Aren't you going to try it?"

"What is it?"

"An orange-papaya margarita."

She sipped it. "Oh God, Sam this is so good. Tell me, how is it that you can throw together these odd combinations and make the best mixed drinks but you can't cook anything?" She got the words out through the second, third, and fourth sips.

He laughed and again the humor went all the way to his eyes. This was the Sam she'd been hoping would come back. No one else had arrived yet. Maybe she should say something now. She opened her mouth—

Sam spoke. "I can't cook because that involves heat. Sam no good with fire."

Rae laughed, too. But just then she heard the front door.

Sam called out. "Who is it?"

"Alex!" Then their friend was pushing through the door into

the kitchen, happily stealing her moment, even though he didn't know it. "Whatcha makin'?"

Rae held out her glass. "Orange-papaya Margaritas."

"Okay, that's really orange." Alex looked skeptical but tried it anyway. Then smiled. "As usual Sam, that's great. Get me one?"

Sam did as bidden, and the three of them went about setting the table with chips and glasses and the pitcher. Lisa had promised to bring most of the food since it had been her turn to host anyway.

At eight o'clock, Sam changed the channel and paused at the beginning of the show. Not their usual Crime Night tonight. This week, their shows had been usurped by a pageant that Lisa insisted they watch. No one worried too much about getting there right on time. They usually planned to start a few minutes late so they could just fast forward through the commercials.

But within five minutes they were all there, settling themselves around the couch, and Sam pushed the play button. All the contestants lined up, smiling, waving and stating their names and stats in whatever accent was appropriate for their home state.

"I think the tall one with the auburn hair is the prettiest. Hands down." Sam cast his vote. He could *not* believe he had just said that and God didn't have the decency to remove him from the earthly plane by lightning or spontaneous combustion at that exact moment. Hands down, he was an idiot. They all knew exactly what he was thinking. Though he wondered if they'd known before.

He had clearly chosen the contestant who looked the most like Rae. Pressing his lips together, he told himself to stay silent, but he didn't last very long. The Rae look-alike tripped. "Oh, Damn. There goes my five bucks."

He was leaned back against the couch, not as far away from her as possible, but not sitting near her feet either. Not that there were any connotations there, he thought as a commercial break came up. Not that anything happened. He was just an idiot with a crush. He watched as the screen jumped, made a few bleeps as it jumped the commercials and left a blond woman standing frozen with a horrible expression on her face as she held up a bottle of aspirin. No one started the show again.

Alex barked, "Lisa!"

"Wait!" She smiled that big, beaming smile of hers. Sam could see how Jack had gotten lost in that smile, the perfect blond hair, and the long legs. There was no denying that Lisa was a gorgeous girl. But in his mind, it was all a cerebral thing. Anyone could look at Lisa and see her beauty. Rae was a visceral reaction. She was tied to some strange knowledge that there wouldn't ever be anyone else. That and a twisting desire to be near her. If he had the nerve, he'd admit to himself that that included possessing her. He liked to think himself a man of the new millennium. But apparently he wasn't. He wanted Rae to be his. He was already hers.

Apparently, Lisa wasn't of the new millennium either. "Okay, I got *this* . . ."

She pulled a mini pot of petroleum jelly from her purse, "After Sheree announced last year that they all used vaseline on their teeth to keep smiling, I thought I'd bring this and let anyone who wanted the real Miss America Experience try it."

"Ooooooh." Sheree scrunched her nose as if the pot was full of wriggling worms. But she followed Lisa's suit and dipped her finger in before passing it to Rae. Rae was the only one who hesitated. She didn't make horrified faces, she just didn't dig her finger in.

"Oh, you have to. We all will." Sheree egged her on.

But it was Jack who replied. "Tell me which 'all' you were referring to."

Sheree grabbed the pot and handed it to him. "What? Afraid that you're not man enough to handle it?"

Sneaking its way onto his face, the grin gave Sam away. That was the downside of having such a small tight-knit group, they knew your weaknesses just as thoroughly as they knew your preferences. And they rarely hesitated to use them against you.

Clearly, before he realized what was happening and how he was getting manipulated, Lisa and Sheree had conned Jack into participating. The man couldn't turn down a dare.

Nor could he face one alone. He held the stupid little pot out to Sam and Alex, goading them into taking fingerfuls of the goo, too. Lisa had paused the show which had already run through the section of commercials and was going to start again without them. For a brief moment he cursed his TiVo. The girls wouldn't be holding them hostage by dare without it.

"Okay. Here goes." Lisa called it. And like the true friends and idiots they were they all rubbed the stuff on their teeth. Sam felt the bottom of his stomach roll but managed to suppress it. To the pageant girls' credit, it worked. His lips would not go near his teeth. He looked up at Jack and Alex and figured he looked like as big an idiot as they did. They both had obvious globs of the goo on their teeth. He wanted to ask them if he did, too, but he couldn't speak.

Unlike them, the women turned and flirted at each other. Their smiles were wide and bordering on natural, if a little glossy. There must be something in the female genetic code that led to the proper application of this junk. Like Rae's makeup shoot. There was definitely something to it. And none of these guys had it.

They all turned and looked at each other, Jack and Alex clearly feeling more masculine for having screwed it up. Sam just felt like a fool for getting conned into trying it in the first place. He started to say so, but once again his lips wouldn't obey.

Come to think of it, no one was saying anything. They couldn't, their mouths wouldn't close. Lisa started laughing. Sheree and Rae followed suit, laughing even harder when Sheree managed to get out "my cheeks hurt." It was garbled, but understandable. Sam shook his head, and forced his lips closed. The vaseline squished and at least had the decency to be tasteless, though the consistency was something he never wanted in his mouth again.

Shaking his head, he got up and headed to the bathroom. Thank god he was at his own house, none of these poor saps had toothbrushes. But Lisa stood up. "Oo-ait!"

He figured by the look on her face that that was vaseline-ish for 'wait!'.

He watched her mouth and heard her voice, but it was nothing like the English he had grown up with. After some serious thought he managed to figure out what she was saying. It was "How much do you love me?"

A smart remark would have sufficed, but he couldn't make it with his mouth full of vaseline. He just grimaced as she produced a six-pack of cheap toothbrushes and a huge tube of toothpaste. She popped the package open and tossed him a purple brush. It didn't look like it would survive more than a few scrubbings, but at least he wouldn't have to chuck his regular brush for being vaseline infested. He headed off to get rid of the goo, so that he could speak again.

After three scrubbings and nearly being forced out of his own sink by jabbing elbows, he managed to breathe easy again. Half his tube of toothpaste was gone but that was well worthwhile. He might inherit the one Lisa had brought, so no loss. Sheree, Rae and Alex crowded around the sink with him, all brushing and spitting. Lisa and Jack had headed upstairs to the bathroom that adjoined his room, and no one dared to ask what was going on up there.

Sheree spoke first, "Ahhhh," followed by, "Well that was a nasty rumor."

"Rumor?" Alex had finally gotten his teeth clean again. "I thought it worked really well, I couldn't do anything but pull my mouth back and bare my teeth. I don't know how this one got his lips closed." He gestured to Sam.

"It didn't work on you guys. You all looked like rabid dogs." Rae piped up.

"Fine." Alex threw the toothbrush into the trashcan with a little extra vengeance. "But you and Lisa and Sheree looked like you were doing okay."

"Sure, but they'd never use it in a pageant." Sheree argued.

"What makes you say that?"

She and Rae exchanged that female look. That *How can they not understand?* look. "How would they ever get through the interview portion of the pageant? I couldn't have talked to save my life."

Shaking his head and regretting the entire experience, Sam headed for the hall closet, finding Lisa and Jack emerging from the master bedroom suite. He reached into the closet and wrapped his fingers around his own idea of Miss America fun. "All right, that was the ladies choice of pageant activities. Now one for the guys." They all eyed him, but he continued, pulling a large roll of silver duct tape from the closet. "We can all tape ourselves up."

Jack and Alex cheered him, but the girls tossed him dirty looks and headed back to the couch. "Oh really, it's no worse than vaseline on your teeth!" Jack kept trying but he wasn't going to get anywhere.

Sam hit the kitchen desperately searching for something to eat. Not that he was hungry, but there was this little after-feeling from the Vaseline, like a faint coating on his teeth, and he just had to get rid of it. Apparently, Alex and Rae felt it, too. They turned down lemonade and corn chips. Rae contemplated the apple for a moment, then decided it would clash with the lingering mint of toothpaste. Then she snapped her fingers. "Popcorn. What else?"

"You're the queen." Alex bowed before her. "Sounds like it will do the trick."

She had left the bag of stovetop popcorn here from before and knew just where to find it and the butter. She was probably the last one who had used them. Sam handed her a pot. Well, the only one he had that would work, not that he understood why. A pot was a pot, right? But not to Rae. He found himself with his arms folded across his chest, propped against the counter, watching her watching the popcorn heat. A quick glance told him that Alex had left somewhere between the real butter and the soft patter of kernels into the pan, and he hadn't noticed. *Uh-oh.* He had definitely wandered into the land of the obvious tonight.

Rae shook the pot again, placing it over the heat and staring down through the glass lid. But then she looked up, her hair falling in easy waves around her face. Briefly it registered in her expression that they were in the kitchen alone. Sam tensed and tried to hide it, waiting for what she would do. For what he should do.

But she smiled. A winning grin. Her eyes flicked here and there for a few seconds and then settled on him, accompanied by a deep breath. "Can I tell you something?"

"Sure." The word had come out with no cue from him. It was just the appropriate response to the question and his mouth had given it. But he couldn't say he was sure he wanted to know what she wanted him to know.

After another deep breath, she shook the popcorn pot and started talking. "I just wanted to say that I'm sorry for pushing myself on you when you were sick."

"Oh, that's okay, you can push yourself on me anytime."

Where had that come from? He raised his eyebrows, trying to appear as flip as he sounded.

The tension ebbed a little with her laughter. "Don't get me wrong. I wouldn't change anything. I'll take you alive any day."

Take me any day, any way, but this time he managed to keep the thought in his head.

"I didn't mean to make you so mad at me. It's the last thing I want. But it scared me." She looked back at the pot and shook it. She looked more like she was trying to make a sentence than make popcorn, and so he didn't interrupt. Sam's chest clenched, unsure if she would say something of importance, one way or another.

"I just had never imagined you could get sick. I mean, you're—"

She stopped, mid-sentence, like she was on TiVo and he had hit his pause button. But there was no way to make her continue.

He wanted to yell, *I'm what?!?!*

Slowly Rae's finger raised to her lips indicating he should be quiet. Then she gestured a circle with her hand and mouthed a few words to him. It took a moment, but he deciphered the motions of her lips to be "play along." He nodded, unsure what he was playing along with, or why.

"*Sam!*" She sounded surprised.

He was simply confused.

Again, her finger rested against her lips for just a moment. Then she pointed at the swinging door. He shook his head, what? He motioned it, shoulder shrugging, hands palm up, but her voice cut the silence again.

"Ohhh, Sam." It was a purr, low and sexy, and every muscle in him tensed. He had heard her say that at least a thousand times. In his head, in his musings, but never for real. He was starting to melt. He was in trouble.

She moved closer, trying desperately not to laugh while he frantically fought to figure out the joke. But she said it again. "Sam." It rolled, all breathy and soft, from her lips. She was inches from him. And he was inches from grabbing her. Only the knowledge that she thought this was all a game kept him from actually doing it.

Rae put her hand between them and silently gestured for him to speak. His mouth opened, but nothing came out. There was only a tension and a realization that he didn't understand anything. That and the awareness that he didn't really care. He just wanted to grab her and kiss her. But by her smothered giggles, that wasn't what she had in mind.

She gestured again. And he spoke the one word he could muster. "Rae." It was tense, tight, and full of frustration. And involved no acting whatsoever.

Apparently, it was what she wanted. Her eyes widened, and she gave him a huge thumbs up. "Sam!" This time there was an undercurrent of surprise to her voice. She followed it with a breathy gasp, the kind he imagined she would make if he touched her . . . just . . . so, although he hadn't moved. In fact, he would bet his life savings that he was physically unable to move right now. Her voice was twisting him up.

And she only continued. "mmmmm. Ohh." She made the noises into her hand, and he was grateful that she didn't look down to see that she had also made his jeans tight. Rae just continued talking, a mysterious humor in her eyes but straight sex in her tone. "Sam, we can't. . . . on the counter? . . . they'll hear us!—ohhhh."

He caught on, finally, although he was quite unsure how that had happened when his brain had clearly ceased all normal function. But he decided to play along. Even if he wasn't really playing. He didn't figure he really had a choice. "God, Rae, I can't help it, I just want you."

He saw it for the briefest movement, something flashed in her eyes. It looked as if she knew he wasn't kidding, but it was gone before he was sure it had ever been there. She took a few deliberate steps, bumped a drawer—probably just to make some appropriate noises—and then was speaking into her hand again. "Aahhh."

She beckoned him to take his turn and this time he was ready. "Come on, Rachel." His voice sounded liquid even to himself. How could she think he was acting? "I want to make love to you. Now."

But she had already turned away and was creeping toward the door. As he finished his line her fingers curled onto the edge of the door and she jumped back, swinging the door wide into the kitchen.

Sheree, Lisa, and Jack tumbled in, falling into a human pile of guilt and laughter. Only Alex managed to remain on his feet, but at least he had the decency to look sheepish doing it.

"Ha!" Rae shouted. She sounded utterly gratified. Sam only wished he felt the same. "I knew you were listening in. It was too damned quiet out there. You guys suck!"

At least his pants weren't two sizes too tight anymore. Sadly, though, it was over, his little game with Rae. He hardly moved as he spoke. "Even the popcorn is very upset with you guys."

"What?" Rae swung to face him, confused.

He pointed to the stove. "It burst into flame in protest."

"Oh, my god!" She jumped to grab a potholder, but he held his arm up and motioned her away. She'd just catch the potholder on fire. He and his blackened sink had learned that one by experience. In a few seconds, he had the little fire extinguisher out from beside the fridge and, pulling the pin, he doused the crackling and popping corn in white fluffy foam. It would be a bitch to clean up, but wasn't everything?

Sheree was just collecting her laughter to where she could stand, "You actually have a fire extinguisher in your kitchen?"

He shrugged and turned to Rae. "Sam no good with fire."

With a small laugh followed by a shy smile, she gingerly

picked up the white and charred pot and carried it to the sink. She rinsed it out, slowly dumping black and foamy potfulls of water and dead popcorn kernels down the sink. The others dusted themselves off and returned to the couch without so much as a single apology. So he stood there with nothing to do or say until Rae picked up a sponge and soaped it up.

"Oh, don't." He pulled the pot out of her hand, brushing against her wet skin while he did and nearly losing his voice in the process. How did she do that to him? It was only getting worse, too. He was *not* getting over her.

"What?"

He had to look down at the pot in his hand before he could remember where the conversation had gone. "Don't ruin a perfectly good sponge for this." He tossed the pot into the trashcan. Her eyes widened. "I'll just get a new one."

Still Rae didn't speak.

So he did, maybe just to fill the void. He gestured into the trashcan. "Have you ever tried to clean out a burned pot? Not just burned food, but actual fire, like this?"

She simply shook her head.

"Clearly, I have. I even have the fire extinguisher to prove it." He motioned with the little red canister, before putting it back in its place.

With another small laugh and a smile that set him on fire in ways it probably shouldn't, Rae set to cleaning off the stove top. And Sam began berating himself. He had just proved to her that he wasn't helpless. He could handle a fire and keep her out of harm's way.

Or else he had just proved that he was an idiot. One who burned things often enough to need a fire extinguisher in his kitchen. A man who was so helpless that he routinely caught his food on fire. Well, shit.

In a few minutes, they were all back out on the couch. Chips were now the food of choice to remove the vaseline residue. No matter how hard he tried, Sam couldn't get comfortable. She was always there in his peripheral vision. He didn't dare turn his head and look at her straight on. Her voice echoed in his brain, his name, over and over in that breathy, heady tone. He was almost surprised that the others couldn't hear it. He figured it would take a strong chemical cleanser and a sturdy wire brush to clean that one out.

CHAPTER 31

"I don't know that eating before performing spells was the best idea," Sloan said it right before she stabbed a steak fry with her fork.

Rae wanted to use her fingers, but the fries—morsels of the gods if you asked her—were covered in minced and roasted garlic and some kind of parmesan cheese sauce. The burgers had been good, but the fries were what she came for. She used a fork, too. There was no telling what the ladies teaching the beginning class would pick up if she came in smelling of garlic and cheese.

"Isn't garlic used in spellwork?" Sloan asked, mirroring her own thoughts.

Rae shrugged. "We haven't used it in class."

"True, but we've only been to a few, and it's in one of the spellbooks I bought online."

"What!" Rae wanted it to be a question, but it hadn't come out that way. "You bought spellbooks online? And why not get them at the shop? Get a professional recommendation."

She was shaking her head while Sloan looked sheepish.

"I don't want to give them all my money. We don't know them from Adam, Rae."

"Sure we do. Adam would never do witchcraft. I'm pretty sure that's clear in the Bible."

Sloan just raised her eyebrows. Sloan was right. They'd been raised as Catholic as the day was long, though only parts of it had stuck. Her mother had performed elaborate prayers the whole time they were growing up, and she'd treated what her girls could do as gifts from God. But she'd worked those gifts like witchcraft.

Rae nodded and her mind drifted back to something her mother had said about a year before she died. That she'd left Italy because she'd gotten a reputation. For a long time, Rae had assumed her mother meant an undeserved reputation as a slut. Rae had been wrong on both counts. When her mother cleared it up, she learned that the reputation was for being a witch and that it was deserved. Though her mother attended mass regularly, apparently everyone knew she was the one to call when something went missing.

Bianca Woodward found lost keys, misplaced objects, things that had once been at a grandparents' home but had been sorted through the generations, and even a missing child. She'd assured the family he was fine and he'd come home soon. He did. But it was the missing husband that did her in. She wouldn't tell where he was. She knew, and they knew she knew. That was when the cries of "Witch!" started coming out.

They said she knew he was dead, she said he wasn't. They said he was in danger, she said he wasn't. They asked if he was having an affair and when she wouldn't answer they accused her of being the other woman. As her mother had told the story, she held it in until the accusations were too much. When the woman had come forward and called her a slut, publicly shamed her for something she hadn't done, spread lies and rumors and worse, the truth about what Bianca could do, her mother burst like damn.

"He's with your fucking sister!" She'd screamed at the woman, in front of all her demanding friends. "Your sister came to visit and he left with her. She's pregnant!" Bianca had let it all tumble out. When the crowd turned on her, she turned on them. "Maria, your husband is cheating with Benedetta! Yes, your best friend." She'd turned and glared at Benedetta who was ghost white. She told about one woman and how she was broke and lying to all her friends. She told about a third woman covering up for an alcoholic husband that beat her and her children. Bianca Woodward laid them all bare in her anger.

And she'd never lived it down. She couldn't go out in public. Her family was humiliated, even though Nonna apparently understood. They'd retreated to their farm and closed ranks. Things subsided when the people learned that everything Bianca had told them was true, but it never got better and her mother had been the point of ridicule. When an American man came through town, they fell in love, and she left with him.

She was pregnant with Sloan before they even reached the states, she'd said. Her family was better off. Emilia's social status was returned; her mother and father were welcomed in society again; and Bianca had been more than a little angry. Emilia was far more powerful than she, but her little sister kept her mouth shut better.

She'd been angry, not knowing that her sister was sick. That she disappeared and died before her family even told her what was happening. It was only later that she'd learned Emilia had a baby and gave it away. It had been a harsh lesson that Rae still found unfair and unforgiving. Bianca had warned her daughters about their gifts, about giving them away.

Rae had told no one except Sloan. Ever.

This foray into the magicks shop was strange. But she and Sloan had decided it was Los Angeles. Mama and Papa were gone; they couldn't be hurt by a bad rep. And in this day and age, who would care if they were outed as witches? Who would believe? So they'd gone to a few classes. That didn't make them witches any more than it made Brittany-of-the-modeling-career one. Though, Brittany sounded like she was doing pretty well these days. So maybe her spells were working. Rae almost smirked at the thought, then she almost smirked again at the idea of Sloan ordering books online.

She told Sloan exactly that. "You're the one who kept warning me not to get in too deep. Were you warning yourself?"

"Maybe." She paused. "I don't know. But I was thinking about what you said about Nonna being a Tavani. I looked up the family names and you're right. We come from a long tradition in the old country. Mom ignored it."

"And look what it got her."

Sloan tipped her head in acknowledgment then turned as the server came up with the bill. Rae was stuffed and about to groan. She considered calling off class tonight. She smelled like garlic and she was so full how was she going to find the focus Allison asked of them?

Sloan picked up the whole check over Rae's protests and leaned across the table. "I didn't tell you what I saw."

Uh-oh. That sounded ominous. And why had she waited this long? Rae leaned in, too, keeping her tone low. "Tell me."

"I checked out scrying in the book I got and it was almost the same as what we got in class. So, I just did it at home."

"What were you scrying for?"

"Him, that guy—Luke." She looked both ways, like a criminal, but kept going. "It's been a week and they haven't called. Right?"

Rae shook her head. "I've been checking, but no."

Sloan nodded, "Since they didn't come to us, I went looking. And I saw Allison and Yasmin talking about us."

"I thought you were looking for Luke."

Sloan about threw her hands up in exasperation. "So I suck at it! I'm new. Look, I saw Allison tell Yasmin that we were natural witches. That we were the ones who had the most potential in the class. And Yasmin was saying she was having us investigated."

That made Rae pull her head back. "Investigated? Us? Why?"

"Because we claimed to be the lost relatives of her husband, that's why. We're crazy chicks who turned up in their store with a batshit story to tell."

Sitting back, Rae tried to absorb it all. "Do we keep going to class?"

"Don't we have to? If we stop, we look suspicious. There's no reason they would know that we figured out we're being investigated."

"So you're better at scrying than me." For some reason that's what Rae latched onto.

Sloan shrugged. "You feel things, I see them. It's always been that way."

"Then I guess we better get to class. And they better offer that damned *Parking Karma* session again." She sighed and got up, feeling like thanksgiving turkey. She thought again about her mother and the ramifications of letting the world know what she could do. Were she and her sister playing with fire?

She told herself they weren't. But she didn't quite believe.

CHAPTER 32

Sam's voice was reverberating in her head. It had been for days. *Come on, Rachel, I want to make love to you.* She shuddered a little, unable to stop the tingle that scaled her spine and rested inside her. Taking the left hand turn at the light, she steered herself and Sheree toward Sam's for Tuesday night. Somehow, he'd been left holding the basket again.

"Cold?" her roommate's voice cut into her thoughts, dashing them to pieces around her.

Rae answered "yes," as it was far easier than the truth. The truth was long and fragile. Friday had given her the opportunity she had wanted, then stolen it right back. She hadn't ever gotten the chance to finish her conversation with Sam. She'd managed to lay only the first part of the path before she heard noises beyond the swinging door. It was difficult enough for her to have the conversation without an audience. Looking back, she had turned to humor out of fear. It would be hard enough to place it at Sam's feet in private. It would be way too much to lay her heart on the line with everyone looking on.

From the corner of her eye, she saw Sheree looking her up and down. But she found any grace for a witty comment gone.

So she said nothing, and was thankful when her roommate kept the silence.

In the kitchen last week, when she'd started her opening gambit, Rae had only wanted to see where the path would lead. She would follow if she wanted. Instead she found herself staring into molten blue eyes, while the perfect mouth told her he wanted to make love to her. She could still hear the sounds, the lilt of it, the undercurrent. Just the memory of it turned her to jelly. But what she heard in her head was merely what she had heard that night. The way she had heard it, and she knew that wasn't necessarily the way it had been spoken.

She had turned to open the kitchen door, her breathing all but stopped, and her ability to continue as though it were a joke completely gone. It had taken every effort to laugh and be outraged at her friends, and not betray the way the core of her had fallen, elevator crazy, straight through her.

Rae watched as her hands rotated the steering wheel in front of her. They knew the way. Sam's again. She had driven by twice in the few days between. Wracked her brain for a good excuse to drop in unannounced, to call to need his help. But nothing even semi-legitimate had come to her. So she'd waited. Had done a short, two-day surveillance for Lincoln. Printed photos for the show. Gone to the gallery and agonized over which frames to have them put on which pieces. Gone to her witchcraft class with Sloan and not heard anything from Yasmin or Luke. And she'd stared, lost, at the print of Sam standing by his car.

Still, she didn't know what she wanted from him.

That wasn't entirely true. She knew what she wanted, like she had never known anything in her life. She wanted Sam, body, heart, and soul. But she didn't know how to get from friends to forever. Or at least the chance at it. Was Sam the forever guy? That would mean kids and mortgages and old age.

But she'd seen him with his niece and nephew and he sure looked like he was all that and more.

Feeling the smile spread across her face, Rae turned to look out her window as they waited at a light. A date? The idea had crossed her mind. But even in her imagination it went horribly awry. He would pick her up, the perfect gentleman. She would barely be ready, her closet in shambles on her floor. He would take her somewhere nice and they would eat a sumptuous dinner. And barely say a word.

It was awkward even in her best musings. What would they say? *So, what do you do? Do you ever want to play football again? Surveillance, huh?*

It all loomed before her. The decisions she couldn't make. The worry that she wouldn't get a chance to finish talking to him while he still might harbor any feelings for her. Then, the thing looming in front of her was his two story brick townhouse.

"We're here!" Sheree popped open her door and then spoke to Rae over the roof of the little red car when she got out. "Just be more talkative tonight, okay?"

She laughed. What must her friend think? Aside from thinking that Rae must qualify as clinically insane. "I promise."

Her feet carried her up the stairs, following Sheree. It was a good thing, too. Otherwise she might have simply stood and stared. The door opened and he stood there, looking like a god on earth. Chastising herself for being melodramatic, Rae took a second look. He looked like a man, a chestnut-haired, sky-blue-eyed hunk who desperately needed her kiss. Suppressing a sigh, she followed Sheree past him. If only it were true.

"Popcorn!" Sheree took a handful from the bowl Sam was holding.

Nodding sheepishly, he explained. "I didn't get a chance to buy a new pot for Rae, I had Jeremy working all weekend." He turned to Rae and held the bowl out. "But it's not microwave, it's that stuff in the foil that you do on the stove top."

"At least." She took a handful. Thinking it didn't taste quite the same, then berating herself for not being more genial. He had noticed her preference and made an effort to do his best, and she was bordering on rude. Her mind was not in the right place. Turning back to smile at him, she saw he'd turned away. *Shit.* Rae realized that she had missed her opportunity and desperately wanted to kick herself. She had never been good at seizing a moment right as it came up, only at kicking herself after it had passed. Yet she'd never regretted it as much as she did right now.

Rae looked around the room, it seemed they were the first to arrive, and they bordered on being late. "Where are Lisa and Jack?" Alex was always a little late. He didn't like the first show anyway.

"Lisa's sick." Sam set the bowl down. "Jack called earlier."

Hanging her coat near the door, she turned. "He's not coming either?"

"Duh," It was Sheree, settling herself into the couch. "Of course not, he's staying home with her. That's what you do when the person you love is sick."

Rae let out an exasperated sigh, but let her friends believe that it was a statement about Jack, and not a commentary to when they had all pestered her about spending so much time with Sam when he'd been ill. They must all either be blind or rude. Not that she was any better.

Without much fanfare, the three of them started into the first show. Rae realized that she must have had quite a thing for Sam for longer than she'd even admitted. She could hardly follow the plot and didn't recognize a character who appeared by his amount of screen time to be a regular. No, she had spent her Tuesday nights daydreaming about the man on the other end of the couch. She curled more tightly around herself and munched the popcorn.

There would be no opportunity to talk to Sam tonight. She would have to haul him away and abandon Sheree, or wait until Alex showed and pray that the two of them just wandered off together. That wasn't going to happen.

Just then Sam's phone rang. He didn't even pause the show as he stood to fish the phone out of his back pocket and move away to answer it. "Hello?" followed by "Hey" then a few words, and "Don't worry about it. . . . Friday then?"

Sheree waited with eyebrows raised until Sam hung up and explained. "Alex. Ran into an old friend today and won't be making it." He sat himself on the other side of the popcorn bowl from Rae. "Looks like it's just us, ladies."

Well, now there was definitely no chance of speaking to him tonight. Her hopes melted into a little puddle inside her. When would there ever be? She munched and planned. No more waiting, then. Rae would have to simply call him and ask him out on a date. Oh, that was so scary. Maybe she could ask him to meet her for some made up purpose or help her out with . . . . Maybe she could say she needed to show him the photo for the gallery show and ask his permission to use it. Oh yeah, like she'd really be able to keep her cool in her darkroom.

Three little beeps indicated that Sheree was fast forwarding through a set of commercials. So Rae pushed herself off the couch and grabbed a can of Sunkist from the fridge. Her favorite. She wasn't sure if he was paying attention, or just had it left over from when she had helped him watch the twins. Dear god. There was no help for her now. Her mind was on overanalysis overdrive. Trying to suss out whether a man's fridge contents meant he liked her bordered on batshit crazy, so she yelled out over her shoulder, "Does either of you guys want a drink?" At least she could try to be useful while she sank into insanity.

"A coke."

Rae jumped. His voice was right behind her. She probably needn't have shouted her question. But she managed to pull her head out of the fridge and hand him a can.

His lips smiled at her. "Thank you." With that he turned and walked back to the living room. Nothing else said. No secret look, no twinkle in his eye.

She needed a knife. To put herself out of her misery.

As she entered the living room, electronic playground music came out of nowhere. The TV was paused so it wasn't that. She looked to Sam, it was his house making the noise, but he seemed as confused as she was.

"Oh!" Sheree jumped up as though she was surprised and rummaged through her purse. "It's my phone. That's the tone for the other teachers at school. They never call. . . Ackk!" After a frantic moment of searching, she pulled the frog green cell phone out and answered. "Denise?"

After a few, 'no's and 'oh!'s she said "I'll meet you there. Bye."

"Rae?"

She looked up at her friend and waited.

"Can I take your car? The principal is out partying tonight and she never comes out, I should put in an appearance. Maybe up my chances of getting third grade next year."

"Okay." There was an odd tone in her own voice.

"What's so great about third grade?" Sam asked from over her shoulder.

But Sheree was looking at her hair in a little makeup mirror she'd pulled out, so Rae explained. "It looks like fourth is going to be a split fourth and fifth grade class next year and Sheree doesn't want it." Turning back to her friend, she dropped her keys into the outstretched palm. "You'll come back to get me at eleven?"

But Sheree shook her head, her dark curls bouncing. "I don't know how late I'll be."

"Don't worry. I'll drive her home." Sam's voice heated her even from behind her.

"Thank you! You're a doll." And oblivious to the envy it generated in her friend, Sheree grabbed Sam's face and planted a kiss on his cheek. Then she ran out the door.

Rae made her way back to the couch and sank down. Just like that, they were alone.

Just what she had wanted. But now, faced with all the time in the world, and him to drive her home, she didn't know how to start. So she watched TV and sipped her soda, and tried to think. She had to come up with a way to start this conversation. She had to find a way to be brave.

It turned out, she didn't have to. Not five minutes later he paused the TV and turned toward her. "What am I?"

"Huh?" Wow. Eloquence was not her forte tonight.

"Friday, before you realized everyone was listening in, you said I was . . . but you stopped. What am I?" He didn't look in her eyes. He followed the line of her collar, the edge of the popcorn bowl, but not her face.

Still not one-hundred percent in her head, she couldn't remember what she had meant to say. Then it popped into her head. She couldn't imagine him being sick. He was . . . so strong. Solid. Manly? All the words she could think of wouldn't do to just blurt out to him.

"Healthy." It was passable. It worked in the sentence and fit the idea, but as Sheree always said, it didn't really convey the spirit of the message. It didn't tell him how she felt. So she tried again. "I just had a hard time believing a big, strong man like you could be sick. It really scared me."

His nod was slight, "I'm okay now."

Her eyes closed, then opened and somehow she found herself looking right into his baby-blues. "I'm glad."

CHAPTER 33

S am was toast. He was sitting on his couch with Rae, and
they were looking right at each other. And he was so . . . so
lost. Was she uncomfortable because she didn't know what to
do with him anymore? If only he could see inside her mind.
Yeah, like that would clear anything up.

He was so busy thinking that her voice caught him off guard.

"Listen, what I was trying to say the other day, and why I
jumped to help you babysit, was that you don't have to avoid me
anymore." She paused in the middle of making no sense
whatsoever and then continued before he could say anything.
"I'm sorry I made you so uncomfortable, I didn't mean to. But
you don't have to—"

He jumped in. "I *was* uncomfortable. But I'm over it." He
squirmed, belying what he'd said about not being uncomfortable.
Just like when he was a kid, and the teacher was waiting for an
answer. He was still nervous and he wanted that to go away.

"Was it because of when you were sick?"

"Yes." This time he managed to quell the discomfort, on the
outside at least.

She shook her head, and he was only vaguely aware of the TV playing on in the background. "I didn't mean to smother you, I just . . ." Her shoulders hunched into a small shrug.

"You didn't smother me, you *mothered* me. And the last thing I wanted from you was for you to mother me!" By the time he'd hit the end of the sentence some of his irritation had bled through.

She was almost mad. *Mad?* "You know, someone had to take care of you! Even the doctors said you could have died!"

"I just didn't want it to be *you!*" Oh God, now he was fighting with her and he'd obviously hurt her feelings.

She nodded and started to move off the couch. Like a lump, he sat there and watched, wondering what she was doing until she started to reach for her coat. How had he messed everything up so much?

"Don't leave."

"Why not? You've been pretty clear." She slipped her arms into her jacket as she spoke. "Apparently anyone but me would have been a better choice."

"Yes, they would have." He jumped up too but didn't explain. The words were hard to find. He started to tug her jacket off her shoulders, which probably was too pushy, but he didn't know what to do. He was knee deep in it now. He'd have to explain. "I just didn't want you to see me like that."

"How did you want me to see you?" She was still standing near the door, as he hung her coat back up. But that was the kicker wasn't it? How could he explain how he wanted her to think of him?

Sam tried the coward's way. "Not so weak I can't stand."

Rae was suddenly very still. "That scared me to death Sam."

But he glossed by it. He added, "Not in a bathtub with a handtowel to cover myself." He couldn't even face her anymore, as he drudged up all the ways she had seen him at his worst. It was a good thing he wasn't looking at her, too. She started laughing.

His heart caved in on itself. The air left his lungs, and they just stopped functioning. He stood stock still for God knew how long until her giggles slowed. His mouth hung open and he couldn't turn to face her. How could she be so cold as to laugh at him?

Finally, she stopped. "I'm laughing at *me*." It was breathy, on the tail end of her giggles. Slowly his heart started to beat again. It had to. "Liam had better be right."

Liam? He didn't ask it. What did Liam have to do with any of this? Oh yes, that kiss at the bowling alley that he had managed to push to the furthest corners of his mind. And even though he didn't think his chest could sink any lower, it did. "You'd better get back to him. Don't let me keep you."

"I'm not with Liam."

Finally, when he thought he could manage nonchalant, he turned to face her. Her cheeks were still a little pink and she was smiling. "Yeah, well, his tongue in your mouth says otherwise."

She shook her head. "There was no tongue."

"Sure looked like it." Could he give himself away any more?

"It was meant to."

He had no response to that. All he could do was shrug and wait. Rae saw his expression and filled the gaps. "Give me a minute. First, let me explain about the bathtub."

He sighed. Just the subject he wanted to revisit.

"I was so scared that evening. I sat outside the bathroom door and cried and prayed. And halfway through my prayer I thought 'Dear God, please get him healthy again. It'd be a sin to waste that body.' I felt like such a perv."

"What?"

She shook her head and looked him in the eye for the

briefest of moments before turning away. "Even sick in the bathtub, you're hot."

"What?" He was scrambled inside and he dared not hope she was heading where he hoped she was heading.

"Seeing you sick didn't change what I think about you."

"What do you think about me?" He tilted his head to the side, trying to catch her eyes, but she wasn't having it. She just kept looking away. So he filled in the missing space. "You don't think about me. You think about Liam." He hadn't meant for it to come out like that.

But apparently it worked. She looked right at him, a little desperate. "No, there's nothing between Liam and me."

"It didn't look like it."

"He was trying to make a point."

A wry smile twisted itself onto his face. "Oh, he made his point all right."

"No!" Rae grabbed at his shirt sleeve as he tried to turn away. He couldn't remember ever being this wound up and this confused. "He was trying to show me that you were interested in me."

"*He was showing you this with his tongue?*" He had said it in a moment of anger, but it made her laugh.

"No, he didn't. He pointed out that everyone else was cheering and that it just made you mad." She stopped laughing. "Liam said there's only one reason a guy would get mad about another man kissing a woman." She paused and waited for him, but Sam didn't know what to say. Her voice was soft. "Tell me he was right."

He still wasn't facing her. Thank goodness, because he was cornered and the words just tumbled out. "He was right."

She yanked against his sleeve and scrambled around to face him. "*Really?*"

"Really."

He looked at her again, his heart beating like a drum solo,

and surely just as loud. He had seen so many expressions on her face in the past fifteen minutes and now this. "Why are you grinning like that? This is the most twisted, convoluted conversation I have ever had with anyone—"

Her fingers had found their way to his hair and she had pulled his head down to her. She lifted up on tiptoe to meet him and fused his lips with hers. Every confusion melted away. Every piece of him melted into her.

Sam felt his arms tighten around her waist and lift her to him. He kissed her back with every ounce of himself, and didn't stop to wonder if it was real. Rae's hands moved along him until her arms were clinging around his neck.

He leaned against the back of the couch, pulling her with him, never once breaking their kiss. There wasn't enough of this in the world, and he found his fingers laced into her hair, holding her head to him. But he had to be sure.

With all his willpower, he pulled them apart, held her head gently in his hands, but away from his mouth. Her green eyes were limpid but confused. He had to be sure. "There was never anything between you and Liam?"

She shook her head. "He's just a friend. I—I— . . ." She took a breath and Sam waited. "I want there to be something between me and you."

"Okay." It was a silly and unromantic answer, 'okay.' But he forgot about it in the heartbeat it took to kiss her again. Her lips parted beneath him and her mouth was liquid heat in his. The kiss was crazy and long, their hands roving over each other.

He smoothed his fingers across her shoulders and down her arms tracing the planes and angles of Rae. Then slipped his fingers inside her cardigan and pushed it down and off, already forgetting it as it piled onto the floor. Her spine passed beneath his touch through the t-shirt she wore as he pulled her closer, flush up against him. She had to feel what she was doing to him. She gasped lightly, and he kissed it away.

For the slightest of moments, he paused just to look at her. Rae, in his arms, kissing him back. Ten minutes ago, he wouldn't have thought it. Actually, he didn't want to think about it now, he just wanted to kiss her more. And more. He wanted her laid out the way she had been the morning after she'd stayed over, peeling her own clothes to get to him.

He told himself what he'd believed that morning was good. He hadn't been wrong.

He traced the edge of her ear with his tongue, then left a tiny trail of wet kisses and groans as he tasted the side of her neck. With a soft sigh, her head tilted to the side allowing him more access. Tightening her arms pulled her breasts up against him and they both had to feel his jeans get tighter. God, what she did to him.

God, what he was doing to her. With a will of its own, his hand traced down her hip then back up again. He felt her breath suck in as he brushed past her ribcage then up to trace the underside of her breast. She sucked in air, and her mouth opened as her eyes widened. They both leaned in for another mind-altering kiss.

She pressed into his hand, and so he did the only thing that came to mind. He continued, until the edge of his hand was against her ribcage and his thumb brushed her nipple. His mouth caught her slight gasp, his other arm pulling her close against him. There was a warmth invading him, knowing that her fingernails dug into the backs of his shoulders.

Raising up on his toes, he pulled her with him, leaning over the back of the couch and falling sideways onto the cushions, Rae on top.

"Ahh!" She started laughing and squirmed a little to get upright. He didn't let her. He just pulled her down for another kiss, as he felt her knees slide to either side of him. Even through all their clothes he felt a jolt the moment she slid against him, her hips flush against his own. Her own shift in breathing indicated that she felt it too.

"Rachel," His voice was far away, and laden with sex. "I want you."

"I want you, too."

The sound of her voice, saying those words, replaced the echo that had been haunting him. This one was real.

CHAPTER 34

"Stay tonight." He was looking at her. His hands molded to her hips, holding her against him.

Rae took a deep breath and felt him move just the tiniest amount beneath her. He was about to set her off like a rocket. It was all she could do not to groan.

"Please." He took her breath away. That Sam wanted *her* was almost beyond comprehension.

She pushed against his chest until she sat upright, still straddling him, "No."

"*No?*" He pushed himself up to face her, their limbs still entwined. His hands cupped her face as he searched her eyes, confused. "I thought . . . I'm sorry, I—I thought you wanted to."

"I do. I do." She felt so frantic. Like he might bolt if she didn't explain right away. The words gushed out of her. "I just think maybe we shouldn't have sex tonight. I mean, we just got this sorted out. Barely."

His hands didn't leave her face and he smiled. She wouldn't need heat to melt the butter next time she made popcorn. She could just get Sam to smile at it like that.

"So stay, I promise no sex. But I want you here."

"Let me get this straight. I'm going to stay over, in your bed, with you, and there will be no sex?"

He nodded, "If that's how you want it."

"That's never going to happen!" Rae was incredulous.

Sam actually looked offended. As offended as a man could legitimately look while a woman was straddling him. "I promise. If that's what you want."

"Well, maybe it's no trouble to keep your hands off of me—"

"It would be difficult." He interrupted, "But if that's the only way to keep you here . . ."

"See, the problem is I don't think I could keep my hands off of you."

She couldn't believe she'd said that. It was true, but she wouldn't have just blurted it out like that. But the smile she was rewarded with heated her like the sun. She should blurt things more often. She had the same thought again as his lips took hers.

After a moment he spoke again, "Then tell me why we're not doing this."

Rae had to push away from him. There was no way she could explain why she shouldn't do what she desperately wanted to do with his lips that close to her. She was utterly swayable. But she knew where her common sense was, even if it was slipping further away with each touch. She grasped at it. "We're not doing this because thirty minutes ago I thought you didn't care one way or the other. Because I have to get up in the morning and go to work and you do too."

His fingers slithered along her waist giving her the best chills. "What you're saying is that it's not perfect."

"No," She shook her head, already missing the feel of his lips on hers. The thought of staying was so very tempting, and getting more tempting with each touch of his hand. "It doesn't have to be perfect. But I know I won't want to get up early in the morning and have to leave . . ."

For a moment she was afraid she had gone too far. Taking the talk from 'sex' to something more. Something that involved the whole night and the next morning. Rae froze inside, waiting for his frown. But it didn't materialize.

"So when?" His eyes blinked slowly. Bedroom eyes. But he didn't even need a bedroom.

"It seems so odd to schedule it." But when, then?

"Friday." His fingers still caressed her lightly. "I don't think I could wait any longer. I've waited long enough already."

Laughter bubbled out of her. "Yeah, that last twenty-five minutes was killer."

He didn't laugh with her and her giggles died at the serious expression he wore. His voice was soft in the air. "I've waited months."

"Months?"

He nodded. His hands slowly clasping around her hips.

It was sinking in. All those nights she'd thought of him, he'd been thinking of her, too. "So that Christmas kiss wasn't a fluke?"

"Oh, God no. I just wish it hadn't taken so long to get to this." His fingers caressed the back of her head and she felt him tug her down to meet him. His other hand remained at her hip, holding her while he moved the slightest bit. Just as the little moan escaped her, his mouth found hers and so did his tongue.

He kissed her into some sort of hazy, sex-laden oblivion. Then abruptly, he sat upright and pushed her away. His breathing was heavy and labored. "I have to take you home."

She felt her confusion seeping in at the edges of her lust.

But he smiled, strained as it was. "If I don't take you home right now, one of two things will happen: I'll break my promise or I'll spontaneously combust."

She looked at the clock on the TV. It was already after eleven. "Yeah, it's about time, if Sheree's already back she'll wonder why I'm late." She would give him his space. Or not.

Grabbing the front of his shirt she pulled him to her for another kiss. God, she was drunk on him. On this. Finally, she pushed him back, separating them. "Yeah, I should go."

It took all her willpower to stand and put her jacket on. But it appeared she was in better shape than Sam, who was having trouble walking. She would have laughed if the thought didn't tempt her so much. But she opened the door and let the chill night air cool her down and force a layer of sense on her.

Then they were in his car, not having said anything. Rae knew it was all she could do not to jump him. So she kept her mouth shut.

"I'm finished at four on Friday."

A happy laugh escaped her. "Four-thirty. But we should go out with everyone."

"Why? They all abandoned us tonight."

Closed in, safe in his little coupe, knowing more about how he felt about her, she felt that she could say these things. She looked out the window at the streetlights and palm trees going by. "I want things to stay as normal as possible." Then she looked down at her hands, but still not at him, "As much as I want this, I don't want to forsake all my friends. I made that mistake a long time ago, and it has never sat well with me."

His hand closed around hers, how it could be so warm was a mystery. But Sam was always warm to the touch. He turned her hand over, running his fingers lightly on her palm, and having no idea what he was doing to her. He would have jumped her there in the cramped car if he had known.

"So we'll meet up like we always do, then we'll head back here, after. All right?"

A silly smile plastered itself across her face, she had a feeling it was a new permanent fixture. "You're on."

"Oh, I'm on all right. That's the problem."

〜

Sam bit at his lip. He was nervous, and he kinda liked it.

It had been ages since someone had gotten him this keyed up. He was zinging.

Rich odors wafted up from the Chinese food he'd bought on his way over. All the little boxes were stacked neatly into the paper bag tucked into his arm. Having no idea what he was heading into, he rang the bell again. He liked the idea that she would be happy to see him. He was leaning for the bell again, having followed someone through the front door, and this time he thought he heard the faintest of voices. In his head it sounded like her. Maybe she was in the darkroom.

So he tried the knob, finding that it turned easily under his touch. The living room was brightly lit, but no one was there. "Rae?"

"In the darkroom!" It was faint but there. "Don't come in!"

What he did was set the bag on the table and go pound on the door. It was supposed to be a small den or big closet but Rae had converted it. He wouldn't dare let the light in and ruin her work, but he sure as hell would yell a piece of his mind through the door. "I can't believe you left the front door unlocked! What if someone wandered in!?"

"What? Like you?" Her voice was too jovial.

"No, like a criminal, for God's sakes Rae! What if I had been —" he stopped himself. She had flung the door open and was standing square in front of him, making his heart have to do its best just to keep beating. He pulled her smiling face to him and kissed her hard before yelling at her again. "I don't know what I'd do if something happened to you!"

That only made her smile. "Hmmmm." She wasn't contemplating anything, so he waited. "Sounds like when I was upset when you were sick."

"So?"

"So, that's when I realized just how head over heels I was for you."

Every tense muscle softened. "Really?" How had he stayed away all day?

She nodded before backing into the red lit room. Then turned and used the tongs that she must have had in her hand the whole time to pull a photo from one of the baths. Sam just looked her over.

Her hair was pulled into a high ponytail and fell in a dark cascade, catching red highlights like mad in the glow. Her little t-shirt didn't even make it to her belly and her sweatpants had been rolled down at the waist. Had she been expecting him? Was this some torture designed by god?

"Look."

He did and was surprised by his own face smiling back at him. In the huge black and white print she held up, he was standing at his car and laughing, his long dark coat pulled against him. "Wow." It never ceased to amaze him how much she could put into a simple two-dimensional piece. The small room was strung with line, covered in her photos clipped up to dry. They all glowed in shades of gray as they hung from string and clothespins, on display around the tiny room.

He turned and was greeted by a wall of women's faces. Each contorting one way or another as they applied this powder or that cream. He could tell by the richness of them that they were color photos, although it was really just a gut feeling due to the red light. "Rae, these are great."

"Thank you." She clipped up another one. "They'll be even better in order." Transferring another photo from one bath to another and setting another timer she turned away. "The gallery has to get thirty, identical, thin, plain, black frames. We picked the wood and they have their guy on it, but it's going to take a while. I probably have to do all the mats myself."

"I'll help." It had tumbled from his mouth, but he didn't regret it. She wasn't mad at him for coming over unannounced. Or for yelling at her about leaving her door unlocked. But in the brief moment after he let himself in, he had feared that anyone else might do the same. That someone might get to his Rae.

When she had become 'his Rae' was anybody's guess. But he couldn't stop thinking of her that way. He liked it. His hands reached for her hips, but, still peering down into the bath, she held up her tongs to ward him off. "Do not touch me."

"What?"

"I have three more photos to go."

"So why can't I touch you?" And how had she seen that coming?

"Listen." She turned and smiled sweetly at him. "I have to finish this batch tonight. After I'm done, then I am supposed to pine away for Sam and wish he was here for the remainder of the evening. I can cut that from my schedule and squeeze you in. But this can't be changed."

His grin was goofy, and his hands itched to touch her, but he kept them to himself. "I brought food."

"Ohhhhhh." She'd sniffed at the air and let out a mouth-watering moan. "You're playing dirty."

Okay, that about drove him over the edge. "Remind me to bring Chinese more often."

"I was actually just thinking about orange chicken before I heard you knock."

"I have orange chicken."

"You are a god among men, Sam." The bare flesh at her waist teased him. But he had promised: not until Friday. Tonight, he was here because he hadn't been able to stay away. Not to break his word.

He jammed his hands into his pockets. He would feed her every bite.

CHAPTER 35

Rae's hands gripped the steering wheel. She had work to do. Even though the show was still several weeks away, her work was due much earlier. Photos needed prepping. Decisions had to be made. In her moments of honesty, she could admit that any decisions she would be making now wouldn't be good ones. So here she was out driving around, with a bag of fresh groceries occupying the passenger seat.

The music of her cell phone ringing startled her from berating herself. The screen lit up the number and her smile lit up her face as she answered it. "Sam."

"Hey, I was just thinking about you."

His voice was smooth and far away and turned her to putty. For a brief moment she regretted the absence of his hands to do something with that putty. Before she could say anything he started talking again.

"I'm sorry I barged over there last night. . . . I just wanted to see you."

"Don't be sorry." She grinned in the dark of her car, even though no one would ever see it. "You completely made my day."

"What are you up to?" There it was, just what she had longed for. The thought that had drifted off to sleep with her for so many nights. The casual conversation she had been yearning for from him. The 'how was your day?' or the 'I missed you.' It would have been perfect had it been accompanied by a hug or a snuggle, but over the phone would have to do right now.

"I'm headed out to a friend's house. I thought I'd make dinner." She sighed. "She's been working a lot lately and I haven't seen her."

"Oh. . . Well, I can't wait until tomorrow." She felt as well as heard the small sigh at the end of his words, and it tugged at her. He wanted her with him, and that sigh spoke volumes.

"Me either." She pulled up and parked across the street, then hauled her grocery bag out with her, the small cell phone tucked awkwardly against her shoulder.

There was the briefest of pauses while she climbed the stairs. Then his voice came to her again across the line, it was liquid in tone and in words, and held a longing that tugged at her. "I missed you after I left last night. I know that sounds silly, but I just want you here."

Her breathing slowed, but still she managed to find something to say, rather than fall into a swooning puddle on the doorstep. "I understand." Covering the microphone with her thumb she knocked on the door before moving her finger and speaking again. "Having you leave last night was difficult. But going to work this morning would have been harder."

"Yeah, I know what you mean, it just doesn't make any of this any easier."

The door before her swung open, and Sam stood framed in the light. His head was tucked into the phone at his shoulder, and for a brief moment he was still too busy paying attention to the phone to really see who was at the door. But then he caught sight of her and his mouth dropped open. Regret sagged through her that she didn't have her camera to capture his face. But it would remain burned in her memory forever.

Holding his phone up toward her he looked confused. "I thought you were . . ."

With a huge smile she thumbed her phone off. "I was just trying to throw you off the scent."

"It worked." He looked at her and, without looking, tossed his phone onto the chair. Pulling the door back wider, he gestured her inside, his face as open as his home. She was proudly sauntering by when he caught her and tugged her to him. With the door still thrown open and the bugs probably coming into his house, he kissed her senseless, his arms encompassing her and his tongue searching for hers. He sighed and she could feel him smile as she kissed him back. Glad to be safe, tucked into his arms. Until he jerked away suddenly, causing her to frown until she saw that he had reached down to save the groceries from hitting the floor.

"Don't drop that!" He peered in the bag, "What did you bring?"

"Food." Rae closed the door behind her and slid out of her jacket, before heading into the kitchen, glorying in being greeted with such a kiss.

He looked wary. "Why did you bring me groceries? I can get my own groceries."

"Just what I need to make dinner."

Instantly his expression changed to stunned or awed, she wasn't sure which, as he set the bag on the counter and started setting out the contents. "You're going to make me dinner?"

"Mm hmm." Rae knelt down beneath the countertop and began sorting through his pots looking for the largest. When she stood up with her prize in hand he still looked a little shocked. "What?"

"You don't have to."

"I want to." She replied, the words rolling off her tongue

with a certain smug satisfaction, until a thought knifed through her, that maybe he didn't want her here. She forced her mouth to speak, "Do you have work to do? Or . . ." She couldn't even ask it—Oh *God, did he have another woman here?* "Should I go?"

"No!" He shook his head, his answer rapid. Rae let out a sigh of relief. "It's just that I grabbed Chinese take-out last night and you're actually going to cook for me. That doesn't seem fair."

Rae laughed. "There is no *fair*. Besides, I've seen you cook. And I—" *love you, but—*, she caught herself, swallowing the words before they left her mouth, "I wouldn't eat your cooking."

"That's probably a wise decision."

She filled the pot with tap water and set it back to boil before reaching in to the cabinet to grab the salt. It was always there for the popcorn. She had brought it some time ago and found that it still gave her a heady sense of satisfaction to have something of hers in Sam's house. She'd never let her self-satisfaction show before though. Rae didn't want to have to explain about why she had always looked so smug at the salt. She simply added some to the pot and put it away.

After a few moments, she became utterly disturbed by the sensation of him staring at her. Again she questioned the brass she must have had to just buy groceries and come over. But he had shown up on her doorstep last night, so she could do it too, right? When the sensation of being stalked didn't stop, she turned around, to find whatever sense it was to be telling the truth.

He was leaning against the counter by the fridge, his arms crossed in front of him. His hair falling, a little too long, over his brows. The blue of his eyes was boring holes in her, even when she'd been facing the other way. "What?"

Nothing moved except his mouth. He was completely unnerving her with every word. "I just can't believe that you are here in my kitchen, making me dinner."

A huge attack of the nerves swamped her. "Did you already eat?" It was after seven.

"No." Still he didn't move, just watched her as if she were his entertainment.

"Then what?"

Finally, he shook his head. More like he was clearing cobwebs than saying 'no.' His arms unfolded and he lost that searing heat. "Just ask me later."

"Ohhh-kaayyy." Rae handed him the knife she was holding still looking at him sideways, still unsure of herself. "Well, at least make yourself useful."

"In the kitchen?"

"Uh-huh." She accompanied it with a smile. "You can chop things. They don't have to be neat." She pulled a package of Italian sausage out of the bag. "Here, cut these into pieces."

"What are we having?"

He took the bag from her and began cutting the wrapper with the knife. She tried so hard not to cringe. No wonder all his knives were so dull. She didn't even bother to ask if he had kitchen shears. He didn't. "We're having lasagna."

"With sausage?"

"Yup. Obviously, it's Italian sausage. My Nonna would roll over in her grave if I did it any other way. Though there is an acceptable eggplant and spinach version, I wouldn't make it for you."

He had finally hacked the package open, and he stopped, looking up at her. "Am I so easily categorized then?"

"In this instance, yes."

His eyes narrowed at her. "What if I'm a vegetarian?"

Rae shook her head. He couldn't win this one, and she wondered why he was even trying. "I saw you eating that *two-pound* burger Alex made you last summer. You will never be a vegetarian." Taking the knife from him she cut off a round from one of the large links. "Cut them about this size."

"Okay." He set to work, slowly but surely. She turned to face off against the mushrooms. In no time they were cut into slivers and the water was boiling. She cracked the lasagna noodles into the pot and stuffed them underwater with a fork. No pasta spoon here.

She opened the ricotta cheese and stuck a soup spoon in it for later, then pulled the protective top off the parmesan and opened a small spice box of premixed Italian spices. If she had brought hers there would have been way too much to carry and she didn't want to stock Sam's shelf, knowing it wouldn't get used again until she cooked.

Rae set out the foil pan she had brought, the largest she could find since she had seen Sam eat before and just wanted to be sure she made enough. Then she started looking for the 'broil' knob on his oven.

"What are you looking for?"

Like he would know. "Broil."

"What's broil?"

"That's what I thought." She found a button on the old machine and pushed it. Then set about slicing the bread.

He stopped, finally finished with the sausages. "You don't think much of me, do you?"

She froze. Had she really given him that impression? "Oh God, Sam, I think a lot of you. I just don't think much of your *kitchen skills*. But then again, I have a lot of skills lacking myself. I still bet my football games on which team's quarterback has the best butt." She paused, unsure if she should continue, but then voted to throw caution to the wind. "I think you're amazing." She felt the knowledge climbing in her chest, and decided that was as much caution as she could afford to throw around, so she capped it off with a lame attempt at humor. "And I have to say you earned me a lot of money when I was in high school."

She turned back to the counter to hide her red face. Caution to the wind? That was caution carried off by a tornado.

She grabbed the jar of sauce and started wrestling with the lid. It didn't give. She told it a few choice swear words, but it still didn't budge.

"Want help with that?"

She didn't want help. She wanted it to open for her. At home she always won sooner or later. But after a few more tries, she gave up. "Fine."

The jar nearly disappeared in his hands, and watching his muscles flex—because she sure wasn't ready to see the expression on his face—while he popped the lid just served to point out the differences in them. She had been fine up until then, but now she just turned to jelly. It was all she could do to not drop the jar when he handed it back to her with the lid off.

She handed him the other. "Here." And she just stood there watching like a slack-jawed idiot while he opened it. It was silly and girly and anti-feminist, and it was great.

Sam handed the jar back to her with a little glint in his eye. Shyness flooded her and she turned to check the noodles. Thank God. They were just done. If she'd ogled him any longer they'd be mush. Like her.

"All right." She set out the pan and set to making layers. Sauce, then noodles, then cheese and sausage and mushrooms, then another round.

"You know," It was all she could do to not jump. His voice was standing right by her shoulder, and she became instantly aware of the exquisite tension of having him stand so close to her. His voice flowed over her. "I was just thinking about the last time we were in this kitchen alone."

She laughed. "When I burned the popcorn?"

"Burned? You made real fire!" But then his tone changed. "Although, with the way you were talking something was going to burst into flames. It was almost me."

Sprinkling the last of the cheese and seasonings across the top of the lasagna she turned to face him and found her nose in the middle of a thickly knit t-shirt, warmed by the man behind it. "You?"

His smile was soft and made her think of heat. "I think any man would have combusted to have you talking to him that way."

She scrunched her nose and turned to load the pan into the oven. "Not me."

"Yes, you." He waited just until she closed the oven door and then turned her around. "I've seen men around you, and you're a bit of a flirt. But that doesn't change the fact that any one of them would take you up on it if you acted the slightest bit serious."

"That's not true."

"Yes, it is. Although I don't know why I'm telling you this. Why don't I just write you an instruction manual to run off with another guy?"

She had to laugh. "I'm here. I'm not going anywhere and I don't want to be anywhere else." She busied herself checking out the broiler and seeing that it was working she turned it off for later.

His arms slid around her waist, and he stopped just inches from her, reaching for something over her shoulder. "How much time do we have?"

"Forty-five minutes." Over her shoulder he punched buttons on a sleek looking timer that was the most useful thing in this kitchen and set it on the counter. Her breathing was already faster. God, what they could do in forty-five minutes.

His mind was riding the same track. "I can think of a few ways to work up a good appetite." He grabbed her hand and pulled her into the living room behind him. He left her on the couch, disconcerted for a moment until she watched him flip the shades closed and come back to her.

Slowly, he came to where she was perched, almost nervous, on the edge of the cushion. He knelt down before her, sending her heart into little flutters, and when she thought she couldn't stand it anymore and she should just grab him, his arms slid around her again and his mouth found hers. How had she lived all these years without this?

He kissed her senseless before carefully pulling the tiny clips from her hair and setting them on the sofa. Not that he once looked away. His fingers weaved through her hair, then fondled it softly.

Sam gently removed her from her perch on the couch, kissing her slowly the whole time, until she was lying across him on the floor. Every nerve sizzled, and the only thought her brain could process was that they were fully clothed. How would she even survive a moment next to him naked? Or would her heart just give out from it?

He rolled her over beside him and rested his elbow on the floor, his hand cradling his own head. She'd thought that she would be able to breathe again when he stopped kissing her. But leave it to Sam to prove her wrong. His finger traced her cheekbones, her eyebrows, her lips. The softest of touches that held her in the tightest of trances.

His mouth followed his finger around, leaving a trail of small kisses, and her breath issuing soft sighs. His hand trailed over her shoulder and down over the rise of her hip. Then, finally hooking his finger behind her knee, he pulled her leg up and over his. Holding her pressed firmly against the heat of his arousal. Blue eyes looked into her soul.

And she panicked.

Her palms firmly against his chest, she pushed away and scrambled to her feet, leaving him lying on the floor looking like he was way beyond confused. "Rae?"

"I'm sorry." Her mouth worked up and down but she

couldn't make the right words come. "I'm in way over my head here. I— . . . I . . ."

He sat up and rested his elbows on his knees. "If you're not ready that's okay. You don't have to be ready tomorrow night. I can wait for you." But his eyes betrayed more nervousness than his smooth voice gave away.

She was standing, towering over him, watching as he worried. And she worried, too. Sinking to her heels, she joined him on the floor, only this time with a little distance between them. She watched him as her fingers twined together in worry. "It's not about being ready. It's about being clear."

"Clear?" His head tipped to the side, but she still couldn't look him in the eyes.

"I . . . I . . ." She paused and gathered her thoughts and a deep breath. "I don't sleep with someone unless we're exclusive, and we haven't talked about that."

"*I'm* not seeing anyone else."

Rae shook her head a little. "Me, either." He must have been able to tell that there was more. Even though she didn't speak, he didn't either. He just sat, waiting. So she blurted it out. "I don't want you to be exclusive with me just because you want sex."

Finally, he moved. His supple form rising until he kneeled, he moved the distance between them on his knees. His hands found her jaw and he planted one soft kiss on her mouth before he said anything. "I can't tell you how desperately I want to make love to you."

She started to reply, but his thumb moved quickly to cover her lips and shush her.

"*But* that's not why I want to be with you. I want you willing and comfortable, and more than that I just want you with me. Whether or not there's any sex."

Rae fought back the wetness in her eyes. She was being whipped to extremes. From the languid puddle in his arms to the tense bundle of nerves when she had something important to say that might ruin everything.

His voice was as soothing as his hands running down her shoulders. "I'll do this however you want, but you should know that there's only you. And that I haven't even thought about anybody but you for a long time."

"Really?" How could he be saying this? She was tempted to pinch herself. The words were better than she had even hoped for. As she sat there, she felt it—the flutter at the back of her brain. What she often thought of as a finger sliding down was now that same soft touch sliding up. Not warning her of danger but . . . that she was safe? That this was good? She trusted that touch above all else. And she trusted Sam.

"Yes, really." He tucked her head against his chest, under his chin, both of them still on their knees. It was the smell of him that did her in. His aftershave and something uniquely Sam. She felt his lungs expand and his chest move as he spoke again. "When you're ready you tell me how you want this to go."

Soft as a whisper, her own voice floated out of her. "I want to stay here tonight, but I won't. For all the same reasons. It's just I'm afraid I'll say something stupid and it will all fall apart. Or maybe I'll say something real and we'll realize we aren't meant to be."

For the first time she admitted to herself how desperately afraid she was of getting her heart broken. In that same moment, she realized that she should just leap ahead. If anything happened she was already doomed to be suffering a major heartbreak. Might as well enjoy it while it lasted.

His laugh was both a sound and a motion. "The only thing that's going to mess this up is you saying 'Sam, go away'. Until then, I'm here for whatever you want."

"I'll come home with you tomorrow." She hugged him around his broad chest, remembering sleeping in his arms and waking up next to him. She added to that the anticipation of tomorrow night being relatively sleep-free.

After a few deep breaths she turned her face up to find him staring down at her, but he didn't make a move. She understood that, after all that, she needed to be the one to initiate things. It was definitely her turn. With a small bite to her lower lip, she gently shoved him down to sitting, his back against the base of the couch. The intake of his breath as she moved her leg astride his hips was pure satisfaction to her.

She brought her face within inches of his, noticing how his eyes dilated, how his breathing sped up. "That was really all I was worried about. I want to be here. Right here." She shifted her weight a little and watched his eyes darken. With wet lips she kissed him until it wasn't enough. Until his hands clutched at her waist and she was grabbing fistfuls of his shirt.

His palms were liquid heat as they came up to cup her breasts, but she didn't stop him. Couldn't stop him. Rae simply tucked her own fingers under the hem of his shirt and was rewarded with hot skin. As soon as she freed him from his own shirt, Sam dove for the front of her blouse, his fingers trailing the flesh exposed by each button as he went. Just when she thought it had taken forever, he pushed the front open exposing skin. The silk bra didn't hide what he did to her.

His eyes told their own story, roving back and forth from her face to her chest. "Oh God, Rachel." Quivers shot through her at the thought of it. Sam Brock seemed to think she was some sort of prize. She had fallen into an alternate universe.

She didn't care what she had fallen into a moment later when he touched her again. His lips making a hot trail along her collarbone then down her chest. He pushed her bra out of the way to make room for his mouth, and the cry that she heard had to be her own.

It wasn't until he stopped that she realized she was digging her nails into his shoulders. Her chest heaved with every breath, matched only in pace by his own. He kissed her again, his mouth sweet and steamy. She shuddered against him as his fingers trailed down her front, to her waist. She heard and felt the snap of her jeans being popped, right before a loud 'ding' snapped them both to attention.

"Okay." She swallowed a few gulps of air. "Lasagna's done."

He nodded slowly, sucked in a deep breath, and leaned his bare torso back against the couch. "Probably a good thing if we're going to make it until tomorrow."

With great pains, she extracted herself from his arms, taking a few awkward moments to re-snap her jeans and close up her bra and shirt. Sam seemed occupied hauling his shirt back on and making a few adjustments to his jeans. It brought a small smile to her face.

CHAPTER 36

Sam had been waiting at the table alone for a full fifteen minutes by the time Alex showed up.

"What? No booth?"

"Wasn't available." He lied. He was more likely to be able to sit by Rae at a table and so he had requested it and even waited the extra five minutes. Not that he didn't feel like a heel for lying, but he didn't feel like enough of one to tell the truth.

Alex ordered a beer and Sam commented on Alex's comments about his new project at work, his new boss, and the possibility of a promotion. Trying to be jovial and his usual self, Sam fought off the jitters that Rae just wouldn't show up. At least he had made it. He had harbored a 'Love Affair' fear ever since she'd left the night before. He was petrified some horrible fate would befall him and she would think he just hadn't shown up.

After a few more minutes, Lisa and Jack arrived. They scooted their chairs together and held hands and made him pray that he and Rachel made it to that point.

"Lisa, feeling better?" He threw it out simply to start a conversation in a very lame attempt to occupy his mind.

"Huh?" She looked utterly confused. "Oh, yeah, yeah."

That didn't seem right, but then it didn't matter, because Rae's voice came from behind him. "Hey, everybody." Casually, she pulled out the chair beside him and draped her jacket over the back before sitting down. No special glances, no goofy eyes. His world contained only her, but apparently her world still contained everybody else. She had even said she wanted it that way the other night, so he backed off to give her some breathing room.

In another ten minutes' Sheree had arrived completing the group and drinks showed up and the banter around the table started to its usual high decibel. Talk turned to Sheree's junior science fair and her shot at third grade next year. Then to the wacky redecorating that Lisa was foisting off on Jack, swearing that he'll like it. "I'll like it if it gets me laid more!"

Lisa punched his arm, but it didn't change his expression. Rae's mouth fell open and she quickly moved to cover it. The ringlets she had curled into her hair bounced as she laughed. It was pinned up in about ten little pins or clips of some kind. He was going to have so much fun taking those out. His thoughts were running away with him.

Though he tried to steer himself back to normal, the thought train took off without his permission. Rae had hardly even looked sideways at him. Maybe she was really nervous. It was endearing.

Nachos and potato skins and french fries arrived. Clearly, it had been Jack's night to choose. All American fare, all finger food, and beer served in the bottle. Sam nursed his one beer; he didn't want to have to stay any later than necessary. When Rae gave the word, he would probably bolt without so much as a goodbye to the rest of his friends.

He ate with his left hand, keeping his right hand free. He could see Rae's fingers twisting in her lap like she was worried. The gesture was completely under the table, hidden from the others. His pinky reached out in search of hers, and for a moment her demeanor relaxed. But then, just as quickly, she yanked her hand back and started gesturing as she spoke, leaving his hand sitting there alone.

He said something inane to Jack who was asking about the legal ramifications of knowing that his boss was screwing the woman who had just been promoted. The conversation deserved more attention than he gave it. But Jack knew he wasn't a sexual harassment lawyer. And usually Sam gave out whatever basic advice he could anyway.

Now he was really just concerned with the fact that he was resting his hand on Rae's knee. Her bare knee. Short skirt. But it seemed that she wanted it gone. She tried shaking him off, maybe. He wasn't sure. Until she discreetly and deliberately picked his hand up and put it back in his own lap.

That was when his world started to crumble. He didn't even know what he had done, but she clearly didn't want any attention from him tonight. Sam made a quick decision to follow along like she wanted. He would pay attention to her only when she was speaking to him directly.

It all seemed so juvenile, but he wasn't in any situation to clear things up without airing their private laundry in a very public place. Praying that things would work themselves out and worried silly that they wouldn't, he did the stupidest thing he could think of. He downed his beer. About three quarters of the longneck had been left. It wasn't even cold anymore, but it was beer.

Rae was fielding questions about the art show. Talking about how she hadn't been able to find mat board today. Not thirty, all alike, that were high quality *and* looked like what she needed. She might have to special order them and pick them up. Maybe pay extra for expedited shipping.

Sam wanted another beer, and he began looking for the server. It wouldn't matter if he wasn't in any shape to drive home. If he didn't go home alone it would be because he'd gotten himself a designated driver.

Finally, their server appeared at the edge of the table. Her bare midriff was right at the diner's eye level. Probably a planned maneuver on her part. Looking up with a sigh, Sam begged her, pretty please, for a black and tan.

She smiled as a few of the others ordered more drinks or appetizers and Sam excused himself. He knew the men's room had to be back here somewhere. It wasn't so much that he had to go to the bathroom, but that he had to go *away*. It was the only thing he could think of that wouldn't send up a red flag. Although it was highly possible that his mood had been plastered across his face all evening.

He let out a mad breath a few times before finding the correct door and going in and relieving himself. Relief? Not from what was really bothering him. What he'd thought was going to be the single best night of his life was turning into the shittiest. Maybe he'd just go home.

As he exited the men's room a few minutes later, he spotted Rae in the line for the ladies room. She looked angry. Just another unexplained new development for the evening. He looked her in the eye.

When she shook her head, he couldn't resist. Better to get the news now than to let it drag on, right? "What?"

Through her teeth, she spit the words out at him. "Could you have flirted with that waitress any more?" She instantly looked disgusted with herself and took the whole thing back. "Nevermind. You don't belong to me. I don't have any say in who you flirt with. I shouldn't have said anything."

The doubt that he had barely managed to hold at bay was creeping in. "I thought I *did* belong to you."

"Then why were you flirting with that waitress?" She waved another woman who was waiting ahead of her in line, and stayed, looking at him, arms folded across her chest.

"I wasn't. But maybe you could explain why you've been such a cold fish."

"*Cold fish?*" He was impressed that she could actually look surprised that he thought that, but then her features hardened. "Sam you were all over me."

"I'm sorry if I wanted to touch you!" *Why was he apologizing for that?* He was about ready to remind her, in public, exactly where his hands had been last night and just how she had responded.

"It's not like we're Lisa and Jack."

He took a deep breath, as though oxygen were the thing keeping him alive. "That's just it. I want that."

"Well we can't!"

Everyone in the line was getting an earful of them, and at least she didn't care. At least she was talking to him. Not that it would solve anything. She waved another woman past her and into the restroom.

"Why can't we?" He was exasperated and hurt and all he could think was *this better be good*.

She stared him right in the eye and delivered the blow. "Because then everyone will know."

He blinked a few times as though he had been slapped. Slapped would have felt better, he was certain of it. After a couple of breaths, Sam felt his blood cool. It went straight through cold without stopping and froze in his veins. His voice went soft. "I'm sorry. I was so excited that I wanted everyone to know. I thought . . ." What had he thought? Whatever it was, it had been wrong. He turned and started away only to feel her fingers tighten on his arm.

"No, Sam." Her voice pleaded with him. He could barely make it out over the thunder collapsing in his head. "It's not like that."

When he turned to look at her, he saw fear. It didn't make any sense, but he was on the border of completely not caring.

He tried to pull his arm away, but she had him with two hands now. "Sam."

Softly, she continued. "Not like that. I'm not ashamed of you. I . . . I want to shout it to the world. But then they all get let in on this and it isn't ours anymore. They'll interfere and . . . what if it messes everything up? What if I tell the world and then have to go back and say I was wrong? I'm not ready to share you yet."

The world came back to him in focus. He put his hand on her shoulder and squared her up to look in his eyes. "I wasn't flirting with the waitress."

"Okay."

"If you still want to, you tell me when you're ready to go."

"If?" Her shoulders slumped. "I didn't mean to make you think 'if'." Her smile was sheepish. "I do actually have to go to the ladies room. But I'll go soon. Will you meet me in the parking lot after about ten minutes?"

"I will do anything." How had that happened? How had everything turned on a dime, then turned right back?

He decided not to question it. Just went back to the table and pushed the black and tan out of reach. He wouldn't be needing it after all. Sam tried to hide the goofy grin that now threatened to consume his face. He could only hope that none of their friends had been paying attention to him.

CHAPTER 37

She hopped from one foot to the other for what seemed like an eternity. Why she didn't just climb in her car and start the engine was beyond her. Well, no, if she was going to be honest with herself, she didn't want to miss seeing him walk out of the building toward her. Rae loved the way he moved. The way he would look around for her. And the smile she would see when she spotted him.

To think she had almost messed everything up tonight by being silly and stupid. She still didn't want to share him, but she'd handled it poorly. Sharing him beat the hell out of losing him any day. Which was just another reason to hop around out here in the cold. *Don't make him come out and look around and not see you.*

When he did finally emerge, he set her blood on fire. Across the parking lot, his eyes found hers and she smiled, the biggest smile that would fit on her face. And not one ounce of it insincere.

Sam wasn't smiling when he finally got to her. He just stared her in the eyes and spoke, his voice low and calm. "Are you done with them now?"

She nodded. She and Sam were here. And the others were all inside. Out of sight and out of mind.

"My place?"

Rae nodded again, but didn't even finish the movement. Her face was in his hands and his mouth found hers. She melted in and kissed him back for all she was worth. She just hoped it was enough.

After a few minutes, he pulled away and laughed at her. "Okay, I have to get out of this parking lot! This isn't the romantic interlude you wanted." He tucked her hand in his and started to pull away, "I'll drive."

But she tugged against him, staying at her own car. He spun around, his eyes betraying the instant wariness. She wished she hadn't caused it, but Rae shook her head slightly, as if to say 'no, it's not what you think.' "I didn't get a chance to grab anything, and I don't want to leave my car here, and I should leave Sheree a note." Dear God, she was babbling! "Do you think you could follow me to my place and then drive from there?"

His brown hair fell forward into his eyes. The stark blue of them shocked her, as did his voice, low and thick. "I can do that." He let go of her hand and pointed to his coupe. "I'm over there, swing around and I'll follow."

With that, Rae found herself alone at her car. She shoved in the key and, unlocking it, quickly climbed in, thinking that she should take a moment and think everything through. And then realizing that nothing needed to be thought about. She wanted this. This was Sam. Not Roger that she'd never been quite certain of. Sam.

Pulling through the parking lot, she watched his headlights as he followed her out to the main street. He waved at every light, and Rae just prayed that she had the mental faculties to follow all the traffic signals. It wouldn't do to have Sam have to pull over with her or have to explain to a cop just what the man in the black sports car was doing to her senses. She thought she could see his eyes smoldering in the rearview mirror. But, even noting how silly that was, she still would have sworn she could see it.

Luckily, her apartment wasn't far away. In a few minutes she was clicking the garage gate open, and Sam followed her in, pulling into Sheree's space. Turning off her engine, Rae spoke over the top of her car. "Do you want to wait for me here? Or come up?"

He slammed his car door. "I'm not waiting here."

"Okay." His fingers found hers and laced through them. The keys to the lobby door tried to slip away from her. It would have been far easier to loosen her other hand from Sam's warm grasp and use two hands, but she refused to break the contact. Finally, she got the building door opened, and she led him in and pushed the call button for the elevator.

The sliding doors revealed that the car had been waiting there and closed behind them with no one else on board. Rae barely got the '3' button pressed before she was in his arms and could feel his heat through her slightly oversize jacket. On her tiptoes she leaned into his touch, hungry for every ounce of him she could devour. When the floor bell rang they nearly tumbled out into the hall and barely managed to make it to her door.

Rae cursed under her breath as she fumbled with yet another key. As she was searching for the right one, Sam turned her away from the door and then pushed her up against it, his mouth covering hers, probing. And she opened to him, pressed herself down the length of him, and kissed him back until he moaned.

She reached for the keys again, the only sane thing to do. "I'd better get us inside."

"Okay." It came out through heavy breaths. His fingers found her waist under the jacket, stealing her breath away. He hooked her belt loop, breaking her concentration, making a simple key that much harder to operate.

When she did finally get the knob to turn, they barely managed to stay upright as they fell together into the front hallway, laughing. Rae shucked her jacket then peeled Sam's from his wide shoulders.

He didn't seem to notice, just pushed her gently against the door they had just come through, clicking it into place.

With her fingers at the small of her back, Rae turned the center of the knob to lock, then had the one clear thought she had managed since seeing Sam come out of the bar, *What if Sheree comes home?* She reached above her shoulder and grasped for the bolt. After a few tries she managed to manipulate the bar. She heard and felt it slide home as Sam's fingers found their place at the front of her shirt. He carefully unhooked her top buttons, finally breaking their long kiss to come up for air. But with that look in his eyes Rae didn't think he needed air any more than she did. She just needed him.

What little oxygen was in her lungs escaped in little breaths as his fingers brushed the insides of her breasts, undoing buttons as they went. She felt her own hands stumbling down the front of his shirt, clumsily opening it, and feeling pure heat radiating from his chest. She hit the last button she could get to before starting to grab handfuls of the material and tugging it out of his waistband. Finally, it was free as he pushed her own shirt wide open to her shoulders. It would have chilled her had she not been so on fire.

"Mmmmmm." He was looking at her, and she was somehow frozen in place and yet boiling at the same time. He must have noticed the new red lace bra. Soon he'd find the matching panties.

Rae yanked at the last two buttons on Sam's shirt and shoved it back off his shoulders. She never finished the job, the buttons at his cuffs wouldn't budge and she gave up, leaving his shirt hanging from him. He was kissing her again, his tongue seeking and finding every corner of her mouth and soul, while his hot hands had crept up her ribcage. Until they held both her breasts and apparently her sanity, too.

Her back arched to him. She would have done it anyway if she had had *any* control over her body. But her mind and her body wanted the same thing. She wanted Sam. *Now.*

As she pressed into his hands his leg moved between hers. She felt the soft touch of the denim he wore slide up the inside of her bare leg, moving her until she came flush against the heat and hardness of his erection.

Sam groaned, and the knowledge that she had caused it turned her bold. She reached between them, running her flat palm up and down the length of him.

"Rachel." She heard everything in his voice. Everything he wanted, everything he intended, everything he couldn't hold back. For just a second, he stood rock still. Then everything changed. She hadn't thought he could get any steamier, but he did. His eyes darkened, his mouth tasted hers in the slowest, softest way. She didn't even realize that he had shoved the stretchy lace of her bra away until he made a wet trail down her neck and took one breast into his mouth.

She heard the moans. Maybe they were hers. Maybe they were his. Rae didn't really care. Her hands searched the broad expanse of his chest, tracing the smooth skin and tangling the light dusting of hair. She followed the trail down until it disappeared out of reach.

When she looked down past her own cheeks and open lips she could see the top of his head. She could feel what that mouth was doing to her breasts and she was caught in the bluest of eyes when at last he looked up at her, his mouth curled into the faintest of smiles.

Even through slow, languid blinks she couldn't break eye contact. Finally, he did. Sam turned his hot mouth back to her skin and made his way up her neck. She might be lost, but she still knew what she was after, and slowly the waist on his pants was getting closer to her straining fingers.

Rae was so pleased with herself at the way his eyes widened, almost imperceptibly, at the sound of the snap being undone, followed by the purr of his zipper and her pushing his pants just wide enough that she would be able to get her hands inside. She couldn't remember ever feeling so pulled under and yet so safe. She couldn't remember anyone ever looking at her like Sam was now. Almost like she was his salvation, and she wanted to be that to him. Whatever he wanted. More than anything.

Her hands skimmed, palm wide, down either side of him, his hips passing beneath her motions. Boxer briefs. It was her turn to smile. He looked so captivated. His lips were parted, his breathing heavy, his hands planted on the wall on either side of her head. Somehow a space of about six inches had come between them, but she intended to put that to her advantage. Boxer briefs wouldn't stop her for long. At her arms full length, she stopped her downward motion with her hands and skimmed them back up to where she had skin to skin contact on his abs. When she pushed her hands down again she made sure her fingers skipped under the waistband. And again she slid her hands down the length of him. The heat from his skin surged up her arms, pushing his breath out on a ragged, sensual noise and her even further over the edge.

In every part of her body, she felt the pulse of every beat of her heart. And when her fingers curled around the hot length of him she could feel every beat of his heart as well. His head tipped back, making her heady with power as he leaned toward her, presenting a perfect neck in dire need of her mouth and tongue. Rae did just that. Eliciting groans and her name several times. All of which she felt pass his throat in tiny quivers before coming to life above her as full sounds.

One of his hands slid down the wall until it made contact with her shoulders. Then slid further, and further, brushing past the tip of her breast and making her gasp. The heavy hand slid past her waist and over her skirt. But Rae got caught up again in the feel of him beneath her fingers. How he moaned and moved just the slightest bit as she stroked him up and down.

She didn't notice that he had pulled her skirt up to her waist and slipped inside the red lace underwear, until he touched her. Her body jolted at the pleasure he sent surging through her. Her head went back, slamming the door, and she heard it make a loud crack.

"Rae!" He cried out, suddenly alarmed, but she shook her head. She didn't feel anything. Just his hand moving from against the wall to cradle her. She leaned toward him for a kiss and closed her eyes, reveling in every sensation. Between her legs, his fingers roved over her, probing, teasing and finally slipping into her.

Everything inside her exploded. Vaguely, she knew that she grabbed him tighter. Knew that he watched her face with eyes molten from her touch, that her mouth was open, that she writhed. Everything disappeared except the man holding her, doing this to her. As her eyes focused again, she was staring into a face that was watching her soul.

"Rachel."

There was still more, and she wanted it. Wanted him to have what she had.

"Please." She sighed it. Breathed it. Wanted it.

That was all it took. His fingers left her and found the waist on her panties, shoving them down. She wriggled the slightest amount until they hit the floor, all the while her hands freed him from his trappings.

He breathed in, a sharp empty gasp, as he moved back. "*Shit. I don't have a condom on me.*"

Neither did she. "I'm on the pill."

He was trying to make his mind work. But hers was

functioning without her and it controlled her mouth. "I've been tested for *everything*."

"Me, too. Recently." Still he didn't move. He stood with his hands on her, her hands on him, perched on the edge of the precipice. He couldn't decide and wouldn't move.

She knew by the cadence of his words that he was trying to say *Are you sure you want me to . . .* but with his ragged breathing all he got out was "Are you sure you want me?"

So she answered that question. "Yes, I want you." Curling his shirt tight in her fists she pulled him to her, closing the space between them. For a brief flare of time, she felt the hot rush of his skin on hers. Her chest pressed into him, his intimate flesh touching hers, the run of a finger down the back of her thigh. He raised her knee to his hip before pushing deep into her, driving out any rational thought, and any memory of any man before him.

Their eyes locked again, and she knew right then that there wouldn't ever be anyone else. She also realized that her other foot wasn't touching the floor. So, slowly, braced between him and the door, she raised her leg, tracing up his pants with her toe, savoring the exquisite feelings that motion produced inside her. And clearly in him as well. When she had both legs wrapped around his hips he began to move again.

His rhythm controlled her breathing, in and out, until she was dizzy from the sensations whirling in her. His hands found her ass, holding her up, moving her against him. His hot mouth found hers, and she was joined to him in so many ways while they stroked together. Breaking the kiss, he pulled back to watch her face, his own eyes lucid but stormy, his breathing a rapid staccato. His motion driving her to the brink. Then she saw him start to tense, and he thrust deep inside her, his orgasm taking him over. She watched his face, and smiled. At least she planned on watching him, until one of his quivers snapped something inside her and her own head fell back, the world spinning again, her voice calling his name.

This time when the world faded back to color from the blinding white she had seen, she made out the sensations of his harsh, rapid breathing in the hollow of her neck. Rae settled her cheek against his, and had the briefest musings wondering when she had gotten as tall as him. She realized that he was still holding her up against the door, and she could now feel the tense muscles of his arms wrapped around her back, holding her tight against him. Her own post-marathon breathing rushed in her ears. Her chest heaved against his with each quick intake.

He sighed and she felt his expression in her collarbone. He pressed his eyes shut and tightened his lips. Not good.

"Am I too heavy? Should I get down?"

"No." It was low, and dejected sounding and Rae opened her mouth to ask him about it, but he looked up into her eyes like a lost puppy, and she realized that when he was lost, she was lost, too. His voice was thick. "I'm sorry."

That jolted her. She'd never been apologized to about sex before. "For *what* exactly?"

He shook his head and couldn't look at her. He gingerly set her on her feet, between him and the wall, and the cold of not being so close to him that she thought she was part of him opened a gaping hole of fear.

"It wasn't supposed to happen this way." He stepped back, zipping his pants, shoving his shirt into the waist, and looking far too tense.

"Huh?" Her blood cooled from boiling and crystallized into solid ice. He couldn't be finished with her?

"It wasn't supposed to be up against a wall. Jesus, it's not even a wall. It's a door." He plucked at her shirt. "It was supposed to be perfect. Isn't that why we waited?" He walked a tight circle, waving his hands, not seeming to realize that what he was accomplishing was winding himself tighter into her heart. This she could fix. But he kept talking, "I acted like a *boy*. I couldn't wait. God, I don't think I even got one piece of clothing off of you."

Her mouth quirked. "My underwear."

"No, it's still around your ankle." He looked dejected as he pointed at it. As she spotted that he was right, she couldn't stifle the laugh that erupted from her. This wasn't normal Rae, leaning against a door, her shirt open and bra askew. Her skirt hiked up and underwear around her shoe. She'd set all that to rights in a minute, but for the first time in her life she wasn't worried being exposed in front of a man.

But she didn't have time to revel in her new confidence, she had to fix his heart first. And she loved that she had it to fix. So she carefully stepped back into her underwear and pulled it up, smoothed her skirt down, and unwound her bra, putting the lace back from where it had been shoved away. He clearly didn't know what to make of her.

After a split second deliberation she decided, not to button up his shirt and tuck it back in for him. What was there to deliberate anyway? He was gorgeous, leave the shirt open, she told herself. She pointed at the floor. "Sit."

He looked at her warily but did as she ordered. Rae then lowered herself to sitting in front of him, but quickly realized that wasn't near enough. Not for what he needed to hear, and not for what she wanted. She moved his knees, climbed closer and shuffled around until she was sitting in his lap, facing him, legs draped around his waist and arms around his shoulders.

His hands tentatively moved to hold her and at that moment she realized that each of his hands nearly spanned her back, making her feel small and treasured. And she intended to return that feeling. "Now, tell me what went wrong here, because I don't see it."

"What? The part where we waited and then I lost control and threw you against the wall in your *entry hall*?"

She smiled and looked around. "I sure will never look at the hall the same way again. And, yes, I still fail to see a problem."

"Well, hell, I could have done that on Tuesday."

"No." She held his face, making him look at her. "Wednesday morning, I would have had to climb out of bed and leave."

He didn't speak.

"Sam, what part of this are you missing?" He still didn't see it.

"This was not what I intended to do."

"Me either." Before he could respond, she spoke again. "It was better than what I intended. God, it was *hot*. I came *twice*, Sam. I've never done that before." She kissed him, holding him tight to her.

"Really?"

"Really."

Silence.

But at least he didn't seem quite so keyed up.

"I want to leave Sheree a note that I'm out, and grab a few things, and I want to go back to your place."

"Yeah? You're okay with this?"

"Yeah." She kissed him again before disentangling herself. Standing, Rae stretched, feeling positively liquid. "You should button your shirt. I'd do it, but I'd probably just wind up unbuttoning it again, and then before you know it the hall floor is seeing some action, too."

He started to laugh. Good. Rae turned and made her way down the hall to her room. She felt utterly alive.

CHAPTER 38

He thrummed.

Sam felt a live tingle in every part of him.

Rae had gathered her things, and they held hands in the hallway and walking to his car. Even shared a few soft kisses in the elevator, then a laugh and more kissing when they got stuck without the garage door opener and had to wait for someone to pull in so they could sneak his coupe out.

He couldn't believe that she was sitting next to him in his car. Going to his house, to stay the night with him. The rough edge seemed to have disappeared, and that was good. Although it was replaced with some regret about how things had happened. But Rae seemed to have forgiven his caveman mentality. Sam still couldn't figure that one out.

While they had been relatively quiet for the first part of the drive, his mouth just had to go and mess it up. He blurted, "I just can't believe you're giving me a second chance."

"I can't believe you think you need one."

He shook his head. "You won't convince me that every woman just dreams of being thrown against her wall."

From the corner of his eye he watched her turn from

indignant to shy, even her voice altered. It was softer, lower. "Actually, there are a lot of us who do."

He couldn't believe his mouth was betraying him this way. It was like he was trying to convince her to go back home. But he couldn't shut up. "You're telling me that women fantasize about being manhandled? I couldn't control myself, it was like I was in high school again." *Stupid mouth.*

"I bet all the girls were happy if that was what you were like in high school." She shook her head, "But, the being taken up against the wall like that, . . . that *is* the fantasy. That a man would want you so much that he couldn't keep his hands off you." Again, her gaze darted out the window momentarily. "I just can't believe that *I* made *Sam Brock* lose control."

His hand made its way across the gear-shift and found hers. He snaked his fingers between hers and the warmth of just holding her hand made him happy. He just wouldn't shift gears all the way back. That now seemed like a good solution. "You have got to be kidding me, Rachel. You walk down the street and men lose control."

Reaching up, she pressed the palm of her hand against his forehead and he laughed when he realized she was checking for fever. She'd probably find him warm, but not from fever. "Sam, you are certifiable. That doesn't happen."

"Yes, it does." For a few seconds he spared a glance away from the road just to look at her. She seemed content. He wanted passionate again, but he made a real effort to keep it in his pants this time. This time it would be slow and sweet. Perfect. He tried talking. "Most men just don't lose it in front of you. The few brave souls that do usually come across as arrogant jerks. But I've seen the way you turn heads, all of them."

She narrowed her eyes at him, as though looking to spot the lie. But he wasn't lying. "I should just shut up before you realize that you could have anybody you wanted."

Again, her voice dropped a pitch. "I do have who I want."

He couldn't look at her. But as his fingers squeezed hers, he could feel himself jumping to attention again. *Down, Boy. Perfect this time. Slow and Soft. Long.*

He turned the last corner as she spoke again. "You exceeded all my expectations."

He laughed. "You must have had some low expectations."

But she didn't laugh. "No, really Sam, it was perfect."

He waited while the garage door opened. Then pulled into the dull yellow light of his freshly cleared garage. He'd been concerned that he might peel her clothing off her as he exited the coupe, and so he'd made room inside, just in case. "There's more."

Her smile was huge, but he had to get her out of the car. Do the right thing. He clicked the garage door closed, and while it rambled its way down, he opened her car door, slung her bag over his shoulder and held her hand while one long leg touched the floor, followed by another, then her face appeared bearing a liquid smile. She let him pull her up, and let him hold the door into the front entry for her. She climbed the two steps up past him, and he watched her perfect shoulders pass his eye level before he followed.

He was where he had planned to be earlier this evening. Only not really how he planned to be here. But if 'wild' had characterized their first lovemaking, then he had one word for now: seduction. He had to sweep her off her feet, had to make her think he was amazing. He had to convince her that she'd never want to leave.

The lights were on dimmer switches throughout the townhouse and he'd set them all on low when he went out this evening. Rae turned and looked up at him with those sexy green eyes, like she knew something was up. But he just took her hand again and led her up the stairs behind him. At the top, he opened the door to his room and reveled in the gasp of surprise from her lips.

Huge pillar candles burned low on every surface, he had prayed continuously that the place didn't burn down while he was out. New Calvin Klein sheets and a comforter, as soft as he remembered hers had been, adorned the bed. The old bachelor black just didn't seem appropriate for her. She wasn't that kind of woman, not to him, and he didn't mean to treat her like it.

He had called Christy and begged her to help. But all the advice she had given him was that champagne and rose petals were only appropriate if it really was what he would have thought of to do. He knew it would seem out in left field. So he had bought a new popcorn pot, chilled her favorite soda and threw a bottle of champagne in the fridge with some strawberries, just in case.

Finally, he had decided to leave her a note on the pillow, propped up with one word scrawled in his horrible handwriting across the front of the card: *Rachel*.

He watched as she climbed onto his bed and crawled toward the pillow, probably not realizing what that sight would do to him. Watching her was probably the only thing that saved him from his own explosive embarrassment. The only thing that kept him from jumping up and snatching the note from her hands and begging her to just forget about it. It had been a stupid idea and he wanted to take it back. He should have gotten roses and . . .

She rolled back against the pillows with the paper in her hand, looking sweet and rumpled from his earlier touches. Rae opened the card and her mouth opened. He had written four words: *make love to me.* He had gotten rock solid just writing it and had hoped she would find it as sexy as he did. Now he stood at the end of his own bed, his hands tucked in his pockets just to put them somewhere. He was staring. Nervous. Hard. Waiting.

She mouthed one word to him.

Yes.

Like water, it drained away. All the nervousness left, every uptight muscle loosened, replaced by a new kind of tension. His belly tightened as he kicked off his shoes. A wry thought passed through his head that he was already more undressed than he had gotten last time. It had been less than half an hour, and already he wanted her again. Just as badly as before.

Now, a tight wire feeling held him in check.

Sam lowered his hands to the bed, taking her ankle and undoing the sandal strap, before slowly sliding the shoe off her slender foot. Her feet must be cold, going out in those sexy shoes before the season really got warm, but they were only a little chilled. He tossed the shoe and reached for her other foot. He shucked the other shoe in a different direction and played with the thought that they would have fun finding all their clothes in the morning. Or maybe not.

He dragged his fingers up the smoothness of her leg, and watched her mouth widen as he crawled up beside her. Lowering himself along the length of her, he realized that he could still smell himself on her. He almost snapped. But with a moment of deep breathing he quelled it, then proceeded to enjoy the primal feeling of possessing her.

The fingers that had followed her leg now traced over her hip and found a small run of exposed flesh where her shirt had never quite been tucked back in. That was from him, too, he knew. She belonged to him, with him. He moved his hand softly along her upper arm, up the curve of her neck and finally brushed his fingers across her lips. Rachel's eyes watched him with deep interest, but her mouth had never closed, her hand had never let go of the card, and she hadn't moved a muscle. As though she were mesmerized by his touch.

Slowly, so he could savor every second, he lowered his mouth, and replaced his fingers against her lips with his own. He had the faintest knowledge that she had reached out and dropped the card off the edge of the bed, before wrapping her arms around him. She kissed him back with a wicked intensity, but for the first time they weren't starved for each other. They would take their time.

He didn't know how long he had kissed her, or how soft and pliant her mouth could be. He didn't know there were so many ways to take her mouth with his and be taken by hers. He only knew that when he finally moved his head away one of the huge candles had sputtered and its flame gone out. Sam's was only hotter.

In the dwindling light, Rae's thoroughly kissed lips parted, and looked even more inviting than they had before. He kissed her once, lightly, concluding that she was the sweetest thing his mouth had ever encountered. Then proceeded to watch his hand trace every line on her face, then her ear, then her neck. Next, he kissed every place he had touched.

Rae let him. She reveled in his touch. He could see it in her liquid stare, hear it in the small, breathy moans, and feel it in the tiny quivers he sent through her.

When he had worshipped every exposed bit of flesh he could find on her, he let his hands roam over her shirt. Her nipples were already hard and tight before he ever touched them. He touched, he rubbed, and he watched as her breath came faster. Ever so slowly, he claimed her with his tongue, turning the fabric wet as he went, plastering it to her, until he had made a wide, wet circle around her nipple. Then took the whole thing into his mouth.

Her back arched up off the bed to him and then settled back down on the soft new comforter. He leaned back and admired his handiwork. The wet fabric and bra concealed nothing even in the deep yellow glow of the candles. He opened her shirt, reverently this time, and wrapped his arms around her, pulling her upright so he could remove it.

Slipping her bra away, Sam took her wrists and pulled them

away from his neck. He held her hands down by her side and fought her natural urge to cover herself. "You are the most beautiful woman I have ever known."

A small smile started at the edge of that perfect mouth, and Rae leaned forward, with Sam still holding her hands loosely at her side, and she pressed that mouth to him along every pulsepoint she could find. At last when he let her extricate her hands, she began undoing the buttons on his shirt, starting with the cuffs then trailing down the front. Slowly he waited, enjoying every brush of her fingers through the thin fabric and occasionally on exposed skin. Rae pushed the shirt off him as she kissed him, her tongue finding his and playing a wicked game.

Her arms moved as she threw the shirt off the side of the bed then pressed herself against his bare chest. She was warm and sensuous, touching everywhere she could.

Sam let his fingers trace the waist of her skirt, until he located the zipper in the back, tugging at it until it had no further to go. With a little movement he managed to pull it completely off, and watched as his hand dropped it off the foot of the bed. Then he turned back and caught sight of her, all air escaped from him.

Rachel lounged against the stack of pillows, wearing nothing but the red lace underwear. Everything about her body said she was ready, the way her legs pulled up towards her, how her arm moved over her head, the way she was unable to be completely still. He watched a few small undulations pass through her while she waited for him as he stepped off the end of the bed and removed his pants.

The feeling of power overtook him as he walked, completely naked, to stand beside the bed. Her eyes watched him, widened as they traveled down the length of him, then turned murky and deep as they found his own gaze.

With slow, aching hands, he reached out and tugged the red

lace underwear off, then lay beside her, as he had when they had started. But this time, the feel of her flesh sizzled against him. All of him. Unencumbered by clothes, doubts, or fears.

Moving one knee over her leg, he pulled them closer together and propped her legs slightly apart, allowing his hand free range to roam. He touched her here, flat palm feeling the heat from her, a finger taking in the soft silk of her skin, and finally when he slid his finger into her soft folds he found her wet and wanting.

As her arms wound around his neck he let her pull him closer, until he was on top, pressed completely against her. As her legs moved he pushed deep inside her, claiming her, branding her. Branding himself.

Her head turned from side to side, and her hair glowed with a fiery red in the candlelight. They moved together so exquisitely, each knowing what the other needed and wanted.

She called out his name several times, and he heard hers in a low hot voice that barely seemed to be his own. It seemed they moved that way forever, pushing towards release. When it finally came, it shook him to his core, and stayed with him long enough to make him wonder.

After a while, lying there, entangled, he felt her shiver a little and pulled the covers up over them. She curled into him and was soon asleep against him. He held onto her, content to breathe next to her, his fingers in her hair, her arm across his chest.

Sam lay awake for a little longer marveling at the way she just seemed to belong there. Suddenly it was her room, too. Not that she had claimed it, but that it would be empty without her. He realized that he qualified under the same rule. A smile played softly across his lips as he guessed that made him hers, too.

CHAPTER 39

It was eight a.m. when Rae wandered downstairs to the kitchen. Opening the fridge, she found a cold orange soda that made her smile. She was wearing Sam's shirt from the night before. She had simply scooped it off the floor as she left the room, thinking it wouldn't do to wander the house completely naked. She sure hadn't tried very hard to find her own shirt, as wearing his was so much more appealing.

She made herself at home, knowing where most everything was already, and pulled a box of crackers from the pantry. Knowing Sam wouldn't mind, she pulled out a small handful and munched them to stop the rumbling in her belly while she foraged for more substantial fare.

Rae had smiled upon opening the fridge and finding a cold six-pack of Sunkist, as well as a gold-rimmed plate mounded high with strawberries. In the back was a black bottle of champagne. Her lips twitched in a small smile as she considered fixing a mimosa, a treat she would never have made for just herself, except that it was a special morning.

She pulled the champagne from the fridge and was peeling

the foil when an overly loud bling sounded a notification on her phone. She hadn't even thought to turn it off. And where was it?

Her purse was near the front door and her phone wasn't in the pocket it belonged in. Rummaging through, she hit the bottom of the bag just as her phone pinged loudly again. She bolted upright, it was on the . . .

Turning, she looked and spotted it face down on the table just as the light faded away. When had she put it. . . ? She didn't even know, but she grabbed it and hit the button, trying to put the settings lower. Rae hoped that she hadn't woken Sam.

She had come awake fifteen minutes before getting out of bed. Full of energy and unable to stay still next to the sleeping bulk of her new boyfriend. Watching him had satisfied her for quite a while. Then he had shuffled around a bit in his sleep. It seemed he'd heard her stomach growling, but it didn't fully wake him. She'd slipped out of the bed, refreshed by the air that was much cooler than the heat that swamped her next to him.

Her fingers reached up to touch the smile she could still feel lingering on her mouth. *Sam was her boyfriend.* The thought sang its way through her head a few more times as she scrolled her way through the new social media posts on her phone. There was an ad for a nearby theater, and she looked at the trailers, dismissing most except for one film she thought she and Sam might enjoy together. Like a real date. She looked up local restaurants and parks.

Then she froze. Maybe she was getting too far ahead of herself. They had agreed to be exclusive, but they hadn't agreed to anything else. They were here, but where was here? Just at the very beginning of something. What if it didn't last? What if it was over as fast as it began?

But that was just her mind trying to scare her. This hadn't begun fast at all. Maybe her subconscious was trying to keep her from getting in too deep, too soon. But the fact was that it was

Sam who had stocked the fridge with a bottle of champagne and a plate of strawberries. He had been upset with *her* for not being willing to share all this with their friends. He wasn't going anywhere soon.

The smile returned, playing softly on her face as she realized that all their friends knew now. Sheree had a note that Rae was staying at Sam's and not to expect her home last night. Rae toyed with the thought that she should have added the word *'ever'* to the end of the message.

But if Sheree knew then everyone knew. The girl could keep a secret but only at great cost to herself, and only if told explicitly, in no uncertain terms, that she was not to repeat what she knew. She hated secrets and being wise to herself she usually refused such information. Rae had thought about just saying she was out, trying to keep Sam to herself for a little longer. She could have said she was at Sloan's but lying to Sheree didn't sit well. So yeah, they all knew now.

Rae scrolled a little further and stopped. An ad for The Webber Gallery popped up, announcing its next show, all photography, all by five new artists. Her heart leapt into her throat and the room closed in.

It was the first time she really felt the pressure of the show as a physical presence. She knew that she had to have all the photos perfectly printed, had to have everything framed and ready weeks prior to the show. The Webber curators were looking through the prints now, telling her what she could keep and what they couldn't show. They were drawing up tags and price lists and she had to approve them and inspect them and they were deciding where her space would be and how things would be arranged and so on and so on and so on.

Rae took a deep breath and another swallow of the soda, polishing it off. The handful of crackers she had found earlier had quelled the grumbling noise, but it still wasn't quite breakfast.

The can made a small clunk into the trashcan in the kitchen as she passed through. She knew exactly what she was doing. Rae was seeking the heat of Sam, and his ability to help her shut out the rest of the world. She didn't have the rest of the weekend as she had thought. She had to get to work. But not quite yet.

Climbing the stairs, she was looking forward to the door and seeing him in that bed, asleep and waiting. But as she opened the door, his expression wasn't what she expected.

"Rae!" He was sitting bolt upright in bed, looking like he might have woken up while he was in the process of sitting, and he looked flustered.

"What?"

"Nothing." His smile was a little slow to take hold, and she made her way across the room to sit on the bed next to him.

"What?" She wouldn't let him off that easy.

"I just . . . it's nothing."

"It's not nothing." She let him take her hand but looked him in the eye, wondering what had disturbed him even more now that he thought he should hide it.

In barely a whisper he told her. "I thought you had gone." His voice gained strength in defense of his silly assumption. "I woke up and you weren't here, and there weren't any noises from the shower or . . . I didn't see that your clothes were still here until I sat up and you were coming in the door."

"I'm right here. I'm not going anywhere."

"Good." His arms enveloped her and tugged her down to the bed. "I was afraid it was all a dream, and I kept waking up and checking all night."

"It better not be a dream." She kissed him reassuring herself that everything would be all right.

"What's this?" He had been stroking her arms and made it all the way down her arm where her phone was still tucked between her fingers.

Rae sat up, near enough to still feel the heat of him, but far enough away to not brush their lips together and to think. "The Webber Gallery just announced the show. There's no backing out now." She held up the screen to face him and he read.

"Announcing new artists . . . who cares, blah blah blah, . . . and Rae Woodward." He smiled, but then glanced over the phone at her expression and stopped. "Nervous?"

"Very."

"But you're an amazing artist."

She sighed, and nodded.

"You're not convinced."

She shook her head this time. "No offense Sam, but photography isn't exactly your area of expertise." Oh god, what a horrible thing to say to the man she had just spent the most incredible night with. "I mean, I'm glad you like it and all—"

His fingers covered her lips as he smiled. "Stop scrambling to apologize. I understand and I'm not offended, and you're right." He shrugged. "I wouldn't come to you for legal advice, either."

She laughed as he continued. "But my mother *is* an expert in this area and she says you'll be a big hit. She doesn't think you'll have to do any more surveillance work after the show at all."

Rae was incredulous. "You told her about that? That's such a seedy job, what will she say?" She buried her face in her hands. What would the Brocks think of her? Did he tell them that she had surveilled her ex-boyfriend who turned out to be married?

"She thought it was a great way to make a living and get lots of practice with your camera. She said it was a brilliant plan."

Her brows pulled together. They didn't condemn her for that kind of work? Maybe not. She didn't think any of the Brocks would ever have need of that kind of service.

He didn't let her get in a comment about it. He did spend the next hour letting her know how glad he was that she hadn't left.

And while she was still breathing heavily on top of the covers beside him, he suggested bagels and coffee.

"What about the strawberries and champagne?"

"They're not substantial."

Neither were her thoughts as he traced her belly with one finger.

Rae took a deep breath. "Then why are they there?"

"They were nervous afterthoughts while I was getting ready to have you come over."

"You were nervous?"

He chuckled, and the sound heated her. "Crazy nervous."

She couldn't respond. *Crazy* was the right word. He would have to have been to be nervous about her. She kissed him into a sigh then sat up. "All right then. Let's suit up."

Rae pulled the spare set of clothes from her bag, grateful that she had been smart and packed warmer items. Hot coffee would hit the spot. They buttoned each other's shirts, and managed—just barely—to not start unbuttoning them again. The crackers and soda hadn't really held her for long and she would be ready to eat by the time they made it out.

Her stomach growled right as Sam looked at her like he was about to change his mind. He ushered her down the steps and to the front door. Buttoning her into her jacket, he kissed her nose and shrugged into his own.

Rae wondered why they were at the front door. "The car?"

"We'll walk. It's two blocks." He opened the door and nearly made it out before his own phone beeped. From back in the kitchen. He sighed. "I almost forgot my phone and my wallet. You make me crazy. In the best way. But that would be awfully rude if I told you I was taking you out for bagels and then couldn't pay for it."

He ducked back in, grabbed his things and was coming back outside as Rae's phone pinged, too. She frowned at several tiny pictures as they popped up in her texts. It was in a group message that they were all on.

The first one was an animated heart that said "Rae and Sam." Well, if she'd ever thought it would stay a secret, she'd been a fool. It sure wasn't one any longer. Lisa was leaving them notes. She sighed and watched as he opened the same message, wondering what it could be. She next clicked on the picture that popped up, opening it to the full size of her screen.

Then she shook her head. It was a photo of Lisa, Jack, Alex, and Sheree out at a club, or so it seemed from all the odd lighting and the people dancing in the background. Rae and Sam frowned at each other, and after a second he hit a few buttons and read the message underneath.

Before she could even see what it said, he rolled his eyes and shook his head, and just handed her his phone while he locked the door. "Last Tuesday night" was followed by "We love you guys. Good luck. Sheree, Lisa, Jack, Alex."

"Last Tuesday night?" She handed it back to him with a frown.

He nodded and held the photo up for her. "Lisa doesn't look very sick does she?"

Rae got it. "We were set up."

Sam nodded and slid the phone into his pocket, now ignoring it. He started down the steps but Rae couldn't follow. Her gut churned. "Doesn't that bother you?"

Coming back up to one step below her, he looked up, his eyes bright. "It's Saturday morning, and look where I am. Who I'm with. I don't think anything could bother me." He kept talking even as she came around. "If they hadn't left us alone we might still be sorting things out, instead of getting coffee and bagels." He grabbed her hand and pulled her along after him.

Rae couldn't budge the thoughts though. "But they knew all along . . ." She hadn't hidden anything! And once again she'd thought she was so slick.

"It's not like they're looking in the windows. But I don't care. I'm crazy about you, Rae. I don't care who knows."

That brought a huge grin to her face. "You're right." Let the world see what a catch she had. "Let's go make everyone at the bagel shop jealous."

He laughed. "Now you're talking!"

CHAPTER 40

Rae felt like she was going to hyperventilate. She'd come home too early from Sam's to get things done for the show. She had shifts to work for Lincoln this week. Though Mrs. Brock seemed to think the show would solve all her financial concerns, Rae had to keep eating and pay her half of the bills until that money showed up. And she'd have to keep paying her half of the bills if the show was a bust, too. Add in that she'd spent a ton getting the set of mat boards shipped, and she was about broke.

Sheree had been wonderful. Though Rae paid a little extra to turn the small closet-sized den into a darkroom, Sheree was graciously allowing her to stack the frames around the edges of the rooms. She'd picked up the set of thirty from the Webber, glass insets and all. That had probably taken five years off her life. She had the mat boards laid out on the kitchen table, and nothing else could go near them. She couldn't risk a spill or stain or anything on them.

She'd found the perfect shade of pearl gray and now she had to cut it. She had a professional mat board cutter, but the measurements were a bitch. Everything had to be perfect and she was procrastinating starting it because she was afraid she'd screw it up.

Sheree had been doing a good job of keeping her calm, but she'd disappeared this morning and Rae had no idea where she was, and she had no one to tell her to just breathe. She thought about calling Sam, but she couldn't tell him about the problem she was having right now. She picked up her phone and ground her teeth as she hit the buttons to call her sister.

"Rae?" Sloan answered as though she knew something was up, but clearly she didn't understand that her little sister was about to burst, and not in a good way. "What's going on?"

"Are you alone?"

Rae paced the small space while Sloan found a spot to talk freely from. The whole time Rae felt horribly claustrophobic, as though the frames were inching in closer and closer with each step. When Sloan said she was ready, Rae gushed like a waterfall. "Sloan! I used my *Big Wish* spell on the gallery!"

"I know. I remember, what's wrong?"

"I don't want it!" She was panicking. How could she undo what she'd done?

"What? You don't want people to come to the show?" Sloan clearly didn't understand and Rae didn't blame her. The ramifications hadn't hit her until just this morning. She'd woken up in her own bed, sadly alone after leaving Sam's yesterday, and she'd suddenly realized . . . everything.

"I don't want people to come to the show because of some kind of spell. I don't want them there because I made it happen. I don't want anyone to buy my work because I cast on them." She was stumbling over her words, trying to get everything out there. "What if it happens and then it all goes bust because no one wanted it anyway? What if it happens and I never know if I was a talented photographer or just a talented witch? I—"

"Rae, slow down," Sloan almost whispered it. "You've got this—"

"No, I don't!" She was borderline on yelling it. She should not be yelling at her sister, but the last thing she needed right now was a pep talk. "I don't need you to tell me it's okay, because it's not. I would not be okay if I ever found out that I'd been manipulated into buying something that way."

"Honey, that's called advertising and it's done to us every day." Her tone was wry and it turned the tide, giving Rae a small laugh and a breather from her own fears. "But I get what you mean. Do you want to come over and we'll check my book and see what we can do?"

"Your book?" Rae was confused, but only for a second. "Your spell book that you bought! Does it have something in it?"

"I don't know, I'm not home. Want to meet me there? I'm about thirty minutes away."

Rae was convinced she'd never agreed to anything faster in her life. She was out the door, purse slung over her shoulder, before she could even think further. Her main goal was "don't hurt anyone on the drive over."

She couldn't even enjoy the day, though it was the first good, truly warm day of the new season. Not that LA had real seasons. She told herself good things while she was stopped at lights on the way to her sister's place in West Hollywood. The fires hadn't started yet up north, so that was good. The Santa Ana winds had stopped for the year. The sun was out and she didn't need a jacket. And she had a show at the Webber Gallery.

She was partly afraid her spell would go sideways. They'd been warned in class not to do anything too big, not to cast on individuals, because sometimes new witches messed something up. Rae had visions of schoolchildren in uniform pouring into the gallery show. The Hasidic Jews, coming over from temple— it wasn't that far from the Webber. Or that every last one of Sheree's teacher friends showed. None of those people would buy anything of hers, and she would have ruined the show for herself as well as the four other artists. They probably already didn't like her, because she'd turned their one-quarter space into one-fifth space.

Fighting back tears at what a mess she'd made, even if she didn't get a gallery full of goths who hated her work, she pulled into her sister's building. Right on West Hollywood, it was five stories tall and had a rooftop that Sloan said they could go up to for air. She parked just down the block and almost ran to the front door. There was no need for it, but she was frantic to find out if Sloan's spell book could undo the *Big Wish*.

She had a key to the front door, even though Sloan had only been given one and it said "Do Not Duplicate" in square stamped letters. The key guy had just put it into the machine and made her the copy. Rae let herself in and hit the elevator button. She stood, tapping her toe and debating taking the stairs, as she watched the numbers come down.

A leathery old woman came slowly out of the elevator, and Rae had to smile. "Hi, Magda."

Magda nodded back at her and offered a little wave. The woman knew who she was, she just could never remember Rae's name.

"You tell your sister I said hello," Magda offered before heading out the front door in a housedress the likes of which Rae had never seen anywhere except on Magda.

Slipping into the elevator, she jammed the button with a little too much force and rode up to the fourth floor. Her sister had a two-bedroom apartment to herself. No need for roommates when you made decent money like Sloan did. She tried the knob and found it locked. She must have beaten Sloan here. She let herself in with a second key—also not to be duplicated—and was barely into the kitchen before she heard a knock.

It wouldn't be Sloan. She opened the door and was startled by Ricky, who was just about as startled as she was.

"Rae!" He remembered her name. But then again, Ricky was awesome. She barely managed a smile before he asked, "Is your sister home?"

"Any minute."

"Excellent. It's Sunday, and we are doing our fabulous Lasagna, Bitches."

Oh, that sounded good. He wasn't calling her and her sister "Bitches," it was the name of the dish, and she'd had it before. Just the thought was wonderful. Maybe if the spell worked and she could be around people. She was opening her mouth to say something, not knowing what other plans Sloan might have for the day, when the elevator dinged.

Ricky turned and saw Sloan come out just as Rae spotted her. But Ricky wasn't on the verge of falling apart. He greeted Sloan with a hug. "Well, speak of the devil. I was just inviting your sister here to Lasagna, Bitches."

"Oh," Sloan looked on the verge of accepting, but her eyes darted to Rae and she held her tongue. In the end, they agreed to let him know later and Ricky went down the hall knocking on a few other doors of bitches who apparently deserved lasagna. Sloan came in and pulled the door shut behind her.

She didn't offer hugs or platitudes or even hellos. She just went to the bookshelf—because she had one of those, she was Sloan after all—and pulled a beautiful, thick hardback book out. For a moment, Rae was entranced, but she found she was almost holding her breath as Sloan took forever to look through the index. It was maybe thirty seconds. When her sister looked up, Rae waited.

"Well, it looks like we can do a general containment spell." She flipped to one page she'd marked with her finger. "It's supposed to pull the spell back and not let it have effect. Or—" she flipped to the other spot she had marked as though Rae could see the difference. "—we can do a reverse version of the *Big Wish*."

"I don't understand." Rae shook her head afraid that none of this was going to work and that she'd already screwed it all up.

Luckily, Sloan was calm and steady. She always had been, and Rae was never more grateful than right now. Sloan read from the page, "An *Undo* spell uses all the same pieces as the original spell, but a few alterations completely erase the original from the universe, almost as if it never was. It won't erase the effects, but it will take away any future reactions and remove anything another practitioner might look for to see if they'd been cast on."

Rae felt her eyebrows go up. "That sounds a bit sinister."

Sloan nodded. "So which one do you want to do?"

Shit. "Whichever one we can get supplies for. We have to go back to the store!" She wanted to smack herself. The store wasn't even open on Sunday evenings. They'd never make it in time. She'd been right there. Right. There.

"Hey, it's okay." Sloan reached out and touched Rae's arm. "I think I have what we need for the *Undo*."

"You have dried Sage, Lavender, Chickory, non-iodized salt, and a witches blade?" Rae rattled off what she remembered from the other week in class. It was an "athame," the blade, but she still wasn't calling everything by its correct, witchy name yet.

"I do."

"What?" Rae almost couldn't believe her ears.

"I bought the book and got more stuff since I wanted to try some of the spells. I got myself a little pantry started." She walked Rae down to the smaller bedroom she used as an in-home office and opened the closet. Shelves had been added into the corner and they were stocked with glass jars tied with twine bearing brown tags. There were bundles of herbs hanging upside down by white ribbons and small wooden boxes with labels in Sloan's neat handwriting on the front. Each item was stored exactly as it was supposed to be for maximum potency.

"When did you do this?"

Sloan shrugged. "This week?"

"When do you have the time?"

"Unlike you now, sister dear, I'm single. I don't have that cool group of friends you managed to rack up. I work and I fill in the time with projects."

"So your latest project is to become a witch?"

Sloan stopped for a moment, the conversation turning from what a strange hobby she'd picked up to something more serious. "Isn't that supposedly what we already are? We're Tavanis from the old country. Did you know my birth father's family is big in American witchcraft?"

"Yeah, I'd seen the name 'Ellis' more than once." Rae nodded, starting to understand.

"I've always done this. I've always *seen* things. Mom shut us down." Her tone changed from wistful to understanding. "I know what she went through, and I don't blame her, but I want to believe it's different now. That it's different *here*. I'm not shouting it at work or anything, but . . . I want to explore it. See if it's real."

"You already know it's real, Sloan. You know what you see. You know how we both are and we've never been wrong." Rae looked into the closet again, really taking in what her sister had done. "I think it's good. I think it's a way of being close to Mom and Nonna and finding out maybe what we really are."

"Then let's go do an *Undo* and see if we can make you feel better."

"I already do." Rae hugged her sister and they started pulling things off the shelf and heading into the living room. Sloan thought they didn't need the roof, and with her new investment, she wasn't calling herself a dabbler anymore. She didn't want to be seen. They ran the spell, following the book, right there on her sister's coffee table.

When they finished, Sloan looked up and smiled. "Done. Let's go get some Lasagna, Bitches, with Ricky and Rob."

"If this spell is half as good as the lasagna, I'll be okay." Rae finally had some hope.

CHAPTER 41

No matter what Sam did or said, Rae looked ready to burst into tears. She'd had this expression on since she'd fled his apartment early Saturday afternoon.

He'd spent four days reassuring himself that it was the show and not anything between them that had her so on edge, so upset. She'd broken down and cried at least once and even now his heart was breaking for her. But it swelled as she came over and took the large, black frame out of his hands and curled into his embrace.

He felt her breath through his shirt warm on his chest. Heard her sniffles. Stroked her head, running his fingers down the ponytail she wore. After she calmed down, she started to pull away, but he didn't let her. Cupping her face with his hands —and feeling pleased at how well it seemed to fit there, and how her huge eyes looked up at him that way—he kissed her. Just for a moment. Before she turned and went back to work.

Sam turned back, too. He had the "pearl gray" mat board spread out on his table now. They'd carefully transported all of it here after Rae had complained that it was taking up all her space and she was going to have to move the glass around too much because she couldn't spread it all out. They had twenty two mats cut. Eighteen of the final pieces from her make-up series were assembled and in the frame and ten of those already were wired and completely done. They had eight more to cut. The large mat sheets had to be cut down with an artist's blade. He couldn't mess up; it had to be perfectly straight, and exactly the measurements of the specific frame it was going into. Since the frames had all been hand made for her photos, they all looked alike, but were often off by half a millimeter. Rae, it turned out, was a damned perfectionist at this.

Then she told him what the set was priced at and he almost fell over.

"No one's going to buy it for that," She told him. "I'm very aware that I'm not well enough known to command what I'm asking. However, *if* anyone does, they cannot find shoddy work inside a frame they paid that much damned money for."

Sam suddenly agreed. Even if he hadn't, it wouldn't have mattered. It was for Rae. He turned back to the rig he'd set up on the table so he could cut clean through the mat and not scar the nice wooden table he'd invested in years ago.

He'd never been more glad that his mother had made him help put wallpaper borders up in their house. He actually had some practice with cuts like this and knew how to use the damn knife well enough to do what Rae was asking. He did the big cuts and she was on the floor, sliding them into a huge paper-cutter she had, the likes of which he'd never seen. It had bumpers and stops and a rolling blade she'd already replaced twice, declaring the used blades not perfectly sharp. She could tilt the blade, and he'd watched her do the first one, making cut after cut, rotating the board and making sure not to bend or nick a corner or edge. When she'd done all four sides, she touched it and the middle fell out, leaving her a beveled mat just the right size for the picture. He'd been impressed. Then she'd sent him back to work.

They'd already had a moment when he'd come out because he heard Rae crying. She'd been upset, making a jagged cut and leaving a sliver hanging on the side of one of the mats. She'd been doing the big cuts he was now assigned to, and he'd been afraid she would take off a finger. She was crying because she ruined the edge and didn't have enough mat board to finish. Apparently it wasn't just gray and you couldn't just go get more. But a little math and they realized they could shave the bad cut and make a perfect mat for one of the slightly narrower frames. That left them with enough mat board.

He'd taken over the straight cuts. Taller than her, he had a better angle to lean into the cut anyway. And he now knew far more than he ever thought he would about framing art. But he found he like it.

Luckily, she was a whiz at setting all the layers into the frames and securing it all with glazing points as well as setting the wires sturdily into the back. She had put the first photo, the one of his mother, together first, and showed him the finished product.

"It's gorgeous, Rae." It was clearly a professional piece and was simply an amazing photo. Somehow, with just a face on a pale background, Rae had captured everything that was his mother. Then she broke his train of thought by whirling the whole thing, frame, photo, and glass around by the hanging wire.

After a yelled, *"What the hell are you doing?"* and a quick duck for safety, he listened to Rae explain that every wire had to be stress tested. They couldn't go into the show and fall off the walls, now could they?

Sam had consoled himself that at least she was in a better mood. Even if it did appear that she was trying to decapitate him with their hard-won work. But that had been eight a.m.

Now it was eleven-forty-five. And everything had to be at the gallery, ready to be hung, by five tonight. And Rae was feeling the stress again. He understood. This was a thirty photo series and she said if one picture didn't make it, then the whole thing didn't show. No pressure there. But he was sure they would finish. They were almost there.

Glancing into the living room, he found her standing over the five frames she had laid out. She was checking something, but he noticed she was bent over at the waist, her round butt high in the air. Sam turned back to his last mat. He hadn't been able to touch her in four days. A state that he had endured before, but was infinitely worse now after having had her in his bed Friday night. And Saturday morning.

The frames. They *had* to finish. He *needed* to touch her. To be inside her.

Two hours later, his frustration level was much higher, as he watched her put the final pieces into the last five frames. At last she stood up and pronounced, "Now all we have to do is get this to the gallery with no mishaps."

Rae smiled. The first, genuine, full smile of the day. But Sam didn't smile back. Just approached her with the paint thinner, and began rubbing it on her hands and wiping it away with the already stained rag he had been using. He rubbed at a spot on her cheek, unsure how she had managed to get it there, but concerned only with the heat in her eyes.

Until she pulled away and started to gather up the scraps of mat that had been shaved off and discarded onto his floor. She happily cleaned, ponytail bouncing. Frustrated, he tried to be helpful even though he didn't care about the mess.

Rae was on the couch, her dark head leaned over, lost in thought over her list on the coffee table. She was scratching off items and muttering. "Shower, dress . . ." She cursed under her breath.

Sam stilled her hands with his own. "We have some time to

kill. Do you think maybe you could come up to my room and we could ease that tension a little?"

Her head snapped up. "Sam Brock, I have to get these to the gallery. This is not the time to think about getting laid!"

His jaw clenched as he leaned back. "You know Rae, it really wasn't about getting laid." Her eyes were already wide, and from her expression she clearly wanted to take back her words, but he didn't give her a chance. "You looked tense and you said that you wanted to go in this afternoon looking like you've done this a thousand times before, like you were dropping off your laundry. I thought maybe a rosy glow in your cheeks and smile on your face would help that out."

He hadn't realized how mad he was, until now, so he kept going. "If it was just about getting laid, I'd have let you cut your fingers off and gone somewhere else long before now. You've been chipping away at my ego all week."

She had come down all the way to positively contrite during his little diatribe. Her voice was nothing now if not meek. "Really?"

"Yes." At least he was done ranting, but he did explain, "You haven't trusted a word I said about how to do this, or when I assured you that we would be done on time," He pointed to his watch, they had hours to spare, "I understand that I haven't done this before, but I timed your process and calculated it, and I *can* do that. Every time I have even tried to touch you, you just shoved me away."

"I'm sorry." She stood up to come to him, but he backed away, not sure why he had said all those things. Not until the words had fallen from his mouth did he realize that in speaking them he was baring a little of his soul. He'd just handed her the power to make it okay or wound him deep.

But she kept coming, until she had her arms wrapped around his waist. "Sam Brock, you are the greatest thing that has ever happened to me. This wouldn't be done at all, and they wouldn't be anything near what I wanted without you. I'm sorry I was such a bear. Can you forgive me?"

"Of course." His arms held her to him and his face buried in her hair. She was his. He didn't want the feeling to leave again.

He felt her breathe in deeply, once, twice. Then her voice came to him. "I think you were right, too. I am too tense. Maybe we should head upstairs and take the edge off."

"Rae." It just didn't feel right to him, like this. "You don't owe me sex."

She smiled up at him. "You're right. I don't. What I owe you is about five massages, for all your hard work and for putting up with me."

He smiled at her, trying to hide his regret that he wasn't going to get to haul her up to his bed.

She kept talking. "What I would like more than anything is to give you that first massage in the shower, after you take me to bed."

He started to lift her in his arms, his smile growing even as his pants got tighter. But she stopped him. "I've been a fool for the past several days, Sam. I just thought that if I slept with you I'd never get out of bed and I wouldn't be ready. I'm sorry."

"Stop apologizing and make love to me."

Rae laughed, but pointed over his shoulder, instead of kissing him.

The front window blinds were wide open. He shut out the outside world, twisting the blinds without looking at them. Grabbing at her knees, he toppled her, leaving her sprawled on the couch. With a little help from her he had her stripped inside of one minute. Still fully clothed, he stood and admired her. She was breathing heavy, and it was making him breathe heavy, too. Even though he hadn't touched her yet. Her eyes were wide and dark, and he felt something dominant and fierce inside him that she would allow him this. Giving her no warning, he yanked her to the edge of the couch, pulled her knees apart and tasted her.

He enjoyed the noises she made and the way she writhed under his mouth, until the incoherent sounds became "enough, enough!"

Frowning, Sam looked up into her eyes, only to find her hands grasping at him. With a strength he didn't know she possessed, Rae hauled him to his feet, only to throw him back on the couch. Then she stripped him. When her hot little mouth closed over him, he thought the world just might collapse. And that would be okay.

Rae and Sloan made it to Monday night class at Blessed Be, but they were parked far enough away that they'd be walking in the door at the last minute. They spent the two blocks talking about what they were going to do.

It had been two weeks. Luke supposedly had their information, but hadn't reached out to them. It was Sloan who posed the possibility that Yasmin hadn't even told him. Rae had to admit she'd wondered the same thing.

They'd been around the shop enough for class that they'd heard about Yasmin. She was supposed to be a powerful witch.

"But if she's so powerful," Rae asked, "and she's got an investigator, then why hasn't she reached out to us?"

"I don't understand." Sloan was shaking her head.

"Because if she's investigating us, she'll find out we're decent people. That we're exactly who we say we are. That Mom is from the part of Italy we said and that her sister was Emilia. Either Luke is or isn't that baby. Why the wait?"

Sloan was nodding by the time Rae finished her rant. But there wasn't much she could say as she pulled the door open. As usual, the little bell tinkled as they entered, and also as usual,

Rae could not find the bell. She was looking up as Sloan took her by the arm and dragged her toward the back room. They were going to be late and she didn't even know what tonight's spell was. The door was already closed. Sloan was turning the knob when Rae felt another presence behind her. She turned.

"Yasmin." For a moment, she was hopeful. Then she caught sight of Yasmin's expression. It might have been angry, or just curious, but it wasn't welcoming.

"I need the two of you to come with me."

Rae's heart started pounding. What did this mean?

Yasmin led them around the corner, back into the store then down another hall to several offices. One of the doors had a Y on it. It was open, revealing a very small space. Luckily, she took them across the hall to the door that had a T on it. Yasmin knocked.

In short order, the door was opened by a handsome man with curl in his brown hair. He was the one they'd seen at the dog park when they'd been babysitting Sloan's boss's dog Gruber. "Hi, I'm Tristan."

Hence the T, Rae thought, but before she could get further, Yasmin was admonishing them for something they hadn't even done. "And don't hit on him. He's taken, by a very good friend of mine."

Rae just frowned, getting angrier. She wanted to meet her cousin, but this was looking more like the Spanish inquisition. She didn't add that she'd already seen him with his girlfriend. "No one has hit on anyone," Rae snapped back. She had a shorter fuse than Sloan did, that was for sure. "So you might want to consider removing whatever crawled up your ass."

Tristan started to laugh, and Rae liked him instantly. Yasmin didn't find it anywhere near as funny. Which *was* funny, because Sloan was also horrified. But Rae had enough of this shit. "Look, just tell us that Luke isn't our cousin and we'll go look somewhere else. But stop stringing us along."

Sloan still hadn't said anything, but Rae had crossed her arms and was taking a stand.

Yasmin matched her. "We don't know anything about you except that you showed up here after mysteriously turning up at our wedding."

"That's not true. You know plenty about us." Rae countered. "You've had us investigated."

"How did you know that?" Tristan asked before Yasmin blew a gasket.

Rae froze. *Shit shit shit.* She had not meant to out her sister. She didn't say anything. Sloan stayed frozen. Yasmin was about to start in, but it was Tristan who spoke up. Rae got the feeling that Yasmin had brought them in here to have him mediate and he was going to do the job come hell or high water.

"You did some kind of spell. And you found out Yasmin was having you investigated."

"We didn't do a spell." Rae said. That was true. Maybe she could take the blame.

"You did. I can see it on you." At least he stayed calm while he accused them. "You've gathered a full witch's complement of herbs and altar pieces and you've been casting outside of class."

"We asked you not to." Yasmin pointed out.

Yeah, well, she and her sister had politely declined. What Rae said though, was, "And we asked you to give our message to your husband."

"I did."

"We didn't cast a spell to see that you were having us investigated."

"I know." Yasmin's arms remained crossed, and she was looking at Rae now like she was a specimen. "If you had, I would have seen you looking at me."

Well, shit. She was scarier in her ability than Rae had counted on. She'd expected some double, double, toil and trouble stuff, but not this.

It was Tristan who once again tried to soothe things. "They're powerful witches, Yasmin. They were born with it."

This time Yasmin turned on Tristan. "But powerful doesn't mean decent. I don't know what they want with my husband."

Rae felt that one in her heart, and she didn't like the way it felt. She could feel Sloan's heart breaking, too. They'd just wanted to find him. Not really paying attention to what she was doing, she reached out and touched Yasmin's arm.

Nothing.

No finger up, no sliding feeling down. Yasmin wasn't bad. She wasn't mean. She didn't pose any threat to Sloan or Rae. She pulled her hand back, not sure what to do with the results.

"What did you just do?" Yasmin was pulling her own arm back.

It was Tristan who intervened. He sounded a little awed. "She was testing you."

"I didn't see a spell." Yasmin spoke to Tristan but didn't take her eyes off Rae.

"Because she didn't cast one. She just read you. It's an innate ability. She didn't have to cast. More like Megan than the rest of us." Tristan was looking her up and down, then suddenly he turned to Sloan. "You're even stronger than she is."

Sloan didn't respond. Rae had had enough. Screw class, she wasn't ever coming back. Yasmin didn't want to talk to them and there was nothing she could do to force it. But her heart hurt. And a lot of times when her heart hurt, her mouth opened. "Look, our mother died five years ago. She regretted nothing except that her little sister got sick and died and she didn't even know until a year later. She didn't even know there was a baby until about fifteen years ago."

Rae took a pause, but no one stepped in. She went on. "Our mother was driven out of her home and away from her family to another continent. That's why she didn't get to keep up with her sister. She wasn't a bad sister. From the moment she found out that the baby had been given away, she looked for that baby. She never found her niece or nephew. We've been looking."

She shook her head and fought back the tears that threatened to roll out. Fuck them. "We only wanted to know that the baby is okay. I fully understand that baby is a grown adult, older than me or Sloan. But we promised our mother we'd keep looking. I no longer give a fuck about meeting your Luke. I'd just like to know if that baby grew up okay or if we made a mistake and we should keep looking."

Yasmin still stared at her, but it was different now.

"We don't want your money or even your time. If he's that baby, then his mother was Emilia Tavani. She was eighteen when she had him and she had cancer. She died shortly thereafter and our family story tells us that she willingly gave the baby to a family she knew and loved. That's about all we know. But Emilia was an even stronger witch than our mother was. So he may have . . . skills, talents, innate whatevers—" Rae waved her hand. "Just thought you should know."

Yasmin paused a second and said, "He's that baby. His mother was named Emilia. And he does have skills. They're under his command now. So you don't have to worry." For all her words, Yasmin still wasn't friendly. "He's okay. He grew up fine. But you should know, he has a family. He never came looking for you because he didn't feel the need. He has everything he needs."

Well, shit. It was good and it sucked. She'd said she just wanted to know and now she did. She had to hold to what she said and let it go. "Thank you. We'll just leave."

She was turning to go when Sloan protested. Sloan, who'd said nothing this whole time, suddenly spoke up. "That's good. And I'm glad he grew up well with a family he loves. But you should know, we didn't come because we thought he needed us. Maybe he doesn't need a family, but he's all that we have left."

With that, she turned and walked out the door leaving Rae to follow. She trailed her sister down the street silently. They'd said what they needed to. They'd found him. It wasn't how she wanted it, but she would tell her Mom tonight that they'd done it. Sloan was at her car door before she said anything, but what she said was, "I just want to go home by myself, if that's okay."

Rae nodded and climbed in her car.

CHAPTER 42

S am picked up his phone and smiled at the screen. "Hey, Rae."

"Do you want some company tonight?"

"From you? Always." He'd smiled and puttered around while he waited for her to show up. She didn't take as long as he expected and he threw open the front door to greet her, only to be jumped by a ravenous she-devil who didn't want to speak.

Since the one peeling his clothing without a word was Rae, he didn't protest. She pushed him backward, walking him up the stairs and somehow getting them both undressed in the process. By the time she shoved him back on the bed he was naked and practically on fire, so when she climbed on top of him, settling warm and wet around him, it was all he could do to hold off and not come right then.

Her fingers dug into his shoulders, his into her hips, and he tried, dear God, he tried to hold back. But she was riding him like a bronco and he wasn't sure he was going to be able to get his brains back in his head after she was finished. When he was certain he couldn't hold back any more, he opened his mouth to say so—or say anything in any language, he wasn't sure—she threw her head back, shouted his name and came apart. Sam quickly followed suit.

Long minutes later, he was in his bed, under the covers with Rae curled up beside him. He honestly wasn't quite sure how he'd gotten there, but he had no complaints. Just questions.

"What was that?"

She shrugged. "I just needed you."

He frowned. "Is this something with your sister? I called the line at your apartment when you didn't answer your phone. Sheree said you went out with Sloan every Monday night."

Rae nodded slowly and he was a little surprised when she answered. "Sheree picked up the landline? We only have that for the cable package."

It didn't answer his question. He tried again. "Are you okay?"

"Not really."

"Jesus, Rae!" He was on his elbow, looking down at her with renewed purpose. He checked for bruises, marks, any telltale signs of what had her upset. "You have to tell me—" He tried again. "What happened? I—"

"I don't even know where to start."

"Are you physically okay?" He said it slowly, trying to hide his fear, his anger at whoever had upset her, and if someone had actually hurt her, he didn't think anything would stop him.

She nodded. "Physically I'm fine." She stopped and took several breaths and he held his tongue, hopeful that if he waited, she'd tell him. "So, my mother had a sister . . ."

It was not the beginning he'd been expecting. Not as ominous or scary. So he pulled her in close, loving the weight of her there, scared that something had happened and he didn't know what it was.

She told him about her Aunt Emilia. About a baby she'd given away, a baby that would be Rae's cousin. She told him about seeing the pictures of Luke and then running into them here. "Is it weird, running into them?"

"I don't think so. It's Los Angeles. I've run into people from my hometown in Georgia, just walking down the street. Breathless is *not* that big. But LA is. If you came from another country, chances are pretty high you'd wind up in New York or Los Angeles. So it's no surprise that your Mom did and that he did."

Rae nodded and he wondered if that was good enough. It was a hell of a coincidence, but they did happen. "So, did you find out if it was him?"

"It was. It is. But he loves his family that he grew up with. He doesn't want anything to do with us."

"He told you this?" How could someone—

"His wife did." Rae rolled over. "I told her that we didn't want their money or anything from them. We just wanted to know that my aunt's baby grew up okay. And now we know. So I guess I got what I wanted, right?"

Sam understood. It was heartbreak, and an unexpected one. "Only as soon as you got it, you realized it wasn't all that you wanted."

She nodded. "Sloan and I are all that's left of my family. Except him. But what can I do?"

"You can have my family." He kissed her hair since she wasn't looking at him. "Christy is always foisting babysitting onto me. My dad tells the absolute worst dad jokes ever and he genuinely believes he's very funny. My mother can move mountains at her will. Just pray you always want the mountain moved."

"You speak from experience?" Rae rolled over to look at him, a small smile perched on her lips.

He nodded. "You know, I've never met Sloan. Can I tag along one Monday night?"

"No." Her answer was fast, and not what he'd hoped.

"Oh, are you doing sister things?" He tried not to be upset. He had no right to be upset, he knew it. But it still bugged him a bit.

"We go to a class. Or at least we did." She rolled away again.

"Well, maybe I can meet her some other time then." He watched the subtle movements of Rae's head as she nodded, but she didn't speak. His hand reached up and stroked her hair. She felt bad, he understood. She'd thought she might be finding her only remaining family and she'd been shut down. Maybe he could just keep her talking. "What kind of class were you taking?"

She shrugged.

It was odd. Why wouldn't she say? He started guessing. "Knitting? Scrapbooking?" She shook her head at each guess. "Welding? . . . Dog training?"

"I don't have a dog. You won't guess it."

"Then tell me. Why not? I won't judge." He was beyond curious, if only because she didn't want to say. It took a moment before she rolled away and looked at him. She seemed to be assessing something. But finally, she said.

"Witchcraft."

He blinked. No, he would never have guessed that. He tried not to frown.

She spoke again before he could comment. "We are in the beginner's class. Luke's wife works at the shop. We do baby spells."

"Oh, so you were just going to see the wife and get to know his family." That made more sense.

But Rae looked away.

"Are you a witch?" He was not ready to process that. His brain roiled. Was she casting spells on him? Did she have a . . . cauldron? He didn't even know what it meant. Only that it was wrong.

"God, no. I don't even begin to qualify." She was moving farther away from him though. "We did a *Big Wish* spell and we missed the class on *Parking Karma*, so I still can't get good parking spots."

"What? There's a spell for parking?"

"Apparently. Not that I know how to do it." She shrugged, but it was halfway, still tentative in her assessment of him.

He wanted to both change that and pull her close, but he was also concerned about this sudden revelation. "What's the *Big Wish* thing?"

Another small shrug. "Something you want to happen."

"Like, on people? Do you try to make other people do your bidding?"

"Jesus, Sam, no." She was shaking her head at him and he could tell he'd handled this all wrong. "It's Wicca. It's a whole religion if you want to get into it. And the first rule is you can't harm anyone. It's not okay to bend people to your will. In fact, they make you sign a contract that says you won't do the spells on people. Just for things to happen." She looked away. "It doesn't even matter. I did my spell, then I freaked out and undid it."

It was starting to sink in. "You went to meet up with Luke's family, and they're into this? It's their store?"

"More or less."

He physically felt the relief as it hit him. "You won't be going back? Now that you know he's not interested in getting to know you and your sister."

"I don't see why we would." She didn't look happy and he could understand that.

He rolled off the bed to a standing position, suddenly feeling restless even though he couldn't pinpoint why. Running his hand over his head he thought for a moment, then held it out to her. "I need something to eat. Come downstairs with me?"

He didn't want to leave her alone. She needed company, and he needed to figure out how to give it to her. Rae didn't take his hand, but she nodded and pulled on her shirt and underwear while he did the same. He sighed and the words tumbled out of his mouth, whether they were helpful or not, he couldn't tell.

"Honestly, Rae, if that's what they're involved in, maybe it's better that you aren't getting mixed up with them."

She just nodded solemnly and Sam grabbed her hand and pulled her downstairs while he tried to think of ways to make her less sad.

~

It had been a week since she'd gotten the email from Yasmin, but they'd already missed two Monday night classes. To her, it would feel weird to go back. Rae sat at a booth at Chili's with Sloan as they ate basket after basket of chips. Sloan must be as depressed as she was.

Sloan had something to say about that email. "You know the tone of it was so hard to read. I mean, we can come back to class, it's okay."

"I couldn't tell if she was trying to be nice or get our money." Rae dunked another chip in one of the several dips they had ordered. There was no need for actual foods or for trying to figure out how many calories this "dinner" involved. She was drinking beer, too. She'd have to quit after this. "And what was that bit about 'Luke is a DEA agent.' I didn't get that."

Sloan shook her head. "I think she was just trying to offer an explanation for why he doesn't want to see us. Like he sees the bad in people so much that he . . . I don't know. Assumes we're bad, too. Do you want to go back to class?"

Sloan looked at her watch as though they might actually make it tonight. It wouldn't happen. They wouldn't make it with traffic and both of them were on their second beer. "No, I don't think so."

What would be the point?

They lapsed back into silence, eating chips and just being with each other. Rae broke it. "I wish we could tell Mom. I mean we did find him and he grew up well and loved. And he seems to be married to the love of his life, so that's all good."

"Yeah. That would be nice." Sloan lapsed only for a second. "Okay, we're moving to a better topic. There's talk of transferring me to a different division in the company."

"That's fantastic. I mean I hope it is," Rae offered around a chip heavy with salsa and ranch.

"I don't even know. It's just different. I can't meet any men at work, as that would be wrong. Maybe it will be a good change. I'm just so bored where I am. If I get it, I'll get to travel more."

Rae nodded, understanding. She and Sloan had polar opposite lives sometimes. Rae was fascinated by her work, doing a lot of exactly what she loved. And sometimes she only had money for Ramen Noodles. Sloan on the other hand was easily bored at her job, but not bored enough to leave behind the steady paycheck.

"Well, here's hoping it goes well." She held up her beer and they clinked the bottles. "So, how's your dating situation?"

"Oh please. Let's not even start on that. My favorite men in my life are Ricky and Rob and they're married to each other." She sighed. "But they are excellent neighbors. Tell me more about Sam. I have to meet him."

"You do. He asked to meet you."

"Is he good in bed?" Sloan blinked. "Okay, gotta stop the beers, can't believe I asked that. I'm just living vicariously through you."

"Amazing," Rae replied. "The sex is through the roof."

"Is he just for fun? Is that why I haven't met him yet?"

"Oh no. He's definitely the long-term kind." Rae smiled just thinking about it. About Sam. "It's just . . . me. Lately, I've been nervous about the show. It's only a week away now. On top of it, I'm totally depressed about this Luke thing. I wanted it to be a big family reunion. And we *said* all we wanted was to know he was safe and grew up well. So I just don't feel like I can push. But we lost that before we ever had it."

"I get that. What's the 'but'?" When Rae didn't respond right away, Sloan tried again. "It sounds like there's a 'but' in there. Something about Sam?"

Rae nodded, admitting it to herself for the first time. And that hurt. That was the problem with new relationships. They were new. You learned new things about the other person. You could find things out that tore you apart. And there was nothing you could do about it. She confessed what was bothering her to Sloan. "He said maybe it was a good thing that Luke didn't want to get to know us."

"*What?*" Despite the beer, Sloan's reaction was swift and almost violent. "Where does he get off—"

"No! Not like that," Rae interrupted, holding her hands out as though the gesture could ward off her sister's negative thoughts. "It was because they own a witchcraft store. He was raised in this small town in Georgia and I didn't realized they had opinions about that, but it turns out he does."

"About doing a class?"

Rae thought for a minute. She didn't want to betray Sam, which was a new feeling for her. It had been the same way when they started dating and she didn't want to share him. Something about Sam made her want to protect what they had. But she also had to tell Sloan. "He was really put off that we were doing spells. He didn't say that exactly, but it was on his face. So he thought it was a good thing that we wouldn't be doing them anymore."

"But we are," Sloan countered. "We've just been doing them at my house. And with no guidance, I might add."

Rae loved that Sloan had bought the book online so as not to be influenced by the culture of the store, but now wanted a guiding hand. "I didn't tell him that part."

"That's not good, Rae."

"What am I supposed to say? By the way, my sister and I think we might be actual witches. So we've been practicing at her coffee table. Oh, and come over for dinner at her house. She's dying to meet you. I should say that?" He'd already expressed his displeasure with her doing simple spells for parking. She'd not mentioned the scrying on purpose.

Sloan was opening her mouth to say something, but her phone rang. She pulled it out of her purse. "Well, speaking of devils. It's Yasmin."

Rae perked up, but she couldn't hear anything. She traded sides and closed ranks with her sister. Sloan held the phone up so they could both hear. She'd clearly missed the opening salvo.

Yasmin was speaking. "—changed his mind. Maybe you could bring your dog and meet us at the dog park tomorrow night? Just for a little while. Just to say hi."

"We don't have a dog," Sloan put out there. It was the truth, but Rae thought it was a little creepy.

"Why would you stalk us at the dog park? We have cats." Yasmin's tone turned cold and with all the beer in her system— two was plenty for her—Rae could think a little more clearly. Yasmin had good reason not to trust them. Rae had turned up at her wedding, then in the lingerie store, then they'd run into Tristan and Megan. It was reasonable to think Rae was a stalker. Sloan was explaining.

"We were dog sitting. We should meet somewhere else if none of us actually has a dog."

Rae almost laughed, she could hear the wry tone in Sloan's voice and that wasn't like her sister.

"There's a park down by the Hollywood Rec Center. Want to meet there?"

They set up a chance to meet. Luke had changed his mind!

Rae's heart soared. Then it stumbled a bit. What would Sam think?

CHAPTER 43

Rae sat at the picnic table at the Hollywood Rec Center. She twined her fingers together nervously, wondering if Yasmin and Luke were going to show up. Next to her, Sloan tapped her leg against the seat, looking even more nervous than Rae did. They looked around, watching as other people went by, taking kids and families into the Rec Center, but they didn't see their cousin and his wife. Not yet.

Sloan leaned closer. "Do you think they're going to show?"

"I do," Rae answered. Yasmin had called them. Yasmin had set this up. Surely, they wouldn't back out now. And she was too excited. This is what she had wanted. She wanted to meet her cousin. She wanted to meet the man that Aunt Amelia's baby had become.

So when she spotted a car pull into the parking lot, she almost stood up. Sure enough, Yasmin and Luke stepped out on opposite sides and began looking around. Luke was easy to spot in his teal colored shirt and purple tie. Once they saw Sloan and Rae, they walked toward them, a bit of hesitancy in their steps. Rae could understand. Still, she stood, wiped her hands on her pants, and tried not to look as nervous as she felt. Surely, they all were, right?

As Luke approached, she held out her hand like a stiff fool and said, "Hi. I'm Rae. And this is Sloan. And, well, I've seen you a few times before, but I've never spoken to you. I'm really glad you changed your mind."

Luke looked back and forth between the two sisters, maybe as if he was looking for resemblances to his own face. Still, he held out his hand genially and answered, "I'm sorry. I should have said 'yes' sooner." He paused, looking at his wife Yasmin and then back at Sloan and Rae. And for a moment, all four stood there awkwardly looking at each other. Then Sloan suggested they sit, and just start asking each other questions.

So they settled on opposite sides of the table almost as though they were at a debate or some formal legal setting. But Luke apologized again, "Look," he said, "I work for the DEA. I see people constantly screwing over the other people in their lives. Even family members. So when someone came looking for me and when they kept showing up, I assumed the worst."

"I understand" Rae answered. Next to her, Sloan nodded her head, and they let that sit.

It took a moment, but Sloan was the first to ask a question, though it wasn't a question really. "Tell me about your parents. Were they good people? Were you happy growing up? I know those are things my mother really wanted to know." And once again Rae found herself wishing that she could tell her mother that they'd found him, that they'd found Aunt Amelia's baby.

It only took Luke a heartbeat to start answering. "Yes. My mom and Dad took me the moment I was born. I am the youngest of seven siblings, all of whom are dark-haired, dark skin southern Italian, chefs, cooks, you name it. But we are a big loud boisterous family and I'm pretty obviously adopted. Still, I never felt adopted. So when more family came looking, I had a moment of thinking, I didn't need more family."

Rae nodded at him. She understood. Or she wanted to. With only her and Sloan left, it was her head that followed his logic. Not her heart.

For nearly 15 minutes, they grilled Luke about his brothers and sisters, about moving from Italy, about settling in Los Angeles, even about meeting Yasmin. While they talked, Yasmin jumped in periodically. She told part of the story about how she and Luke got together. She told them of a shooting and some surprising witchcraft. But she told the story without arrogance or exaggeration. Rae found herself beginning to like her a little bit more.

It became clearer as they spoke that Yasmin had merely been protecting her husband. She was the wife of a DEA agent. She understood what he saw and how he reacted when people came out of nowhere. But now, as they spoke, she seemed a little warmer, a little more welcoming, a little more understanding, and a little less standoffish.

At that point, though Rae hadn't expected it, Yasmin and Luke turned the tables on them. They began questioning Rae and Sloan about their lives and for the first time Rae found herself speaking openly about her mother, about how she was run out of town for having told some of the townspeople the things she knew. That she'd met and married an American man and wound up in Los Angeles, how Sloan's father had died, then their mother met Mr. Woodward and they'd had Rae but Rae and Sloan had always been full sisters in their hearts.

By the time they'd spoken for almost an hour, the sun was setting and the weather was turning cooler and it was time to wrap things up. Though Rae would have liked to have invited them out for a drink, it seemed maybe it was a good time to let the first meeting pass peacefully and not let it possibly run into trouble.

As they said their goodbyes, Yasmin made sure to extend an invitation for them to return to class.

Though she smiled, Rae was beginning to think better of it. She replied, "That's very nice of you, but it may be better not to mix business into this. We'll think about it."

Yasmin nodded as though she understood and then pointed out that they wouldn't be charged for future classes. "It's not business anymore. There's no fee for family."

~

Rae was a wreck. She'd touched up her makeup about five times. Then she decided to change her dress. Why she decided to change out of the dress she'd specifically bought for the gallery opening, she couldn't have said. Next, she decided that since she had chosen this dress when she was sane that she shouldn't re-decide now. Logically, she understood that was the best decision, but what she really wanted was to just sit down and scream for a minute.

That would be impossible, Rae thought to herself, because Sam was coming to pick her up, since they'd both decided she'd be too nervous to drive. Before she could blink, he was leading her by the arm through the front doors of the Webber Gallery. Where she was to spend the evening being gracious and telling people about her pieces. And not consuming too much wine, she thought as Mr. Webber himself welcomed her and handed her a glass.

Sam was warm and calm and happy—all the things she was supposed to be but was too nervous to muster up. Taking advantage of the space before the doors opened to the invited guests, he walked her around the gallery and got them introduced to three of the other artists. The fifth had begged off with a family emergency. *Yeah, like a case of stomach upset. I should have thought of that.*

Busy thinking to herself, she almost forgot to put her hand out and meet Alexander Reno, and then Thomas Cole.

That startled her, "Thomas Cole?" She looked the man up and down, taking in his brown hair and warm green eyes.

Sam leaned in between them, appearing almost nervous. Rae suppressed a smile of satisfaction at seeing him nervous. It made her own nerves seem less abnormal. By his voice he was clearly surprised. "You two know each other?"

"No," Rae shook her head. "Thomas Cole was a famous Hudson River School painter."The other photographer nodded. "No relation, strictly coincidental."

"It doesn't hurt though, does it?"

"No, I'll take any help I can get."

Rae laughed, glad that she wasn't the only artist with a little case of nerves at her first show. Not the only one who would have to scrounge her way up. She glanced back to Alexander Reno, taking in the purple leather jacket and slim, deep gray pants with creases. He was a study in contradiction. He'd probably planned it that way, all the way down to the bright yellow ponytail band that held his long bleached-blonde biker locks back from his face.

Her own slightly flirty little black dress wouldn't make her stand out from the crowd in any way, she suspected. And that was exactly why she had chosen it. She wasn't one for splashy outfits in her everyday life, why start now? In fact, a bit of shyness probably had everything to do with choosing photography as her medium.

She felt a slight shiver run up her spine. A physical manifestation of her nervousness she was sure. Until she heard the voices behind her. No, it had been an actual gust of cold air as the door had opened, letting in the first invited guests to the opening. After tonight, the gallery would be open to the public. But for the opening they had gathered up all the local elite as well as anyone who had bought from the Webber before. Rae felt she was in good hands, but still, the physical shiver due to nervousness followed close on the heels of the other.

It seemed that she blinked and the gallery was full. There was a cocktail party in full swing in the atmosphere. None of these guests were the quiet, subdued gallery goers seen in films. They talked and exclaimed and oohhhhed, and even occasionally made faces of distaste or argued. She wondered again if she and Sloan had managed to undo her *Big Wish* spell. This sure was a huge crowd. Had she been responsible for it? Surely not. That would be assuming her original spell had worked as intended and in a big way. She wasn't in Yasmin's league. So it couldn't be.

Sam's hand ran down her back and it occurred to her that she'd invited Luke and Yasmin to the opening, but hadn't told Sam. But before she had realized what had happened, she had been pulled from Sam's side and was answering questions about her work. The question *How was she inspired?* led to the telling of the makeup series, and watching Sheree put on all her products one morning, and all the contortions she had made.

Time flew by, with one question after another coming at her, and Sam appearing occasionally to replace the wineglass in her hand. Finally, with water. A genuine smile grew wide across her face until a tall gentleman clad in an entirely black suit turned to her, his mouth flat and dour. He didn't look at all pleased. "This has an entirely familiar feel. Where would I have seen it before?"

It was all she could do to not choke on the ice water she was sipping. How did you respond to that? At my high school art show? As the evening had worn on she had come to realize that the other artists were new to the area, but she was the only one in her *first ever* show. Rae didn't know how to answer the man. She didn't want to give away that she was such a novice.

He leaned in closer, his breath near her, and she backed up until she ran into the solid wall of Sam's chest. Thank God he had been standing silently behind her all night. Right now, she appreciated his physical and moral support more than ever as she tried not to shrink from the questions the man in black was pressing her with.

"It has a feel like I've seen it before, is it a copy of another artist's style?" He waved his hand.

At least Rae was beginning to get the impression that he was merely untactful and not downright trying to be rude. But to insinuate that she was purposefully copying some other artist's style was about to make her explode.

Another Brock rode in to her rescue before she had to tell the rude man that he couldn't possibly have seen her work before, and force her to confess that it hadn't been anywhere. Mrs. Brock touched the man's arm making him turn to her just to be polite. "You've seen her work before Frank. Think where else you've commented on such a marvelous eye for composition. . ."

He squinted at her. But Mrs. Brock just smiled at him, and Rae watched the exchange, praying that one day she possessed such social graces as to turn an old stodge to a friendly guest with a few sentences.

But the man just squinted until Mrs. Brock sighed. "The New York scape that was in my home. You tried to buy it off me." She smiled around the side of his hulk at Rae. "It was Miss Woodward's piece."

"I thought that was a male artist."

Mrs. Brock shrugged, and Rae had to stifle a laugh, knowing that Mrs. Brock had made the same mistake herself. Then her laughter stopped. The old coot had tried to haggle Mrs. Brock out of her artwork? *Wow.*

She felt Sam's mouth near her ear and reveled in the feel of his breath as he whispered to her. "See, I told you you were good."

The man in black didn't say anything to her, just turned and stared intently at walls, scrutinizing each grain of each photo. He made Rae nervous, but just as she was starting to flutter a little, she heard Sam's voice, and felt him move away from her. *Not now, when she needed him here.*

Then her head turned at the familiar sounds she loved. Sheree, making loud comments on the wine. She saw Jack and Lisa wandering off and talking over each other. And Alex, giving an art gallery level 'hello' to Sam. Soon they were all converged around her, praising her work, and commenting how they hadn't seen her for nearly a week. Sheree was starting to say what a pain in the ass she had been, until Rae silenced her with a look.

That was the last thing she needed. The entire crowd at her first opening knowing that she had cried in frustration three times this week. That she had made her boyfriend help her finish her framing, that she was such a novice at all this. Not like she wouldn't blow her own cover. She wasn't sure when, just sure that she wouldn't get through this night without everyone knowing she was a fraud.

She was trying to keep it together when she felt that touch on the back of her brain. She looked up toward the doorway again and spotted Luke and Yasmin coming in the door. Yasmin wore a black dress and Luke looked bright on her arm in a peach colored shirt with a yellow tie. Her heart leapt at the idea that her new family had made the time to come see her art. It shouldn't matter if they even liked it or not, but she found her nerves sinking back in.

Just as she was getting ready to head toward the door to say hi, she was touched on the arm. One of Mr. Webber's assistants, who was extremely tall and intimidating for an assistant, asked her to step aside. A brief panic flared deep in her belly. They were going to throw her out. Her and her art, sitting in a puddle in the back alley, she could see it now.

Surely that wasn't what it was about. So she followed Miss Prim as the woman scooted her glasses back up her nose and walked Rae up to the man in black. "Mister Lundberg here would like to know if he can make you an offer for a particular piece of work."

Her eyebrows raised of their own accord. The man who'd tried to beg her work off Mrs. Brock wanted to barter with her now? "Everything is already tagged and the tags stand." She wasn't coming down. Maybe later, but as she swept her eyes around the corner of the gallery where her work was displayed the throng of people revealed that there were already at least three small red "SOLD" tags on her pieces. Her heart did a little flip flop.

Miss Prim didn't notice her discovery and she continued. "There is a piece not tagged. Mr. Lundberg would like it."

Rae's brows narrowed together. A piece not tagged?

The assistant looked down at a small notecard she had been clutching. "Yes, A Cold Day in July."

It took Rae a moment to recognize that it wasn't a phrase, but the title of a piece. The piece of Sam standing in his jacket by his car, laughing and happy in the oddly chill LA air that day. It was an old piece, and she had titled it that, thinking that he seemed so happy and content and that she thought she might never find that with someone. She had even forgotten that she had given it that title, her print had hung in the back of the darkroom for so long. She'd had to flip it over to look for a take date, and found the phrase, when she reprinted it for the show.

She shook her head. "It's not for sale. That's why it's not tagged."

"I thought everything in the show was for sale."

"Not everything." She couldn't sell Sam. Although it wasn't like she couldn't just print another one. But it was her dream, and it had turned out to be that she was finding it with the man in the photo. She glanced over to find him watching her, before he turned back to pay attention to Sheree.

"I am prepared to make you a very nice offer."

"I'm sorry." Her hand fluttered to her collarbone, unsure if it was a wise decision to antagonize anyone at her very first ever showing. But she couldn't sell Sam. And she couldn't bring herself to think of the sale of the photo in any other terms.

He held his hand out, palm up. A business card tucked neatly between his first and middle fingers. "Call me at the office this week. We'll talk."

She didn't take the card. "I don't want to sell that piece."

He shook his head in disdain. "Clearly." But it was the first time he had looked like anything other than an angry curmudgeon. "Call me."

This time she took the card.

CHAPTER 44

As he woke, Sam felt his heart do little flip-flops in his chest. Rae had been exhausted last night, and had barely made it out of her dress, before passing out across the bed. He had to wake her back up to make her put one of his button-down shirts on. It would have been a long hard night with her next to him, blissfully asleep in nothing but her underwear while he was awake having a . . . well, a long hard night.

Sam had gotten some sleep after a while, curled around her and had woken up entangled. He'd carefully extracted himself just to get to where he could lie here and look at her. Rachel had held her own last night. She had been a nervous wreck in the car, leaving him worried she was going to vomit, she was that anxious. But she held it together. Then she'd lifted her chin and walked into that gallery like she owned it.

A few times she had shot him a look. A look where she clearly was saying *I'm so out of my league, get me out of here.* But it didn't show to anyone else.

They hadn't made love, but that was all right. The very fact that she was here was enough. It said what she thought of him and them that she wanted to be here just to sleep. It was far more than he had expected just a few weeks ago. Sam sighed and ran his fingers along the soft skin of her arm, up to her pulse at her wrist, but she didn't move. He wanted to wake her up this morning in a rain of passionate kisses. He wanted to tell her how proud he was of her. How much it meant that he was the one on her arm the night before. He wanted to tell her . . .

But she wasn't having it. She was sleeping, unaware. Maybe he shouldn't have handed her so many glasses of wine last night. If he hadn't stopped when he did, they might be in the ER treating her for alcohol poisoning right now. She would have just kept drinking whatever he handed her. Thank god he was paying attention.

Sam didn't think that she knew he had come up behind her when the man in the black suit was bothering her. Rae had cringed, just a touch, when he spoke. And the man had no tact whatsoever. He had been just about ready to play angry boyfriend and place a solid hand on the man's arm and tell him to stop bothering his lady . . . well, not in *those exact words*.

He had been coming up behind her, when the argument, if it could even be called that, had reached his ears. Then he had put it together. She wasn't selling the picture of him. Wouldn't even run off an extra print to sell. Almost, he had stepped in and said "Sell it, Rachel, he's offering you good money." But then the bricks had hit, crashing down around him.

She wouldn't sell the picture of him. She was hawking the people on the street. She was hawking her series, his mother, Lisa, Sheree. Other photos of them, one of Lincoln. One of Liam, taking a photo of another person. All brilliant, all with an eye into her world, but not the one of him.

After she bumped into him, then found her spine and stood up on her own, he turned and walked away. He had the feeling that he was finally holding all the puzzle pieces, if he could just see how they fit together. Sam knew that he was missing something stupid. That everything fit, he just didn't see it. It had something to do with their fight the first Friday night, and her not wanting their friends to know . . .

He'd wandered off to the men's room. Looking in the mirror, it was the reflection of his own face that triggered it. When he wondered what the hell she saw when she looked at him. And he found it.

He was in love with her. He felt all the puzzle pieces shift inside him into one cohesive picture. With it came the realization that he would do anything, *literally anything*, for her. He almost laughed at his reflection. All the times he had thought he was in love. In high school, once in college. Then he wised up. He'd decided to go with the *you just know it when it happens* theory that anyone who had ever been in love had told him. And he had given up on finding it. But right then he had known.

And, under the "do anything for her" clause, he didn't want to tell her last night. It was her night, she was nervous, and she didn't need him declaring undying love in the middle of it. Besides, it was for him that he would say it. Not for her. She would get every last drop he had to give, whether or not she knew why. But he was bursting at the seams.

So he lay here beside her this morning, still bursting, and having her not able to listen. Instead, he said it softly. "I love you, Rachel."

She didn't move. But he liked the way it rolled off his tongue. The way it settled even just a little deeper in him with the words said. When she woke up, he would tell her. And so he watched, patiently. She needed the sleep.

Maybe he dozed a little. Maybe he really did just stare at her for over an hour. At last, Rae's eyelids fluttered. And he was waiting, ready to tell her. "Good morning, Sunshine."

Her lips curved into a sensuous smile, a cat with cream. "I'm still alive? They didn't eat me?"

The laugh was his own. "Nope, Sugar, you sold quite a few

pieces last night. No one could have taken a bite out of you if they had tried. Believe me, they didn't dare."

"I was soooo nervous." Her arms snaked over her head and he felt her stretching long from fingertips to toes.

Tracing her nose, then her lips, he replied. "I only know because you kept telling me. No one else had a clue."

"Really?" The stretch had ended and she slipped one arm over his shoulder.

The feeling settled a little deeper. This was where he belonged. "Really. I want to tell you something."

"Tell me later." She rolled over on top of him and he lost all coherent thought.

Rae pulled up in front of Blessed Be noting, with a touch of irony, that one of the cars in one of the prime spots right in front of the store was just now pulling out. Of course, she would get primo parking the first time Yasmin offered her a chance to park in the back with the staff. Luke was running late. While she, Sloan, Luke, and Yasmin had met up for dinner once before this was only going to be the second time that the whole family had gone out to spend the evening together. But with Luke running behind, Yasmin had offered them a chance to meet up at the store first. Since Sloan was caught in traffic, this meant Rae and Yasmin were the first two there which made Rae a little bit nervous. She and Yasmin hadn't had the best start. She'd looked a little bit like a stalker from the beginning she could admit.

Following Yasmin's directions, she pulled around behind the store and found a clear spot. Turning off the engine, she wiped her hands down her jeans to remove some of the sweat from her palms. One of these days she was going to have to get to a point where she could meet her new family without being nervous. Deciding not to let the emotion rule her anymore, she opened the door and followed the instructions through the back door of Blessed Be.

The shop looked a little different from this angle. There were extra offices and storage space back here that she hadn't been aware of before. But she easily found her way in and found Yasmin's office clearly marked by the big Y on the door and knocked. This time, like the last couple times, Yasmin's reaction to her was wholly different. Her new cousin-in-law had apologized several times and Rae had forgiven her for everything that Yasmin had doubted in the past. She understood, but this time it was Yasmin who led the way.

"Hey Rae," she said as she jumped up and offered a hug—another surprise. "It looks like Luke's going to be another 15 minutes so make yourself at home and let me know if there's anything I can do for you while we wait." Rae found herself wandering into the classroom. She hadn't been here for several weeks despite Yasmin's invitation for them to come back to class. She figured maybe now was the right time and she began looking at the board to see what kind of spells would be offered for the next week. She figured she still needed to catch up on the *Parking Karma* class. As she was checking the list, she was surprised to see Yasmin come up behind her.

"We can rearrange it if there's something you want. You know, not something that's too soon since the last time we taught it, but let us know and we'll see what we can do," she offered. It seemed once Yasmin had come around to accepting them, as Luke had accepted them, that they weren't after anything other than just meeting their family she'd opened up quite considerably.

Rae offered a wry grin, "I have to admit the one spell I really want to know how to do is the *Parking Karma* one."

Yasmin looked at the board, "Ooh, it's going to be a little

while before we can repeat that one, but as soon as we get the option I'll make sure that it's on a night that you can make it."

Rae turned and looked at the other woman, "Thank you," she said, hoping her deep level of sincerity was apparent in her voice, "It means a lot to me that you and Luke have decided to accept us and to make a place for us in your lives."

This time Yasmin didn't apologize. This time she said, "When Luke and I sat down and really talked about it, we realized you two had spent over a decade looking for him and it was the least we could do to offer you a chance to find the family that you'd been wanting. And you know what? It's always good to have extra family."

Rae agreed. Then she decided since she had a little extra time, she'd ask Yasmin for some help. "Hey Yasmin, do you remember that *Big Wish* spell that we did?"

"Of course."

"Well, I was wondering . . ." she wasn't sure how to broach this. She'd been doing witchcraft beyond the shop's walls, which was something they had asked specifically that the practitioners not do.

This time it was Yasmin who said, "Look, I know you guys countered your *Big Wish*."

Rae was surprised. Then again, why should she be? Yasmin was a witch. Yasmin was teaching people how to do spells. So at what point would it be a shock that Yasmin knew something? "Yes," Rae replied, "that's right. Sloan and I tried to do an *Undo* on it, but I was never sure that it worked."

Yasmin nodded, "It did."

Frowning, Rae asked, "How could you tell? My *Big Wish* was to have everybody show up at my gallery opening. It was to have the whole place packed. Since it was, how can I be sure my *Undo* worked?"

Yasmin motioned for Rae to come over to the back of the classroom. The wall was covered with post-it notes signed by the classroom participants. Rae had even signed several herself.

Yasmin pointed, "This is why we have you sign your name along with your spell and put it on the wall at the end of each class. Remember how you're not allowed to use your own pen?" Rae nodded. She'd found that a little odd at the time. Now she was thinking she should've looked at that a little more closely.

"Well," Yasmin continued, "there's a certain ink that we use. We track you guys. We keep tabs on all of our beginners. We really feel that it's our responsibility to make sure that we put this information—'power' if you want to call it that—into the right hands and that we're careful to keep it out of the wrong ones. It's not our place to make a decision for whoever shows up to class, but it is our place to monitor. And if we think something's going wrong, to step in. So this is how we monitor." She gestured to the wall behind her and all the post-it notes that were up there. She found a spot and started looking and then pointed. "See? Here's your note for the *Big Wish*."

Rae looked at it. "How can you tell? That one's blank."

"Look, it's right next to Sloan's. Remember?"

Rae blinked suddenly. She had signed that paper in the blue ink with the pen they had handed her, so why was it now blank? Yasmin smiled and shrugged, "It disappeared. It does that. Well, it will fade if you try to erase your spell. It disappears if you're successful."

Rae looked at it for a moment wondering if maybe the post-it notes had been traded out. Sensing her skepticism, Yasmin motioned her forward and suggested Rae put her fingers onto the note where she could feel the impression and see the faint shadows from where her signature had once been in a nice bold blue.

"Wow," Rae said, "I really did it. Everybody who showed up at the gallery opening was there because they were really there."

"Yes," Yasmin replied, "you're really that good of an artist and the Webber Gallery is really that good at packing their floor on opening nights. It's not the first time Luke and I have been, but have to admit I wish we could afford more of the art in there." Yasmin seemed amused that Rae was more concerned with the fact that the people at her gallery had been there to actually see her artwork than with the fact that the shop was keeping tabs on their beginner witches or that they had a spell that could show exactly when any witch had undone their own spells.

Still, Yasmin was content it seemed to let her go on for a few minutes about her pride at actually having completed a spell appropriately and having packed the gallery. Then Yasmin turned and said, "Come here. Take a look at this one. It's from several weeks earlier."

Following her over, Rae looked as Yasmin traced some more of the post-it notes looking for something in particular. Once again, Rae's and Sloan's post-it notes from the scrying class were up in positions side by side with each other. Rae could read both pieces of handwriting pretty clearly. "Those are still there."

"Right," Yasmin said, "you both passed scrying class. Nothing has happened to your scrying abilities. However, take a look at Sloan's."

Rae looked, noting that Sloan's ink was now darker than most of the other ink around it. In fact, several of the inks for the scrying class had gotten darker than the average or maybe hers was lighter. She asked Yasmin about it.

"Well, with the scrying class it's not about enhancing or undoing the spell, it's more about practice. So you can see as your ink is only slightly faded your ability remains, but you haven't done much to practice with it. And if you look at the other signatures from your class you can see a few of them have gotten darker so we know which witches are practicing and which ones have basically gone home and left this as a Monday night hobby as well."

"Oh wow," Rae said, "that's really cool."

"Yeah, but here's where it gets amazing. Take a look at Sloan's." Rae looked again. Though some of the other classmates' inks had darkened a little bit Sloan's was nearly black.

"Wow," Rae said, "I didn't know that she's been scrying that much."

Yasmin almost laughed. "That's the interesting thing. I don't think she has been."

"Then why is the ink black?" asked Rae.

"It went black almost the first night."

"What? Rae asked. "So she just went home and scryed on everything? Would that be enough to make the ink get that dark?"

"That's just it," Yasmin said, "I don't think it is. I think what the ink identified here was a natural ability."

"Oh," Rae said, but she didn't say more. It wasn't her place to out Sloan's skills.

The pause between them was a little bit unnatural and Yasmin let it sit for moment before she said, "Look, I don't know what you and Sloan can do, but I know you can do something. I know you came here and I know you cast spells that worked on the first try. That's not very common. Generally, it takes a natural witch with a little bit of inherent ability at least to get something like even our beginner spells to fly on the first try. Then you went home and you managed to undo a *Big Wish*. Who did you ask? Did you pay somebody, or did you guys do that yourselves?"

That was something Rae was willing to confess to. "Well, Sloan bought a book off the internet. She's Sloan, so she probably did a lot of research before picking this particular book, but we looked through it and she's gotten herself a miniature witch's apothecary, so we had everything we needed. We just sat down in her living room at her coffee table and undid my *Big Wish*. Or at least we tried. I guess we succeeded.

SAVANNAH KADE

That's news to me though. Honestly, we were just following the recipe from the book."

"Exactly," Yasmin said, "Almost nobody can do that with the kind of success you guys had right off the bat. You don't have to tell us what your other skills are. Or if you want, you can tell us when you feel like it, but we've had our eye on you since the first day you walked in. Given the fact that you had been showing up wherever Luke and I were, it was a little disconcerting to see someone with that kind of skill, that we didn't even know what it was, keep turning up different places."

"Oh," Rae caught on for the first time. She hadn't even considered the possibility that she might look like a threat. It wasn't just that she was stalking Yasmin and Luke, it's that they saw skill where Rae and Sloan had always seen oddity.

It was a surprising conversation as she and Sloan had been raised never to speak of it with anyone outside of the family. So while she and Sloan talked freely about things they saw, things they felt, why they'd made certain decisions based on it, they'd never even mentioned it to anyone. In fact, Rae's little foray into the topic with Sam was as close as she'd ever come to speaking about anything that she felt with anyone outside her family. These days, that meant everyone beyond Sloan. Although, apparently it was starting to include Yasmin and Luke.

Yasmin must've decided that Rae and Sloan had become trustworthy. And she must've decided that Rae might be more willing to talk about herself if Yasmin opened the conversation. "I'm a naturally powerful witch. Although I don't have anything in particular that I seem to have as a skill. I'm just good. I cast spells and they work. Like you, my spells generally worked from day one. I once hid my house from Luke, but that's a fun story for another day."

"What?" Rae asked.

"Later," Yasmin said. "Luke, on the other hand, doesn't do any witchcraft or spells at all, but he's a Dream Walker."

306

"A what?"

Yasmin clarified. "The things he does when he's asleep sometimes happen in real life. He's able to connect to other people. He's able to go places while he's sleeping and control it and see what's actually happening in other places. On the one hand, it's helped him tremendously as a DEA agent. On the other hand, it's really hard to explain where he got some of his information when he tries to convince his bosses that a sting is necessary. And honestly he's seen some things that he can't unsee."

"Oh my gosh," Rae said, "I hadn't even thought of it that way. I always just seem to know when people have my best intentions or harm at heart and I knew when I felt where you and Luke were nearby that something was important. I couldn't even tell if it was good or bad. It was just that you were important people and I needed to get to know you. Of course, once I saw Luke he looked so much like my grandfather, I really started to wonder given his age." She was talking and before she even figured it out she'd told Yasmin exactly what her skill was. It was right then that Rae felt the other presence in the room. Turning, she saw Sloan and the look on Sloan's face that said she hadn't been quite ready to talk about it yet.

CHAPTER 45

Rae turned the small, cream colored business card over in her hand. It was really non-descript. Black Print. Normal type. *Edward Lundberg. Acquisitions.* And the number. It was only the following Tuesday. But she was going to call. She had worked surveillance for twelve hours the day before, as a favor to Liam. He was on twelves with another of Lincoln's people, but needed a shift off. She was tired of looking at the little card as well as just plumb tired.

She'd wanted to talk to Sloan about it, but that wasn't happening. Sloan wasn't not speaking to her or anything like that, but she was angry. And Rae understood. Though she had every right to talk to Yasmin about herself, and that was all she'd done, talking about herself was—by extension—talking about Sloan. And Sloan hadn't been ready. It didn't matter if Yasmin could figure it all out for herself. Rae had screwed up.

Sloan had made it through dinner that night and she participated pleasantly in the conversation. But she hadn't been herself. She'd been hurt. And now she was mad. Though Rae couldn't figure out specifically what she could have done better other than shut Yasmin down, she understood Sloan's side of it, too. Rae had really wanted to talk to Yasmin. She had questions about things she'd never talked to anyone but Sloan and their mother about. She'd wanted to make her connections to Yasmin and Luke stronger, and witchcraft was something they now had in common, so it was a natural point of conversation. But Sloan wasn't happy with her these days. Rae didn't know how to fix it. So she was here with a business card and no big sister to call for advice. She was on her own.

Still she was unsure why she should really call the man. He wanted to buy a piece she wasn't selling, and she had said no. Rae had thought she'd done it in no uncertain terms, too. So, here she was, yawning, wanting to call Sam, but not wanting to interfere with his normal life. And not wanting to call this Mr. Lundberg to tell him what they both already knew.

But for the sake of not burning too many bridges, at least not beyond repair, she pulled her phone out of her purse and started dialing.

"Lundberg's." The voice was almost nasal and Rae suddenly realized that she hadn't recognized the area code.

"Yes, I'm calling for Mr. Lundberg." Well, duh. *Smooth moves, Miss Professional.*

"May I ask who's calling?"

She refrained from saying 'yes, you may ask.' And instead replied, "Rae Woodward."

"Oh." Just the slightest gasp was in the girl's voice and that put Rae off kilter a bit. "I'll put you right through."

There was only a moment and a few quick clicks in which to be surprised. He must really want *A Cold Day in July*. Which would make it all that much more difficult to keep turning him down. But she had made up her mind and had decided that she wouldn't sell out and she was sticking to her guns. No matter what he offered.

Rae kept repeating that thought.

She didn't even finish it. His voice was liquid silk today. "Miss Woodward?"

"Yes." Rae found herself wishing that she had prepped herself a little better for this. He was out with honey this time.

"I thoroughly enjoyed your show last weekend."

"Thank you." She waited for whatever he was about to offer.

She didn't wait long. "Tell me you haven't sold *Eye of the Beholder*."

The makeup series? He was interested in that now? "You would need to check with The Webber, they would be handling that."

"I just got off the phone with them about fifteen minutes ago." That shocked her, but he kept talking before she could comment on it. "I meant to a private buyer."

"No, I haven't." It was like the clocks had stopped ticking. She was so confused. What could he possibly want with the make-up series? It was too much for a private home. It was meant to simply be a show piece. She didn't dare hope that he had another show for her.

"Well, that sounds like good news to me."

Okayyyyy. But she didn't say anything, just waited through the pause.

"Are you familiar with Artesia Printing?"

"No, I'm not." Dear God, he was going to offer her the chance to do nude photos or posters of dogs in roller skates. She stifled the noise of her sigh. He might as well ask if she wanted to join a coupon club or a commune.

"I'm a buyer for Artesia, and I'm looking to purchase *Eye of the Beholder* for them. I am assuming that it will be in other shows and that you do not want us to release it for perhaps six months to a year. We'll hammer that out. I—"

"Excuse me? Release what . . . ?"

"I'm sorry. We create many of the posters that people buy. No dogs in roller skates—"

Rae just laughed. Had he read her mind? In spite of this ridiculous offer, she was beginning to like him.

"Excuse me?" It was his turn.

Rae couldn't help it. She confessed. "My greatest fear is that I should be asked to take pictures of dogs in roller skates."

"Oh, I assure you, we handle nothing of the kind. Frameable, quality, poster sized prints. Never rolled."

Rae blinked to herself a few times. Was he saying what she thought he was saying?

Mr. Lundberg continued. "Now that doesn't mean that *Eye of the Beholder* won't end up on every college dorm room wall. But we do produce quality pieces. . ."

He kept talking, but Rae didn't hear much. She finally hung up after telling him that she would have to think about it, and then *she* had to reassure *him* that she wouldn't sell to anyone else in the meantime.

Blinking again a few times, Rae stared at her phone as if it held the answers. She was certainly awake now, if still utterly confused. Perhaps she should go back to bed and wake up and start all over. Now she really wanted to call Sam. Turning to check the microwave clock, she noticed for the first time the icon on her phone indicating that she had several voicemails. Vaguely she recalled a few clicks during her surreal conversation with Mr. Lundberg. Maybe it was Sam.

With a spurt of excitement at the offer, she started clicking through the options. After a few clicks and beeps and a request for her code, a voice that sounded a little too upper-crusty to actually belong to anyone who might actually be that blue of blood, spoke. "This is Melissa Westland, from The Webber. I was simply calling to let you know that I received a call from Trent Lindley with the Martch Gallery in Chicago. I gave him this number as you had stated that we could give it out. Thank you."

The machine clicked off. Rae found herself disbelieving her

ears again. So why she kept blinking her eyes was beyond her. She was hallucinating sounds not visions. Just then the phone rang in her hand, startling her. She'd drifted into her thoughts to the point that the vibration startled her.

After two rings and a deep breath, she answered once again wishing it was Sam. She needed some stability, but she didn't recognize the number.

"Hello?"

"Yes, may I please speak to Rae Woodward?"

"This is she." She didn't sigh this time. Who knew what was waiting on the other end of the line for her today? Weirdness, that was for sure.

Sure enough, it was. "This is Trent Lindley with the Martch Gallery . . ."

Thirty minutes later, she was getting dressed in a haze. She wasn't going to call Sam. She was going to drive over there and sit on his doorstep until he came home. At least that way, if she got more mind-boggling calls, she wouldn't have to drive afterward. Rae pulled on her pants, and shucked a sweater over her head, amazed by the difference in the very simple acts. She had been asked to show her work in Chicago. Someone wanted to pay her good money for *Eye of the Beholder* and he said he couldn't guarantee that it wouldn't end up on the wall of every college dorm room in America. God, she should be so lucky.

And, to top off the whole thing, she had Sam. The rest of it, she had worked hard for. She'd been working toward this for a handful of years now. Just plying her way to her dream. She knew this might all just be just a flash in the pan. But Sam. She had no idea how that had come about. Certainly, with little help from her. Snatching up the keys by the door, she raced outside. The sun was out and the day had hit that point of perfect L.A. weather. Go figure.

She was driving like a madwoman and she knew it. But she didn't hurt anybody, and her tires made only a medium level squeal as she skidded to a halt in front of Sam's townhouse. Throwing the car door open, she threw herself out and slammed it behind her, taking the front steps two at a time.

But no one answered her breathless knock. Or the second one, either. Finally, Jeremy emerged from the garage with an oily rag in his hand and a curious look on his face. It changed to a scowl when he realized he was being watched.

His expression changed again when he spotted her. His lips curled up into a sneer that was obviously meant as a come-on. His arm braced against the side of the garage, and the rag dangling from a carefully placed hand on his hip. If she hadn't been so excited, Rae would have just bust out laughing at this kid trying to pick her up.

"Don't move!" She called to him, entirely upset at his look of startled surprise. It wasn't the same expression. She needed the first one. She fumbled the key into the lock on her car and yanked her camera out of the backseat. Slinging the strap over her head just in case she clutzed up and dropped it, she sauntered back to the front steps, readying the camera as she went. Already she felt calmer. As if the earth had started turning again.

"What's that?" He looked rude, and it wasn't matching the snapshot captured in her head from when he first rounded the corner.

"I'm a photographer." She smiled sweetly, then realized that she'd have to ply her victim. "Can you give me that first look again? When you came around the corner?"

"What look?" *God, he was an arrogant little thing.* And she wanted to get that on film so bad.

Ply harder, Rachel. "That . . .uh . . . hot, sexy look."

"Ohhhh." It all came back. He draped himself against the garage door opening, and smiled that young, greasy, come-hither of his. "Like this, Baby?"

"Yeah. That's it." She decided to ignore the 'baby' part. And she snapped off about fifteen shots from mildly different angles and zooms. Then she stopped and let the weight of it drag the camera away from her face.

"Thank you." She started up the steps again, then turned back. With a grin that she even got to ask it, she tossed out the words. "Can I have your permission to put this in a show?"

He wiped his hands, looking a bit unsure about the fact that he had smiled his best smile and she had just thanked him and walked off. "What do I get for it?"

That was a good question. Rae shrugged. "Fifteen dollars now or fifty if I sell it." She thought she had that much cash in her purse. Although she wasn't sure that she had her purse with her. It hadn't exactly been a stellar morning for her common sense.

"Can I think about that for a while?" He rubbed at his hands a little absentmindedly.

She nodded. "Do you know if Sam's home?"

"He's in court this morning."

"Ohhh." Rae nodded again, and sat down on the cold steps, amazed by the letdown she felt just because he wasn't home. What did she expect? That he just lived his life when she was around, and the rest of the time was spent waiting until she could show up again?

"—if you want to wait." Jeremy's voice broke into her thoughts.

She'd missed most of what he'd said. "I'm sorry. What?"

"The garage door is open. You can wait inside."

"Thank you." Rae smiled at him. A real smile, just to let him see what one looks like. As she stood and dusted off the butt of her jeans, contemplating going in, Jeremy spoke again.

"You're his girlfriend, right?"

It took just a moment to answer. "Yes."

~

"What do you think?"

Sam tried not to bite his own tongue. He had been waffling back and forth about what he thought for the past three weeks. He knew what he felt. Even though he hadn't ever gotten around to telling her. And Rae hadn't asked.

So here they were, out at dinner celebrating the sale of a large number of her pieces from the Webber and the acceptance at the Martch Gallery of new ones. He particularly liked *Petty Theft Auto*, her new one of Jeremy standing at the entrance to his garage, but he had no idea when she had taken it. Just as he had no idea when she had moved out of his social circle.

Rae was about to be a world-renowned photographer. He could feel it in his bones. Chicago was three days away, and Rachel was right in front of him, wanting to know what he thought of the whole thing. He shrugged. "I don't think I really matters what I think."

"I think it does." Her voice was soft and carried to him on a warm drift from where she was snuggled next to him in the too-large restaurant booth.

This time he turned to look at her, as always taken aback each time he saw her or touched her, that his memories never did her justice. "I think that this is your dream and that you worked really hard for it, and paid your dues, and you deserve it." He left out a whole lot of what he thought, but that much was truth at least.

"What about you? Could you come with me?" There was a tremor in her voice. It was the first time she'd asked him, and she wasn't looking at him. Just smoothed the question into the conversation between bites of goat cheese ravioli.

Part of him wished it were otherwise. But part of him was glad that it wasn't. "I can't leave. My practice is here. There would be too many court dates to reschedule." Besides, after a while of him being her lackey she would get tired of him.

"Is that all?" It was a whisper he wasn't sure he had heard, until he looked up from his food again and saw the fear and the question in her eyes. Her hand held tightly to the fork at the side of her plate, giving away a tension that wasn't seen in her face.

"No, Rachel, it's not anywhere near all."

"Then what? Will you miss me?"

"What?" He felt like he was exploding, but his voice was quiet. How could two people who got along so well and seemed so in sync have one person think the other wouldn't miss them? Maybe they weren't as in sync as he had thought.

Her voice got softer with each question, but he still heard it. "You said that you were crazy about me. But you never said you didn't want me to go, or that you wanted to come, or even that you would miss me. . ."

He felt and heard his entire chest heave. Setting his fork to the side of his plate he turned and took her shoulders in his hands, squaring her to him. "Listen, when I said I was crazy about you, it wasn't the whole story."

She blinked a few times, and he continued. "I'm not *just* crazy about you, I'm in love with you. And that means that I want you to have your dream . . ." He had more to say, but just watching Rachel's lower lip tremble stopped him.

"But I had two dreams." She shook her head.

That was news. There was still more? He had told her how he felt. The next move was hers. "What was the other dream?"

"You."

That didn't make a hill of beans worth of sense. So he waited.

"I wanted someone to curl up with at night, who was in love with me and wanted to be with me—"

He started to interrupt her. He started to say *Someone will*, but she wasn't having it.

"And then I realized that I wanted that person to be you. I need that person to be you. And I want you to come with me."

"But I can't." At no time had he ever thought it would come to this. That they couldn't be together and still have what they wanted. It had just never occurred to him that she couldn't be a world-class photographer here. "See, Rae, I have this dream, too. But unlike you, I didn't know it from the start. I already have mine. I worked hard for it and I gave up the spotlight and I gave up the high-paying, ninety-hour-a-week job. I'm finally in a place where I can help people, and I get to only take the cases I want and I can arrange other payment options for people. And I'm good at it. I—"

He tried again. "If I followed you, I would have to give that up. And I couldn't be useful the way I am here. I can't do this from a traveling location. And if I couldn't do this, I wouldn't be me. I'd be your little . . . assistant? I don't even know what they call it. You wouldn't want me." He had so little to offer her, he thought. But he had learned long ago about being true to himself.

It broke his heart to even think it. But if Rae didn't fit into that picture, then she didn't. He would have to see her off at the airport and go home and cry like he hadn't cried since he was five. Then spend the rest of his life wondering where she was and how she was doing. He told himself this many times each day. Because it was just so tempting to pick up everything, throw his cases to other attorneys and follow her like a lap dog.

"But you would be useful to me." She sounded pleading, and it twisted at his heart how much he wanted to say yes.

"Out of everybody, you were the only one who never tried to convince me that I could go get a corporate job and make way more money. You never once told me I was a fool. Everyone else has. Even my own parents. But not you."

Rae nodded slowly. "You're right. I can't take that away from you." Her sigh was heavy with sadness. "That's why I took that picture of you, you know. *A Cold Day in July.* Because you were so happy right where you were."

He nodded to her. Thinking how unhappy he was right now with her leaving. What was it he really wanted? Her? He tried to convince himself. "I have my friends, and time for them, and clients who have me when they don't have anyone else. . ." Maybe he could just change the subject. "The judge dropped the charges against Jeremy. The kid actually cleaned up and they gave him community service, finding some good civic projects for him."

The smile that spread across her face was slow and sad and full of loss. It wasn't what he wanted for her. His heart would break less if she got on the plane happy and excited. She was paying about as much attention to his change of subject as he was. She looked on the verge of tears. "I love you, too, Sam."

Again, he felt the urge to just hug her and tell her he would go with her. He wanted to get his cell phone out right here at the table and call the airline. He could transfer his clients. Unfortunately, he could also see himself lonely and bored in hotel rooms around the country, sight-seeing Chicago by himself while Rae worked, playing the dutiful, what?—husband? —on her arm. He didn't know how wives did it, following their husbands from city to city . . .

His own voice was steady and gave away nothing of the fact that he was breaking into pieces. "You can stay with me until you go, if you want."

CHAPTER 46

Rae sat bolt upright, blinking into the dark of the room around her. For a moment, she was disoriented, unsure where she was, what time it was and, for a moment, even who she was. She only knew that something was wrong, very wrong. Then she realized she was at Sam's.

Sam became her first concern. Was he okay? She couldn't see, the room was pitch black and it took a moment for her eyes to orient while her hands reached out to her side, patting around until she felt the lump next to her that was her sleeping boyfriend. Though she reached out and touched him, Sam didn't wake. He continued sleeping heavily beside her, unaware of the heavy pounding of her heart and the terror that was slowly taking over.

Though she could hear him making soft sounds, she left her hand on him for just a moment to feel the steady breathing of his deep sleep, reassured that the problem wasn't with Sam. She tried again to figure out what might possibly be wrong. Taking a deep breath, Rae sat back and leaned into the pillows against the headboard of the bed. She tried to steady herself so she could be open and maybe gain some understanding of what was going on. Despite the wild beating of her heart and the firm knowledge that something was horribly wrong, she knew how to do this. She'd done it before.

First, she closed her eyes again, even though it didn't make any difference in the darkness of the room, and she asked herself, "Is it Sloan?" The feeling at the back of her brain moved upward, no. Sloan was safe. Next, she asked if Sheree was okay and the feeling went downward this time. No, Sheree was not okay. Sheree was who this alert was about—even if Rae didn't know what the alert was, where Sheree was, or what might be going wrong, only that something was. She had learned a long time ago to double check. Knowing that something was wrong with Sheree might not be the whole story. If Lisa was with Sheree, or if Alex was, there were things Rae could check from here at Sam's, things that might help make the problem clearer. So she checked everyone else she could possibly think of.

She asked the universe about Yasmin and Luke. She thought about Lincoln and his family. She went through everyone that she could conceive of, that she might be getting a warning about in the middle of the night. In the end, only Sheree gave her that strong feeling, the sensation of a downward swipe at the back of her brain. So Sheree was in trouble, and only Sheree was in trouble.

Next, Rae had to try to pinpoint Sheree. Unfortunately, this was nothing she had any talent with. That meant her first order of business was get dressed and go home. She wanted to fling away the covers, flip on the light switch, throw on her clothes, and run out the door. However, that would mean waking Sam up and truth be told, she didn't know what she would tell him.

Why was she running out of his room, out of his house, in the middle of the night, frantic? He would want to know and she didn't have any answers he could handle. So she fought the overwhelming urge to rush and slowly peeled back the covers, sliding her legs down to the ground, opening her eyes again. She waited long painful minutes for the light in the room—the very, very dim light—to adjust until she could see her underwear, her pants, her shoes, her shirt. She didn't think about a bra. She didn't think about socks. She would come back for them later. She didn't think about the need to explain such decisions.

She needed to get out. Something was very wrong with Sheree. Quietly getting dressed, Rae then crept over to the door, slowly turning the knob and creaking the door open, hopefully without waking Sam. She tip toed down the stairs, gathering her purse, keys and phone that she'd left by the door, grateful that she hadn't carried them up to the bedroom, grateful that the light by the screen of the phone didn't wake her boyfriend. Even so, she was turning the knob to go out the front door, wondering how she would lock it behind her when she heard the stairs creak behind her.

"Rae," he asked, "Where are you going? It's 3:00 A.M."

She didn't know how to answer him other than to tell the pieces of the truth that she could begin to make sense of.

"I'm going home."

"But why?" He clearly couldn't understand her need to rush out the door. The problem was, neither could she.

"I forgot something," she stammered. It wasn't a lie, but it wasn't the truth either, and Sam wasn't having any of it.

"What could you have possibly forgotten, that you need, in the middle of the night suddenly?"

"I just," she paused and tried again. "I just ... I have to go. I have to go home."

This time, when she started to open the door, she felt his hand on her arm, stopping her. She wanted to shake him off, throw his hand away, and bolt but she froze instead. This was Sam, he deserved better, even if she couldn't explain what better was.

Being Sam, he offered better. "Rae, please, tell me what's going on. I want to help." She stared at him, thinking about that offer for a moment. Sam had not had a good reaction when she told him she was taking witchcraft classes. She hadn't told him that they'd been having dinner with Luke and Yasmin. Having been pulled aside like she was at the gallery opening, she hadn't even had the opportunity to introduce him to them. His last impression of her cousin and his wife was that they were running a witchcraft shop and Sam didn't think it was a good idea for Rae to fall in with that crowd.

Now, here she was in the middle of the night, with nothing other than this dead set feeling that something was very, very wrong with her best friend. How was she possibly going to explain this to him? She looked at him again, "Sam, I can't say. I just ... I have to go home. I have to check on Sheree."

She paused then, wondering why the last part had fallen out of her mouth. When had her mouth gotten ahead of her brain? When she had decided that it was okay to tell Sam? Because it wasn't. She'd never told anyone.

He shook his head at her, "Why do you need to check on Sheree? Sheree's fine. I'm sure she's in bed right now, just like she is *every* night, in the *dead, middle of the night* Rae. What's going on?"

She shook her head at him. "I don't think she is. I don't think she's okay."

Sam looked at her, finally seeing her terror, her panic and whether or not he believed, he understood that she felt it. "Okay Rae," he said, "Let's do this; let's call Sheree first. Before you run out of here frantic and get behind the wheel and maybe hurt yourself, let's just call Sheree and let her tell you she's okay."

It wasn't a bad idea, Rae thought. Sheree would answer the phone, she would say everything was all right and then Rae could go back to sleep, only, she watched as Sam dialed Sheree's number and she knew, Sheree wasn't going to answer the phone because something was very, very wrong and Rae had never been wrong about that.

She was still standing by the door, Sam still standing a few feet away, looking at her, no longer holding her arm but definitely concerned about her panic when he hung up. Sheree hadn't answered. He looked at Rae and said, "I'm sure she doesn't sleep by her phone. I don't. You don't. Why would she answer the cell phone in the middle of the night?"

"You're right," Rae said. "Call the house. We have that stupid land line that comes cheaper with our service and for whatever reason, we never turned off the ringer. Call the apartment. She'll hear it in the middle of the night and she'll freak out, but she'll answer."

"All right," he told her, turning around, pulling up his phone again and picking another number out of his list. He waited, still staring at Rae while she still fidgeted her keys. No matter how desperately she wanted Sheree to answer the phone, she knew her roommate wouldn't and a moment later, when Sam hung up, he said, "I don't know why you're right but, you're right. She's not answering. I've called twice. She should have heard the rings and gotten out of bed. Wait for me. I'll drive. Just give me a minute, Rae."

Rae shook her head. "I've got to go. I've already wasted too much time," but that was the panic speaking. She took another deep breath. Again, she'd been here before. She'd had these anxiety attacks, she'd known when things were wrong and honestly, when it had been her mother dying, she hadn't known what was wrong but it had already been too late. What if it was too late for Sheree?

She couldn't stomach the thought, but she did try to be rational. "Okay Sam, you can drive, but run. Go now. Go get dressed. Get your shoes. I've got your keys. I'm standing right here, I'm going to go climb in your car and wait, but you have to be fast."

He bolted up the stairs before she could finish the sentence and she had never been more grateful in her life. This time, she bolted the front door and headed for the door through the kitchen that led to his garage. She plucked his wallet and keys from the table where he'd left them, right by where she'd left her purse originally.

Then she went into the garage, started the car, and climbed into the passenger seat, yelling out to him, "I've started your car, Sam. I have your wallet. Hurry." Then she sat in the car for a small eternity while apparently, Sam took his time getting dressed.

That was unfair. She knew he was fast. He was downstairs so disheveled that it was impossible he'd taken any time at all. He barely had shoes on his feet and she was grateful for that, glad she hadn't said anything. She even opened the garage door and it was just finishing its upward grind as Sam climbed into the car and reversed at high speed out of the driveway, making a quick turn, automatically hitting the button to close the garage door and curling out onto the street.

He didn't ask questions. He knew the way to Rae and Sheree's apartment by heart, just like she did. On the drive, she fought panic at every stop light. She fought the panic when the apartment's garage gate didn't want to open because she didn't have the clicker with her from her own car. They parked on the street, illegally. Both of them climbing out suddenly, slamming doors. Sam hitting the button and making the inordinately loud bleeping sound as his car locked and they ran up the street, half a block, to her front door. The key didn't want to fit in but at last, it did. She didn't wait for the elevator, just headed up the stairs. She threw open the door to her own apartment, running in and yelling for her roommate.

"Sheree," she called. "Sheree, wake up." Even though she went through the apartment, directly to Sheree's door and threw it wide open, it was clear the bed had not been disturbed and Sheree had not been home. So Sheree was out very late and she wasn't answering her phone. Rae's panic climbed a notch, another confirmation that not only was she correct, but she still hadn't located Sheree. When she hit a maximum panic level, Sam grabbed her shoulders and turned her to face him.

"Look, Sheree's probably okay. So she went out and partied late, she does that. You and I both know that sometimes, you don't come home and sometimes she doesn't come home either. If she's sleeping by her cell phone, she probably turned it off and so she's not going to answer it till morning or late. She'll answer it when she wakes up. There's nothing else we can do."

Rae didn't buy that and she didn't know what to say. This was Sam. This was the man she'd told that she loved him. How could she love him if she couldn't tell him everything else? It spilled out of her mouth because she knew. She had to do everything she could for Sheree. She couldn't live with herself otherwise. But would she have to live without Sam because of it? She didn't know, but she started talking.

"Sam," she said. "Things are not okay with Sheree and I *know* it. We have to go find her."

He shook his head at her. "How would we even do that? She's not answering her phone. L.A. is huge. Do you have any idea where to start looking?"

Rae shook her head.

Sam continued, "I don't think the phone company will triangulate her cell signal for us. We're not even family. What are we supposed to do?"

Only for a moment did she enjoy the fact that he didn't call her crazy, that he didn't tell her she was completely nuts but she wasn't able to enjoy it for long. She had to find her roommate.

Sloan. She would call Sloan. That's what Rae did when things got truly horrible and she couldn't figure out what was going on. It didn't matter that Sloan was mad at her. She would come. She dialed her sister's number and found that her sister wasn't home.

"Shit." Trying to calm her still racing heart, she stepped back for a moment, removing Sam's touch from her shoulders, put her hands by her side and worked desperately to calm her nerves. *Sloan?* she asked the universe, but got the result that Sloan was okay. Sloan was fine. Sloan was the one who simply wasn't answering her phone in the middle of the night and Sloan didn't have a landline. They'd have to have a discussion about this later, if Rae hadn't turned into a blubbering ball of mush.

Rae took another deep breath, dialed Sloan again and once again, when she got her sister's voicemail, she did the only other thing she could think of. She looked at Sam but didn't say anything. Then she clicked through her phone, found Yasmin's number and dialed.

CHAPTER 47

Rae heard the click on the other end of the line, her heart pausing in its frantic race, as she heard Yasmin's voice.

"Rae," Yasmin asked, "is everything okay?"

"No." It was the only thing that came to mind, and she knew if she told Yasmin anything else, none of the rest of this would make sense. "It's my friend Sheree, I don't know what's going on. I've got a terrible feeling, and when this happens I call Sloan. Sloan can *see*. She can help me figure out what's wrong. But I can't find Sloan."

"Oh, my God," Yasmin replied. "Is Sloan okay?"

"Sloan's fine. I just can't find her. And she's on the other side of town. I don't know where you are. Are you maybe closer?"

It took a moment for the two of them to relay addresses and realize that yes, Yasmin was close, and perhaps she could help. Honestly, Rae would have driven straight to Sloan's apartment, but she wasn't even sure if Sloan was home. It was entirely possible her sister had gone out into the late hours and was in a club not answering her phone. Rae was beyond grateful for Yasmin's help.

"I've got you covered," Yasmin said. "I'll do whatever I can, but honestly, it might be better if we meet at the shop. How fast can you get there?"

Again, it took a moment to coordinate it, but Rae and Sam realized they could make it to Blessed Be and meet Yasmin there, cutting the time in half from trying to get to Yasmin's house.

In a moment, with things worked out, Rae hung up the phone, and she and Sam raced out of her apartment, back down out of the front door, and into the car. It only took a few moments to get around the corner to the shop. Once there, Yasmin would have everything she needed, if she couldn't see what had happened to Sheree. Rae had no idea what skills her cousin-in-law might possess. She'd only said she was a natural witch.

Rae considered telling Sam to just drop her off and go home. She didn't want him to see this. But, so far, he'd been reacting to her panic and doing whatever she needed. Even he had become concerned about Sheree, though his concern level was clearly much lower than hers. He knew only that it was three a.m. and no one could get a hold of his friend. To him, this didn't mean something was wrong.

Once parked in the back of the shop, they hopped out of the car and began huddling at the back door in the chill of the night. "Sam," she tried, "You should go home. Get some sleep."

"I'm not leaving you in the back of a Hollywood shop in the middle of the night, Rae."

"But when Yasmin gets here—"

"No. I'm not leaving you when you're this upset."

She tried again and again for several minutes, but Sam kept refusing ending the argument only when Yasmin arrived. Screeching her little car to a halt, Yasmin jumped out and, keys already in hand, opened the back door, bolting into the shop.

Before Rae understood what had happened, Yasmin had the

lights on and was inside the classroom, tugging Rae along behind her. Only it wasn't the classroom. It took Rae a moment to realize she was standing in a room dedicated to spells. Not a room for beginners. Yasmin had dragged her into the center of a circle permanently cut into the floor. In fact, it looked like it had been burned in. Salt filled the round crevasse like a moat.

Inside the circle, a pentagram—a five-pointed star—reached out to exactly touch the edges of the circle. Though Sam tried to come in with them, Yasmin held her hand up and motioned him back. Though he looked utterly confused, he did as he was told, waiting by the doorway as the two women stood in the middle of the strange, inscribed floor.

With deep breaths, Yasmin placed her palms into Rae's hand, trying to make a connection. Rae, too, tried to slow down her breathing, tried to calm her thoughts and let Yasmin pick up anything that she could.

After a minute, Yasmin shook her head. "It isn't working. Stay here. And you, stay there," she motioned to Sam.

She darted out of the room, coming back with a pendulum and water that she'd fetched from somewhere. Rae hadn't heard any running. Yasmin pulled a bowl from the back of the room. Rae hadn't even noticed, but supplies lined all kinds of shelving along the back wall. Coming back into the circle, Yasmin motioned Rae back, poured the water into the bowl, and kneeled in front of it. She motioned again for Rae to sit down on the opposite side of her.

Holding the pendulum over the water, Yasmin repeated words in a sing-song chant. Rae had never heard or seen anything like this. Then again, she'd only had the beginner class on scrying and Yasmin clearly knew what she was doing.

After a moment, Yasmin stared deeply into the reflection on the surface of the water. "Look, Rae," she whispered. "Look. What do you see?"

Rae saw it then. It was Sheree's car, twisted and mangled,

wrapped around a tree. There were no street lights in the area. The darkness concealed almost the entire image, and no cars appeared to be going by on the street. Rae looked up at Yasmin frantic, "Where is this?"

Across the room, they heard Sam, who was utterly confused. "What is it? What are you looking at?"

Looking up, Rae noticed that he was staring at the two of them and it made sense. All he could likely see was two women staring into a bowl of water, but she didn't pay any attention to him. It didn't seem there was time to explain. She looked back at Yasmin. "I have no idea where that is. What do we do?"

"Hold on," Yasmin said, pulled the pendulum back out and started again. But she sighed in exasperation and shook her head after several tries. "I don't see anything more. You look."

She left Rae there with the bowl showing her the picture of the car. Though, now, she could see motion in the image. She could see Sheree's car taking the turn just a little too fast. She could see sand on the road—maybe gravel or water, *something*— causing Sheree's tires to lose traction and her car sliding ever- so-slightly sideways, hitting the shoulder of the road, and sliding into the edge.

Rae heard the sickening sounds as the front of the car slammed into the tree, the tree taking the brunt of the force, and the engine crunching, the hiss as it gave up its steam. Yasmin was gone. Surely, she was doing something important, but Rae tried to gather every bit of information she could.

Without knowing how she did it, she managed to replay the scene. The shoulder of the road was narrow. There was barely even any gravel. The side of the pavement disappeared into a very narrow path that appeared to be for joggers given the dirt was pounded down. Beyond the jog path, the ground dipped sharply and fell away. Trees grew up out of the slanted slope, and in the distance, Rae could see city lights.

Shaking her head, she watched again. Could she recognize the lights? Could she figure out where Sheree was? Even as she tried to determine what little she could, Yasmin darted back into the room. The pendulum still swung from her fist, but this time, she carried a full-size map of the city.

"Move over," she said to Rae and Rae did, taking the water bowl with her, two to three steps to the right, until she'd made enough room for the size of Yasmin's map.

Yasmin knelt down again. Holding the pendulum above the map, she let it swing until it fell, silent in one spot. Stepping back, she put her palms flat on her thighs, took a deep breath, and closed her eyes, and then did it again. The pendulum fell onto the same spot. The third time, she swung the pendulum in a different direction getting the same result. She looked up at Rae. "Is she possibly on Mulholland?"

Rae took a gasp. It explained everything, the lights in the distance, the lack of shoulder on the road, the jogging path.

"Yes!" But she paused. Mulholland was so long. "Where?" she whispered to Yasmin.

"One minute." Yasmin went back with the pendulum again until she could narrow the space to about half a mile of road. "Let's go."

They left everything there in the middle of the room, abandoning their spells, grabbing Sam by the hand, and running out to Yasmin's car. It was Yasmin who took Coldwater Canyon Road up into the hills, then swung a left onto Mulholland. She took the road—with its steep curves, sharp turns, and missing edges—far too fast for the middle of the night. The lights were on bright, and it took only five minutes of chattering teeth, clenched fists, and eyes darting everywhere, for Rae to yell out from her passenger seat, "There! That's Sheree's car! There she is."

Yasmin managed to stop the car about fifteen feet beyond

where Sheree had her accident. It was far too dangerous on Mulholland to just slam the brakes. They might run off the road, and if they did that, if they hadn't hit a tree like Sheree did, they might have tumbled over the steep side, killing everyone in the car.

It was difficult to maneuver the car to the side of the road, and Yasmin had to do it carefully. The concern, of course, being that they might run into Sheree's car, making whatever accident Sheree had already had only that much worse. As soon as Yasmin had the car at a stop, Rae opened her door to bolt out, only to realize that—as she went to put her foot down—there was no ground beneath her feet. Yasmin had parked as far to the side of the road as she could, trying to leave the road wide open for other drivers that might come by in the night. The slope was too steep for Rae to get out on her side.

"Rae, this way." Sam held out his hand, motioning for her to push her seat back, close her door, and climb into the back with him. That way she could get out on the driver's side, where the road was fully under the car. Her heart beat faster, but she followed him out, taking his hand and letting him tug her along.

It was Yasmin who arrived at Sheree's door first and began tugging on the handle. The door wouldn't open. The car was crunched, though the main body of the car appeared to be relatively intact. Looking into the window, using only the moon as their guide, they could see Sheree slumped over the wheel, blood coming from her forehead. She didn't stir despite the noise they made.

Rae joined Yasmin in yanking the door. This time it was Sam who asked Yasmin, "Do you have a device in your car, one of those rescue things? You know, with the seat belt cutter and the window breaker?"

He struggled to find the words, but Yasmin nodded. "I do. Hold on." She ran back toward her car, opened the driver's side door, and reached into the pocket.

She returned instantly with a tiny device. It looked too small to do anything, but Rae watched as Sam pulled back and cracked it against the driver's side window, once, twice. On the third time, the glass gave way, showering down, and Sam managed to reach in and find Sheree's pulse.

CHAPTER 48

R ae blinked in the dark. The clock read four a.m. Her alarm would go off in just under half an hour.

Last night, she'd hugged Sheree good-bye at their apartment. Jack, Lisa, and Alex had all been there for a group send off over dinner. Sloan had come, too. She wasn't comfortable in groups where she knew almost no one, but she wouldn't have missed it. She gave Rae a present and told her how proud she was and how proud Mom and Dad would have been. Rae had been fighting back tears.

They'd found their peace again, a steady rhythm between them as sisters. Sloan was the only one she'd told about her fears. About the fact that Sam was holding back from her. That he seemed wary of her now. He knew she was in touch with Yasmin. He seemed to think Rae was turning to witchcraft—and he wasn't wrong. What he was missing was that she'd always been aimed that way.

He'd only asked her once how she'd known about Sheree. They'd been in the hospital. Sheree hadn't needed surgery, but she'd been whisked away through the ER and had been observed for almost two days before she was declared well enough to go home. Her roommate might have died if she'd been left there until someone discovered her in the morning. Her body temperature had been dropping. But when he'd asked, Rae had only shrugged and said, "I don't know. I only know that I *knew* it."

He'd walked away nodding. Gone home. Changed. He'd come back, but everywhere except bed, he'd been distant. So this, lying in Sam's arms, *this* was what she would really miss. For a moment she closed her eyes, not sure if she was trying to will herself back to sleep or simply taking a moment to burn it into her memory.

She was naked beside Sam. His arms, heavy in sleep, were draped around her. But she'd been graced to be here often enough to know that those arms looked casual, but were steel bands that wouldn't let her go. Not until he was awake. Then he would open them and step back. He said he was setting her free.

Last night they reached for each other until they had no strength left. She should have slept like the dead. But each time he touched her, and each time she touched him, she was certain something was getting lost. She was afraid this would be the last time they were together. Last night, he'd loved her like he thought that, too.

She wanted him to come with her, but he was right. He couldn't. She had no right to ask it of him. If she wasn't willing to stay for him, then why should he be willing to go for her?

She had to go. She had worked too hard for too long to let this drop when it was finally coming her way. She would be miserable staying here and doing P.I. work and just barely paying the bills if she let this slip through her fingers. Sam, on the other hand, had just *happened* to her. He also might be walking away anyway. He didn't seem the kind to be able to deal with what she could do. There was no way she could guarantee it wouldn't happen again. It had already happened twice. What if they had kids and she had to tell him they couldn't go to a certain daycare or something because she had a *feeling*? He wouldn't believe her.

Rae felt her teeth press together. The problem was, his changing feelings didn't change how she felt. And just because he hadn't been something she planned, or had worked hard to get, didn't mean he was any less precious. Her eyes opened and she looked over at his sleeping face. It was better when she didn't have to see his eyes. When she didn't have to see his expression of knowing she was leaving. When she didn't have to wonder if the other layer she saw there was relief.

His saying he loved her hadn't brought the joy that statement should have. She'd only felt the weight of it. Like finding out your lost lottery ticket was worth twice as much as you thought.

Several days ago, she printed herself a wallet sized version of *A Cold Day in July*. She had cropped it so she could see as much detail of him as possible and stuck it into the clear inserts on the back of her art bag. It was supposed to be for an ID card. This was her ID. Already she bumped against it several times a day and saw his face, happy and content. She wanted him to be that way again after she left. And yet she didn't. Maybe that was why she had told him that she loved him, too. Not so he would be happy, and not to hear herself say it. But maybe to tie him just a little tighter to her.

She shifted in his arms and they moved with her, adjusting to a new hold, just as deceptively loose as the others. She buried her nose against his chest and prayed. Now that the day was upon them, maybe he'd finally change his mind. She could imagine still frame photos of the two of them at the airport. Him dropping her off, her finding her seat on the plane, and him showing up in the aisle. Saying something like he just couldn't wait. He couldn't live without her. Maybe he could beg her not to go, then when she said she had to, he'd say "Fine, but I'm coming with you."

Even there in bed, the thought brought a smile to her face. It was fleeting though, as she expected it never to pass. Sam had court tomorrow. He was still defending the man ·who had invented the ski rack. That case hadn't finished yet. He had people who depended on him, which was how he liked it. How could she be so selfish as to think she could take all that away to drag him to a cold hotel room where he would rot while he waited for her? What would he do during the day? Hold her equipment?

She amended the photo series in her head to include her telling him to stay. It was the right thing for him.

She'd be gone for three weeks. And the three weeks in and of itself wasn't so bad. Except that she'd already fielded calls from two other galleries. Both out of state. He knew how his mother could promote an artist. Sam had even told her that none of his mother's previous projects had stayed put. Mrs. Brock had a knack for moving her artists up in the world. And they moved— sometimes to the big cities, sometimes just around—but they never stayed.

Just then, the alarm began its mechanical beeping song and Rae felt like wailing to cover the sound. Sam reached out and fumbled to turn it off and woke with a heavy sigh. There was no moment of disillusionment, no second chance where he looked at her and was just happy. His expression changed even before his eyes opened, revealing that the first thought of the day was about her leaving.

Rae sighed in kind. "Morning, Handsome."

"Morning, Gorgeous."

She wanted to smile, but there was no smile in his voice when he said it. And she didn't really feel like it.

They forced themselves out of bed and got dressed. They were silent through breakfast, and all the way to the airport. From his face she was pretty certain that he was waiting just like she was. He would be able to break up with her for the distance. Whether it had anything to do with the classes or her new ties to family and witchcraft, she wouldn't know. She figured that was the point. This was a way out for him.

At the airport, he waited in line and helped her check her bags and held her hand all the way until she had to get in the security lines. He kissed her without passion, only longing. Still they didn't talk about waiting for each other. Neither asked and neither volunteered. They both knew this was just a first step. Then he stepped away.

With a small smile he said, "I love you, Rae."

Then he turned and was gone before she could even say that she loved him, too. She watched him retreat until another passenger tapped her on the shoulder, motioning her to move forward with the line. Sam didn't once look back.

Friday night Sam crawled into bed by himself. Just like he had every night all week. Tuesday, there had been a bit of a pall over Crime Night. Everyone missed Rae. It wasn't like when someone was sick or out for an evening. Rae was out for a while.

Sheree had also commented that Rae was getting calls from galleries all over the country. LA wasn't what people thought of when they thought of art, but it was apparently a great springboard if you hit right. And Rae had hit.

He, on the other hand, had become a wet blanket. He was out with their friends, and she was out hobnobbing with a gallery full of people she didn't know. Next week she had a dinner with the gallery patrons. After that, a public event. She'd done some whirlwind shopping, spending some of the money from her art sales. She'd wanted to bank it, but didn't want to get out on the road and not fit in either.

He'd been an idiot. He should have gotten her a necklace to

wear. Something to remind her of him. Something close to her heart. What she had instead were text messages and the occasional selfie. But "Sam in front of courthouse" for the third day in a row wasn't inspiring. Neither were his messages that always sounded whiny in his head. He missed her like he would miss a limb. Or maybe more.

He wasn't sleeping well. He tossed and turned, having managed in a short period of time to get used to having her in his arms. But aside from a few texts once a day, he didn't know what to do. She'd pulled away. She'd physically left.

At three a.m. he'd reached the part of his routine where he reminded himself that while she'd not technically lied to him, she'd pretty much done just that. They'd agreed that she was better off without her cousin and his wife. Witchcraft wasn't anything any decent person got involved with. She should know that.

He'd understood because she wanted to find her family. But she'd found Luke. Apparently, he'd been raised by witches or something, but he was alive and safe and not on the streets or doing drugs. Sam understood that Rae and Sloan had wanted to reach out. But when Luke and his wife hadn't wanted any contact, it seemed for the best.

So why hadn't she told him that she and Sloan were seeing them? That she was going back to that class that was silly at best and flat out dangerous at worst. Then she'd done that scary-as-hell thing when she'd bolted up in the middle of the night, talking like she was possessed and frantic about Sheree.

Then they'd gone and done some dark ritual in the middle of a freaking pentagram burned into the floor! He was glad they'd found and saved Sheree, but it didn't seem safe. Had she sold her soul or something? He didn't really believe in that, but he didn't believe in what Rae had done either. He'd been reading his Bible at night again. He hadn't told his mom.

He sat up at four a.m. blinking.

He'd worried that Rae had cast a spell on him. She said she'd been going to the class for a while. She said she hadn't done that. But could you trust a witch? Could you truly trust someone who sat in a pentagram with salt all around it? Now, suddenly, it occurred to him that she'd cast a spell on his mother and it made his heart race.

He spent the next hour talking himself down. He alternated between "Rae would never do that," and "My mother is okay, even if she got heinously taken advantage of."

By the next hour, he'd wondered if Rae hadn't cast a spell on him. Maybe he was just so in love with her that she'd seen him as a tool to get to his mother. His mother was a name maker. Rae could have— No. He told himself to stop.

And he tried to stop, but his thoughts ran off the rails. He didn't know what time it was that he finally got to sleep, but he woke up what felt like only five minutes later. The light was pouring in around the curtains, the angle telling him he'd missed most of the morning. His head pounded and he wanted to curl up and not think about any of it.

Then the pounding came again and he realized it was his door.

What?

Who came to his door?

Shit. Jeremy. Jeremy's mother. His mother? Had she figured something out about Rae?

He was out of bed, and running halfway down the stairs to get the door, when he realized he was in his underwear. That wasn't really appropriate for any of the people who might be standing on the other side. He yelled out, "I'm coming. I need a minute!"

The pounding stopped and he bolted back up the stairs. As he'd never made it to the bottom, he still had no clue who was on the other side. He slid into jeans, and pulled a shirt on as he dashed back down the stairs a few seconds later. He was breathing heavily when he pulled the door open, the only thing stopping him was sheer surprise.

"Sloan?"

He'd only met Rae's sister the night before Rae left for Chicago. Though Sloan was blonde-haired and blue-eyed compared to Rae's auburn and mossy green colors, there was no mistaking that they were sisters.

Sloan nodded at him, her face set and she marched into his living room without an invitation. She looked down at his bare feet and up at his just-rolled-out-of-bed hair and said, "So help me God if there's a woman upstairs, I will go through my Big Book of Witchcraft and turn you into the ugliest fucking toad ever."

Startled, Sam jerked back and closed the door behind her, propriety taking over where reason completely failed him. She was sitting on his couch before he said, "There's no woman upstairs. I just slept late because I can't sleep at all because I'm in love with your sister."

Sloan narrowed her eyes at him as though she didn't believe him. Clutching her purse on her lap, she looked even more uncomfortable than he felt. Then he looked at her more closely as the gears in his brain clicked and he asked, "The Big Book of Witchcraft?"

"We're beginners!" she almost snapped it. "I bought it online because it sounded simple enough for us to do."

This time he plopped back into the chair across from the couch and eyed her warily again. "You don't have to lie to me Sloan. There's no Big Book of Witchcraft and obviously Rae isn't a beginner."

She sighed a heavy sigh like she was put out with him. As though she had a right to do that. She'd barged into *his* house! She sighed a second time and said, "That's what I came to talk to you about."

"About the fact that she lied to me? She and I talked and we agreed that it wasn't smart to get mixed up with witches!"

Sloan blinked at him. "She never agreed to that. She told me that you told her it wasn't a good idea and that it didn't matter because they didn't want anything to do with us. She never agreed." Then she gave another heaving sigh. "I know about you. Good Southern Boy, raised Baptist. Thou shalt not suffer a witch to live."

"Well, I wasn't raised in a voodoo shop!" He was standing now, and he watched as she rose in a fluid motion.

"We're Catholic, you moron!"

He blinked. "No, you're witches."

"No, we're Catholic. We're taking classes in spellwork."

He was totally confused now, and she seemed to read it on his face. "Sit down, it's clear you don't understand anything about my sister."

"I—I . . . I thought I did. I thought I loved her. What don't I know?"

"Do you really love her?" Sloan was seated and leaning forward. She stared at him, hard, waiting for the answer.

"I do." It was the softest of confessions, thought it was strong in his unsteady heart.

"Then listen up. Really *listen*."

He nodded. What else could he do?

"We're Catholic, just like you're Baptist. We just started going to these classes. Rae never lied to you. Never. But she did withhold some things."

Sam sat back and tried to absorb what he could as Sloan told him about the classes. About how the spells weren't that different from some of her Catholic practices. "I mean, as a kid I went to a certain candle and lit it with a certain kind of wood, I said a certain prayer over it . . ."

"But not in a pentagram!"

"What's wrong with a pentagram, Sam?"

What wasn't? "It's a sign of the devil."

"Educate yourself. Look it up. An *upside down* pentagram is considered that, yes, but so is an upside down cross. The only people who are immune to that crap are the Jews who were smart enough to make a religious symbol that you couldn't invert!"

He blinked at her for a moment, then he laughed. Then he pulled out his phone and googled it. She was right. His search triggered another problem. "You can't be Catholic and Wiccan!"

"Witchcraft is the practice of spells. Wicca is a full religion, but honestly, I don't see why not. You can be Baptist and Wiccan." She motioned to him. "I mean you're supposed to be nice to people and be the stewards of the Earth and protect it and protect those who can't protect themselves. Doesn't sound that far from your own religion, does it?"

"Aren't they Satanists?" His heart was still beating out of time. He didn't like this conversation, though, like Sloan, he knew the necessity of it.

She bust out into laughter. At him, he realized. "What?"

"Do you not read the news? Or the online articles? Jeez, Sam, even the Satanists have a good game these days. Their commandments are pretty much the same. You and me? We got the outdated ones."

He frowned and tapped at his phone for a minute, before looking at her sideways. She couldn't make him see things on his phone, could she?

"Jesus, Sam, phone a friend, they'll tell you the same thing!" Apparently, he was not getting educated at a rate fast enough for Sloan Ellis. He was tempted to call though.

Then her expression turned more serious. "Here's the thing, Sam. And this is the part where you get to decide if you can accept her, because I don't think either she or I are going to give this up. It fits. It answers questions we've had all our lives. And isn't that what religion is supposed to do?"

He only nodded.

She took a deep breath. "I'm breaking my own trust with Rae to tell you this. I'm only doing it because I think you're a good man. No, I *believe* it. I believe that you're in love with my sister and I want her to have that. But you have to accept everything that she is if you're going to support her."

Well, shit. That hit him in the solar plexus. "Go on."

She told him about their mother, about her being driven out of town and not speaking to her family again. Rae had told him the same story, but let him believe her mother had been falsely accused of being a slut. He hadn't realized her mother had "skills" like this, too. He absorbed it as Sloan went on. He only interrupted once.

"Wait. She's been able to do this her whole life?"

Sloan nodded. "She found Luke with that feeling she gets. She just *found* him! And . . . and she made you go to the hospital because of that same feeling. Sam, her powers saved your life."

He felt everything in him wilt.

He'd doubted her. He'd been just like everyone else, but he didn't have time to berate himself. Sloan was still talking.

"We never told anyone what we could do. Not *anyone*."

"You told your cousin," he countered.

Sloan shook her head. "No, she told us. She welcomed us! Even without thinking we should be her cousins, she told us our powers or skills or whatever you want to call them weren't bad, that they weren't shameful, and they weren't anything we had to hide from the people in the shop."

Oh, shit. Sloan hadn't said it. She hadn't had to. Rae had felt she had to hide from him. And he'd played a big part in that. She'd tested him, and he'd failed.

"I don't know if it's because we're a younger generation, or because all the tech means we can cover it better, or if it's the difference between the diversity of Los Angeles and small, old, conservative towns in Italy, but Rae and I want to be more

open. We aren't going to run around yelling that we're witches."
She offered a wry smile. "Honestly, neither of us has the skills to
back that claim up! Ha. But we aren't hiding anymore. She told
Sheree, and Sheree just hugged her and said, 'Thank God you
were able to find me.' Sheree made Rae promise to help look
when she loses her keys."

Sloan blinked, and he saw what this meant to her even
though it wasn't her own friend. "Neither of us has ever been
accepted that way before." Then she took another breath and
suddenly stood up, startling him. "So you need to make a
decision, Sam. If you really love my sister, you need to act like it.
Because this is who she is."

With that final word, she turned and was out the door before
he could get himself together to even be polite enough to see
her off.

She left him sitting in the chair half-stunned, half-ashamed,
and wondering what he would tell his family about his decision.
His mother loved Rae. His father thought she was the best thing
that had ever happened to Sam. What happened when they
found out?

CHAPTER 49

R ae ordered room service—lobster, since she was going all out. Also since she could actually afford it. She laughed after she hung up the phone, the prices did still floor her. It was insane to pay that much money for one meal, but she wanted to.

The hotel was nice, if the weather was cold. Just when things had started to warm up back home, she had to come to Chicago. The heat was cranked up, the lobster was on the way, and still the room felt like it faded at the corners.

Nothing here felt real. Not for the two weeks that she had been here anyway. She was getting great photos of Chicago. The Martch had a darkroom where they let her develop her pieces. She was trying to hide them, none of the shots were show quality. They all lacked spark and she didn't want them to think she lacked actual talent.

There was a knock at the door. The lobster had arrived. Somehow, she'd sat on the bed, lost in thought for all this time, and hadn't even managed to do the one thing she needed to do: dig out some cash for a tip. Although it rubbed her the wrong way that the lobster would wind up costing even *more*. But she would not untertip.

This man deserved his tip. Dressed to the nines and impeccable in behavior, he wheeled in his cart and snapped out a fresh starched tablecloth onto the small dining table in the room. Rae grabbed for her camera and felt the smile cross her face.

She quickly asked permission, her days as a P.I. had taught her well that photos made a *lot* of people angry. When he agreed, she began snapping away. The man was a gold mine. Perfect in form, with just a hint of a ham in him that showed up after the first two clicks of the shutter.

When he had the lobster laid out, steaming, for her, she quickly shucked the camera and scrambled for the tip she had shoved in her pocket. He nodded and turned away, a consummate professional.

"Wait!"

He startled at the sound of her voice, but composed himself quickly and turned. By the look on his face he was ready to help with any problem although he clearly didn't think he'd forgotten anything.

She smiled again. A genuine smile with real human contact. "I'm a photographer."

He nodded, not adding an *I gathered that.*

So Rae continued. "I have a show at the Martch Gallery right now. And I would like to get your name so that I can pay you for modeling for me."

There! She'd flummoxed him. The unflappable was flapped. She held out her new business cards that Mrs. Brock had printed as a gift. Mrs. Brock was a godsend. Rae jotted a quick note on the back and signed it before handing it over. "You can get into the show with that card. And bring a guest or two. Although you might want to wait about a week. I suspect some of the shots of you will be up by then."

"Really?"

"Yes, feel free to call me—" she pointed to the number on the card, "and check." Then she asked for his name and address so she could contact him if the piece sold. It only seemed right to pay the people who modeled for her.

After a few flushes of red across his face and an embarrassed "thank you," he left the room, and Rae settled in to a dinner of lobster. Juice was everywhere by the time she had the shell cracked. She ignored it as it ran down her fingers. She sucked down slivers of lobster meat, dunking her fingers into the drawn butter with the shellfish. Even the green beans went down without utensils.

Heavenly. The food was heavenly. She almost moaned. Until about halfway through the meal when the silence began to roar in her ears and her eyes were heavy with tears. She wiped at her face with the back of her hand, the only part not covered in her dinner.

She looked to the walls, but they didn't look back. She could turn on the TV, once she washed her hands. But that wouldn't solve the problem, just mask it with noise.

Biting her lip, she could barely see past her own hand as the tears started coming freely. And of course just then it occurred to her that it was Tuesday night. They would all be sitting around watching Crime Night. Without her. She was so lonely.

More lonely than she had ever been in her life. And she hadn't spoken to Sam since she had left. They had never said so, but there was an implicit agreement that it would be easier for them not to make plans to see each other again. So though they'd texted a little, she hadn't heard his voice in weeks.

She washed her hands, ignored what was left of her dinner and crawled onto the bed and sobbed. She bawled for a long time. Long enough for her dinner to get plenty cold.

Then, suddenly, even though tears clouded her vision, things were clear. All she knew was that she had chased the wrong dream. She had screwed up royally and she wasn't sure she could fix it. She hadn't told Sam the whole truth. It was a risk and she hadn't been willing to trust him. She'd screwed it up, and now she was half the country away and barely texting him while whatever love he'd had for her grew colder.

Rae cried until she curled up into a little ball. Until she realized that she wasn't cut out for the dream she thought she wanted. She couldn't travel the world and take pictures of it. Not by herself. Not like this. And she cried until she found herself hoping that Sam hadn't moved on.

He wouldn't have, would he? Not in the two weeks since she had been gone. Not in the two weeks when she had walked out and gotten on a plane and some part of each of them seemed to have agreed to not look back. What had she done?

Her stomach turned at the thought that he might have sought comfort from someone else. She was seven kinds of fool. She cried when she came around to being glad that she had at least given it a chance, even if it hadn't worked. She wouldn't wonder 'what if she hadn't chased this dream?' But she would wonder 'what if she hadn't left Sam to do it?' 'What if she'd told him her secrets?' Could he be trusted with them? She wanted to say yes, but if she didn't try, she'd never know.

Her breath sucked into her lungs and she sat upright on the bed. The tears stopped and with a quick wipe on her shirt sleeve they were gone from her face. Her feet swung around off the bed and quickly she shucked her clothes and hopped into the shower. She was a mess.

Five minutes later, she emerged, clean, never having cared so little to linger in the warm spray. She put on a little makeup and brushed out her hair, thinking she would let it air-dry, then cursing the cold Chicago weather before spending almost half an hour getting the mass to something she could wear outside and not die from exposure. She had never hated her hair so much.

Rae packed up her supplies and pulled out a comfy pair of jeans, then slipped into an old t-shirt and her little zip-up sweat jacket. She shoved her feet into socks and sneakers, and began folding and packing everything she could grab. A quick glance at the clock told her it had taken all of five minutes since she emerged from the bathroom. She was flying.

Picking up the phone, Rae waited with utter impatience for the maybe twenty seconds it took the front desk to pick up and agree to send up a bell-hop. This way he should arrive just as she finished packing.

Rae stopped, and slumped. The Martch Gallery had some of her work in their darkroom. She would have to wait until tomorrow to claim it. Tears welled up again. She wanted to leave. Now. She could be home a few hours after the next flight out. Maybe she could see Sam before sunrise. But not if she had to wait.

She sniffed back the new tears and decided to leave her work behind. She could send for it. It hadn't been very good anyway. The new, good pictures were still in her camera. Everything had been packed. In record speed mind you, but it was still a little disturbing that her life could be folded up so quickly. It was a sign. A sign that she shouldn't be here.

After an interminable time had passed, three minutes according to the clock, a knock sounded at the door and Rae jumped up to let the bellhop in. She swung the door wide not checking at the peephole.

Then her face fell. "I'm sorry, you have the wrong room."

Once again, room service stood before her. This time it was a woman in a starched shirt and cummerbund, with a tray holding chilled champagne and a big bowl of strawberries. She checked the ticket, looking confused. "No, this is the right room."

Rae shook her head. "Something got mixed up. I ordered a bellhop. I'm checking out."

"Why are you checking out?" Her breath caught and her eyes pulled all her attention to the figure emerging beyond the doorframe. That voice.

She screamed his name, "Sam!" And nearly knocked over the room service tray trying to get to him. Flinging herself into his arms, she held him tightly to reassure herself that she hadn't fallen asleep waiting for the bellhop, that it wasn't all just a dream.

When she finally managed to unsqueeze her eyes and look up at him, he lowered his face to hers and kissed her. He wasn't with someone else. He had missed her, too.

When he set her on her own feet he looked around, but the hall was empty. The tray had been wheeled into the room and room service had left them standing there, kissing in the hall. He asked her again. "Why were you checking out?"

"To go home. To you."

He smiled just as she slugged him in the chest. He turned, "What was that for?"

"You should have called. If it hadn't been so cold and I hadn't had to dry every last piece of my hair I would have been out the door already."

The easy smile came back. "I would have caught up to you at the airport. The next flight out isn't until two a.m."

Why did he know that? She must have frowned because he read her like a book, like always. "In case you had someone else in your room, or hadn't missed me, or couldn't forgive me, or—"

She cut him off. "Sam, that's impossible. I haven't been happy here at all without you." Rae plopped down on the bed, but didn't let go of his hand. "I can't do this. I can't travel like this and not have a home. Besides, my shots are utterly uninspired here."

A knock came at the doorway, and Sam went to answer it. She loved having him here. Her skin felt cold from where he had heated her simply with the touch of his hand. He tipped the bellhop and sent him away, asking that the front desk be notified that Miss Woodward wasn't checking out after all.

He came back into the room, after turning the deadbolt.

She smiled up at him, but his expression was dead serious. "Can you forgive me for the way I reacted?"

"What? When?"

"Jesus, all of it. When you told me about your cousin and that you and your sister were taking classes in witchcraft. When you saved Sheree . . ." he trailed off. "When you saved *me*. And you didn't tell me how you knew I had to go to the hospital—"

She frowned and interrupted him. "How did you know about that?"

"Well, I've been doing a lot of research. And . . . your sister came and set me straight. I owe her, big time." He stood up and stuffed his hands in his back pockets. "I'm sorry, Rae. So sorry. I can only say that I was raised one way and I—"

"I understand. You think one thing and it's hard to get out of that. It's okay."

"No," he protested, "it's not. Not believing you and listening to you and even just asking you about it in the first place means I let other people make decisions about you and me. About what I thought about you. And that's not okay. We have to come first to each other. And I didn't do that. But I want to. I can do that now. I won't make the same mistake twice. Can we be that to each other, Rae?"

His eyes were wet. He was scared. She could see it. And she knew this was a photo she would keep in her head, in her heart, forever. Along with the moment she said, "Yes, Sam. We should be that to each other. That's what I want, too."

His smile was all she needed. She reached up for him and found herself engulfed in his arms as he whispered, "Please don't keep things from me in the future. Please forgive me, I promise I'll be better."

She whispered back, "There's nothing to forgive you for. I should have trusted you more. Take me home, Sam."

"But I arranged five days off. We should stay."

All the pieces inside her clicked. "Okay, but I'm going home with you at the end of the five days."

She tried to kiss him, but he wouldn't let her. "Only if that's what you really want."

A nod and a smile would have been fine, but she needed to tell him. "I'm in love with you. I have never been so lonely as I was here. It isn't right being here without you. I just want to go home and cancel all the shows."

"No way." He laughed. "I came because home isn't right without you there. I decided I'd be happier following you around."

"But it isn't what you really want."

"Just like being at home all the time isn't what you want. Why don't you go to open the shows then come back to me?"

Rae shook her head; it wasn't enough. "Maybe. If they still want me, then maybe we'll go visit the shows whenever you have a few days without court. We could go together. Is that all right?"

He nodded. "We'll think it through. I don't know what we'll do, but we'll figure it out." He made a satisfied sound as his arms came all the way around her. He filled up her entire vision of the world, and she decided that she liked it that way.

"It just feels right to be in your arms again."

"Tell me about it."

CHAPTER 50

They sat at breakfast the next morning in the restaurant downstairs. It was open to all the comings and goings in the lobby. Sam spotted the couple he'd met the night before as they came into the restaurant area. Waving his hand to them he called them over, "Mr. and Mrs. Vanderpool!"

The older couple was smiling as they approached. Sam introduced them to Rachel and her to them. "They snuck me into the elevator to get me up to your room. Then they waited outside the door, with a cell phone in case I was a stalker and you weren't happy to see me."

Rae smiled though she wanted to laugh.

Mrs. Vanderpool turned thirteen shades of red. "Well, you never can tell these days."

"No." Sam put his hand out on her arm. "Don't be embarrassed. It was a wonderful thing you did. I like to think that if anyone else had come for Rae, you two would be there to watch out for her. Would you like to join us for breakfast?"

"Oh no." She declined, "To tell the truth, we're a little surprised to see you two lovebirds up and around this morning."

He looked back to Rae, her smile was wide and her eyes held some sort of shimmer. He got to be the lucky guy who knew it was for him. He smiled back at her, then spoke to the Vanderpools again. "Please. We haven't even ordered yet."

Rae couldn't hold it any longer, she just blurted out. "We'd like to invite you to our wedding. . ." Then she flustered, all cute and red. "We don't know when it is yet, but we almost missed each other and we would have if it hadn't been for you two. Please say you'll come."

The Vanderpools spent a few moments congratulating them, before sitting down and joining them for breakfast. They were even more interesting than he had found out in the elevator on the way up to see Rae.

Somehow his hand had snuck under the table and laced fingers with hers without his knowledge. She was excited and she was about to burst with it. It was almost unfathomable that she could be so wound up about spending her life attached to him. But she was.

She was *his Rachel*. Those children he had imagined, with auburn hair and those lucid green eyes, they would happen. And his Rachel would always know if they were okay. When she told him to be worried, he would jump. He might get to jump fairly soon if things went according to the plans formulated late last night. But what was a plan anyway? All he was sure of was that, if he was a smart man, he wouldn't let her spend another night away from him.

She'd told him so much last night. So much more than Sloan had even filled him in on. She said she'd never cast a spell on him and never would. But then she confessed, she'd thought about it. She'd found one that would bring him to her: the SoulFire spell. He'd laughed and said there was no need to cast it. It wouldn't do anything. He was already hers.

Thank you for reading! I love romances with real love and believable characters, and I hope you found all that in these pages. I want to fall in love right along with the characters, and I do, while I'm writing it.

About Savannah

I started writing when I was eight--I hand wrote an 80-page novella that I believed to be (adult) romantic suspense. I'm proud to say, I've gotten a lot better since then. I've grown up to be a nerd at heart! I love neuroscience and people watching, and if you look, you'll find some of that in each Savannah Kade book. Most days you'll find me in my office, looking out my window at a handful of the neighbor's cows, or watching my dogs or my cat roam the backyard.

Follow me, find me, ask me questions! I would love to hear from you.
www.SavannahKade.com
Savannah@SavannahKade.com